KINGDOM OF MONSTERS

BY
JOHN LEE SCHNEIDER

SEVERED PRESS
HOBART TASMANIA

KINGDOM OF MONSTERS

ISBN: 978-1-922551-66-5

"It was surely well for man that he came late in the order of creation. There were powers abroad in earlier days which no courage and no mechanism of his could have met. What could his sling, his throwing-stick, or his arrow avail him against such forces as have been loose tonight? Even with a modern rifle, it would be all odds on the monster."

The Lost World
Sir Arthur Conan Doyle

CHAPTER 1

Jonah and Naomi had been traveling the mountains for three weeks when they saw the military chopper passing above.

The sudden roar of rotor blades was like the shriek of some giant predatory bird. Naomi's hand instinctively dropped to the pistol at her hip.

That was the thing about living post-apocalypse – even once-familiar sights became fearful and threatening.

"He's coming in low," Naomi said. "It looks like he's landing."

It was not the first chopper they'd seen. The two of them had been following the path of military transit, sticking to the highland passes. These days it was the safest way to travel.

When you lived in Tyrannosaurus territory, you learned to mind your surroundings.

Jonah quite vividly remembered the first time he'd wandered out of the general store to find a *T. rex* waiting in the parking lot.

He had seen all the old movies – everything from stop-motion animation, to rubber suits and animatronics, to fancy CGI – but instead, he'd discovered tyrannosaurs were really more like giant road-runners – he'd barely out-distanced the thing in his pick-up on a paved mountain road – and both of those were luxuries you couldn't expect anymore.

Not since the end of the world.

In a purely detached way, it was remarkable how quickly the world of humankind had receded. Although, when you thought about it, ninety-percent of people lived – *had* lived – in major population centers, which had been the hardest hit.

At first, there had been lingering radio reports of varying credibility, wild speculations involving everything from genetic experiments gone wrong to beasts and dragons from the Pit.

Personally, Jonah doubted he would ever live to know. He had lived like a hermit *before* the end of the world – a rustic cabin high in the mountains – and if he hadn't come into town after fishing that day, he might have missed it.

That was one of the more subtle, yet jarring differences, Jonah thought – the end of the flow of information. There was no news anymore. The Internet and cellphones had been replaced by CBs and walkie-talkies, and a lot of wide-open space in-between.

All Jonah really knew was that, one day, monsters had just walked out of the woods, right into the cities and towns, as if they'd been out there waiting all along.

On the ground, it didn't matter whether that day had come because of Biblical judgment, or all-too-human bio-genetic-buggery – either one got you there.

And either way, Jonah had found himself running ever since.

Naomi had been running right beside him – neither by choice or plan – only the simple happenstance of walking out into that same general store parking lot, and escaping with him in his truck, just as a prehistoric beast that had no business being there, bore down on them like a train-engine with teeth.

Their old lives had been torn away in an instant as they fled the apocalypse together.

Naomi had been the wife of a fighter pilot – one of those genuine American heroes.

Lieutenant Lucas Walker had died fighting the apocalypse. In his final breath, he had delivered a nuclear payload that likely preserved what remained of human life in the majority of the western states, releasing his missiles even as the winged beasts in the air, as terrible as *T. rex* on the ground, finally chased him down.

Naomi had watched his fighter destroyed, exploding in the jaws of a giant flying dragon.

Jonah, ten years divorced from a woman who had traded-up without looking back, could only imagine the grief of losing a genuine soulmate.

He also knew he was a poor substitute – a reclusive, backwater guide pilot, who flew rust-bucket choppers and propeller planes, but preferred traveling by boat. It was perhaps understandable that Naomi might be a bit indignant at the fates for saddling her in *his* company. She had certainly not been shy about saying so.

Still, the end of the world was a bonding experience, especially after an ill-fated jaunt in Jonah's rusty, tin-bucket chopper. Hoping to find their way to Naomi's husband's Navy base, they had instead discovered pterosaurs would go right after a chopper.

They'd crashed in the mountains along the Oregon/California border, and were forced to travel cross-land, walking through the Apocalypse on foot.

But in the end, they'd made it back to Jonah's cabin, which remained miraculously untouched, and really not looking much different than before the world ended.

Naomi, of course, had set about putting a change to that. As was her way, she settled in, and in short order, began making the place her own.

A woman's touch on the rustic cabin was undeniable. Jonah was reminded of college – the sorority palaces and the fraternity dives, often sharing a fence, right next door to each other.

The cabin was also high in the mountains, which made it relatively safe.

Funny thing about the Mesozoic-era – it was an oxygen-rich, fertile-world, quite unlike the arid climate of modern Earth. A Cretaceous creature like *T. rex* didn't like the thin air in the mountains.

So the beasts didn't bother them, and they settled into a routine – hunting, fishing – Naomi started up a garden.

It had seemed a strange interlude, perhaps even a reward.

Jonah had thought so, right up until their one night together.

To speak the truth and shame the Devil, Jonah had been in love with her almost from the moment they'd met. Naomi, naturally, was perfectly aware, and fine with it, as long as he clearly understood that, even as the last man on Earth, she was *still* out of his league.

Jonah, for his part, was fine with sleeping on the couch in his single-bedroom cabin.

Then one night, just over three weeks ago – Jonah didn't know *why* at the time – he had come back in from the river, his back aching, cold, tired and wet, to find her halfway into a bottle of wine.

He'd frowned. Naomi could get a little chirpy with alcohol. But tonight she just seemed melancholy.

Thinking about the husband again, he thought, tiredly. That always bode trouble.

Jonah had referred to him as 'her ex' once – a mistake he'd not made twice.

"He is *not* my *ex*," she had hissed, rounding on him, her eyes flashing venomously, as she held up the ring she still wore on her finger. "He *died*."

But tonight, she had a fire crackling, and had folded herself in a nest of blankets on the couch.

Jonah tossed off his jacket and wet boots, and sat down on the floor in front of the fireplace, his cold skin prickling with goose-flesh at the warm gust of flame.

Sliding behind him on the couch, Naomi touched her hand against his cheek.

"You're chilled," she said.

And remarkably, he felt her fingers touch his shoulders, which were tight and sore, and began to rub.

"You're also tight as knot," she said.

Jonah looked at the half-bottle of wine as her hands now stole down onto his chest.

He started to turn, and suddenly she was in his arms, slipping down off the couch and pulling him down with her beside the fire.

Her eyes were wide as her arms circled his back, drawing him close.

Half-a-bottle of wine, Jonah thought.

"We shouldn't do this," he said, without conviction.

Those dark eyes had blinked once, looking up at him, half-lidded.

"*Shouldn't* we?" she murmured back.

As if it had ever been in doubt.

Jonah would later wonder if nobility was strained, or would he simply have been foolish to turn away a good thing?

Push came to shove, he found he didn't care.

All he knew was that, whatever came next, he now had that moment etched in his memory, where she pulled him down beside her and they first touched.

That was a moment he wouldn't give up for anything.

Perhaps symbolically, he was awakened the next day when the earth moved.

A rumbling in the ground was cause for alarm these days. The entire region was a semi-active volcanic range, and seismic activity had recently increased tenfold.

Of all the loose nukes that had been tossed about in the immediate aftermath of 'KT-day', Jonah had heard reports that at least one of them, by accident or design, had hit dead center on the San Andreas fault.

He also had it from multiple sources that the resulting tectonic shift had finally delivered on the long-promised collapse of southern California into the ocean.

And neither had the earthquakes stopped. Far from it. Instead, tremors seemed to step-up in tempo by the day, and long-dormant forest-covered mountains suddenly began burping smoke and ash, as their bowels boiled with molten pressure from down below.

Jonah had almost learned to ignore the semi-regular tremors, much the way they once had in southern California before it collapsed into the ocean – not that attentiveness would have made a lot of difference.

But as he was stirred awake, Jonah's bleary consciousness registered something was different about these tremors.

The second thing he realized was that Naomi was gone from his side.

As he blinked away the fog of sleep and looked around, he saw her sitting at the window, legs folded, her feet curled up beside her. She was wrapped in her robe, as if she'd been up for a while.

He sat up to greet her but saw the furtive look in her face.

"That's not a quake," she said.

Jonah paused, listening, even as he felt the impact again, followed half-a-tick later by the heavy booming sound, echoing like a delayed pulse of distant thunder.

Like footsteps, Jonah realized. Heavy enough to shake the mountain.

Even big *T. rex* were only nine or ten tons. They couldn't do that.

This was something else.

Jonah and Naomi quickly dressed, and had hiked up to the edge of the ridge, where the trees cleared, offering a view of the surrounding terrain.

On the very opposite peak, less than half-a-mile distant, a giant shadow loomed.

It *wasn't* a quake – not from the Earth.

The first time you saw one of these beasts, you found yourself just sort of standing and staring, the way you would at an incoming storm – or like an avalanche moving down a mountain – almost disassociated by the scale of it, until you realized it was coming right at *you*.

To Jonah, it looked like a giant cloud, blocking out the sky.

This cloud was in the shape of a giant rex – a rex that reared its head more than two-hundred feet high, its unguessable tonnage shaking the earth with each lumbering step.

And out of the middle of that cloud, stared two blinking eyes.

They glowed emerald green.

It was a signature tell of the giants – or any infected animal – an odd side-effect.

This creature would have once been a normal rex, before the rabies-like progression of the infection – which Jonah had noted was passed on, at least to some degree, by ingestion, a cycle that could take anywhere from weeks to months.

Among the drifting rumors echoing over the barren airwaves, Jonah heard it called the 'Food of the Gods' – another contribution from the 'genetic-engineering' faction of the tin-hat theorists.

But it was what *really* destroyed the world.

A normal rex might top out at forty-feet, nose-to-tail. The largest sauropods, on the other hand, approached two-hundred feet.

An *infected* sauropod might stretch *two-thousand* feet or better, and a herd of these rage-infected giants would rampage until the madness burned its cycle and the beasts finally died.

Weeks to months.

Entire cities had literally been trampled flat. These infected behemoths had barely noticed humanity's efforts to add to the destruction with missiles and bombs.

Now, as the giant rex perched on the opposite hill, just as abrupt and sudden as an avalanche, Jonah could see this beast was in the very late stages.

The rabies-madness set in once growth topped out, as if whatever chemical-biological reaction percolating the DNA just kept forcing more and more energy into the system, like a constant diet of cocaine and steroids, until the infected organism finally died.

This rex had passed the last of the *rage* phase – or more properly, lost the physical/cognitive ability to continue acting upon it, simply shambling forward until its failing biological life-process finally allowed its suffering to end.

That day had also been the first time they'd seen military presence in the area.

As the rex began moving down the hill, there came the buzzing drone of rotor blades, and two choppers appeared above, like giant wasps, hot on the tail of the infected giant.

Naomi had stiffened at the sight – her husband's colors.

The rex didn't seem to notice the buzzing metal bugs as they circled and flew past. Jonah hoped they wouldn't attack – if the beast noticed at all, it would only piss it off, perhaps even summoning up one last maddened rampage.

But instead, the choppers circled back, disappearing over the horizon in the direction they'd come.

Obviously, someone in the military had learned futility. There was no point in engaging an already-dying giant.

As the rex trundled the downward slope, it stumbled.

The staccato footsteps were replaced by a rumble, like rolling boulders, as the giant rex collapsed forward, an avalanche all on its own, and an entire swath of timber was wiped away as the massive beast crashed to the forest floor.

The impact continued to reverberate beneath their feet for nearly a minute before it finally stilled.

In the beast's eyes, the green glow of the Food of the Gods faded as its life left it.

Unfortunately, it wasn't over.

Because now they were looking at an ecological time bomb.

Here was a mountain of free meat, and its scent would carry like ringing a dinner bell for miles around.

But it was infected.

Jonah and Naomi worked their way further down the hillside, hoping for a better view. They moved with caution, judicious in any wilderness, although Jonah had learned to treat it like any lifetime woodsman – it was no different than knowing where the bears were when you lived in Alaska.

The *T. rex* didn't like the hills, but would follow you there if they got on your tail – and they could be damn stubborn about it.

Which caused Jonah to wonder, what might *this* big beast have been following?

He did not, however, question what had drawn the first of the valley's other predators.

Naomi pulled at his shoulder, pointing to the big rex' path along the opposite peak.

The dying giant had likely been casting chemical messages in the air that its end was near, and the scent would have carried. Any freeloaders looking for an easy meal would be following right behind, prowling like circling sharks.

And sure enough, the first of the *'normals'* appeared on the scene.

The valley south of Jonah's cabin was patrolled by a big rogue male rex, easily approaching ten tons, and it was this mighty beast that followed closest in the dying giant's footsteps.

Likely, the pack of females, who traveled together, would not be far behind.

The senior female would keep the pack in-line until the big rogue claimed the territory – and of course, ate his fill, showing due reverence for the Tyrant King.

T. rex' social habits rather resembled those of some large ground birds. The senior female kept her troop separate from the solitary males, except when she would pair-bond for a period of weeks with the territory's dominant rogue.

Young males would sometimes run in their own small groups once they got too big for the female pack – like many raptor birds, male rex were highly aggressive, and couldn't be tolerated among the more social females – and even these juvie-teenage mini-packs always eventually broke down as every swaggering buck, sooner or later, got too big, too mean, and just *had* to challenge for the top spot, and either be king or be killed.

And the king tended to be right there handy when that moment came. The juvie-packs often followed the rogue's path, always at a respectful distance, waiting to freeload off his kills. In turn, he would let them stand and wait their turn, while he confiscated anything *they* happened to bring down – in both cases, after he'd consumed his lion's share, *and* provided he'd taken a nap half-a-mile away down by the river.

The rogue *allowed* it – just like anything else that went on in his territory.

Very generously, he allowed it, up until the moment, every now and then, when he had to kill one of them.

Jonah supposed, in its way, it was a very stress-free life.

And as far as living around them, on the flip-side, *T. rex* did NOT tolerate other predators.

Jonah had seen that demonstrated time and time again. To be a big carnosaur within the nigh-uncanny scent range of a rex, or *any* tyrannosaur of anywhere near comparable size, was to get your ass bit off.

The rex also seemed to particularly hate sickle-claws – any sickle-claws in scent range, and they would dig out their burrows and dens like bears rooting out termites.

Naomi actually seemed to have become rather fond of the local *T. rex* troops, in an admiring-the-lion kind of way. She had named the big senior female Trix, and called her flock Josie and the pussycats – Josie being the second-largest female, and presumably, either Trix' little sister or daughter. There were also two other adults, likely sisters, Daphne and Velma.

The roving teenage male gangsters were the JV squad. The largest was Big Moose, although the leader seemed to be a smaller, but more aggressive individual Naomi called Rudy. Archie and Jughead rounded the group.

But so far, it was just the lone rogue that made his way down the slope, where waited the massive, inviting feast.

Naomi raised a pair of binoculars, focusing on the rogue, as he perched atop the giant carcass, and without ceremony, began to gorge, his massive jaws tearing out five-foot chunks like a Great White tearing blubber from a dead whale.

And so the clock was set on the first living time-bomb.

Naomi handed Jonah the binoculars, and he zoomed in on the feeding rex.

Just as if lighting up a fuse, he could see the rogue's eyes, already glowing green.

And waiting in the wings, Jonah now spotted Trix, along with Josie and the pussycats, ambling their way through the convenient space in the trees the giant had left in its passing.

The flock paused on the crest, looking down to where the rogue assaulted the carcass, waiting until he worked that initial aggression out of his system.

Doubtless, lingering somewhere, still out of sight, was the third-stringer JV squad, pulling up the rear.

Already a few of the pussycats ventured down the slope, taking their first nibbles at the dead giant's tail, which by its sheer size stretched beyond the rogue's immediate comfort zone.

Keeping a careful eye on the big alpha rex, a number of the female gang began wolfing down huge mouthfuls of meat.

A single infected rex qualified as a regional threat, let alone a pack.

And that was to say nothing of a sauropod. The largest titanosaurs that ever lived could look Godzilla in the eye *before* the Food of the Gods – an infected Argentinosaurus, in the final throes of madness, could knock the Kraken on its ass.

And so the infection would bloom up again, like a slow-motion nuclear strike that spread like a virus.

This time, however, someone was taking steps to arrest that pattern.

From the direction the choppers had disappeared, now came the roar of jet engines.

Fighters armed with ordinary missiles were ineffective against an infected giant.

A napalm strike to burn a corpse, on the other hand...

Jonah and Naomi watched helplessly as three jets came in low, each releasing a deluge of weaponized fire.

In the echoing space of the surrounding peaks, came the screams of the rex pack gathered around the now-burning carcass. The forest around them burned as well – probably the only time of year that the perpetually damp Oregon rainforest *would* burn.

Visibility from below was quickly reduced to near zero as the flames began to spread.

The jets veered back the way they had come – mission accomplished.

Jonah understood the strategic reasons for this burn – an effort to avoid the spread of the infection. Whether it was an effective method or not remained to be seen, but it definitely looked to successfully destroy a wide expanse of landscape.

And looking down at the express-delivered, instant-inferno, Jonah realized the flame was going to overtake the cabin as well.

That had been three weeks ago.

They had fled the area via the river, with nothing but what they could load in a boat and carry in a pack.

Remarkably, Jonah found that Naomi actually seemed to hold it against him – apparently for not stopping a forest fire, a napalm strike, or a two-hundred-foot *Tyrannosaurus rex*. He hadn't moved Heaven and Earth.

Worse, she seemed to connect it as some kind of karmic retribution for their night before.

Either way, she never mentioned being together again, and in the time since, her posture had reverted to what it had been at the beginning – firmly at arm's length.

They were lucky just to escape the fire. The river had only taken them so far and, since then, they'd been on foot.

The fire followed them for days, a towering cloud of ever-present smoke, always at their heels, advancing inexorably, like one of the infected beasts itself.

Then, finally, on the fourth day, there was a heavy rain, which went a long way to extinguishing the bulk of the blaze. Having no better destination, Jonah and Naomi continued north – the direction the planes had gone after they'd destroyed their home.

And just today, they had come out onto a ridge, right at the edge of the mountains, overlooking the greater valley.

They could see what had once been the community below.

As the elevation rapidly dropped, the main highway descended down through the rural farmlands into what must have been a bedroom town outside of Portland.

Naomi had paused, looking down at the houses, all lined up in rows – what had once been families.

Abruptly she stepped aside. As she turned away, Jonah realized she was crying.

Naomi deliberately gave him her back, inviting no comfort. Jonah had learned not to bother her in those odd moments. He obligingly held off while she allowed the sting of tears to dry.

She was just drying up when there came the first sudden blast of air as the helicopter flew past up above.

It looked like a cargo chopper – bulky with dual rotors front and back. It seemed to be following the highway they had seen below.

As Naomi raised her binoculars, peering down at the distant road, she saw several vehicles traveling under the chopper's escort – a caravan, half-a-dozen RVs deep.

The chopper had pulled ahead of the procession, cresting the hill, leaving the caravan to follow the road all the way around.

Once over the peak, the bird's altitude began to drop.

"It's landing," Naomi affirmed, and started up the hill at a lope.

"Hold on a minute," Jonah objected. "What if we're following them into a fight?"

Naomi shrugged. "Would you rather wait for them to napalm us?"

She turned, without waiting for him.

Jonah gritted his teeth as he hurried along to follow.

CHAPTER 2

Just over the ridge was a communications outpost, and what looked like a freshly-built radio tower, set at the highest point that still allowed access to where the main road wound around the mountain on its way down into the valley.

As the chopper circled in to land, Naomi pulled her binoculars and scouted them from their vantage above.

Experience had engendered a modicum of caution. The world was dangerous, and encountering strangers of any stripe carried risk. In their time on the road, there had been at least one attempted robbery at gunpoint.

There had also been filtered rumors about sideways-encounters with military.

Some of these stories were scary, and all plausible enough, given conditions of desperation – but whether some, none, or all of them were true, it was also prudent not to just walk up on a bunch of armed soldiers, executing maneuvers in a combat zone.

Especially now that the whole world was a combat zone.

The caravan trailed about a mile behind, as measured by the windy mountain road, no portion of which could be trusted beyond sight of the next bend.

Topography was not even reliable anymore. The Big One had purportedly left the new southwestern coastline a sheer, broken cliff a hundred miles south of the Oregon border.

On a more localized level, the terrain had shifted and broken, splitting along tectonic cracks. Even minor rumblings could easily collapse tunnels and break apart paved roads.

Adjusting her focus, Naomi followed the pilot climbing out of the chopper over to the outpost's single sentry coming out to meet him.

Three more soldiers followed the pilot, hopping out of the chopper, performing a perfunctory sweep of the area, guns out and drawn – alert, but obviously routine, as they then began to offload supplies, carrying a procession of boxes and crates into the outpost storage bunker below the tower.

One of the soldiers, with a medium-sized crate, stepped discreetly away from the others, and made his way to the edge of the clearing, glancing over his shoulder as he went.

Naomi frowned. "What's this guy doing?"

The soldier unstrapped the crate and opened the front. There was scurrying movement from inside.

"Oh *no*," Naomi said aloud. "Check this out,"

She handed the binocs to Jonah and he zoomed down into the clearing.

Skittering out of the carrying crate were what looked like a troop of miniature plucked emus – short, gangly, little two-legged lizards, no more than two feet tall.

"Oh *no*," Jonah repeated.

They had seen *this* little lizard before.

There had been a lot of them running around after KT-day – seemingly a breed of small sickle-claw, although unique in that its birdlike chirps and screeches could shape their utterances into uncanny myna-birdlike imitations, repeating human phrases like a parrot.

They were disgusting creatures – ghouls, who in the days after the fall, seemed to specifically scavenge human corpses.

It called itself Otto – and they *all* did – in the same strange man's voice.

"*My name is Otto.*"

But they were a lot more than just a parrot.

And the soldier releasing this small troop – it looked like at least three of them – apparently had no idea.

But it was a lesson not long in coming.

The first of the little lizards hopped nonchalantly to the edge of the brush.

All the way up on the ridge, Jonah and Naomi could hear the screeching cry, as the little lizard bugled like a trumpet.

The other soldiers looked up at the caterwauling, and the errant young man stepped away from the shrieking lizard as if startled.

There was a brief pause as the screeching echoed to a stop.

Then the bushes suddenly erupted with a warbling scream.

"Oh my God," Jonah breathed, setting down the scopes and reaching for his rifle. Naomi's pistol was already out and drawn.

A pack of sickle-claws burst from the brush.

Dromacosaurs were a particularly nasty clade, and these were big ones – leopard-sized.

The hapless soldier who had released the little lizards fell back, grabbing for his sidearm. To his credit, he got a shot into the first of his attackers before it landed on top of him and bore him to the ground.

As the giant hooked claws dug into him, the man's scream echoed up to the ridge.

The other soldiers had their weapons ready, and there was the blast of machine-gun fire, but the sickle-claws were already upon them.

From the ridge, Jonah was trying to track the fast-moving beasts for a clear shot. He jumped as, beside him, there was a sharp retort from Naomi's pistol. Down below, one of the sickle-claws dropped.

It didn't matter – there were half-a-dozen of the clawed devils, and they set upon the four remaining men like a pack of bounding kangaroos.

The chopper pilot went first, his throat torn away by an eight-inch foot claw. The outpost sentry was next, disemboweled.

The remaining two soldiers made a fight of it, taking out two more of their taloned attackers, even as Naomi caught another from the ridge – but the last two got through, piling into both troopers at once, their deadly sickles tearing and slashing.

One man fell, trying to wrestle the clawed beast, even as its foot-sickle gutted him. Jonah managed to drop the beast with a rifle shot – a bit belatedly for the soldier's sake.

The other man was already down, and the sound of *ripping* tissue carried all the way up the ridge. Naomi dropped the beast off his chest with a single shot, but it was clear the damage was already done.

Jonah scoped the remaining beast, where it still lay over the body of the first soldier, but it appeared the one shot the young man had gotten off had done its work, and the creature was unmoving.

The little group of Ottos perked, looking up as a troop towards the ridge.

Naomi drew a bead and fired another shot, but the scaly rats scattered into the surrounding brush.

That wasn't good. Any time those little bastards were around, things went south fast.

The fact of the six-dead sickle-claws was also bad – not that they were *dead*, but now you knew they were in the area. And this troop must have been prowling within their scent range all morning.

And as they made their way through the camouflaging bush, down to the clearing, Jonah and Naomi were both unhappily aware that likely meant there were more of them prowling about,

The carnage was typical of a sickle-claw attack. The men who had been hit were hard to look at.

But now there came a low moan.

The first soldier, who had released the Ottos, still lying under the dead body of the dromaeosaur he'd shot, was alive.

Jonah started to roll the lifeless beast away, only to see where both foot claws were buried in the young man's chest, the hand claws clasped onto his shoulders, locked-on for leverage, just beginning the convulsive slash downward – a strike that on a large prey animal would leave ten-inch deep, slashing divots over four feet long.

But the bullet had caught the creature's heart, and it froze stiff, postured in death, in a perfect strike pose. Jonah remembered a fossil had been discovered just like that, – a Velociraptor and a small ceratopsian, with the predator's foot claw buried in its prey's throat.

The young man was conscious, blinking up at them, his eyes full of pain.

Naomi grabbed hold of the foot claws. She eyed the man, her face sympathetic.

"This is going to hurt," she said, and yanked the sickles free.

The soldier shrieked, and blood spurted from the wound. Without waiting, Naomi pulled both hand claws loose, and Jonah pushed the dead sickle-claw away.

"Ohhhh, Jesus," the man moaned. "That *hurts*."

"He got you pretty good," Naomi allowed, leaning over to inspect the wounds. Jonah began rooting through his pack. After a moment, he handed Naomi a first-aid kit.

"So, soldier," Naomi said as she pulled a vial of alcohol and begin daubing, "what's your name?"

"Meyers," the young man said, wincing at the sting. "Corporal Meyers."

Naomi nodded at the empty carrying crate.

"And what the hell were you doing letting those scaly little bastards loose?"

Meyers looked uncertain.

"There was this girl," he said. "One of the refugees back at the base. She said it was a lab animal and they were going to dissect it. She couldn't bear it. Said it reminded her of Wilbur the Pig." Meyers shrugged. "It's a scaly little rat. What harm could it do?"

Naomi held up a blood-soaked cloth.

"How does your ass feel?" she said.

"Not too good," Meyers admitted.

"Where are you headed?" Jonah asked, keeping his eye on the surrounding trees.

"I can't give out that information," Meyers said.

Naomi didn't even look up, but her fingers dug where she had been doctoring.

Meyers' face went tight.

"We've got a base up on the mountain," he said quickly. "We're a supply-chain. Delivering to outposts." He caught Naomi's expectant eye. "My Commanding Officer is Major Travis," he finished.

At that moment, Meyers' radio barked static – the caravan calling in.

"Hey, Meyers? Anyone there? This is Bob. Is our path clear? Repeat. All clear?"

Meyers' radio was pinned under his hip, and it was ginger moving him, but even as Naomi started to pull it free, a response sounded – in 'Bob's' own voice.

"All clear," the voice said.

There was a static bark from the tower, and they turned to see one of the little lizards in the window, standing at the microphone. Its parrot-like voice repeated, "All clear."

Naomi picked it off with a pistol shot, sending the little beast spinning.

Meyers glanced at her, brows raised. "Are you military?"

"My husband was," Naomi replied.

Meyers glanced at Jonah. "This guy isn't...?"

"*No*," Naomi said, before he could finish, emphatically slapping a new clip into her pistol.

Meyers' radio barked again – Bob: "Okay, we're coming through."

And from the brush behind them, an exact repetition, with even the crack of static, "Okay, we're coming through."

They turned and the other two Ottos were back, perched right in a row at the edge of the forest, their heads all cocked, birdlike.

"What harm could it do?" the first one said, with Meyers' voice this time, in that same apparently mindless, parrot-like mimic.

And then they all screeched together.

From the surrounding brush, more sickle-claws appeared – an entire pack of the wolf and panther-sized beasts that always seemed to accompany the scaly little bastards, like a prehistoric royal guard.

Jonah guessed at least two-dozen animals. Naomi was a good shot, but in these close-quarters, she didn't have enough bullets in a clip. And Jonah might pick off one or two with his rifle before they tore him apart.

But then there came the crunch of gravel from the unmaintained former highway that circled the ridge, and the first headlights of the convoy came into view.

"We've got to warn them," Naomi said, even as she eyed the surrounding sickle-claws.

"Warn them?" Jonah retorted, watching for the first movement, "Warn *us*!"

The sickle-claws seemed to hang on the moment – and that was another thing that was different whenever an Otto was around – dromaeosaurs were evil-tempered beasts on any given day, but mostly behaved like animals.

But today, they hung like trained attack-dogs waiting on command.

Jonah was frankly amazed there were so many of them. You didn't see sickle-claws much in the valley because the *T. rex* rooted them out, and there was no escaping that tyrannosaur nose. This lot must have been traveling the hills, just like Jonah and Naomi – a disconcerting thought.

Still, *this* many of them? How much longer could their combined scent fail to attract one of the local rex packs?

But even as he thought it, there came the first break in the heavy foliage, beyond the outpost – the sound of a large branch cracking under massive weight.

Jonah had read stories describing how five-ton elephants could stand unseen within meters of you in heavy brush.

But it was something else when a *T. rex* did it.

How could such a giant beast be so damned *sneaky*?

The first to separate from the forest was Rudy, followed by Moose, Archie and Jughead – the JV squad.

Opposite the clearing, the sickle-claws turned to face them, claws cocked.

Jonah and Naomi exchanged a worried glance. Trapped between them in the open ground, there was nowhere to run.

"We might be in trouble," Jonah said.

CHAPTER 3

Even in a world of monsters, *T. rex* was special.

Giant carnivorous dinosaurs came in a variety of forms, but among all flesh-eaters, *Tyrannosaurus rex* stood out like a pitbull in a dog-show.

The massive skull was built for impact – reinforced to take the shock of its own charging attack with its hydraulically muscular neck and skull, while its assault drove home twelve-inch, armor-piercing teeth, scissoring together to CHOMP out a scoop of flesh the size of a fifty-gallon barrel.

The reason *T. rex* didn't tolerate competitors was because they didn't *have* to. Jonah had seen more than one big carcharodont square-off with a rex – with the carnosaur usually holding a clear size-advantage. But faced with a rival predator, the carcharodonts unerringly made the tactical error of locking jaws with the smaller tyrannosaur.

In most cases, the big carnosaur simply had its face bitten away, sometimes with a simultaneous jerk that left its neck broken.

The JV squad were teenage *T. rex* – thin-boned for their size, but that still put them at twenty-feet tall and just under forty feet long. And while they maintained a svelte average bodyweight barely in excess of five tons, not yet filled out into full, stout adulthood, they were pretty damn fast at that size. More than that, they accelerated quickly – built for explosive movement, they could get that five tons coming at you like a white shark hitting a surfboard.

Jonah also saw that their hides were adorned with freshly-healed burns. The napalm-induced wildfire had left its mark. He wondered what happened to Trix and the others. Or the rogue. The fire had obviously separated the JV squad off into the valley.

The painful wounds could not have improved the mood of the already intolerant *T. rex*.

Nor would the presence of sickle-claws.

But as Jonah realized a moment later, that was undoubtedly what saved their lives.

Up the road, the caravan had now come into open view.

Like a rabbit in a greyhound race, the two Ottos darted in their direction.

The sickle-claws broke as a flock, immediately on their heels.

Like five-ton greyhounds, the *T. rex* bolted after them.

Without a sideways glance, the rex pack thundered past, leaving the three huddling humans in the clearing miraculously untouched.

And as much as the tyrannosaurs hated sickle-claws, Jonah knew it was *Otto* they were after.

That was another thing Jonah had seen demonstrated – *repeatedly* – if *T. rex* hated sickle-claws, it LOATHED *those* little bastards. Jonah had seen tyrannosaurs walk through fire and munitions just to stomp a single Otto flat.

And God forbid an *infected* rex get a whiff – entire skyscrapers might fall for even one of the scaly little rats hiding in the basement.

T. rex understood the concept of a flyswatter, but it carried a sledge.

On the other hand, if they had an odd instinctive compulsion to smash those parrot-talking little bastards into paste, Jonah was fine with it – he didn't particularly like them either.

In any case, it had certainly proved reliable behavior.

Reliability that, Jonah now realized, was being exploited.

A rex would chase those scaly rats wherever they went, and right now they were running straight at the convoy.

Recognizing the danger, Meyers tried to sit up, struggling to reach for his radio, but his wounds immediately began to bleed.

Jonah looked grimly after the juvie-gang of *T. rex* chasing the hooligan pack of sickle-claws, and then to the unsuspecting troops, only now coming around the bend.

"Sorry, pal," Jonah said, as he hiked Meyers' weight up enough to pull the radio from his belt, eliciting a painful curse from the wounded soldier. Jonah fiddled with the switches, trying to make it work.

"Oh for God's sake," Naomi said "Give me that!" She grabbed it up and flipped the transmit switch. "Hello? Anyone there?"

"This is Sergeant Robert Jameson," the voice barked back. "Who the hell is this?"

Meyers grimaced as reached for the radio, his voice a painful grunt as he hit the switch.

"Listen up, Bob," he said, "this is Meyers. You've got incoming!"

"What are you talking about...?" came the response, but now the convoy pulled into view and the situation spoke for itself.

The sickle-claw pack was leopard-sized, but when they were attacking, they didn't come at you like mammalian pack hunters – they *mobbed*.

Sergeant Bob's voice sounded over the radio. "Oh *shit*!"

Machine gun fire erupted. The half-dozen vehicles skidded to a halt as the sickle-claws swept over them in a wave.

Barely two-hundred yards away, the outpost clearing provided a clear view.

It was a one-two assault – the sickle-claw mob drew the troops' initial attention for those first vital moments.

A convoy like this would carry munitions that could take down a *T. rex,* but it took a *big* gun – you were talking about a creature the size of an elephant, but *much* more densely constructed, and far more muscular and thicker-boned. Putting one down required bazooka-level munitions.

But the troops' initial reaction was to engage the smaller sickle-claws already upon them – a man-sized animal, more easily dealt with using rifles.

When the JV squad battened down, bare moments later, they simply never had a chance.

Jonah estimated two-dozen men over the six vehicles. Gunshots quickly mixed with screams after the few seconds of the sickle-claw assault.

Then the *T. rex* hit.

"Oh Jesus," Meyers said, covering his eyes.

Jonah had seen rex packs do this to convoys before – they simply bulldozed anything in their path. RVs crumpled like paper under stomping feet, chomping jaws bit cleanly through metal chassis, or were simply grabbed and physically *thrown*.

And a machine gun just pissed-off a *T. rex* – probably the worst move under the circumstances because it attracted their attention. If the troops had simply run, the JV squad would have probably ignored them. As it was, the retaliatory gunfire was promptly snuffed. In less than a minute, the convoy was smashed into wreckage, and the troops along with it.

The rex pack took a few hits, but ignored the angry rash of peppered bullet wounds, as they now turned to the renegade sickle-claws, and in particular, to Otto.

Normally, a sickle-claw raiding party would sensibly retreat once a rex pack appeared on the scene, but today, in Otto's presence, they instead turned to fight – a strategy that proved helpful for the *T. rex*.

As the dromaeosaurs attempted to mob the outnumbered rex, the tyrannosaurs met them face-first, snapping wildly in every direction, like swordfish in a tight grouping of tuna.

Jonah once read you could hear a crocodile's 'jaw-snap' over a greater distance than a shotgun. *T. rex* jaws coming together echoed like a cannon blast.

In another minute, this secondary skirmish was over and quickly followed by several judiciously-placed stomps as the big rex rooted out and squashed the scampering Ottos.

Once the last of the little lizards was accounted for, the rex pack settled down and started picking at the scraps.

Jonah saw Jughead toss a soldier's body down his massive gullet like a pelican swallowing a fish. The others poked and pecked among the wreckage like giant pigeons.

But Jonah knew what came next.

Rudy was the first to turn his head in their direction. Jonah turned a nervous eye to Naomi. She nodded back.

"We've got to get out of here," she said.

Jonah looked around. The radio tower wouldn't protect them from a rex. But trying to escape on foot, they would just be run down.

There was, however, the chopper.

Jonah shut his eyes. He'd become a pilot because he'd grown up wanting to fly. But as an adult, he'd discovered it was not the feeling of a soaring bird, so much as driving a big, heavy truck high up in the air – a rather frightening sensation that he'd never really gotten over, even after getting his commercial license. It was why he preferred smaller aircraft, like his little buzz-chopper, or a little single-engine plane.

This thing was a friggin' flying tank.

"Can you fly it?" Naomi asked, clearly no happier than he was.

Behind them, Jughead was also now looking after them curiously, his head cocked over the smoking ruins of the convoy, a dead sickle-claw dangling from his jaws.

Jonah ran to where the pilot had fallen. Keeping his eyes averted from the gory remains, he rifled through the dead man's pockets until he found the key chain.

Naomi was now standing over Meyers' still form. In her hand, she had his dog-tags.

"He's dead," she said. "Let's get out of here."

Rudy was moving in their direction – not a run, just a casual stride. On twelve-foot legs.

A *T. rex* had good eyes, and they were attracted to movement like cats, easily enticed to chase.

Jonah and Naomi were now the only things still moving.

The two of them scrambled aboard the chopper – and then sat for several excruciating moments, as Jonah first determined the correct key, and then figured out how to start the damned thing.

Naomi twisted in the co-pilot's seat, looking anxiously over her shoulder.

Jughead was following Rudy, a dozen steps and closing fast.

"*Jonah...*" Naomi began.

There was a startling roar as the twin rotors suddenly fired to life.

Rudy answered with a roar of his own, breaking into a lumbering run.

Jonah yanked the joystick – the craft was just as heavy and awkward as he feared, and the chopper threatened to spin, even as the air-blast yanked them off the ground like the jerk of a hanging rope.

Rudy was coming up fast, and Jonah was certain the rear rotors were going to strike the rex as it came charging in.

For a split second, they hung nearly eye-to-jaw as Rudy's four-and-a-half-foot skull split into a gaping maw.

Jonah heard the jaw-snap, like the smash of six-ton anvils, less than two feet from his window, before the chopper launched in a twisting lurch into the air.

Naomi grabbed her seat, shutting her eyes as the forest spun around them, her voice trilling in a low moan. "Ohhhh *God....*"

But as they ascended the tree-tops, the wobble straightened out.

Jonah took them straight up, letting the spinning momentum wind itself out, until he had control.

Jughead joined Rudy below, bellowing angrily after the retreating chopper.

Jonah took a breath.

"Well, *that* was closer than I would have liked."

Naomi was still rigid, looking down at the tantruming *T. rex*. Rudy roared and stamped his feet. Jughead sniffed briefly at Meyers' body and then snapped it up. Naomi turned away, grimly, pointing to the west.

"He told us his base was up on the mountain," she said.

"You sure that's a good idea?"

Naomi indicated the scene below as Rudy and Jughead turned to rejoin the others, pecking clean the last scraps of the convoy.

"I don't want to be on the ground," she said. "We've got to go somewhere."

Jonah had no better ideas, and started to veer west. The big aircraft moved sluggishly, but with an excess of power.

"These things are too big," he said, wrestling with the joystick. "Scares the hell out of me."

Naomi quipped brief laughter. "Scares *you*? I've flown with you twice. You've crashed both times. Try not to make it three for three."

Jonah frowned. There were a lot of extraneous circumstances she was leaving out. One of those incidents had been a pterosaur attack, and the other was the blast wave from a nuclear explosion.

To be fair, he thought he'd done alright.

"We're both still here," he said, "I haven't killed us yet."

Naomi kept her eyes on the hard ground below as Jonah wobbled the big chopper unsteadily.

"Not *yet*," she replied.

CHAPTER 4

Rosa had seen pterosaurs take down choppers before.

That was why their military transport picked up speed as it passed over the peaks of the Rocky Mountains – by Rosa's estimate somewhere between Colorado and Utah.

It didn't matter. Once they got near the trees, pterosaurs came up at them in flocks, like clouds of bats, some of them forty-feet across.

Not that size seemed to make a difference. A four-foot pterodactyl would charge a fully-gunned Blackhawk, diving blindly right through the rotor blades

The transport chopper was flying twelve deep. Besides the two pilots, there were eight civilian passengers – or 'seven-and-a-half', counting the very smallest, who was less than six-months old, and as far as Rosa knew, he was the only newborn in North America – perhaps the world.

There were also two gunmen on-board, and as the mob of pterosaurs flocked in, they slid the side-panel open, letting in the blast of cold wind. In careful, measured shots, they began to pick off the flying dragons that seemed to zero-in on the chopper like moths to flame.

As she saw the first of the pterosaurs drop limply out of the air, Rosa's confidence rose a notch – the gunners were clearly sharp-shooters.

But the freezing wind and gunshots prompted frightened wails from the little bundle, clutched tightly to the breast of the woman beside her.

Rosa had been a doctor in her previous life – Doctor Rosa Holland, MD – and she had met this then-expectant mother on KT-day.

Allison was her name, and Rosa remembered assessing her with a tiredly jaded-eye – body-art and pole-dancer, just showing pregnant – a type Rosa had seen many times – usually druggies – often the sort that delivered meth-addicted babies.

Then there was the man with her – 'Bud' – *just* a bit older – another animal Rosa had known before – the doting, low-rent sucker, who Allison would settle for in place of a sugar-daddy, now that she was knocked-up. Rosa had never asked if Bud was the father, although she suspected his wallet would be acting like he was.

This snap-judgment had been within thirty seconds of meeting them. Since the world ended, Allison and Bud had saved her life half-a-dozen times.

They had all survived together on the road for the past year.

For her part, during that time, Rosa had helped deliver Allison's young son – possibly the first birth in the new world. In the months since, Allison watched over him like a mother bear.

And now the blasts of gunfire, and the cold grab of wind were terrifying.

Allison, herself, was in tears as she tried to calm her crying infant. Bud lay a protective arm helplessly over her shoulder, as the chopper rocked around them.

One of the other passengers, however, rose from her seat – the one woman out of the group of four the transport had picked up on their last stop, only an hour before.

Rosa didn't know what to make of her yet.

The young woman had caught Rosa's eye as they'd boarded and taken the seats opposite the cabin. She was strikingly beautiful, although in the manner of an athlete rather than a supermodel – she moved like a performance artist in a ballet, as she rose from her seat as casually as a passenger on a commercial flight. Her eyes were bright and unguarded, and as she caught Rosa's eye, she smiled gently with the comfortable familiarity of an old friend.

Her companions called her Shanna, and now she knelt easily at Allison's knee, balanced with that dancer's grace, amid ringing gunshots at her ear, the whistling wind, and the chopper's abrupt back-and-forth lurches.

"Shhhh," Shanna said, as she first set a soft hand on Allison's shoulder, and then touched her wailing little bundle on one tear-streaked cheek.

Like a passing squall, the cries faded away.

The little eyes blinking out of the wrapped blankets matched those of his mother as Allison smiled shyly back.

Shanna nodded to Rosa as she sat back down, clutching the side of the rocking aircraft like a carnival ride.

Rosa was frankly amazed. She had known Allison nearly a year, and while perhaps unfairly judging her character, the scars Rosa had recognized in that cynical first appraisal were very real.

Happenstance placed them together on KT-day, trapped among the wreckage, along with a handful of other survivors. But even huddling among the cracks, in the days and weeks that followed, as the apocalypse erupted all around them, Allison had sat away from the rest. Only Bud would sometimes sit apart with her.

But today, when Shanna had bent at her knee, Allison had leaned close, as if huddling by a fire – although, her eyes still blinked away, as if not to stare directly at the burning embers, not quite ready to step fully into the light.

Whatever happened to her in the old world scarred her deep. The most common vices always did. It was possible the apocalypse had saved her life – even the life of her baby, if it happened to have dried her out.

Speculations, of course. These were all questions Rosa had never asked.

None of it mattered after KT-day.

And none of it would have mattered at all but for a swaggering fly-jockey, who just happened to crash his jet almost on top of their huddled group of survivors, and had somehow managed to sheer *alpha-male* them out of the devastated city, all the way to his base.

Lieutenant Lucas Walker – call-sign 'Skywalker' – a chiseled specimen, who represented everything Rosa considered primitive and animal-like about the human male – made worse by the keen, wry mind that piloted his not-inconsiderable physique.

Rosa, an anti-war pacifist, who loathed everything he stood for, had nonetheless found herself swept back to the primitive, and by the time she'd seen the last of him, she was pretty sure she had been in love with him – a married man, no less, who was himself waiting on word of his missing wife.

When he'd left them that last day, Rosa had kissed him goodbye. Then he had gone on to save them all, one last time – and she had never seen him again.

He had told Rosa it was for his wife – that was why he fought – every time.

Rosa wondered if at least some of it, that last time, was for her.

Allison had named her child Lucas.

From Rosa's end, Lieutenant 'Skywalker's' ultimate fate remained inconclusive. She had waited for any of the pilots to return, but none did. The base that had been their sanctuary had been destroyed. And the original group of eight Lucas had trafficked across the apocalyptic tundra had been pared down to just the three of them.

Bud had approached her on the third day after. They couldn't just sit camped out forever.

It was a special cruelty that she would never know.

Rosa realized she should simply be grateful and accept the gift of the life he had saved for her, and not to look the gift-horse in the mouth for not providing her closure.

Still, once they set on the road, she had taken to hailing military lines, ostensibly because that seemed the most likely route to some semblance of civilization – but, truthfully, she had been looking for some word of Lucas.

Now, for her troubles, it seemed they had essentially voluntarily consented to what felt more and more like capture.

She found herself not liking the questions they were being asked – skills, age, fertility.

They were to be taken to a refugee camp but had been informed resources were strained.

Allison and baby Lucas were *in*. Bud, on the other hand, Rosa found herself worrying about. He was not a young man, and the skills of a former journalist were not in great demand.

He was on-board for now, but as one of the soldiers – one of the sharp-shooters – had remarked, he might get 'phased-out' later.

This had been after they had picked up Shanna's entourage.

The soldier, whose badge identified as Wilkes, had expressed surprise that the new group was three-to-one men.

"That's actually the opposite," he remarked, "of our marching orders."

"Pardon?" Rosa had asked.

"When pulling in civilians," Wilkes replied, "first rule – three-to-one, women to men." He shrugged. "The way I understand it, productive females are greater assets than males."

"Assets," Rosa repeated.

"It's tougher for us fellas," Wilkes said, nodding sympathetically to Bud. "On the other hand, we're always at breeding age, so less age-restriction. Fair's fair, right?" He chuckled a little. "Besides, three girls for every guy sounds like a good party to me."

Rosa nodded mildly. "And this is where you're taking us?"

Wilkes nodded back. "They're calling it the Arc Project," he said. "Repopulate the Earth. Except they're trying to slant the odds over Noah's two-by-two."

Breeding stock, Rosa thought. The sort of thing scientists once theorized about – most often in pipe-smoke, spit-ball fashion.

Hypothetical supposition of dystopian extremes were now apparently guiding policy.

Wilkes smiled at Rosa reassuringly. "Don't worry. A doctor? Besides being female and all, you're doubly valuable."

Rosa absorbed this silently. Had the species really been brought so low that such measures were actually in place?

Never mind the *other* implications...

For the immediate moment, Rosa pushed the incoming thoughts away – that was just too wide-open to speculate on, based on the hearsay of a field-combat soldier.

It did not, however, on any level, sound good.

That was when Shanna had spoken up.

"The Arc Project is Dr. Shriver's plan," she said. "I know him. He's basing it all on breeding rates with comparable animals, and minimum genetic diversity necessary, and simply assigning the numbers to humans."

She shook her head. "The problem is, humans need a society. Reproduction is only part of the issue. What he's setting up at the Mount is an ant-farm." She considered. "Well, more like a chicken-coop." She sighed. "That's the problem with myopic *experts*."

Shanna leaned forward across the aisle, offering her hand to introduce herself.

Rosa felt the odd glow, the almost bewitching air about her. While she shook Rosa's hand, Shanna smiled back at her, as if the touch told her more than her eyes.

Clearly, Allison had felt it too. When Shanna knelt beside her, it was like a hissing stray cat cozened right up and purring. And Bud, the guard-dog, allowed her within Allison's inner-space. Rosa had barely been granted that privilege during Lucas' birth.

Shanna's entourage was also an odd cast.

The most obvious was a braggadocios lout, with the nerve to call himself 'Maverick' – a nickname, she hoped – along with an older gentleman, who appeared to be his father, and simply referred to as 'Mr. Wilson' by their third, somewhat milder companion, who introduced himself as Cameron.

All three of them hovered around Shanna like a troop of protective malamutes. And while it was clear they were all *with* her, Cameron seemed to be the one at her side.

"We were traveling west," he told Rosa, "but we got recaptured refueling at a depot in Idaho."

Not 'captured', Rosa noted, *'recaptured'*.

Who exactly *were* these people?

"That was where you picked us up," Cameron said. "We'd been there three days when we got word all civilians were being moved."

The second soldier, a stern fellow, whose badge labeled as Garner, had tapped his rifle butt on the floor like a stomping hoof.

"That's not something you need to be talking about."

Cameron smiled obligingly, sitting back.

Maverick had leaned forward.

"You know," he said to Garner good-naturedly, "I've only known you an hour and I'd already like to kick your ass."

Unimpressed, Garner lay his rifle across his lap.

"You know," he said, "I'd like to *shoot* you." His marksman's eyes leveled back at Maverick's. "Best we don't act on our impulses, don't you think?"

Maverick nodded to Rosa, smiling winningly.

"Hey, honey," he said confidentially, "if you haven't noticed, this guy's a douche-bag."

Rosa nodded back, acknowledging freely that there was no shortage of douche-bags handy.

As if to put a stamp on it, Mr. Wilson reached out and swatted Maverick across the back of the head. "Keep a lid on it, boy."

Maverick cussed, rubbing his head, but subsided.

Rosa found herself wondering what this idiot could have done to make him important enough to be a prisoner. So far, he seemed to be a solid selling point for three-to-one women – an impression that was helped not at all, as he nodded at her with a wink.

Something about his swagger reminded her of Lieutenant Walker, both seemingly overdosed in testosterone.

Of course, the difference was just as obvious – Lucas Walker had been an elite cut of military discipline.

It was a similar discipline that she saw in both Wilkes and Garner.

Still, she wondered what Lieutenant Lucas might have made of the two of them.

There had never been a feeling of being expendable under Lucas' watch. At the same time, he also made you willing to follow him through Hell.

But priorities had changed since Lucas had been alive.

Rosa wondered what the mission statement would be now.

Despite being an 'asset", as Wilkes had phrased it, Rosa felt very expendable.

She blinked, realizing Shanna was looking at her, and when she spoke, she seemed to answer Rosa's own thought.

"We're *all* assets," Shanna said. "That's why we're going to the mountain."

Rosa eyed her warily. She felt an inexplicable impulse towards *liking* this woman, and her analytical mind didn't trust it. Rosa had known charming people before and knew that personality did not presuppose character. There was, after all, the charm of the Devil.

"Why are *you* an asset?" Rosa asked.

Shanna smiled. "Oh dear. As far as General Rhodes is concerned, I am THE asset."

"Who's General Rhodes?"

Sergeant Garner again started to object, but this time Shanna held up a shushing hand.

"You just sit still," she said. "Knowing General Rhodes... and I *do*," Shanna paused, allowing the emphasis to sink in, "I'm sure he wouldn't want to hear that you upset me. You're under strict orders, I'm sure."

Garner frowned.

"Ma'am. With all due respect, you're sharing sensitive information."

Shanna smiled. "I am," she agreed. "My whole life is sensitive information. Now hush."

"Yeah, douche-bag," Maverick volunteered. "Hush."

Garner eyed Maverick darkly, and Rosa saw his fingers tap, just for a second, on the rifle in his lap.

Rosa wondered if Maverick wasn't pushing his luck. In this era of expendable civilians and gender-quotas, might not redundant components be dealt with callously?

Maverick seemed pretty confident in the importance of his own asset, so to speak, but Rosa found herself doubtful if he might not be earning himself a bullet.

For the moment, Garner's patience held.

Then the first of the pterosaurs attacked.

With the same sort of lethally professional movements Rosa associated with Lieutenant Walker, both Wilkes and Garner were at their stations on either side of the chopper in moments. They also took out the leathery flying devils with the same sort of accuracy Rosa had seen Lucas target sickle-claws – elite training.

The problem was that pterosaurs had a tendency to swarm. An entire group might mob a chopper, letting themselves get chopped up, as if the whirling blades activated some basic instinct, like a bug into an electric zapper.

Unfortunately, that most often meant the rotor blades were broken away, clogged with the sheer weight of that much chopped meat.

The pilots seemed to know this – at this point, any chopper pilots who hadn't learned to evade pterosaurs, were probably already dead.

There was a lurch as the chopper arched upward – altitude and speed, established protocol – first evade the mob, and then outrun them.

It would have worked if not for a particularly large individual, with easily a fifty-foot wingspan, that caught them sideways.

Even large pterosaurs were light-boned, but this was still an animal in excess of a thousand pounds, impacting against a flying object the size of a city bus.

It was enough to smash the windshield, and the six-foot beak that came in through the window impaled the pilot like a spear.

The creature itself was killed on impact, neck broken, its beak planted through the pilot's chest into his seat, leaving its own dangling body draped over the windshield.

Rosa felt the chopper lurch into a sudden nosedive as both creature and pilot slumped over the controls. The co-pilot wrestled for the joystick, but it was pinned beneath their combined dead weight.

Maverick was already up and moving, and was met immediately by Garner, his rifle business-end up.

This was the moment, Rosa thought, where Maverick pushed it too far – and he clearly intended to, because as he stepped casually past Garner to the cockpit, he extended a stiff straight punch that knocked the soldier out cold.

Wilkes moved immediately to intercept, but Maverick was already helping the co-pilot pull the impaling beak free of the dead pilot's chest.

Maverick shouted back angrily at Wilkes, "Don't just stand there, ya damned fool. Help us out!"

The plummeting chopper seemed to *lean* into its dive, leaving the passengers clinging to their seats. Wilkes did not so much comply as was thrown forward, and his added strength allowed them to wrench the prehistoric bird-thing loose.

Rosa didn't see precisely what happened next. As the big pterosaur's corpse started to tumble away, it looked like the head – part air-rudder, part fishing-scythe – caught wind and jerked in the tight compartment, catching the co-pilot in the throat.

Blood splattered like a hose. Wilkes sputtered as gore splashed his face.

Maverick shoved him aside, as he yanked the dead pilot out of the seat, grabbing the joystick.

"What the hell are you doing?" Wilkes shouted. "Are you a pilot?"

"Grew up flying my daddy's crop-duster," Maverick replied, straining to pull them level. "How hard could it be?"

Behind them, Mr. Wilson's eyes were shut.

"Ah Jeez," he muttered, "he's gonna kill us all."

Centrifugal force was against them, like going into a tight turn too fast – the moment of vertigo as you began to *tilt*.

Rosa felt the sickening shift in momentum – the drop in the stomach – the grab of gravity after you step out over a height you know is enough to kill you.

The mountain below peaked and dropped off rapidly beyond its south face. At the angle they were coming in, their trajectory either put them broadside into the peak itself, or over the top into the canyon beyond.

The *crash*-part seemed inevitable.

Allison clutched baby Lucas, with Bud's arms wrapped tight around them both. Wilkes clung from the doorway to the cockpit, still standing over Garner, who remained out cold. Cameron and Shanna both buckled in. Glancing out the window at the fast-approaching ground, Rosa did likewise.

Maverick grunted as he strained the joystick and tipped their momentum just slightly over the top of the peak.

The heavy-duty aircraft hit the descending slope, and began to slide down the opposite side of the mountain.

Rosa was just thinking how lucky there were no large trees ahead, until she realized that was because there was a drop-off, and open-canyon beyond.

The impact had crumpled their landing gear, and they were in a free slide.

"Do something!" Wilkes stammered.

"What do you want me to do?" Maverick barked back. "Jump out and drag my feet?"

The spinning rotors sputtered and quit as the big chopper skidded up to the edge of the cliff. The front of the craft slid over the side, dangling into open air.

But just before the weight begin to tip, the chopper slid to a stop.

Maverick let out a slow whistle.

There was a communal escalation of relief from the cabin.

Mr. Wilson shook his head in open disbelief. "I'll say this for him, the son of a bitch is hard to kill."

Allison looked down at stoic little Lucas, who hadn't uttered a sound through the whole thing.

Rosa was a little speechless herself. She actually couldn't believe they were alive.

At that moment, Garner sat up groggily, putting a hand to his swelling jaw.

And Rosa felt the momentum of the chopper shift.

Then it tipped and fell over the edge.

CHAPTER 5

'Monster Island' was always one of the wilder urban legends.

Kate certainly never expected to be going there one day. Yet, there she was, out over open ocean in a little rented Cessna, flying low, so as not to be detected by radar.

It was exactly three weeks before what surviving *homo sapiens* would start calling 'KT-day' and no one on board had any idea they were ushering in the end of the world.

Kate had been skeptical when she had first started receiving mysterious e-mails a few weeks before – broken pieces of messages, attached to snippets of video.

Her first reaction was to assume a put-on. Modern CGI could be convincing, and pranks kept pace with special effects. In 1923, Sir Arthur Conan Doyle had previewed cuts from the silent film, *The Lost World* – subtly implying that the footage was real – and the then-breakthrough stop-motion technology was enough to fool the New York Times.

Kate's reputation as a journalist was already considered a bit sensational – an accusation she maintained was because she commanded a public following independent of any parent network.

She actually laughed at the thought of bringing the networks the brief clip of video, like one of those 'lost-footage' dramas that had become so cliched.

Although, this clip *was* well done. Kate looked closely for pixel lines but could find no tells.

Still, you had what *was* possible, and what was *not* – what she saw on this video was obviously impossible, and so that sufficed as its own tell.

It wasn't until her long-time tech-nerd assistant had analyzed it that Kate had taken a second look.

Recruited right out of college, Betty had hired-on as a data-analyst and because she was highly adept with computers, although both were really periphery-skills of her primary field of study, which had been genetics – with her particular area of interest being medicinal applications of drugs and chemicals.

"The resolution on this footage," Betty pointed out, "is extremely high. Higher than most studios use. It's hard to fake at this level."

She had sat back, absorbing the implications for herself.

"It *looks* real," she said.

For Kate, that was enough to get her going. Unfortunately, she had made the initial mistake of contacting official sources for confirmation – a pesky hold-over of old-style journalistic ethic, that was more of an encumbrance – and the next thing she knew, there were government officials confiscating her computer and her devices.

Then she had made the greater mistake of calling her father.

Four-star brigadier General Nathan Rhodes, semi-estranged from a daughter he'd raised alone, and a man of duty before all else. Kate's appeal had the effect of skipping past the rank-and-file, to a directly-ordered cover-up, right from the top.

She did, however, have the foresight to make a copy of the file, stashed in Betty's purse with her never even knowing, and just as easily retrieved.

Among other cryptic bits of information – broken-broadcast chop, as if someone had attempted to scrub the entire message before it had even been sent – there also contained latitude/longitude coordinates and a map.

The destination lay deep in restricted waters.

No sense going through official sources for permission on this one, Kate had decided It would likely get her in trouble just asking. She would certainly be questioned, and probably detained, General's daughter or not.

Kate was therefore going anyway, and would just skip the asking part.

She had the crew – a little team she'd set-up and kept together in a loose alliance for years.

First and foremost, she had a crazy pilot, willing to fly *any* aircraft, credentialed or not, and hadn't been killed yet. An important first step, all the more ironic in that Betty had been their initial contact.

Kate made wide use of unpaid interns, particularly at the start of her career. As a student at NYU, Betty had operated in this capacity since she was a sophomore.

On this particular evening, Kate was due in Chicago for an on-set interview, debuting her first mainstream film release – an exposé on war-profiteering, that would *really* piss-off her father. It was also intended to be a career kick-starter – the first time one of the major networks had agreed to promote her.

But she had to *get* there, and damned if one of the biggest storms to hit New York in years hadn't up and blown through, shutting down all the goddamn airports.

Kate had called all the charter pilots and found them either grounded or already booked. Betty, however, mentioned a guy she knew on campus – a film-student, whose mini-feature class-projects featured a lot of aerial footage.

"He has a friend who's a pilot," Betty said. "I think they do charter work."

"Is he any good?" Kate had asked.

"Well, he's hot," Betty said. "That's actually why I was talking to his friend, because I wanted to meet..."

Kate interrupted. "Can you get him here quickly?"

Betty produced a phone number – the film-student, who agreed to meet them. With Betty in tow, Kate spent an hour driving through the deluge and flooded roads, out of the city to a small, commercial air-park on Long Island, that catered to small aircraft and private charters.

She was even less enthused when she met the duo waiting with their twin-engine plane.

The burly fellow who was apparently the pilot, introduced himself as Maverick.

"You know," he said, "after *Top Gun*."

Kate had glanced doubtfully at Betty, who shrugged.

His companion smiled reassuringly. "He'll get us there," he said. He reached to shake her hand. "My name's Cameron."

"You're the film student. Why are *you* here?"

"Maverick needed a ride. His driver's license is currently suspended."

His grin widened as he grabbed up their bags. "All aboard."

It didn't get any better once they were in the air, especially after the turbulence *really* started tossing them – out over the Lakes, right around where the Witch of November had taken out the *Edmond Fitzgerald*.

"Where did you get your license?" Kate had asked – *shouted*, actually, over the thundering storm.

"License?" Maverick had replied, playing the wheel, seeming to dodge lightning strikes like slalom flags. "I learned to fly on my daddy's crop-duster."

Kate had glanced back to where Betty was retching into a bag, her voice an involuntary moan. "*Ohhhh* God."

"You might as well relax," Cameron told Kate, as they had barreled along, headlong, "he'll either crash us or he won't."

It was a remark that Kate had not found very reassuring.

But Maverick had gotten them there. In Kate's world, that was first and foremost. And while he wasn't an unpaid intern, he was a sight cheaper than most charter pilots.

Of such auspicious beginnings...

Maverick, as it turned out, was quite reliable, at least, in the sense that she could count on him to be talked into anything – if the cash was there, he did not care.

It dovetailed nicely that Cameron's role on their charter business had been filming the trip for customers, and his film-school skills adapted quite nicely as Kate's personal cameraman.

To her credit, Kate had kept this little Scooby Doo team together ever since. And when she had contacted them this morning, in the very early a.m. – via a text, no less – they were available on a dime.

"Got a communication/tip – you have to hurry – we need to GET there!!!"

When Cameron and Maverick had appeared on-scene, Kate showed them the craft she had acquired, just for the occasion.

It sat at the end of the boat-dock, floating on pontoons. A two-engine Cessna.

"We might need to make a water-landing," Kate said, "so...."

Maverick chuckled. "I've always wanted to try out one of these."

Then she had shown him the route.

"You realize," he said, "that this is deep within restricted waters?"

Kate nodded. "Is that a problem?"

"Well," Maverick asked, eyeing her meaningfully, "what would Han Solo do?"

"Ask for more money," Kate replied, pulling out her checkbook.

They had been in the air in twenty minutes.

The flight should not be more than three hours, the largest practical risk simply being the possibility of flying out into the middle of nowhere and running out of fuel over empty ocean.

They would also have to fly low to avoid radar, which would be harder on gas, and of course, *way* more dangerous.

Fortunately, Maverick was crazy enough on all necessary levels, and didn't require much convincing. And Cameron always just seemed to show up.

And Betty, who sat looking pale-green? Well, Kate hadn't exactly told her about the restricted air-space – or more accurately, she might have implied, by mentioning her father, that she'd gotten special clearance.

Kate operated on the philosophy that, if you needed someone's help, and it involved committing a federal and international crime, *and* you were pretty sure that person wasn't predisposed to do so, it was better not to tell them until after they'd already done it.

Ideally, it wouldn't come up until after they got back. Betty's mind was currently occupied with all the jumps and gyrations as Maverick wrestled with the unfamiliar craft, even as the surface winds from the ocean below tugged at the cumbersome pontoons.

"Jesus, Maverick," Kate barked, as she was tossed in her seat. "Can you fly this thing or not?"

"So far," he called back, and then dipped one wing, knocking them all back into their seats. "Now hush up in the peanut gallery."

Kate bit down her reply.

They'd been in the air nearly three hours. If their destination was there, it should be soon.

If it was there.

The next twenty-minutes would tell.

But then there was a crackle of static as Maverick's radio barked – a hailing frequency. Maverick hit a switch and a woman's voice came on the speaker.

"Attention! Unidentified aircraft. Please come in. You are traveling in restricted airspace in violation of international law. Please come in."

Maverick had tipped an eye to Kate. "Um. Boss? Does anyone know we're coming?"

Kate leaned forward, taking the co-pilot's headset.

"My name is Kate Rhodes. I received communication from Professor Nolan Hinkle, and was provided these coordinates."

There was a pause. When she replied, the woman's voice was doubtful.

"We accept visitors under absolutely no circumstances."

"Well," Kate replied, "we're here."

And for the first time, just ahead, on the endless stretch of ocean, they could see the peak of land-mass on the horizon.

From a distance, it appeared to be a flat plateau, rising out of the sea. But as they grew closer, they realized it was actually the mouth of what must have once been a huge volcano.

As they passed over, they saw the mouth created a circular wall around an interior bay, surrounding a smaller island within – a craggy mass that had likely once been a massive lava-cap.

The radio crackled again.

"Listen to me," the woman said, "you are in extreme danger. Do exactly as I say. Circle north. We have a dock at the lagoon. Maintain altitude. Do not drop below a hundred feet until you pass the reef."

Maverick glanced back at the cabin. Kate nodded.

Pushing the limits of his instruction, Maverick held at exactly one-hundred feet.

As he approached the island, the water below suddenly erupted.

Riding the exploding geyser were a massive set of crocodile-like jaws, attached to an enormous body that blasted out of the brine like a breaching whale.

The jaws snapped shut just below their ponderous dangling pontoons.

There was a second deluge of ocean as the beast crashed back beneath the surface.

"What the hell was *that*?" Maverick had barely reacted before the attack was over, like a croc missing a strike at a passing bird.

"Oh my God," Betty said, staring out the window. "It's all really true."

Cameron belatedly had his camera out, filming empty water where the creature had disappeared.

Properly impressed, Maverick held his altitude until they were well past the reef, and approaching the lagoon.

There was a long dock, probably where supplies were delivered. Maverick brought them in low, touching the pontoons down experimentally.

Kate had almost forgotten it was Maverick's first water-landing, but he promptly reminded them, as the plane skipped the waves like a tossed stone, threatening to tip, roll, and break apart.

Even Cameron held his breath as Maverick lurched them back up in the air, wings wobbling wildly, before finally stabilizing and dropping down onto the water.

"Just like water-skis," Maverick said, as they plowed the surface, and now he circled towards the dock.

He coasted the Cessna to a stop and cut the engines. The plane bumped against the pier.

Maverick turned to the cabin.

"Well," he said, "we're here."

When they pushed open the cabin door, the scent of heavy vegetation was cloying, and the heat hit them like a sauna.

The tropical lagoon sat sultry-still, greeting the four trespassers as they filed out of the plane. The dock led to a small clearing. A path, paved with gravel, was cut into the trees.

But so far, the road beyond was empty.

Maverick tied the plane to the dock. Kate snapped her fingers at Cameron, who was filming the beach and surrounding jungle.

"Camera on me," Kate said, posing in front of the clearing, as Cameron zoomed in on her.

"We have arrived," Kate said, in her best narrator's voice. "We are standing on what modern folklore has called Monster Island."

Cameron panned back to reveal the island behind her.

"Rumors have persisted for years," Kate continued, "dismissed as urban legend, dreamed-up in popular culture, stories of mutations and genetically-bred monstrosities. Scientific mythology.

"Yet today," Kate intoned, "before even landing on this island, we have already encountered irrevocable evidence that the impossible is true."

As she spoke, there was the sound of crunching movement from the gravel road. The heavy vegetation had grown together over-top, hedged together, like a gateway to the rest of the island, and now the bushes lining the path began to shake.

Cameron frowned as something dark filled his viewfinder. He pulled back from the camera, looking up.

"Uhhhh, Boss...?"

Kate saw his expression and started to ask, when Betty suddenly screamed aloud, full throated and shrill.

Beside her, Maverick let out a blue curse.

Kate turned.

Her gaze turned up.

Standing in the road, reared on its haunches, pushing the overgrown brush aside, was a silverback gorilla.

It stared down at the four paralyzed humans from better than twenty-feet high.

Kate sucked in breath and joined Betty's scream with her own.

The giant ape cocked its head, appearing somewhat displeased at the piercing shriek.

"Shit!" Maverick blurted, making a dash for the plane cabin. He emerged a moment later with a rifle. In a single movement, he shouldered it and fired.

In the same moment, Cameron reached up and pushed the barrel aside.

The ape looked startled as the shot zinged past its head. Then its lips pulled back into a growl.

Maverick rounded on Cameron. "What the hell are you *doing*?"

"*Wait!*" a voice cried out.

They heard the revving engine of a four-wheel Jeep as it appeared on the path, kicking up gravel and skidding to a stop protectively in front of the giant ape.

There was a young woman at the wheel, waving frantically.

"Don't shoot him!" she shouted.

The woman, presumably the same voice from the radio, stepped out of the Jeep, offering their first look at her.

Maverick whistled respectfully through his teeth.

Kate frowned at Maverick, although to be fair, the young woman did cut a figure that could distract from a twenty-foot gorilla.

The best description was that she seemed like a walking mirror of the surrounding tropics, radiating a lush, healthy bloom – in the tone of her muscle and the flush of her skin, she almost seemed to glow.

Kate was also struck by her direct, penetrating eyes, as she scanned each of them – narrowing particularly sternly at Maverick, who dutifully shouldered his rifle, holding up both hands apologetically.

She also spared a grateful eye to Cameron, who had diverted Maverick's errant gunshot.

Then she turned to where the giant ape was now shuffling cautiously towards them. The puny humans from the plane shrank back.

The young woman held out her hand. The big gorilla touched it gently.

"Are you okay, Congo?"

Congo grunted. He sat back and began making movements with his hands.

Kate realized the big ape was signing, just like Coco the chimp.

She nudged Cameron in the ribs. "Are you getting this?"

Cameron, filming more or less on auto-pilot, nodded numbly.

"Excuse me, Miss," Kate said. "But who exactly are you?"

The young woman turned, her hand still resting comfortingly on the four-foot palm of an eight-ton gorilla.

"My name is Shanna," she said. "Professor Nolan Hinkle is my father."

CHAPTER 6

"You people are in a lot of trouble," Shanna said.

The Jeep bumped along the gravel road as they traveled briskly through the jungle. As Shanna had loaded them aboard, Betty muttered unhappily to Kate, "You lied about getting clearance, didn't you?"

Kate shrugged.

Betty started to sigh, but instead let out another scream, as she climbed into the back and was greeted by a shrill, birdlike squawk.

From under the seat hopped what looked like a little plucked emu – no more than two-feet tall, with a whiplash tail, and a scaly head and neck like a lizard.

The creature hissed, and while its body was small, its gangly forelimbs ended in large claws, with a wicked-looking sickle on each big toe.

Betty froze as the little lizard-thing hopped into her lap, staring into her eyes like a hypnotizing cobra. Betty chittered like a trapped squirrel, trying to speak.

"Leave her alone, Otto," Shanna said. "Get in back."

In a flash, the obedient lizard hopped over the seat into the open trunk. Its lizard-head bobbed like an ostrich as it peered over the headrest.

Kate gave Betty a little push, sliding into the seat next to her. Betty looked uncomfortably behind her as Otto perched just at her shoulder like a parrot.

Maverick crowded in last, filling the back, and Cameron took the passenger seat in front.

Shanna glanced sideways at the camera on his shoulder.

"You shouldn't be filming," she said. "I'm serious. I already reported in when I first detected your plane. I'm pretty sure they're going to wake a few generals over this."

Kate nodded confidentially to Betty. "That'll piss my father off."

She leaned forward. "Where exactly are you taking us?"

"Up to the compound," Shanna replied. "This island is dangerous."

Kate glanced over her shoulder, where Congo loped along behind them.

The gravel road had taken a dramatic slope upward. As they emerged through the umbrella of foliage, breaking through into daylight, they came up along the canyon wall, and the road continued up into the highlands.

Kate estimated the entire island was no more than five-miles across – a lava plug that had once bubbled over the top of the mountain – a post-eruption regurgitation that had cooled and sealed the volcanic mouth.

It also seemed to have spent the last few thousand years breaking apart. The flat plateau was split by canyons, creating segregated valleys of wetlands, inundated by brush.

And as they circled the cliff, they got their first view of one of the triangulated valleys below.

Kate recognized the view – it was from the video clip that had been e-mailed to her.

Maverick let out a long slow whistle. Betty leaned over Kate's shoulder. Cameron held up his camera.

Monster Island. If the Nevada Desert was Area 51, this was Area 65,000,000 B.C..

These were the beasts on the video.

Even from the hilltop, looking down, the sight was majestic.

Prehistoric monsters, resurrected through genetics, just like the urban legends claimed.

Long-necked sauropods dominated the living diorama below, like elephants might lord over an African waterhole, except some of these creatures approached a hundred tons.

Smaller, but no less formidable, were herds of elephant-sized ceratopsians – mutated reptilian-rhinos in battle-armor.

A bevy of other plated and spiked denizens milled together, in what seemed an over-congested gathering – a lounge-spot where the falls cascaded down from the cliff, feeding the river on its way out to the ocean.

Since she'd first received the video, Kate had been reviewing her dinosaur species.

"These animals aren't just large," she said, "they're all the largest of their kind. Those aren't just sauropods, those are titanosaurs. And Triceratops is the largest of the ceratopsians."

Shanna said nothing, reluctant to speak, as Kate pointed out several other examples, all from different eras, all the culmination of their evolutionary lines.

"And what are those evil-looking critters?" Maverick asked, indicating a troop of decidedly non-herbivorous beasts lounging in the shade, stretched out like a pride of lions.

"Predators," Shanna said, "are mostly inactive during the day. Those are Giganotosaurus – a carcharodont-carnosaur."

"Largest of theropods," Kate said, nodding. "So? No *T. rex*, then?"

Shanna glanced at her in the mirror.

"We keep the *T. rex* sequestered," she said, "rival predators tend to fight."

There was a sudden, startled screech from the back seat. Otto had crept up on Betty's ear, darting a quick tongue in-and-out, prompting a frenzied response, her hands flailing as if slapping at a spider.

Otto hopped back over the seat.

"Leave her alone, Otto," Shanna chastised.

The little lizard ducked out of sight. Maverick grinned at Betty.

"I think he likes you,"

Casting Maverick an evil eye, Betty turned her attention back to the creatures down in the valley.

"These animals are too big for this island," she said. "There isn't enough biomass."

"We have automation," Shanna said, "that sends feed out to the island. We also have heavy vitamin content pumped into the water, saturating grazing fields, as well as hybridized vegetation. The sort that could feed the world if it were mass-produced."

"Why isn't it?" Betty asked.

"Because," Shanna said stiffly, "we don't exist."

They had reached the summit and could now see several structures built on the crest of the falls, right at the point where the plateau split – a hydro-power set-up, obviously, but unlike any Kate had ever seen.

Congo, who had been keeping pace at a galloping dog-trot, suddenly fell back.

"Your monkey friend's taking a powder," Maverick said.

"Yes," Shanna said. "We have a guest in camp right now, and they don't get along."

Kate wondered what manner of *guest* could drive off an eight-ton gorilla.

The compound was mounted so as to overlook the valley – a series of buildings, most utilitarian, but with living quarters perched at the top, and massive fencing built anywhere that wasn't protected by sheer drop-off.

Below the main compound, carved into the cliff so as to allow direct access to the road, there were several enclosures, constructed on stair-stepping levels, like a zoo built into a steep hillside.

Heavy-duty construction, Kate noted. Sort of like what you saw on elephant cages, or aquarium tanks containing whales.

Shanna slowed to a stop, parking the Jeep, and led them on foot to the main gate. The road looked down on the enclosures – they were all empty, except for the one immediately below.

"This," Shanna said, "is our guest."

The tyrannosaur was immense.

It lay in the enclosure, curled up like a big cat – or rather more like a big duck, with its nose tucked tight under one shoulder. It seemed to be sleeping, its huge nostrils flaring with deep rhythmic snores that might have echoed out of a bear's cave.

"He's *huge*," Betty said.

Shanna nodded.

"Yes. By weight, he's the biggest meat-eater on the island." She pushed open the gate that led to the enclosures. "Wait here a moment."

Shanna made her way down the steep stairway to the rex-pen.

The foursome watching from the road above drew a collective breath as she pulled the lock and stepped inside.

"Is she *crazy?*" Maverick whispered, lest his voice rouse the beast.

Cameron glanced wide-eyed at Kate, who motioned to keep his camera rolling.

Kate wasn't sure what she was seeing. Fascinated in spite of herself, she had barely processed the reality of a *T. rex* as a living animal in a cage, but was already assigning acceptable protocol. What she saw below reminded her of animal handlers who got careless around large predators in their care – until one day, the predator suddenly remembered itself.

Shanna paused at the gate, producing what looked like a pneumatic-injector needle, of the type used on large livestock, before stepping fully into the enclosure and marching purposefully towards the sleeping giant.

37

Maverick nodded to Cameron.

"If she sticks that thing, make sure you got that camera on, because I'll want to see the replay."

His voice carried. Shanna looked up from the enclosure, smiling as she felt along the dragon's scaly neck, clearing the needle, and injected the shot into the thick hide.

The rex didn't even interrupt a snore.

"He's been sedated," Shanna said, her voice drifting up. "That was a shot of antibiotics. Tyrannosaurs heal up pretty fast as a rule, but he's had a rough go of it lately."

Betty leaned over, observing the rex' hide, which did indeed seem to be a collage of scrapes and abrasions.

"He's injured?"

"Life's tough for your male *T. rex*," Shanna said, patting the somnolent beast on its massive, over-muscled cheek. "Especially during mating season. He's got bites all over him."

"Other males?"

"The *females*," Shanna said. "*T. rex* packs are lorded over by the females. Males are too aggressive, and the pack will eject or kill them once they reach adolescence. Except for a few weeks during mating season."

Shanna ran her hand over some of the big tyrannosaur's wounds – rather similar, Kate thought, to 'mating-bites' she had seen on large Great White sharks.

"Very few males grow to full adulthood," Shanna said. "Those that do, like Big Rex here, are usually loners. They spend most of their time driving off the competing predators, like the big carcharodonts and the packs of sickle-claws. That's why we have to keep them sequestered. The predators would all kill each other long before they even touched the herd animals."

"So," she said, "in the interest of genetic diversity, being that the island territory is too small, and left to his own instincts, he'd just stake out the whole island as *his*, and bite any critter who thought different..." Shanna shrugged. "We just give him a little time-out up here."

She gave the sleeping dragon one last pat before turning for the exit.

The moment she turned her back, the rex' head suddenly popped up behind her, perking awake like some giant bird.

In the space of a heartbeat, the six-foot head dipped forward.

Kate's voice caught in her throat as she started to shout out a warning – rendered moot, as Betty let out a full-throated scream.

Shanna turned, just as the massive jaws parted – a long, thick, pink tongue lulled out, reaching towards her slender form...

... and licked her from her thigh to her head, a slobbering wet dog-kiss that nearly knocked her off her feet.

"*Rex!*" Shanna blurted, laughing. "Stop it! Lay down!"

And the ten-ton beast lay its head down beside her. A rumble reverberated deep in its chest – a sound like purring.

On the ridge above, the four visitors to the island exhaled as one.

"Big dope," Shanna said, swatting playfully at the rex' gnarled hide. "God forbid he and Congo bump into each other when we turn him loose tomorrow. They're both jealous as dogs."

"Jealous of what?" Kate asked.

Kate scratched the rex behind the ears.

"Of *me*. Both of them want to be the favorite."

Beneath her scratching fingers, over skin that hadn't even noticed a shot from a pneumatic-needle, the big rex was lulled back into a doze. The nostrils again flared into snores. Shanna stepped back.

"Lazy animals," she said. "Worse than lions."

Shanna locked the enclosure behind her – a fairly token gesture to Kate's eye, as the animal within looked fully capable of getting out on its own.

Yet, it lounged peaceably enough.

On the other hand, at the moment the rex had first reared its head, the little lizard, Otto, had jumped from under the seat and scurried through the gate, disappearing into the compound.

"Otto doesn't like the *T. rex* either," Shanna explained, as she rejoined them on the road. "Which, I suppose is fair. Given the chance, tyrannosaurs eat those little guys like popcorn."

She pulled the lever on the main gate – latched, not locked – no particular need for that kind of security.

"Where exactly are you taking us?" Kate asked.

Shanna motioned them all through, closing the gate behind them.

"I have to keep you here in the compound until someone shows up to arrest you." She shrugged. "It shouldn't be long."

"*Keep* us here?" Maverick objected. "What if we don't want to be kept?"

"Well," Shanna said, "I have an eight-ton gorilla that could force the issue. But considering your other option is to wander around in the jungle....?" She nodded down into the valley. "Be my guest."

Maverick looked down where hundred-foot sauropods lounged like scaled-up elephants under the wash of the falls.

"You know," he said, "I would kind of like to ride one."

Cameron patted Maverick on the shoulder, turning him away, nodding placatingly to Shanna.

"Let's not tempt him," he said. "We're fine with being kept."

Kate, however, was not.

"Excuse me," she said, "but my communication was with Professor Nolan Hinkle. I was unaware he even had a daughter."

Shanna frowned, eyeing Kate skeptically.

"I don't know how that's possible," she said. "My father doesn't *have* correspondence. With anybody."

Shanna fell silent as she led them through the compound, until they came to a large building that seemed to be the utilitarian centerpiece, mounted on the ridge, directly above the animal enclosures.

The building was space-age, looking even more bizarre in the tropical prehistoric landscape, with a preponderance of glass, like a clean-room in a high-tech development lab.

Through the thick, transparent-alloy windows, they could see the distorted image of a man puttering about inside, a morphing shadow among an assortment of blinking screens and bubbling cauldrons.

Shanna tapped a button, and the door slid open with a loud buzz.

After a moment, the man inside paused – belatedly, as if the sound took a moment to register – perhaps hard of hearing.

Shanna motioned them inside. The automatic glass doors slid shut behind them.

It was like standing on the bridge of the *Starship Enterprise*, stepping right out of the lost world into a futuristic space-age.

Shanna pressed a second button and two more glass doors slid apart, accessing the main lab.

The man inside turned towards them. He was white-haired and balding, clad in a well-worn lab coat and glasses – short, squat and rather toad-like in his face and form.

The old man blinked, as if confused.

"What's this?" he said. "Visitors?"

"Daddy?" Shanna said, doubtfully, "these people tell me they were invited here by you."

Shanna turned to Kate.

"Miss Rhodes," she said, "this is my father. Professor Nolan Hinkle."

CHAPTER 7

There was only one pair of human eyes on the mountain who saw the pterosaurs take out the transport chopper.

Mark had learned to be wary of his fellow survivors, and he already had a bad history with the military, so when he saw the helicopter in trouble, he *really* hoped he wouldn't be put in a position of having to render aid.

Sticking one's nose where it didn't belong was a lesson Mark had punched into him long before KT-day.

Despite rampaging monsters, dragons, or abominations, or whatever you chose to call them, if you were human, you always had to be watchful of your own species first.

Mark had been making his way through the Rockies for the last few weeks, and was just getting his first look at the downward slope of the current mountain. The Rockies took a brief topographical break right at the triple border between Colorado, Wyoming, and Utah, dipping down into a series of river-cut valleys and lowlands, before rising back up to their full stature as they bled into all three states.

Normally, Mark would avoid the lowlands, but he was already anxious to get out of the general area. Earlier today, he was about to pick a ripe-looking berry, growing just off the path, before he spotted what looked like an exploded squirrel. With its insides-out, Mark could clearly see it had been feeding on the same bush.

As he took a second look, he realized that the foliage seemed odd. He was no botanist, but he'd grown up in the northwest and he knew trees.

The indigenous fauna was being strangled and invaded. He hadn't noticed at first, because the new growth was likewise suited for the surroundings, but with different species of leaves adapted for the same niche.

Mark kicked at the dead squirrel. He'd seen this effect before, whenever a normal animal – didn't matter if it was crow, coyote, fish or insect – tried to scavenge off a carcass of one of the giants.

Normal animals didn't get *infected* – it was fatal – *catastrophically* fatal – on the spot.

Whatever caused this new invasive wildlife to grow into giants utterly destroyed normal organisms, right from the cellular level, like a power-pill that simply overloaded the DNA. Visually, it was rather like every single cell erupting into a zit, and then popping all at once.

Surviving indigenous species quickly learned to avoid the giant carcasses, no matter how tempting the mountain of meat might be. In point of fact, it was advisable to leave the entire area, because, while the carrion might be off-limits to modern scavengers, resurrected prehistoric relics came running. *That* was how the infection spread.

But Mark had never seen it transmitted through plants before.

It was as if this new growth that seemed to have taken over this side of the mountain, winding in among the giant trees like ivy, had absorbed the fatal element/chemical in its very pores.

Was this whole mountain about to bloom?

As he looked around, Mark wondered if a wise man might set a torch to the entire area.

On the other hand, he was still several hard days' travel out of the mountains, let alone with a forest fire on his heels.

Thus, in the pursuit of self-interest, this ecological time-bomb, whatever it was or however it had been set, would continue to tick away.

Mark wondered how many other such ticking mines were hidden out there in this new wilderness.

The thought was enough to get him moving, and he had been hoofing it hard, hoping to vacate the area by sundown, when he first saw the chopper pass above.

He watched as the pterosaurs swarmed, and despite gunshots, and an apparently imaginative pilot, the transport craft piled it in just over the next peak. He could hear the crash.

Once-upon-a-time, his first instinct would have been to run and help. That impulse had been systematically beaten out of him.

The last time he had extended his good Samaritan hand, he'd nearly gotten his ass bit off by a *T. rex*.

Ironic – in a world where he had become a prey animal, his biggest hang-ups were still trust issues.

"*Damn*," he muttered, as he began a reluctant march in the direction the chopper had gone down.

Then, in the bushes, he heard a low hiss.

Mark froze. It was a sound he knew all too well. He scanned the surrounding brush – nothing more than four-feet high, but thick.

Just right for an ambush.

The thing exploded from the leaves like a flushed pheasant, less than two-feet tall, but with chomping jaws like a thirty-pound reptilian pitbull.

T. rex were mean as hell, right from the egg, and Mark had seen *this* little SOB before.

He had his pistol out in a flash.

"Hey there, Junior," Mark said, pulling the trigger, "you little sonofabitch."

The little creature's jaws were the size of German Shepard's, but the teeth could sever his hand like a shark's, coming at him at a sprint.

It knew gunfire, though. After the first shot scraped its hide, the little monster broke its attack, darting back for the bushes, as Mark emptied the clip after it.

One of these nights, that thing would come creeping up while he was sleeping. If a five-ton rex could stalk as soundless as a cat, a four-foot hatchling was as light as a spider.

It would keep coming too. *T. rex* were like that.

Mark knew *why* well enough – just like he knew where it had learned its respect for gunfire.

It was because Mark had killed its mother – a five-ton female he had shot in the head, right in front of her lone surviving brood.

He hadn't *wanted* to, but the thing had chased him for six-hundred miles.

All things considered, Mark knew he was ridiculously lucky to be alive.

Although, *anybody* alive was lucky these days.

Mark had not been ground-zero anywhere on KT-day, but he had been one of the first to encounter what the rest of the world had waiting in the wings.

Ironically, as far as the government was concerned, that had made him an 'asset' – and as such, he had already been in 'protective custody', sequestered far away from the cities, when the day ultimately arrived.

But it was only a temporary stay – the marching apocalypse finally caught up with him too, and the entire base where he had been stationed was stomped flat.

That night, he had also lost a young woman he had cared a mountain for.

Mark and Sally had spent the year together, mostly in incarceration, living on-base like married recruits – just not free to come and go.

They met on a cruise – shortly before their boat sank, just off the Central American Pacific Coast.

Cruise-wrecks were actually fairly common, because they navigated shallow waters, putting them at risk of collision with reefs. It was almost routine – all passengers had made it to lifeboats.

In fact, no one would have died, if they hadn't made it to shore.

Mark had heard stories about castaways landing along this coast and stumbling into anything from modern pirates to Cartel drug-grow operations, and never being seen again.

This was more like a grow-operation of flesh-eating monsters.

Out of the hundred-plus survivors of the wreck, only Mark and Sally had made their way out of the jungle a few bare miles north to a bustling tropic port.

That's how close it was, all along.

They had been taken into custody shortly upon arriving back to the States.

Sally had been raised in what Mark generously called 'polite' society, and was totally unprepared for survivalist rigors. The time in the jungle had taken its toll. Mark watched her wither over the following months, with a recurring, strength-sapping illness, that seemed to take a little more of her each time it came back.

After a recent bout of nausea, she had finally been taken to the infirmary – the first time they'd been apart in over a year.

That night, the beasts had come.

He remembered hearing that steady approach, hours away, like the rumble of encroaching thunder. Except this rumble was in the ground, like an earthquake. And then, somewhere in the darkest hours of the night, the storm landed on top of them.

He never saw any of it clearly.

There were explosions and burning light. Beyond that, there were… sounds – like giant footsteps, accompanied by reverberating bellows that might have echoed up from the depths of a volcano – and then the buildings had tumbled down on top of him.

For a long time, he was trapped in darkness. But eventually, the sounds of the giants faded, followed by a deadened stony silence.

Sometime after that, he began to pick his way through the rubble.

After he'd dug himself free, Mark had made his way across the demolished base. He had gone far enough to see what was left of the hospital.

He stood there long enough to absorb it – to *accept* it – to make it *real*.

Then he had turned and been gone, even as more choppers circled above, arriving on the scene – rescue troops that were hours too late and would have been laughably ineffective if they'd been right on time.

With Sally gone, Mark had no more need of what was left of the old world. He'd never done that well within it anyway.

He had fled into the forest – into a new world – a lost world.

The grow-operation had spread – and the monsters had followed.

Or had it just been like that everywhere? Drug-cartels operated grow-operations in the States too. Just out of sight, on protected lands. Natural preserves. Entire stretches of open wilderness, off-limits to the public, but walking distance to every major city in the world.

It wasn't like people disappearing in the woods was something new.

Mark imagined a hiker that stumbled into a *T. rex* on an off-limits nature-trail would have left little evidence of the encounter behind.

In fact, Mark was willing to bet in the days before KT-day, the odd *T. rex* might even have cleared out a cartel pot-field or two. Sickle-claws would have been a handful too – true, those operations tended to be guarded with automatic weapons, but Mark could bear direct witness that a sickle-claw running at you in the dark was damn hard to hit.

Of course, bullets would just piss-off a *T. rex*.

And you *really* didn't want to piss-off a *T. rex*. For whatever reason, they held grudges.

Having once crossed a mamma rex, Mark sure wouldn't do it again.

Although, it wasn't like he *meant* to, the first time. He had literally just escaped the wrecked base, and after hiding the night in the bushes, less than a mile from where choppers still circled above, he had taken off on foot.

And as if he just couldn't screw himself fast enough, he had run right into the middle of a rex-nest.

For those who had never seen one up close, a *T. rex* yearling was about the size of a golden retriever, with a mouth like a similarly-sized crocodile.

There were half-a-dozen of them, and they came at him like a pack of piranha.

Mark shot them all, reflexively, in quick succession – he had never grouped shots like that together, before or after, in his life, and if he hadn't, at least one would have gotten him, with the last of them dropping literally at his feet, the little beast's jaws snapping shut like a guillotine, bare inches from his shoe.

Then he had looked up to see the mama.

The chase was on from there on out.

Rexy, as he came to call her, ran him a merry chase that day, but it was only the beginning. That damned dragon-beast had followed him halfway across the country. Led by that bloody damned nose, she could ferret you right out. She didn't even have to hurry – just kept walking.

She had tailed him up into the Rockies, where *T. rex* were few and far between, except for the ones obsessively following *him,* and she would have caught him too, but for an unfortunate tumble over a cliff.

Mark had actually ended up shooting the poor stubborn beast as it lay in a broken heap on the rocks below, just to put it out of its misery.

Naturally, *that* was what Junior had seen – lone survivor of Rexy's most recent nesting, hatched right there in the mountains.

Mark didn't know what passed for a mind in *T. rex*, but they clearly followed their noses, and he knew the little beast had imprinted his scent early on.

Out of misplaced sympathy, he hadn't shot the thing at the time, and he'd already lived to regret it.

The little sonofabitch had latched onto him like Hook and the crocodile – except that was just a crocodile. A big rex might grow up to nine tons or better.

It had been Mark's intention to find a working vehicle, a stretch of open road, and put some distance behind him – hopefully out of range of that friggin' *T. rex* nose.

Until then, he'd keep his pistol ready.

He felt bad for the little critter, but he'd still shoot the little sonofabitch if he had to.

Of course, *that* just left his own species to worry about.

Even in a world of monsters, Mark might still lay odds that if he died prematurely, it would be at human hands.

In his time on the road, he had been shot at – he never saw by who – there had been attempted robberies on two occasions, and that was not to mention the scattered encampments of survivalist cult-types.

That had happened fast, and they didn't always look it.

It turned out people got nutty in an apocalypse.

Mark had met a few religious nuts, but they were easy to spot, mostly because it was all they talked about – Judgment and Last Times.

Not that it was a point Mark was particularly inclined to argue.

Of course, some folks started out nuts, and just got nuttier.

Perhaps predictably, Mark had already encountered 'dragon-worship'.

Mark had grown up in Oregon and had known the odd Wiccan – he'd even had nodding acquaintance with more than one self-proclaimed witch. But just during his recent short travels in the mountains, he'd spent the night in a small encampment with a young lady – a sprightly woodland nymph, who called herself Lily – who, along with her troop of 'sisters', had taken the occasion of the apocalypse to not only embrace full on cauldron-bubbling, coven-style black-magic – but to adapt their theology around it.

"Easy enough transition," Mark had remarked mildly. "Devil worship to dragon."

"Witches," Lily cautioned, "are not, by definition, Satanists."

Mark had been lectured on the difference before, by both Wiccans and witches back home.

"But *you* are," he clarified. "Right?"

That relationship had ended after she and her sisters attempted to offer him up as a human-sacrifice to the 'dragon' that had been chasing him.

That was a break-up story he never thought he'd have to tell.

When Mark told Lily and her sisters about Rexy – especially the part about the plundered-nest – they promptly laid him out as bait.

Lily compared it to making friends with a wild dog, by giving it treats.

Unfortunately – or *fortunately* for Mark – Rexy had also drawn the attention of the military. Several gunships that had been tracking the big rex ended up crashing the ceremony with machine guns – a situation that escalated upon unexpected return-fire from the outraged Coven.

Ironically, Rexy actually had no interest in the ensuing battle – *Mark* was her priority, and she had dogged him right to her very last breath – right up to that last tumble down into the ravine.

In the general chaos, Mark himself had managed to slip away.

The last he saw of the Coven, they were surrounded by soldiers, their inexperienced gun-handlers quickly subdued by the trained troops.

On the other hand, Mark had a feeling he wasn't the first fellow that particular cat-crew had fed to a dragon. Lily had made passing reference to their 'men-folk', who were apparently no longer with us.

And now this troop – *Coven* – was surrounded by the inherent dominance-structure of the military.

Pop. Bubble. Fizz.

As good a reason as any to get the hell out of the territory. Rampaging dinosaurs be damned.

But then that stupid chopper had to crash. Didn't they know pterosaurs went after choppers?

Cursing himself for a fool, Mark worked his way through the forest.

For all the good it might do – a plume of smoke indicated something had burned. He would be rescuing charred dead bodies.

He hadn't gone twenty minutes when he again heard the familiar rush of bushes and the sound of skittering feet.

The little SOB wasn't done for the day. Junior had apparently flanked him. Mark drew his pistol.

But this time he was caught by surprise. The dog-sized head burst from the bushes almost right behind him, with snapping jaws zeroing in on his leg. A bite would be crippling or fatal.

Mark twisted quickly, turning his pistol, getting off a single shot – but then a larger shadow rose up behind him.

Junior skidded to a stop in mid-attack, hissing balefully. In a flash, he turned and disappeared into the brush.

Mark turned as the shadow continued to rise, blocking out the sun.

The creature pushed two massive trees aside – a giant gorilla – over twenty feet tall.

Mark looked at the diminutive nine-millimeter in his hand. Backing up slowly, he pocketed the pistol and pulled the rifle from his shoulder.

The big ape saw the gun and snarled, making motions with its hands.

Mark pulled the trigger. There was an outraged roar as the beast brought up its massive arms, covering its face, taking the shot in the shoulder. Mark fired again, eliciting another outraged howl.

The ape lowered its arms, glowering down purposefully at Mark.

Well, *that* pissed him off, Mark thought.

There was, however, one little trick that had worked on Rexy.

Pulling a tin canister from his bag, Mark pulled the seal and pitched it into the giant ape's face.

There was the stench of tear-gas, and before the ape's agonized howl even sounded in his ear, Mark turned and ran like hell.

CHAPTER 8

Tomorrow would be one year since KT-day.

Sally knew General Rhodes wanted to mark the occasion, but was unsure how. Somber, honor the dead? Hope for the future? When Rhodes had called her in, she assumed it was to ask her opinion. He did about most things.

She wasn't sure why – she was non-military, and had only become his personal assistant by virtue of the near-extinction of the species.

Rhodes also seemed to deliberately speak out around Sally, almost as if testing her, perhaps setting leak-traps. It made sense – he needed someone in her position that he could trust. He was the highest remaining representative of her old Uncle Sam, despite rumors that the president was still alive and sequestered somewhere.

But that was different than soliciting her input. And didn't explain why he had chosen *her*.

Possibly it was because, in the old world, she had been a real person. Maybe that kept him grounded.

He had told her once, in order to do his job, he had to think in terms of numbers, but he never wanted to *feel* in terms of numbers.

Especially now that Def-con 5-level survival strategies were in place.

They had been at the Mount for over a month now – they called it the 'Arc Project' – ten miles of tunnel deep into the Colorado Rockies, named for obvious reasons, with human-survival as its stated mission, and repopulation a primary agenda item.

Currently, the facility housed exactly two-hundred soldiers living onsite. There were also three hundred civilian refugees, although that number was expected to grow – almost all women of breeding age.

Def-con 5, remember.

Sally knew Rhodes *had* to think that way. But it didn't change the reality of it. And honoring KT-day in any way was going to be a tough sell. There was already a rumble of dissention among the largely feminine civilian ranks. No doubt Rhodes would want her thoughts on that as well.

It seemed, however, that larger problems had come up.

When Sally stepped into his office, Rhodes was on his speakerphone – *standing*, which meant something requiring action. Sally had seen him like this before, barking orders into his phone, pacing back and forth in his office as if he were right in front of the troops, ready to act on his own orders.

Sally paused at the door.

"I need to know where it went down, Hicks," Rhodes was saying, and his voice had that calm, almost dangerous tone that it did in battle-conditions.

Hicks' voice buzzed back through static.

"We've got choppers out, sir, but it's a big area."

"We have an extreme VIP on board that transport, you understand?"

"I understand, sir. We have all available resources on it."

"Let me know the second you hear anything."

"Well, sir," Hicks said unhappily, "I *have* got word we've got a possible bloom sprouting."

Rhodes shut his eyes. "Give it to me."

"So far, it's just a bud, sir," Hicks said. "Just a single sighting. It can probably still be contained within a burn. But it's within the search range, sir. And it's all a crow's fly of the Mount."

"You know the drill, son," Rhodes said. "Nukes on blooms. Napalm on buds. Get confirmation on what we've got first."

"I've got Johnson in the area, sir," Hicks said.

Rhodes turned to Sally.

"How many active nukes have we got on hand?"

"Um, fourteen, sir," Sally said, flipping her clipboard. "Major Travis has two F-16-capable missiles at our West Coast site – two more non-operational. Captain Mason has reported a dozen long-range capable missiles aboard his sub. We have no way to confirm, but he reports them all fully functional."

"What about Maelstrom?"

"Last communication with the Maelstrom base said they had one silo coming online."

Rhodes sighed. "Five-hundred missiles on that site, and *one* of them is *almost* ready when we need it." He tapped the speaker. "Lieutenant?"

"Yes, sir," Hicks responded.

"Keep an eye on the bud, Lieutenant. Scramble the sub and the planes to be ready on a dime. Have a cleaner-crew ready, strength of detergent to be determined once we know what we've got.

"But," Rhodes emphasized, "priority one is the rescue. Nothing drops until our asset is clear. Is that perfectly understood?"

"Yes, sir," Hicks replied.

Rhodes turned off the speaker, turning to Sally, grimly.

"That was something we did not need."

He grabbed up his clipboard, nodding to Sally. "Follow me on my rounds?"

Rhodes was always careful to speak to her as if asking for a personal favor, rather than giving an order, which was how he spoke to pretty much everyone else.

It was clear, however, polite or not, he expected to be obeyed. Sally followed obediently enough.

She sometimes wondered how he really felt about her. He seemed to personally care, yet remained aloof. He also seemed deliberately paternal, perhaps establishing platonic psychological boundaries. But he *had* taken her under his wing – necessity of resources, notwithstanding, an administrator still needed an office, and therefore a personal assistant to run it. As it happened, secretarial skills were rare among the Mount's battle-hardened combat troops.

And if you were living on the Mount, and were *not* one of those soldiers, then you better fill *some* function – every job needed to be done.

Sally first met Rhodes two years ago, and had the impression at the time the General had taken a liking to her – he had mentioned a resemblance to his daughter, Kate, who he spoke of in the tones of one lost and gone.

For Sally, the idea that she would one day not only be interviewed by a General, but actually consulted for updates on nuclear assets...?

That was the sort of thing she would not have predicted for herself during her sorority days at UCLA, only two birthdays and forever ago.

Her qualifications? She had survived an early skirmish in a war that had yet to be fought – bare months later, she would have been one out of millions.

Before she was a spoiler for the apocalypse, she was a co-ed on a summer cruise – and ironically, if her ship hadn't sunk, stranding its passengers on the edge of a tropical jungle filled with prehistoric dragons, to be eaten alive, then she wouldn't have been in 'protective custody' on KT-day, and likely would have been home in LA when that city was totally and utterly smashed into the ground and then dumped into the ocean.

So, she was lucky that way.

Sally had learned to look for the positive spin where she could find it.

For better or worse, she was now committed to her new station. For more reason than one.

She had already tried to run.

Almost exactly one month ago, when her chopper first touched down on top of the mountain, she had just hopped out and taken off into the woods.

It was the first time in two years she hadn't been surrounded by at least a dozen soldiers – it was a transport craft with one pilot and two snoozing troops – landing on a brand-new base – a staging area for supplies and equipment before transferring down into the caverns under the Mount.

When that chopper hit the tarmac, Sally had simply jumped and run before anyone could move to stop her. She fled into the woods, like a dog escaping its kennel.

Within two days, she was back at the Mount – *rescued* was the word they used – probably accurate enough, all things considered. But she still remembered that rush of freedom. After two years.

She had not, however, fully appreciated all that waited outside the safety of these supposedly imprisoning walls.

Rhodes had been disturbed that she'd tried to run.

Sally expected him to be angry, and had been quite afraid of his reaction, but he actually seemed to feel badly – like dealing with a daughter who ran away from home, and struggling to make *sense* of it, knowing *this* should be where people ran *to*, not away from.

Although, word-of-mouth that drifted through the Mount suggested that, in many places, people had done just that. In some spots, as military installations became known, survivors in the surrounding areas had appeared in significant numbers. There weren't many from the cities, where the initial blooms of giants were concentrated, but out in the sticks, there were those who had managed to hole-up through the worst of it.

Resources for refugees were limited, particularly in the outlying outposts.

It was said that, in several instances, push had come to shove.

Sally was learning military dead-pan.

It was a brass-shield against hard-core reality. *Rights* were not determinant anymore – *scientific recommendation* was now dictate – the justifiable priority being the survival and repopulation of the human race.

Sally, who was just entering her second trimester, was what Rhodes called their 'most precious asset'.

He had told her this in his office after she had tried to run. His eyes were hard as he said it, because while he might try to understand *why* she ran, it still could not be tolerated.

Sally remained unsure of his motivations. While he had mentioned a daughter, he never spoke about any wife. Sally had no idea what any of that meant long-term, but there was no going back now.

Rhodes didn't know why Sally had run that day. And while he seemed to have forgiven her, was even apologetic, she wondered how he'd have reacted if he'd really known.

As her transport chopper had sailed over the tree-tops that day, Sally had looked down at the forest floor and she had seen Mark.

He was running from the chopper like a rabbit from a hawk – just as Sally had seen him fleeing the shattered base that night, even as choppers had landed and troops had circled all around her.

Protective custody had not suited Mark well – nor had it appreciated him.

While Rhodes had taken an instant liking to Sally, he hadn't much cared for Mark.

Sally's father hadn't liked Mark either, in point of fact – Mark, who was a baggage handler on the Pacific Princess, not a passenger, and certainly not good enough for his daughter.

Rhodes didn't seem to think so either. Things started out testy over the course of their year-long-detention, culminating when Mark had slugged Rhodes in the jaw, nearly catching a bullet from the guards.

Before Sally had taken sick that night, she and Mark had been planning to run.

But it had to be *that* night.

Sally actually didn't remember a thing. The nurse had given her a mild sedative, before somewhat sternly escorting Mark away.

Mark, who had been at her bedside all day, had kissed her cheek and whispered, "Keep a candle burning."

Sally must have slept – perhaps even been knocked unconscious at some point, because when she suddenly awoke, it was over, and she was lying among rubble. The entire infirmary had been demolished – the bed she had been lying in was gone, as was the entire med-unit, and its staff.

Simply lying limp, riding out the living blitzkrieg, Sally had somehow survived it – missing the crushing force like a beetle misses a rototiller blade.

Battered, and semi-dazed, she had climbed out from under the pilings of rubble.

And the moment she felt the night air, she became aware of two things – the first were the rescue helicopters arriving on-scene, circling down.

Second was the sight of Mark, running for the perimeter, scaling the fence, and jumping for the forest beyond.

Sally could have called to him, but then he would have stopped, and he would have come back for her, and they would have caught him. So she stayed silent, firmly believing she was never going to see him again.

Then she had spotted him from the air.

When the chopper touched down, it wasn't even a considered decision – she had simply bolted. The chopper had left him miles behind before landing, but if she could just *find* him...

Instead, she had stumbled into a quaint little band of forest-dwelling psychopaths who called themselves the Coven.

As it turned out, Mark had crossed paths with them too, and if he hadn't been running from the mountain before, he sure was now.

It was the second time Sally had seen her child's father leaving her behind – all unknowing, believing her long dead, no longer even searching – and *this* time, most likely disappearing from her life forever.

And, naturally, the crazy bitches who tried to feed him to a *T. rex* were now living with her on the Mount.

All part of the Arc Project. Crazy didn't matter – they were all of productive age. Def-con priorities.

On the other hand, their presence was already an influence on the Mount – a ripple-effect on a community that was adjusting to section-eight-level stress as a daily reality.

Overall, the Arc Project had so-far gone anything but smoothly. Their main depot site up top had been hit by a rex-attack – rare, this high in the mountains – and the beast had done ridiculous damage. An entire shipment of equipment was lost, and nearly a battalion of troops.

Now everybody was housed in underground bunkers, buried hundreds of feet below solid mountain, and reinforced to take nuclear damage.

The residential bunkers were for civilians and soldiers. The officers were housed separately – adjacent, but separated by floors, with the command station nearest the top.

On the residential mall was a centralized rec-area that reminded Sally of a chimp habitat, except instead of a swinging tire, it was tennis courts, and a swimming pool.

And you couldn't go outside.

Sally had been sequestered on bases for almost two years before coming to the Mount, but at least there had been OUTSIDE.

But these days, that was the price of security – and these dark rock walls were going to drive her purely crazy. She had said so to Rhodes, who acknowledged the problem.

It had only been a few weeks and things were already starting to bubble.

Bubble, bubble, toil and trouble.

"Your friends are acting up," Rhodes said.

Friends. What that meant was, after she'd made her break into the woods, she'd spent the night with this band of nutcases, just before they were *all* captured again.

Probably not PC to say so – she couldn't imagine Rhodes taking it well. Certainly not the Coven. And it didn't hurt if that one night spent in that camp, before being taken together, had left them on better terms with Sally than most of the other women at the Mount – a dubious honor, but not a gift-horse to be stared in the mouth.

There weren't many of them – thirty members, all-told – but they were noisy. And they were quickly becoming dominant in a number of subtly deliberate ways.

When she'd first arrived on the Mount, Sally had made friends with a military nurse named Rose, who told her the group of them seemed to have taken over the med-unit.

Everybody worked on the Mount, and one could optimistically see the job-preference as altruism – *except*, Rose said, she couldn't help think it was *supposed* to look that way – the encroachment of the infirmary felt more like infiltration.

"I've known a lot of stripper-types," Rose told her, "who became nurses. Lotta crossover there, for some reason. Raising hell all night, good deeds during the day. Like some sort of Karmic bargain."

Rose shook her head. "*These* crazy bitches are something different."

Sally had also noticed the Coven's presence in the maid/janitor duty-rosters, which seemed surprisingly domestic. She would have thought it unlikely the women she'd met would be so readily acquiescent to such menial, keeping-the-cave-clean, back-to-the-Stone-Age, Wilma Flintstone roles.

Perhaps passive-aggressive submissive types?

Or it could be, they understood the power inherent in those basic essential duties – the hand that rocks the cradle rules the world, and a maid has a key to locked doors.

It was also true that the world was now a place where the chain of command from house-staff to nuclear-authorization had grown significantly shorter.

Nurse Rose had disappeared two weeks ago.

She had simply gone – no trace. It was assumed she had deserted, although Sally had never heard her express the slightest indication of any such intent.

In her place, running the infirmary was Ginger, the oldest of the Coven – late-thirties, at least, even though her body was whip-cord, surfer-girl tight, just like the rest of them.

Ginger was *older sister.* During Sally's one night at their camp, Ginger was the one who had given her the pitch to join up.

Sally's failure to RSVP in the time since had cooled Ginger's demeanor somewhat, although she was careful not to become adversarial, as she respectfully recognized Sally's pull with Rhodes.

And while officially no foul-play was suspected in Nurse Rose's disappearance, at least one member of the Coven had been questioned on the incident – a tall, lithe Amazon called Michelle who, when Sally first met her, had carried a hand-carved spear and a ten-inch hunting-knife strapped to her hip – *and* who, in her first week at the Mount, had stabbed two servicemen with a fork.

Michelle's interview had been conducted personally – and privately – by Rhodes himself. Sally didn't know the details, but in the time since, Michelle had been remarkably well-behaved.

So far, Rhodes had chosen not to engage any of the others, although he clearly intended the suddenly meek and compliant Michelle to serve as an example.

Still, the lot of them continued to stir-up generalized trouble. Just the simple fact of a troop of sexy, nubile young things introduced among a bunch of mostly male troops was a bubbling cauldron all by itself, and the so-inclined could readily take advantage.

There were already accusations of harassment – he-said/she-said tales wafting out of the residential bunkers. Rhodes told Sally privately that, in his experience dealing with such cases, nine out of ten times, the woman was telling the truth. But within that remaining ten-percent, there *were* amoral alley-cats – ruthless and cynical – traits a combat General knew full-well to respect and fear in anyone.

And of course, the world's oldest profession had promptly sprouted up – one of the most basic forms of trade.

All fairly pedestrian stuff, but corrosive. And small, intense factions did tend to take over larger social groups.

And based on short association, Sally had a good idea that this particular faction had been a bunch of end-of-the-world nutcases *before* the end of the world. Now they had actual, physical dragons to play with, and had taken advantage of it.

One of the young ones, a wide-eyed Lolita named Lily, had made past-tense reference to their 'men-folk', and was promptly shushed by Ginger.

Sally had not pressed for details.

She *had*, however, mentioned it to Rhodes, who nodded thoughtfully.

"Witches," he muttered. "Satanists converted to dragons."

"Witches aren't synonymous with Satanists," Sally said, as she herself had been corrected by both Lily and Ginger.

"But *they* are, right?"

Sally nodded. "Right."

Rhodes had leaned back in his chair with a sigh.

"Well," he said rubbing his eyes, "I'm afraid you're going to have to tell your friends there will be some emergency war-time restrictions on their right to practice religion."

But Sally already knew the rest. By Rhodes' logic, they were *still* women.

He had leaned forward.

"They are *assets*," he emphasized. "And they will be tolerated. But not enabled. Please relay that, so I don't have to."

That was another thing – Rhodes seemed to think Sally had some special pull with the civilian population at the Mount – puzzling, because Nurse Rose had been her only friend. Sally was quartered separate from the residential barracks, so her interaction was minimal – both the civilians and the rank-and-file servicemen most often saw her in the company of Rhodes. *That* was her identity.

It was remarkable the roles you fell into.

In her younger days, she was the quintessential sorority girl – they used to call her Delta Dawn.

Now nuclear options were at her fingertips – just a maximum-security door away.

Of course, every door was like that on the Mount. There were locks and codes and procedures – similar to how inmates operated and worked within a prison – only in this prison, the inmates slept a hundred yards away from the warden.

"What's on the docket today?" Sally asked, as she followed Rhodes into the claustrophobic mine-shaft of an elevator, that gave her the horrors every time she stepped into it.

"Going down to see the Doc," Rhodes said, closing the door quickly before she could object.

Doctor Victor Shriver dwelled down within the very bowels of this not-quite bottomless pit, down past the barracks, past multiple equipment and maintenance levels.

At the very bottom of it all, was Shriver's lab. The *mad* lab as it had come to be known, populated by a single individual, who was without a doubt, the creepiest person in the entire complex.

There was an unsettling drop in Sally's stomach as the elevator seemed to fall forever. The tiny electric light was military basic – if it went out, they would be in utter darkness.

Sally could feel the oppressive weight of the mountain around them, only waiting for the slightest shift to crush their tiny lifeline shut forever.

CHAPTER 9

Dr. Shrinker, as he was known among the troops, WAS the science these days.

His comments regarding the Arc-Project were succinct. As he put it, "We aren't *forcing* anyone to get pregnant, but if you put men and women together, it's going to happen. And yes, I'm all for encouraging just that."

Sally, safely knocked-up, standing at the General's shoulder, had another question.

"What if a member of the community doesn't *want* to reproduce?"

Shrinker – Shriver – had shrugged.

"Then that member will have to perform some other function."

His voice was always very neutral as he spoke, as if any inflection at all might corrupt the pure factual logic. Nor did he invite dissent.

"A worker or a breeder," he said. "I think it's fair to call them both work. But you need to provide *some* function, or we can't afford you." He dismissed the point as settled. "It's a tough world," he said.

Shriver's criteria determined who got onto the Mount – total numbers allowed versus gender-breakdown and necessary genetic diversity.

So while Rhodes asked Sally her opinion on most things, here was one of the *other* people he asked. And Sally would daresay, the one he probably listened to the most.

It certainly seemed that his was the weighted voice when it came to dealing with outbreaks – *nuke a bloom, burn a bud* – that was his.

The thought of nuclear weapons being set off, literally beyond the end of the world, was nearly as depressing as the end itself.

Nukes remained a threat simply because of their existence. During the weeks of battles that followed KT-day, missiles had fired that shouldn't have – that *couldn't* have – somehow overriding fail-safes that by simple numeric probability couldn't be overridden. Worse, missiles with targeting systems that had no hackable interactive technology were redirected.

Three things needed to happen for a successful nuclear strike – the warhead needed to be activated, the missile needed to be targeted, and then it had to be launched. Each of these levels was guarded by multiple levels of security.

A sub-launch, for example, would require the participation of nearly every member of the crew – everything from achieving launch depth to the turning of keys – and a rogue launch would require PhD-level understanding to rework the targeting system, even after coding had released the keys. And once a missile was chambered and the sub was at sea, that should have been impossible.

But somehow it happened.

Errant nuclear strikes had been worldwide. The EMP had been as well – and not just a bad one, but *designer*-bad.

The digital-age was gone. All that rot about what might survive? Exaggerated – all of it. Individual pieces of tech survived – items surrounded by any sort of makeshift Faraday cage – a tin waste-basket was often enough – but the networks were gone. And of course, the widespread EMP had been combined with a physical demolition.

At this point, military communication was down to radio-relays and walkie-talkies, dotted with little bits of post-millennium tech.

The surviving nukes, depending on where you found them, *should* still work, but required targeting commands from tech that didn't exist anymore – or barely existed. So each of these surviving missiles would require refitting. And then, whatever came online, by whatever method, also needed to be coordinated through the chain of command.

All this demanded a bit of know-how, and now that ninety-nine-percent population reduction had likely been achieved, qualified experts had been pared thin.

Then there was the simple fact that there had been a hell of a lot of land-based nukes out there, and not the least priority was to find out what was left.

On the naval front, not so much. They had exactly one submarine that had somehow survived. The *Anchorage* had been stationed off the coast of Florida, and its Captain Terrance Mason had only made contact barely a month before.

Rhodes considered the recovery of a submarine a real coupe. Post KT-day, subs were the only possible option at sea. You couldn't have ships, because the Megs would take them out.

Megalodons, the formerly-extinct giant Great White, were just like modern sharks, targeting surface prey. A typical Meg could reach sixty-feet or more, and could already take out all but the largest watercraft. An infected giant could bite an aircraft-carrier in half like a surfboard.

There were also a host of other nasty denizens that had invaded the seas.

Competing with the Megs for the honor of top ocean-predator were pliosaurs – short-necked plesiosaurs. At a similar-size, a big pliosaur could give a Megalodon a nasty fight. Megs probably scored higher on the biggest single strike, mimicking those Polaris-style attacks of modern white sharks, but a pliosaur was like an agile seal, given the jaws of a crocodile.

According to Captain Mason, the *Anchorage* had survived by hovering near the bottom, running on silent, and never surfacing off-shore.

Currently, their most viable nuclear-option was seven F-16 fighters in Oregon, with a total of two working missiles. The rest of the roughly ten thousand nukes nationwide, were currently inoperable. For better or worse.

The Puget Sound depot was utterly destroyed, along with sites in California and Nevada. Their best intelligence suggested that European, Chinese, and Russian assets had likewise already been destroyed or detonated.

The Maelstrom facility in Montana had physically survived, and was currently the most promising of the land-based silos to potentially be brought on-line.

But for the time being, it was a couple of planes and a sub – assets they would have to use sparingly.

Hopefully, they would be looking at more buds than blooms.

Unfortunately, Hicks' last report suggested a potential outbreak, uncomfortably close to the Mount.

They were still a ways out. The general search area probably spanned fifty-miles. But a big bloom could engulf that quite quickly.

The passengers on that crashed transport must be VIP indeed.

There was a ding from the elevator as the sheer-drop descent began to slow, and Sally felt her weight settle back into her feet. Rhodes tapped the intercom as they settled to a stop.

"Doc. It's Rhodes."

There were a few more R2-D2-beeps and the elevator opened.

The mad lab.

Blinking blue-light from computer screens reflected off bubbling glass vials, lined-up in rows, in multi-colored solutions. Simulations ran on every screen – seemingly a dozen experiments all conducted simultaneously.

In the middle of it, huddled over a microscope, was Dr. Shriver.

Sally could picture him wringing his hands over some chained lovely in a dungeon, with a Frankenstein monster strapped to a cot in the background.

Sitting beside him on the table was a small cage. Inside was a two-legged lizard, about two-feet tall.

Sally had seen a lot of these little vermin in the aftermath – it was one of the little reptilian ghouls you always found scavenging human corpses.

Immediately behind the cage, sealed in a transparent vault – some alloy no-doubt much stronger than steel – was a cabinet filled with vials of glowing liquid.

Glowing green.

Every survivor alive in the modern world knew that green glow.

Repopulation strategies and nukes aside, Sally knew this was Shrinker's *real* value.

There weren't many survivors available who could refit a warhead, but it was conventional knowledge, with text that could theoretically be learned.

Such was not the case with the Food of the Gods. Nor the work of Professor Nolan Hinkle.

Sally had never before even heard of Professor Hinkle, and only passing reference to Monster Island, which she had tossed-off in similar categories as Big Foot and Area 51.

Area 51, however, was where Dr. Shriver came from.

Shriver, according to Rhodes, was one of two people alive with any practical knowledge of Hinkle's research.

"Unfortunately," Rhodes had confided to Sally, "he's our *second*-best. And I think the homework has left him a little damaged."

Sally could see evidence of that in Shriver's eyes. It was in the hunch of his back as he crouched over his microscope, the impression of desperation, becoming frustration – perhaps only enough comprehension to make him a little crazy.

Looking too deeply into the workings of creation might be a bit like staring into the eye of God – or even Lovecraftian Elder Gods – enough to drive a man insane at a glance, and turn his hair white.

His hair white, his eyes slightly askew, Shriver sat up, turning to acknowledge his visitors.

"General," he said, "I'm glad you could make it."

"We've just got reports of a potential bud," Rhodes said. "We're seeing outbreaks again. We had a chopper go down, and we think the pterosaur that hit it was infected."

Shrinker was nodding before Rhodes even finished.

"Too many of these blooms can't be explained simply by chance," he said. "We're seeing infection in herbivores. The chemical does not transmit as readily through foraging. It can be absorbed, but tends to kill the local plant life. It would require genetically-engineered foliage. Then there's the speed of the effect. With ingestion, it can take a period of weeks to attain full growth. With direct injection on the other hand, depending on the dosage, it can be much faster. With a sufficient dose by weight, it can be as little as a few hours."

Shriver tipped his hand – *therefore*.

"Madness maximized," he said. "Worldwide rampage."

He turned to indicate the sealed vault behind him, and its rows of glowing green vials.

"And as far as subverting any of that?" Shriver shook his head. "I can't do it alone."

He nodded to Rhodes meaningfully.

"I need *her* to go forward."

Rhodes sighed. "Well, Doc, we're doing our best. But it just so happens a pack of flying monsters took out our transport chopper. Right now, we're hoping someone's alive to be rescued. And we aren't even sure where they are yet."

He returned Shriver's meaningful eye.

"You may have to *go forward* on your own. Like it or not."

"Unfortunately," Shriver replied, "the blooms themselves are only the symptom, not the problem."

"A weapon," he said, "be it chemical or explosive, is just the tool, not the enemy."

Now he turned to the small cage sitting on his desk.

"Which brings us to this," he said.

The little lizard inside perked at the sudden attention.

"This is our problem," Shriver said. "Meet Otto."

Sally eyed the little creature uncomfortably. Besides their ghoulish taste for human carrion, they were known for their myna-birdlike imitations – often human voices, sometimes even screams.

"Why do you call it Otto?" Sally asked.

"It's what he calls himself." Shriver tapped on the cage. Inside, the little lizard perked to attention.

Then in a clear, human voice said, "My name is Otto."

"Whose voice is that?" Rhodes asked.

"I believe," Shriver said, "that is the voice of Professor Nolan Hinkle."

"And they *all* do this? In the same voice?"

Shriver nodded.

"This creature is not like the other beasts out there," he said. "In more ways than are readily apparent. First and foremost, they are non-viable. This animal here is a clone. Created right here in this lab. And they're *all* clones. Duplicates of the same parent.

"More significantly," Shriver added, "they are not an extinct species. They were genetically designed."

"For what?" Rhodes asked.

"For intelligence. Modifications have been made, expanding areas of the brain nature had not yet evolved. The experiment was actually deemed more or less a failure. One problem was how neighboring areas of the brain responded to modification. Who knew what perceptions might be expanded, absent a mammalian-style cerebellum? All translated through the simple alligator instinct of the medulla oblongata? It was rather like trying to program modern coding into an eighties-era program. The basic unit was simply not equipped to process the data."

Rhodes leaned in, studying the little creature, which blinked back, absorbing what it saw, without apparent inflection.

"So how smart are they?" Rhodes asked. "It just sits there, like a lizard or a bird."

"Individually," Shriver said, "I don't think they're much more than that."

Now Shriver frowned, uncomfortable speaking outside the area of numbers into realm of speculation.

"You see, I don't believe they're actually *smart*. They're more like a blank memory chip. And the more of them there are, the larger the memory bank. And when a lot of them get together..." Shriver shrugged. "Who knows?"

"One thing we do know," he said, "what one imitates, they *all* do."

Rhodes frowned. The implications were not encouraging.

"Think about it for a moment," Shriver said. "What if you could infiltrate your enemy like a rat in the walls? How many mice are in this compound right now? What if every one of them was a bug, recording voices, phrases, codes? What could you even do about it?"

"I've been receiving direct briefings from Area 51 for years," Rhodes said. "Why was this *Otto* never mentioned?"

"For the same reason we never consulted you about changing a beaker. They were an early experiment. In the Monster Island project, these were like hamsters – even kept as mascots. And once KT-day hit, there was no reason to focus on this one little lizard when two-thousand-foot sauropods were tearing down skyscrapers.

"That is," he said, "until you looked at the flocks of them riding the giants' backs. Just like birds on the backs of elephants on the Savannah."

The little lizard cocked its head, blinking back at them over the seemingly empty mirrors of its eyes.

Sally was beginning to get the creeps.

She jumped as a loud beep sounded – more droid-language from the security-box, and then there was a voice over the speakers, young and female.

"Doctor? I have your lunch."

Shriver tapped the intercom. "Thank you, Lily."

The security door slid open. Lily stood there with her food-cart and attached janitorial supplies. At her shoulder was an armed escort, a young soldier, whose badge identified as Corporal Stevens.

Lily's eyes widened as she saw Sally and the General in the lab.

"I'm sorry," she said doubtfully. "Should I come back?"

"It's fine," Shriver said. "Just leave the trays. No clean-up today."

In the cage, Otto perked up at Lily's presence. Its mouth opened, speaking in a clear imitation of Lily's voice.

"Aren't you a *cutie*?"

And then a moment later.

"Polly want a cracker?"

Setting out her trays, Lily blushed furiously.

The girl seemed nervous. Her eyes were oddly shy as they flitted sideways in Sally's direction – even as they batted, *just* perfectly over her shoulder at Corporal Stevens, who was obviously smitten.

"I'm sorry, Doctor," Lily said. "It was just a couple of soda crackers."

"It's alright, Lily," Shriver said, nodding to Rhodes. "But I think that illustrates my point."

Dishes rattled as Lily pushed her cart to the door and Shriver buzzed her out.

Otto, denied his cracker, hissed in his cage, watching her go.

CHAPTER 10

As the elevator shut behind them, locking them in the compressed space together, Lily glanced over her shoulder, with just the right touch of shyness, at young Corporal Stevens. As a girl who had been going on forty since she was fourteen, she knew how to smile at men. Stevens smiled right back.

In a way, it was too easy – the Coven wielded many forms of witchery.

The last group of menfolk they'd run with had learned that hard lesson. This one would too.

Still, Lily was nervous. She had not expected to see Rhodes in Shrinker's lab – or Sally. Lily wondered if she should tell Ginger.

She was reluctant. She desperately did not want there to be any problems. Her big sister/mother-figures would frown darkly upon her if anything should go wrong this time.

As much as anything, she coveted their approval – belief in their teachings was almost presumption.

Lily sometimes didn't quite remember who she had been before the world ended.

She had been seventeen on KT-day – already rebellious enough to have been kicked out of her mother and step-father's house, and had been looking forward to being old enough not to need the fake ID at Susie's Bar, where she danced five nights a week.

Lily still didn't know where her mother had been on KT-day, or what happened to her – they hadn't spoken in months. Lily had just been showing up for work.

Where were *you* when the world ended? Swinging her legs around a pole.

It was also, doubtless, what saved her life, because her friends were there. Susie's Bar was a place where Lily found more visible concern and guidance than she ever had at home.

And she had been an eager enough ear that she hadn't overly questioned the motives of *this* sage council.

On the other hand, she really didn't have to. There were witches and then there were DARK witches – those that made no bones about embracing the wild power of destruction.

It was actually an easy sell to the young and angry. It wasn't hard to convince a kicked-around LA-kid the world was a bad place. And if the world was bad, it would only stand to reason any move against it would be a virtue. It was practically built-in scripture, justifying almost any anti-social acting-out you cared to imagine.

The perspective was really quite freeing – throw in a little yin-yang, moral-relativity rationalizing, among a willful community-base, with a few issues of their own – and presto – you had yourself a completely self-enabling ideology.

Lily had never really thought of herself as a 'bad girl' – but it was funny how you got drawn in. One day, you were just *in* it.

And she had indeed been *in* it.

She couldn't say she hadn't done things *before* the end of the world that weren't... questionable.

But she'd never done human sacrifice before.

Although, she was pretty sure the Coven had.

Again, surprisingly not as hard a sell as one might think – *they-had-it-coming* was usually enough. Gang initiations were often worse – and ALL the girls at Susie's Bar belonged. Most were not much more than Lily's age.

Ginger and Luna, however, were older – they were the generals.

And when necessary, Michelle and Christine were muscle.

Michelle was a leggy dancer who could sail her seven-inch clear-heels a quarter inch over a customer's drink, and could just as easily sail that heel into your knee, or your gut, or your face.

Of all of them, Michelle seemed to thrive on the apocalypse. She had been their warrior, cutting quite a vision, with her hair tied back, carrying a spear. And *lots* of knives.

Christine was more practical. She packed a gun.

As elders, however, Luna and Ginger called the shots. And Lily knew she had fallen out of their favor.

Mark, the young man in the woods, the one chased by the dragon – *he* was to have been her first.

Lily had liked Mark. But she'd led him to the slaughter anyway.

One thing had nothing to do with the other. No different than a female spider – something else the girls at Susie's Bar had taught her.

Both Ginger and Luna had greatly approved of her selection. Mark was perfect – young and strapping, and *already* targeted by a rex.

But in the end, he had brought them to this *debasement* at the Mount – the Arc Project – breeding stock.

Granted, it wasn't because of anything *Lily* had done, but in matters of witchcraft, the actions of the fates were incriminating.

But now the fates had delivered something else entirely.

Shrinker called it 'Otto'.

Lily had been entranced right away by the little lizard in the cage – perhaps as the chipmunk is charmed by the snake. She had taken to feeding him crackers and was delighted the first time it spoke back her name – in her *own* voice! – only to be quickly scolded by Shrinker.

It wasn't until later she began to perceive what this little creature really was.

Before they had been taken into the Mount, Lily had adopted a wounded rex hatchling, who she named Junior – and Otto in his cage reminded her of how helpless the little rex had looked, his cracked shin splinted with a makeshift cast.

Never mind that Ginger had been the one who broke the leg, getting him to scream for his five-ton mother to come eat the live sacrifice they'd laid out for her.

Details.

Lilly still felt bad about the leg.

Otto, she assumed, was some sort of test animal, like a hamster – probably eventually to be euthanized – certainly experimented on.

One night when she was cleaning up, Lily had let the latch loose on the little lizard's cage, just to give the little guy a fighting chance.

Then the next day, when she found Otto still in his cage with the door once again latched, she had taken a bolder step.

Shrinker often kept the cage covered – apparently, to keep it from constantly mimicking every sound – and Lily had opened the cage and slipped the little lizard into her cleaning bag.

Once back on the maintenance floor, she had pushed a ventilation grating open in the wall and let him loose.

The next day, however, Otto was in his cage, as usual.

Shrinker had noted her thunderstruck face.

"Something wrong, Lily?"

On the desk, Otto had repeated, "Something wrong, Lily?"

Lily had shaken her head, numbly, quickly gathering up her trays, and following her armed escort to the elevator.

The next day, she had tried again.

And again, the next morning the little lizard was back in his cage.

When she had returned to the maintenance level that day, she had pulled the ventilation screen open and held out a box of crackers.

"Polly want a cracker?" she called softly into the echoing corridors.

She was rewarded by the sound of skittering feet.

The pipe was narrow, but Lilly could see at least half-a-dozen of them, their eyes blinking back the light like little sparking fireflies.

She remembered the first time she had shown them to the Coven.

They had all gathered round – *all* of them – summoned by the Elders, after Lily had gone straight to Ginger.

Lily had opened up the grate in the wall, and introduced them to a talking dragon.

Within this small circle, it might as well have been a burning bush or a crying portrait of the Virgin Mary.

What better way to start a new religion than with Scripture right out of the horse's mouth?

Lily had failed the Coven once. Now she found herself back in favor.

More than that, they were looking to Lily as if she were the prophet's chosen voice – even Ginger and Luna.

The only off-note was Michelle, who had been morose in the couple of weeks since nurse Rosa had disappeared. Lily didn't know the details, but Michelle had been brought in for questioning by General Rhodes himself.

Michelle had not talked about it. And in point of fact, seemed rather cowed.

That by itself, left Lily more frightened of Rhodes than anything since she had been on the Mount.

Ginger had broached Michelle, tentatively, in the time since, but was forcefully rebuked.

When push came to shove, Ginger was *older* sister. In a knuckle-up, Michelle was BIG sister, and so, for the moment, she was allowed her space.

The rest of the Coven, however, were assigned duties – it was not too hard to charm a soldier into doing favors – certainly not anything as harmless as setting a helpless lab-animal free.

Lily had already been one of the first to embrace the young soldiers on the base, Arc Project or no Arc Project – and in fact, she was wondering if she might not already be pregnant. Although, it was *just* possible she might have been a little knocked-up *before* she actually got to the Mount.

No need to throw that on the record, though – certainly not to Corporal Stevens.

The elevator slowed as it approached the upper-levels, before stopping at the maintenance floor.

Corporal Stevens smiled as Lily rolled her cart out.

"See you later?" he asked.

But she shook her head sadly.

"Not tonight," she said, without explanation – just as Ginger taught her. Let him wonder. Stevens looked appropriately crestfallen as the elevator door shut in front of him.

Lily checked her bag. She had gone ahead and made her grab. The small container had been waiting next to the trash. With Rhodes there, she had almost chickened out, and had only grabbed it up because she was more afraid they might find it.

She opened the little box. Inside, were several glowing green vials – along with a pack of pneumatic injector needles.

Something for the next shipment out – and there had been a lot of flights lately.

Still, Rhodes *had* been in the lab.

Ginger, she decided, would have to be told.

Tomorrow, the Coven would honor KT-day – and Lily wanted nothing to go wrong.

CHAPTER 11

The young woman's name was Kristie Morgan, and she had made her way down from Alaska over the last several months, working her way through Canada until she had just now reached the border of Montana, into the United States.

For whatever reason, the northern territories tended to have fewer of the really large beasts – the odd bloom notwithstanding – possibly because of the largely higher elevations. But they *were* well-stocked with sickle-claws.

Kristie had been trapped in her cabin for weeks.

As the Alaskan nights had started to grow long, packs of sickle-claws became ever bolder, even as she picked them off one at a time with an old-fashioned bolt-action rifle she had bought for protection during the polar bear migration. But the polar bears hadn't shown this year.

Perhaps they had already been eaten.

When her supplies low, Kristie had fled across the tundra.

And although she had no idea, Major Tom had watched her every step of the way.

Of all those who had witnessed the apocalypse, Major Tom had the best view.

Major Tom Corbett had been in space for eighteen months – a recently launched single-man station, purportedly designed for communications, but actually a surveillance vessel – dubbed the Eye in the Sky. Tom was hooked into every satellite in space, and he had seen the world end from every linked viewscreen on Earth. In high-definition.

At the beginning, he had received a lot of broadcasts from below – even after the digital platforms were fried there was still ham radio, CBs and walkie-talkies. Some people even broadcast video. Kristie had been one of those. She was also all over the radio waves – at first calling for help and then, over the following weeks, just talking over the air, narrating her life.

That was how Tom got to know her, even as all the other broadcasts faded – and frighteningly quickly.

Once he'd known her name, he'd actually pinpointed her location, and had managed to zoom a satellite camera down to where she lived.

Tom had watched her trek down through the Yukon – all her skirmishes with the hordes of sickle-claws – unable to even speak to her.

At least, he couldn't until just today.

Tom had been effectively trapped on the EITS station once ground support failed. He didn't even have an escape pod – or at least not one that would survive re-entry. The operator of the EITS was not allowed to come and go of his own authority – that's how non-espionage it was. There was the module-entry-pod attached to the airlock, which was the means by which you entered the station, but that was ferried from a shuttle.

On the other hand, there was the International Space Station. The ISS had been on automatic for the last several months before KT-day, after sustaining damage with debris from a junked Chinese satellite, and was absent any crew. Tom had actually picked up the bulk of the ISS' normal duties, networking satellites and such, until repairs were completed.

Tom's module pod could theoretically connect with the ISS and get him on board. *They* had entry-proof lifeboats.

Of course, that still left the problem of what happened when he landed in the middle of the ocean. It wasn't like there was a boat coming to get him anymore.

In any case, staying on the EITS wasn't an option. For whatever reason, the on-board computer was deteriorating badly.

Almost simultaneous with KT-day, and for no technical rhyme or reason he could decipher, his mainframe went haywire, with random glitches, like a cat running on a keyboard. Some functions seemed to work perfectly – he could access satellite-video for example – but at the same time entire spectrums of bandwidth seemed utterly and completely blocked – none of the military bandwidths came in, despite Tom's repeated efforts.

That by itself should not have been possible. He knew factions of the armed forces still maintained – he'd seen evidence of continued skirmishes from satellite-images.

But radio-reception was cosmetic. It now seemed the EITS' life-support systems were starting to get blinky.

He had waited the last six months for the ISS to come in range of his little module-pod. That had been today.

He had projected the very moment the ISS would be in range.

When he had climbed into that module pod, and pushed the airlock shut behind him, it was the finest moment of pure terror he had ever experienced in his life.

There was nothing on Earth that could compare to what it was like to be in space – physically, mentally, spiritually – the weightlessness – the view of the Earth itself below – a billowing blue jewel that was always surrounded by a starscape of permanent night.

Pushing the release, lofting the module pod away from its moorings was like letting go of a life raft.

The ISS was barely in sight. Tom only prayed his glitchy computer possessed the AI-cognitivity to connect with the station's ports.

He hoped the station itself hadn't been further compromised.

The pod's minimal propulsion drifted him painfully slowly across the airless chasm.

When he was within three-thousand meters, he initiated the docking commands.

For long minutes, there was no response.

What would happen if the ISS simply didn't read his corrupted signal? He might collide with the station – or worse, go sailing on past. The thought of arrowing off into space – to just continue to drift on forever – started a bead of sweat on his temple. He wiped it off, watching the droplet float and then split into particles.

Then there was a responding beep and the pod's propulsion fired briefly, angling towards the ISS' own air-locks.

With excruciating slowness, the pod floated until Tom felt the bump of contact as they connected to the dock. There was the heavy locking sound as the units attached.

And then the air-lock opened.

There was a blink as the automated lights in the station clicked on.

Tom took a cautious breath.

After a moment, he let himself into the adjoining chamber – the US module that had been one of the original centerpieces of the station. Over the years, contributing countries had added sections of their own – there had been plans to one day attach thirty modules to the original cluster. No longer to be, of course.

It was the first time Tom had been on the ISS in several years. And would be the first time anyone had been aboard in at least sixteen months.

He blinked as something touched his face – he swatted reflexively, as if at a spider, and came up with an empty candy wrapper, just floating loose.

As he looked around, he realized there was more debris floating loosely – nothing major or mechanical – just loose refuse.

It seemed odd that the departing cosmonauts would have left the place in such disarray. Tom wondered if it was possible the ISS had sustained further damage – perhaps impact from asteroids or other space debris.

Although, this reminded him more of a long-closed warehouse where rats had gotten into the supplies – which seemed unlikely in space.

Tom let himself up through the corridors, arrowing his weightless body like a swimmer, taking a moment to luxuriate in the relative space of the station versus the tiny little EITS. He knew his muscles were likely badly atrophied – his motivation to exercise had been low in recent months.

The main U.S. lab on the ISS was the Destiny module, and the walls were lined with blinking computers that operated mindlessly, careless of the absence of active human hands. Along the floor was a view-portal, looking down on Earth. It was Tom's favorite room on the station.

He pulled himself in front of what had been his own desk for a period of weeks – there were no chairs, but handles to hook your feet and keep you from floating away. Tom tapped the console and the screen blinked alive.

He tapped a few more buttons. Everything seemed to be online. He was looking at an active system.

Whatever had corrupted the EITS apparently hadn't touched the ISS.

Which meant, among other things, he should have access to all available bandwidths.

It also meant he could talk back.

He tapped the screen again, bringing in a satellite feed, focusing the cameras as he had done so often in recent months.

After a few minutes, he found her.

Kristie was on foot. Her trajectory would be pointing her towards the Maelstrom air-force base in northern Montana – perhaps that was her destination – her audio feed had cut out from the EITS station's reception several weeks ago.

Tom had her bandwidth. He realized he could call her – he could *talk* to her.

He actually felt himself freezing up, as shy as a kid asking for his first date.

What exactly was he going to tell her? Hi – I'm Tom and I've been spying on you from space for a year?

He laughed at himself, taking a breath, his eyes turning up and around as he thought about what to say.

As he did so, his eyes happened on one of the other screens.

And he frowned.

He turned from Kristie's image, pulling himself in front of the other workstation – an active station, he realized.

It took a moment for the full impact to sink in.

Something was wrong. Something was very, very wrong.

CHAPTER 12

The screen Tom was looking at was a duplicate of his own console on the EITS. And the surrounding screens were his workstation.

He tapped the keyboard, bringing up his home screen.

Everything was working, as if there had never been a single glitch.

The EITS had interfaced with the ISS mainframe when it had taken over its duties, pending repairs – could some virus have infiltrated at that point?

If so, why was the random haywire only on his end?

Now he realized a number of the surrounding screens were also images from the EITS – a security video log of his own chair – live footage of where he'd sat for the last year-and-a-half.

As if he'd been being monitored.

Tom frowned.

There were several other active screens as well – global maps, highlighting specific geographical areas. These views continued to rotate, reconfiguring moment to moment.

He realized he was not looking at a remote system continuing to operate – this was an active workstation.

Was someone on the ISS?

He tapped the console, bringing up the security screens from each compartment on the station one after the other.

After successive views of three empty corridors, the screen from the module right next door popped up – the *Tranquility* living-quarters.

Tom felt his blood run cold.

The image on-screen was all bug-eyes, teeth, and claws, jabbering at the camera.

He pulled the image back and found himself looking at a little two-legged lizard.

It was a little beast he knew all too well.

When KT-day had hit, and before his system had melted down, Tom still had access to all the least-hackable information in the world, and he knew all about Nolan Hinkle – about Monster Island – and Otto.

"Oh no," he breathed.

Suddenly everything made sense – every malfunction, every glitch. The interface with the ISS had overridden his own system on the EITS.

Behind him, there was the electric hum as the compartment door slid open.

Three of the little beasts, as weightless as butterflies, sprang into the room, claws out, jaws wide and hissing.

Attached to the console beside him was a coffee mug, adapted for zero-gravity with a sealed-top and a metal straw. Tom grabbed it up, and turned to smack the first of the little clawed bastards as they came for his eyes and throat.

The scaly little creature ricocheted with the impact, bouncing off the walls. Bracing against the console, Tom took a second, wide swing, catching the other two almost simultaneously, sending them spinning. One of them tumbled back out the door, but the other caught hold of the chamber wall.

Sealing his grip, Tom lunged forward with his foot, kicking the clinging lizard out after the other, and sealed the airlock shut. Then he turned to the third, which was perched along the rafters, claws extended and hissing. Tom wielded the coffee cup, straw-end first. He also grabbed a sharpened pencil.

The Otto hissed again, balefully. Then it pushed off the wall, making a dash for the door at the opposite end of the compartment. Tom hit the switch. There was a satisfying crunch as the scaly rat didn't *quite* make it through before the airlock sealed.

Tom shivered. He *hated* those little bastards.

He put a hand to his shoulder where a slashing claw had snagged his arm, sending droplets of blood floating like little red balloons.

Then he turned back to the screens, taking a closer look at the maps.

It was actually quite helpful that Otto used the military's own coding. It made things perfectly clear.

Tom glanced back where Kristie's face still waited on-screen – just a touch of a button away.

Instead, he tuned into the military bandwidths that had been so mysteriously blocked for the last year.

"Mayday," he said into the speaker, "this is Major Tom Corbett, aboard the International Space Station. Mayday I have urgent communications for General Nathan Rhodes. "

CHAPTER 13

Mark was ready to get the hell out of these mountains. Besides Junior, he was pretty sure that big ape he'd shot was tailing him.

The last thing he needed was another giant beast with a grudge. A little one with a grudge was bad enough.

There was no amount of self-interest to be served by forging forward on this ill-advised rescue mission, and Mark wanted more than anything to just start putting miles between all of it.

Unfortunately, he had a pretty good fix on the crashed chopper's postilion, marked by a steady plume of smoke, putting them right at the top of the highest available peak – and why the hell not?

He was also pretty sure there were survivors. He'd seen pterosaurs circling and heard the retort of several gunshots. Someone was a pretty good shot, dropping one of the winged dragons with each pop.

Mark guessed at least two miles from his position. Uphill, mountain miles.

And this was clearly no ordinary mountain. It reminded Mark of nothing so much as the tropical brush that had bordered the beach when the lifeboats of the *Pacific Princess* had made shore. More of that invasive shrubbery, much of it latching parasitically onto the giant timber.

He'd already seen the wildlife.

So far, it was giant gorillas, hatchling *T. rex,* and the trees were flush with nasty pterosaurs – some of the real ugly ones with teeth.

He'd also seen *something* had left a pile of shit the size of a minivan.

Mark chose not to even speculate, beyond the affirmation that the area was set to bloom – maybe even a trigger-point.

It was fortunate, at least, that he was coming in from the east. The southwest side of the mountain was a sheer drop, peaking at the ridge, before dropping into a series of forested canyons and valleys – a winding fissure of lowlands that trailed out from the surrounding mountains.

The terrain from his direction was at least hike-able. The brush, however, was either thick undergrowth, or giant trees. And while the slant wasn't vertical, it was certainly stair-stepped. You wouldn't want to lose footing and go rolling, or you might find yourself bouncing down a quarter-mile before you hit a tree big enough to stop you.

And Mark was a *little* nervous just about putting his hands in the thick brush.

He was even more nervous when he heard the heavy break of foliage in the brush behind him – along with what sounded like the snorting of an eight-ton gorilla.

Mark had been navigating a particularly nefarious, near-vertical tangle of roots that seemed to be a hybrid-mutation of thorns and bristles. Already scuffed and bleeding, he had nonetheless hauled himself up and over the worst of it, hunkering down out of sight.

He checked his bag. He was down to one can of tear gas. His pistol was useless. That left his rifle, which he'd dotted that big ape with twice, and the beast had just covered up and taken it in his arms.

It might be different with a head shot.

The wind, at least, seemed to be with him. Mark didn't know what kind of noses gorillas had, although he doubted it was on par with Rexy. Still, his scent might carry.

There was also that big pile of shit for a distraction. Mark hadn't showered lately, but he didn't think he could overpower *that*.

The bushes surrounding the clearing parted and the giant ape shuffled into view.

Mark held still, his rifle steady, his shot lined up right in the middle of the massive domed skull.

He waited for the beast to turn in his direction.

The big ape lumbered over, and seemed to be inspecting the six-foot dung-pile, actually setting back on his haunches and shaking his head.

Mark held his breath, finger tensed on the trigger.

The big ape turned, rising up on two legs, scanning the brush, and for a moment, Mark thought it had spotted him.

Then the beast dropped back down to all-fours, and with a disgruntled sigh, trundled out of the clearing. Mark could hear the crash of brush as the big gorilla seemed to be making his way up the mountain – roughly towards the same peak Mark was headed.

Perfect. Why not?

Mark shut his eyes. Was he really going to follow through with this?

He let himself down out of the brush. The giant ape had left a trail to follow, right through the briers.

"Oh what the hell," Mark breathed as he stepped into the makeshift path of crushed greenery in the big gorilla's wake. He kept his rifle ready.

In the clearing behind him, the brush rustled again, this time from just a few feet above the briers Mark had been wrestling through.

Junior's head poked out from where he'd lain, *for twenty, patient minutes*, plotting his ambush, as Mark now turned in the other direction.

With a grumbling scowl, the little beast hopped down through the brier patch and followed.

CHAPTER 14

Caesar was a fairly young silverback, but was still the alpha of his tribe.

The last time he had been measured by his human keepers, he was just over twenty-three-feet tall, heel to crown, and just under eight-tons.

He was the second largest *Gorilla gigantis* ever measured, but the other guy was a moron.

The ape tribe was not like Otto's saurians – they were not bred into the wild.

Congo had been the original, the one and only, back on the island – a further experiment in intelligence, intended as an improvement over Otto, by virtue of starting with a much more naturally evolved brain.

Caesar was among the brightest of his clade. If measured on a human IQ test, with all appropriate allowances, he would have scored average human – 95 or 100.

Of course, he was still an ape first, and one that had been bred as a potential practical application – the only one ever done with any of Hinkle's work, and one that had been conducted completely within the darkest corridors of Area 51, far from the old man's personal knowledge.

Hinkle had been testy about such things in the past, and so, out of consideration for his sensibilities, the powers-that-be decided not to tell him.

The elders of the ape-tribes, including Caesar himself, had been bred with an eye to their intelligence, combined with size, as a potential form of soldier/attack-animal.

Originally a troop of two-dozen – all given code-names – Grape Ape, Konga, Big Joe, Cornelius, a tubby fellow called Dr. Zaius, and of course, Brutus, who was two years younger than Caesar, but a full twenty-five feet tall and almost nine tons.

But 'Project Donkey Kong' was an utter failure. Apes weren't dim-witted minions, and the larger and more powerful you made them also meant more dominant, resistant to efforts at training, not to mention alpha-male laziness.

Eventually, the project was abandoned, and the subjects ordered put-down. It was an order that had been issued over speaker, in full earshot of Caesar himself.

It was a remarkable trait in humans – they could create him, make him intelligent, and then still not *believe* in him. Caesar had promptly taken the news back to his fellows, and the troop of them had trashed the place and escaped into the mountains.

Of all the genetically-born denizens, lurking unseen in these protected lands, the ape-tribe was the most isolated of all. They knew enough to stay away from humans, and the elevation minimized contact with the saurians.

The apes were also the only animals that hadn't been released as part of Otto's apocalypse.

Otto had been like a mascot at Area 51, and Caesar knew that little bastard well.

And now, for some reason, he could *feel* him.

An awareness, that had seemingly just clicked on.

Just like he could also suddenly feel the *T. rex*.

And *her*.

Shanna.

Inexplicably, he knew her name.

Caesar was not like Congo – he wasn't raised on an island with her, he had never even *heard* of her. But he could feel her presence, just like the warmth of a sunbeam.

And lately, that warm glow had grown. All his tribe felt it.

Unfortunately, there was also that accompanying smelling-salts-burn of Otto.

And probably not coincidentally, just recently, there had been more blooms.

The vegetarian apes had not been at great risk from the Food of the Gods. Caesar had learned to spot areas of infection by what it did to the indigenous animals – scavenging mammals and birds turned inside-out. If you saw that, it was advisable not to consume the foliage in the general area.

Brutus, on the other hand, was perhaps not so wise. He was a big, powerful, alpha-male, which lent itself to also being a muscle-head and a glutton.

The ape tribe had split, pretty much along those lines – the biggest chest-beaters had gravitated towards Brutus – Grape Ape, Big Joe, and Konga – extroverts, who tended to act out.

The bulk of the tribe, however, the more sophisticated, *reserved* apes took Caesar's path. Cornelius and Dr. Zaius, were his primary lieutenants. The separation of tribes was an equitable enough situation and there was no need to fight over leadership – a conflict nobody wanted, with no guaranteed outcome. Brutus was big, but Caesar was anyone's match in a fight.

Brutus had settled up here on this side of the mountain.

He and his troop, however, seemed to be gone.

It also seemed the area had a bloom budding up – and not from the carcass of any infected giant. This was something in the foliage itself. The leaves on this stretch of hillside were different. Brutus and his tribe had clearly not noticed – which was not surprising, if you'd ever seen them eat.

The results were obvious enough. In the clearing, Caesar found a six-foot pile of ape shit that told its own story.

An outbreak of the Food of the Gods was dangerous for more than one reason. The humans had taken to burning entire swaths of forest at the first sign of an infected giant. Several members of Caesar's troop had been caught in recent burns.

Instructing Cornelius and Zaius to lead the rest of the tribe further north, Caesar had gone to investigate the sudden outbreaks.

So far, what he'd found was not encouraging.

And as if he needed another pain in his ass, Caesar also had seen signs of that human who shot him.

Twice, he shot him. The big ape grumbled, touching gingerly at the bullet wounds on his arm and shoulder.

He had seen that little rex hatchling creeping up and had tried to intercede – *T. rex* were feisty, even at two feet tall, and he knew screwing around with the little beast could lose him a finger, so he'd attempted to scare it off with a roar.

That earned him two gunshots for his trouble.

It was likely that human was still around somewhere, working his way over the mountain. Caesar knew he would have to be wary.

And even as he thought it, there came a loud crack of a breaking branch.

Caesar turned, eyeing the twisting roots and tangling briers. He scented the air, but the wind was against him

The big ape scanned the foliage, looking for movement, but saw nothing.

Then he turned to the summit, still a couple miles distant.

She was up there. And as much as he could feel her, he knew she was hurt. That was enough to spur him to action.

With a last glance at the surrounding brush, Caesar shuffled out of the clearing, his eye on the peak beyond.

CHAPTER 15

Trix was pregnant, and feeling a bit hormonal.

During nesting season, and at this time only, female *T. rex* coveted the presence of the male.

Her mate, however, was infected.

Trix could see him from the hillside – the rogue, along with several females that once had been her pack.

And while she did not intellectually understand what had happened to him or her sisters, she had learned to stay clear of the giants, in the way hatchlings stayed clear of adults.

The growth-cycle of the infected rogue and his harem was nearing its peak – madness would soon set in.

Trix only knew the scent of her mate had changed, and she kept her distance.

She was already skittish with her pregnancy, which had likely saved her life, because she had not eaten any of the infected carrion. Something about the scent of the carcass set her hackles up and she held back, even as other members of her pack had rushed forward for the giant free meal.

Her oldest sisters, Daphne and Velma, had stayed back with her. Josie, however, her oldest daughter, had not.

Trix' primitive mind instinctively recognized the significance – it was a rebellion. And Josie led several of her sisters with her. Granted, there was a lot of tempting food, but there were principles at stake.

As senior female, Trix' territoriality manifested differently than the rogue. She allowed no other matriarchs. Once one of her girls got pregnant, she got chased out – off to stake a new territory with her own brood.

Female rex were also not belligerently aggressive the way males were. On average, females were fairly apathetic about other animals unless they were trying to eat them.

But, if you got them in one of their moods, like say, pregnant, nesting, mating – or worst of all, somehow challenged the dominance hierarchy – there was absolutely no bullshit in females. They wasted not a second on roars, stamping feet, or displays of any kind – they went right for the throat.

In that regard, lady rex were more dangerous, because their expressionless faces made it difficult to tell the difference until it was too late – they went from zero-to-kill in an instant. Males at least went through the pantomime.

By leading the others onto the carcass, Josie was jumping ranks, and under normal circumstances, would have been harshly disciplined.

Before any of that became an issue, however, jets had dropped napalm on top of them and lit the mountain on fire.

Trix' hide bore ugly scars, as the clinging flame had burned her skin alive.

Daphne hadn't made it. Trix had seen her stumble, her lungs choking with smoke, snapping a shin as she struck the ground. Crippled, Daphne lay helpless as the flames overtook her. Her screams followed the rest of the pack as they fled the burning forest.

Mercifully, the mountain was bordered by a wide river, which arrested the blaze. Trix, along with Velma, and two younger females, both daughters, stumbled down out of the smoking mountain, soaking their blistered hides in the cold water.

Trix' pack had originally numbered an even dozen. The rest had either gone with the rogue, or else perished in the fire.

Then the wind on the water began to clear the smoke, and Trix caught their scent on the air.

She saw them, a mile upstream, already crossed over to the opposite side of the river.

The big rogue turned his head in her direction.

T. rex' visual acuity was comparable to modern raptors, and even from the distance, Trix could see the green glow in her mate's eyes.

The same glow was mirrored in the blinking stares of Josie and all the pussycats flocked around him.

That had been three weeks ago.

At first, Trix had followed him.

The rogue had been moving southeast at a nearly straight trajectory.

But as the infection took hold, further effects became evident as Trix herself began to *feel* him, as if the sheer energy in his system were cast off like an ambient scent.

Soon after that, Trix herself began to perceive the beacon that drew him.

There was no precise physical sensation, but it was rather hypnotizing, like staring at a soothing light.

It seemed to touch the same part of the brain as that prickly tickle that rankled her sinuses whenever one of those little talking lizards was about – except this was almost exactly the opposite of that nasty, smelling-salts-acid-static she got from those scurrying little rats – that foul, psychic-stench that prompted an irresistible impulse to stomp the little bastards flat.

This was different.

It was... nice.

Like music taming the savage beast, without actual music, just a sense of general wellbeing. A glow.

Trix seemed to sense it a tick before the others, perhaps due to her pregnancy, but now they were all following the beacon together.

Rather than trailing in the hazardous footsteps of the rogue and their former sisters, Trix took her own flock up into the hills, running a parallel track through the highlands.

Tyrannosaurs acted on instincts. Trix gave no more thought to why she trekked the cold and inhospitable, thin-aired mountains than when acting on the impulses brought by hunger or sleep – she followed the beacon for no greater reason than a plant leans towards light.

But there was also something strangely familiar – a presence she must have been aware of subliminally all along, but now had grown brighter.

Trix had no idea what any of it meant, or why she was drawn. She did, however, sense that others were converging on the same site.

Somewhere in the canyons below, the rogue sensed it as well.

Trix recognized his territorial roar, announcing his authority.

Once that claim had echoed across an entire valley.

Now, his voice was the thundering gale of a titan – the echoes might have reverberated halfway across the continent.

But this time, somewhere off in the distance, Trix caught the faint echo of an answering roar.

A challenge?

Was this beacon marching them into a war?

Trix felt the stirrings of an old rivalry – as subliminal as the shine itself, instinctive as a mating urge – or a predator/prey relationship.

The canyons below again echoed with the rogue's commanding bellow.

Again, there was a distant response.

In Trix' memory, few rivals had dared challenge the rogue *before* the Food of the Gods – and none successfully.

The idea that any creature might try it *now* was an affront.

Being that *T. rex* were prideful beasts, Trix found her own ire sparked that *any* might dare.

Somewhere ahead was *their* star, and if they must battle to stand in its light, so be it.

Trix surveyed the terrain ahead. They were near, perhaps not more than three peaks over.

The big female's jaws parted and she let the mountains echo with a challenging roar of her own. Beside her, Velma and her two daughters joined in, until their bellows bounced off the peaks for miles around.

Trix could sense a tempest brewing.

She didn't yet know what lay ahead, but it wouldn't be much longer now.

CHAPTER 16

The cargo chopper was the heaviest thing Jonah had ever flown, and he could feel the difference in every tug of wind, every shift of momentum. It was everything he hated about flying.

He wasn't a fan of the parallel rear rotors either.

"This is like flying with a trailer," he complained.

Naomi clearly wasn't happy about it either, having said so emphatically and repeatedly, as they buzzed the mountain tops, as high and fast as Jonah could manage.

"It's a gift," she remarked, as Jonah struggled with the heavy-duty aircraft. "Some have it. Some don't."

Jonah glanced sideways. He was perfectly willing to acknowledge he was no fighter-pilot, but really wished she wouldn't say things like that at times like this.

"Maybe we can find a *truck* when we land," she suggested. "Or would that be too scary?"

Jonah bit back his reply as he took them up and over the highest peak, giving them their first look at the valley beyond.

The river cut through the mountain, and here it fed a modest lake and irrigated farmlands spread across the hillsides and down onto the valley floor.

Further below was a small town, remarkably overgrown, after only a single season of unmowed lawns, perhaps a few isolated fires – and, of course, certain parts that had been stomped flat.

It was, however, flat ground. According to Jonah's map, this little berg had a number of private runways, along with a small commercial airport, originally for crop-dusters, but adapted and expanded to accommodate full-size commercial aircraft. It also lay not five miles from a wrecked National Guard site.

Corporal Meyers had told them his base was this direction.

The camp would not, however, be on the valley floor. You simply couldn't have permanent structures on the lowlands. They would have to look to the high-ground.

But as they surveyed the peaks, there was nothing obvious. The heavily forested terrain was its own camouflage.

"Well," Naomi said. "This is the area."

She grabbed up the radio.

"Hello? Anyone out there?"

There was a scratch of static and an irritated-sounding whine, before a voice suddenly barked back over the air.

"This is Major Justin Travis. Who the hell is this?"

"Hi there, Major Travis, my name's Naomi. Your convoy got taken out by a sickle-claw raid and a pack of *T. rex*. We took your chopper and got the hell out of there. Now we need a place to land."

There was a brief pulse of static before Travis responded.

"Who's we? Are you civilians? How many are you?"

"There's two of us. I'm a four-star widow." Naomi glanced at Jonah. "I'm traveling with a civilian."

"What about the convoy?" Travis asked. "Were there any survivors?"

"None," Naomi said. "And you lost your outpost sentry as well."

There was another pause and scratch of static. When he spoke, his voice was deliberately neutral.

"You'll need to land immediately. Head west from your position."

The Coast mountains were not as large as the Cascades, but still maintained some respectable peaks. Just a few miles off one of the major highways, where the river had carved out a heavily wooded canyon, was what had once been a state prison, mounted high on an isolated peak above the water, and accessible by a single winding road.

Jonah could see why they had selected the site – the access-road was narrow, with a drop-off on one side and rock wall on the other. The prison itself bordered a sheer drop several hundred feet down to the river.

A runway/landing-strip was built across the modest plateau like on an aircraft carrier, and they could see several fighters tethered in rows. The tower was armed with gun-turrets on all sides, most likely as defense against pterosaurs.

Jonah circled, dropping altitude gingerly, trying not to overcompensate with the unfamiliar rear rotor, but the brisk side-winds took him by surprise. Thirty feet above the tarmac, a sudden gust pulled the chopper sideways.

There was a rush of movement from the gathered troops on the landing strip as the blades of the chopper turned briefly in their direction. Jonah cursed, wrestling the joystick. He had already started his drop when the gust hit, and was not quite able to get level before the landing gear struck asphalt, one side first, jarring them sharply to one side.

Naomi sucked breath as they felt the metal leg break, even as the other strut hit the ground. There was a paralyzing moment where it seemed the chopper might tip and roll, breaking the still-spinning rotors like bladed shrapnel, maybe even tossing them off the cliff into the ravine.

Jonah cut the engine. The chopper rocked itself to a stop.

As the rotors slowed, the troops waiting on the runway surrounded them. They had their guns drawn.

The leader tapped on the chopper's cabin. "Please exit the aircraft."

Jonah glanced at Naomi, who shrugged, unlatching her seat-belt, turning to push open the cabin door. Jonah followed, stepping down out of the chopper behind her as the soldiers circled the chopper.

Jonah looked around uncomfortably. This was not quite what he was expecting.

The soldier who had spoken before raised his radio.

"We've got them, Major. They've landed."

"Thank you, Sergeant Meyers," the radio barked back. "Bring them up."

"Meyers?" Naomi said. "We met a Corporal Meyers on the convoy."

The sergeant's eyes were grim.

"My brother," he said, in a tone that suggested he'd already gotten word.

Naomi reached in her pocket and held up Corporal Meyers' dog-tags. She offered them to his brother.

The sergeant frowned. He lowered his rifle and took the tags.

"You're going to need to come with us," he said. He motioned with his rifle, still hung ready over one shoulder.

As they walked, the rest of the armed escort followed

A second soldier stepped up beside them with a clipboard, asking their names and ages.

And then to Jonah he asked, "Do you have any special skills?"

"Well," Jonah said, a little uncomfortably, "I'm a pilot."

Beside him, Naomi snickered. "They *saw* you land."

"You're not helping," Jonah muttered.

The soldier with the clipboard shrugged, making a notation. He then proceeded to ask further questions about Jonah's health, family history, blood-type, and whether he'd ever had children.

He seemed satisfied just with Naomi's name and age.

Jonah could guess why.

He was a liability who would have to pull his weight. Naomi, on the other hand, was the most precious resource left.

Naomi's face was touched by a shadow of a frown, and Jonah could see a little of that boundless confidence evaporate with the awareness that things were not as before.

The former prison readily adapted itself for a fortress. And as they were marched into the main compound, it felt very much like they were off to see the warden, perhaps in anticipation of solitary.

Cages for human beings, Jonah thought, looking at the oppressive bars around him.

Naomi seemed unbothered.

Major Travis was, in fact, waiting in the former warden's office. Sergeant Meyers handed the Major the clipboard with their – or rather *Jonah's* – information before stepping outside and closing the door.

Travis perused the notes briefly.

"Alright," he said, setting the clipboard down, "I'd like to hear how all my troops are dead and you're flying their helicopter."

"We were onsite when the rex hit the outpost," Naomi replied.

"And what were you doing on our outpost?"

"Well," Naomi said archly, "we've been on the road for the last three weeks, ever since you people burned us out of our home."

Travis frowned.

"You were caught in the last burn," Travis said. He shook his head regretfully. "You were collateral damage. For that, I'm sorry. However, your presence here is a bit of a problem, and I'm not sure what to do about it."

The Major sat back, hands folded.

"This is a high-security base you've stumbled onto," he said. "We don't take refugees here. And since you now have operational knowledge of our assets, you have officially become a security risk."

Naomi chirped derisive laughter.

"Security risk? Who are we going to tell?"

Travis nodded. "Well, that's part of why I'm not sure what to do with you. Regulations dictate you be detained. And that rules out transporting you to any refugee facilities."

"If this base is so high-security, why did you let us land?" Naomi asked.

"Because we'd lost contact with our convoy and you were flying their chopper," Travis replied thinly. "We've also had several other convoys hit in the last few weeks by apparently random rex attacks, just like this one. And we need to know why."

Jonah had been silent, but now he was shaking his head.

"Major," he said, "your convoy wasn't hit by a random attack. The *T. rex* were lured."

Travis' eyes narrowed. "Lured by what?"

Jonah glanced at Naomi, who shrugged.

"Tell him," she said.

"Intelligent lizards," Jonah said. "They ride sickle-claws. You've probably seen them eating human corpses. They talk like myna birds."

Travis absorbed this quietly.

"The *T. rex* hate them," Jonah continued. "They'll pretty much charge through fire – or a military convoy – just to get at one of them."

Jonah eyed the major's reaction, which was so-far totally non-committal.

"And," Naomi added, "it was your Corporal Meyers that let the things loose."

Travis regarded them a moment longer before leaning forward and touching his intercom switch.

"Security? I think we're done here."

"You don't believe us?" Jonah said.

The Major sighed.

"Oh, I believe you."

Sergeant Meyers appeared at the door with two guards. Travis nodded to Jonah and Naomi.

"Would you please take these two to holding," Travis instructed.

"Are we prisoners?" Naomi asked.

Travis shrugged. "I'm not sure yet." He nodded to Meyers. "I need to talk to the General ASAP."

"Sir," Meyers said, "the General's already been in contact. I came to tell you. We're on alert."

Travis frowned. He nodded to Jonah and Naomi.

"Take these two to holding," he said, "then get me a wire."

Jonah exchanged a nervous glance with Naomi as they were ushered out of Travis' office, down the caged hallways of the former prison.

And not a hundred yards away, out where Jonah had not-quite crashed, the runway crews were clearing away the chopper.

As they loaded the damaged bird to be towed, there was a rustling as the cargo in back was disturbed – none of the work crew paid any mind.

Only one of them looked up briefly when he thought he heard the sound of skittering rats.

Half-a-dozen little lizards scurried discreetly out of the cargo hold, out onto the runway, and immediately bolted for the surrounding foliage that bordered the site, slipping quickly through the barred gate into the forest beyond.

CHAPTER 17

To look at Otto, you would not have guessed intelligence – and perhaps that wasn't quite the right word.

While they clearly operated under studied actions, they seemed to act, both individually and in groups, as if programmed – living drones.

It was also difficult to say if their actions were precisely planned so much as studied impulse.

In truth, Otto's pre-avian/post-reptilian mind was not capable of advanced thought.

But if you got enough of them together...?

Well, they destroyed the world.

The destruction had even been a bit more total than anticipated, because Otto, himself – *them*selves – were unexpectedly stamped out with it.

Tyrannosaurs had done that – wherever they had them – not all *T. rex* – Tarbosaurus in Russia and Asia, Albertosaurus and Gorgosaurus in Canada – all consistent with their historical geography as the Mesozoic world was imposed on what had briefly been a land of humans.

Otto's presence could influence most of the other beasts, to greater or lesser degree of usefulness.

Carnosaurs were willing enough soldiers, including the big carcharodonts that populated Africa and South America, but damned if they hadn't nuked large sections of both continents.

Then there were the herd beasts, but they were mostly limited to trampling and goring, depending on the clade, and didn't have many buttons beyond *go*, *stop*, and *eat*.

Humans, of course, continued to be a problem, but without their technology, they were highly dysfunctional, and at the numbers the species had dropped to, *should* already guarantee extinction.

The biggest problem, by far, were the *T. rex*.

Otto could never even have made it across the tyrannosaur-dominated territory by land – the rex would have rooted them out.

Tyrannosaurs, and *T. rex* in particular, instinctively resisted domination – which should not have been so terrible as a single clade of only a few species versus the rest of the implanted ecosystem. But the rex were an especially DOMINENT element of that ecosystem, and tended to kick the shit out of Otto's own foot soldiers – to the tune of four-to-one versus a large carnosaur.

Big herd animals could be weapons against them, but were much more mentally primitive. They could be angered and set into motion, but with no particular nuance.

It was the presence of the *T. rex* that had caused the Food of the Gods to backfire so badly.

A rex was hostile towards Otto by nature, but once they became infected, suddenly any Otto within perception-range became the subject of a search-and-destroy mission.

And unique to the other infected giants, an infected rex became *focused*.

So while humanity had been largely stomped out, Otto had been stomped out with it – and not just stomped, but hunted, rooted out, and eaten.

It followed that the next logical step, then, was to eliminate the rex.

Again, it was not a conscious decision exactly, so much as an instinctive response – acting on the simple goals of any computer chess game.

The rex, unfortunately, guarded their strongholds. The West Coast, and the northwest states were particularly dense population centers.

Sprouting blooms in the area was dicey, as the last thing they wanted was an infected rex.

On the other hand, they applied opportunism when it presented itself.

At first, they had started burning forests themselves, skulking into the territory, in small raids, minimizing their presence, and of course, always accompanied by a pack of sickle-claws. But the combination of the smell of smoke, and their own psychic-stench, alerted the rex to their presence, and invariably got them rooted out and stomped. Neither did the damp forests of the northwest readily burn out of season.

Just as it was easier to hitch a ride cross-country on their choppers, it was easier to get the humans to do it – they could be reliably counted on to dump napalm on the slightest presence of the Food of the Gods. And the largest bloom initiated in the region in the aftermath of KT-day, the humans had taken out with a nuke.

The rex packs were also quite predictable. In Otto's presence they would attack unrelentingly.

In this regard, *T. rex* was even more reliable than humans.

And if it could be depended upon, it could be factored and used.

The troop of Ottos began hooting softly, mimicking the bird-calls in the surrounding forests, not drawing undue attention yet.

But it was not long before the calls were answered by a rustling in the brush.

Sickle-claws from all the surrounding areas had been drawn in, just for the occasion.

Just as Congo and the rex responded to the lady, the sickle-claws and the meaner, more primitive beasts, responded to the lizard.

The dromaeosaur-packs remained just out of sight.

Over the last hour, they had systematically eliminated all the guards and sentries along the road leading to the prison, as well as the border fence.

Acting in the trained-dog fashion they always did in Otto's presence, they also took out the security cameras that lined the perimeter.

Thus there was not the early warning there might have been when Rudy and the JV squad separated from the forest and began making their way up the now-unguarded road.

Otto and the sickle-claws began flocking as a group through the perimeter fence, ducking between, over and under the gates, flooding all at once into the humans' compound.

Reliably enough, Rudy and the JV squad would be following along behind.

They could be trusted to charge through machine-gun fire for the chance to stomp a single Otto flat.

Had the fire separated them to the other side of the mountain, the JV pack might have been part of the exodus with Trix and the others, following Shanna's empathic light, but on this side of the mountains, the most poisonous, acrid smell was *them* – that foul sting in the sinus.

The rex pack knew the humans were up there too, and were quite aware the troublesome hominids were capable of inflicting a lot of pain.

Not that it mattered. A Triceratops could dish out a lot of pain – a *T. rex*, like Rudy, was used to tolerating pain.

The only thing he wasn't prepared to tolerate was that scaly little rat-bastard breathing his air, and too bad for anything standing in his way.

CHAPTER 18

Rosa could hardly believe they were alive. She also had to hand it to Maverick, who had utterly no shame in taking credit for what she judged to be almost blind luck.

Two things had saved them, the first being their mangled landing gear tangling with the vegetation, which served to check their fall into half-a-dozen broken lurches.

More significantly, the cliff had broken off in layers, and stair-stepped onto a narrow ledge approximately a hundred feet below. The chopper had landed nose-first, and still remained dangling, tail-up, from the mass of roots torn away from the cliff wall. The fuel tank had been punctured, and some of it had burned.

Miraculously, no one had been killed, although Wilkes and Garner were both the worse for wear. Wilkes had been in the cockpit, and was dotted with broken glass and shrapnel. Garner had been thrown forward, hitting his face on the back of the pilot's seat. Maverick had reflexively belted himself in when he'd taken the controls, and didn't have a scratch on him.

Most of the others had been tossed roughly. Allison had belted in, with Bud wrapped over her, the both of them a protective ball over baby Lucas. Mr. Wilson had tumbled and was nearly thrown out of the open side door.

Rosa's seat had torn completely loose, narrowly missing Garner, nearly landing in the inverted cockpit. The seat landed bottom first, otherwise she would have been crushed.

But the only one that was really injured was Shanna. When the chopper hit the ledge, she was thrown on top of Cameron, and the two of them tumbled awkwardly. Cameron ended up on the bottom, taking the brunt of the fall, as well as Shanna landing on top of him, and gained a pretty good assortment of cuts and bruises of his own. But it was Shanna who earned herself a broken leg.

Rosa had set the leg as best she could – a break just above the knee that should heal just fine – but Shanna would not be walking anywhere soon.

She wouldn't be climbing, either, Rosa thought, as she looked up at a hundred-feet of cliff.

To the other side was a dizzying drop of a thousand feet or better.

None of them were quite sure yet what to do.

For the moment, they had a fire going, and were using the shelter of the crashed chopper against the chill mountain wind. Allison had Lucas practically bubble-wrapped in blankets. Cameron set up a similar cocoon for Shanna in front of the fire, her injured leg propped up.

Maverick pulled the dead co-pilot from the cockpit and tried to cover him up, but the scent quickly attracted pterosaurs, that began to buzz the ledge. While Wilkes and Garner pot-shot the circling dragons, Maverick simply tossed the body over the cliff.

"Sorry, pal," he muttered.

Wilkes and Garner had both already tried their radios but had gotten nothing.

"We're on the opposite side of the range, and tucked into a little pocket of volcanic rock," Garner said. "No telling what natural properties might be interfering with the radio. We need to get up top, over to the other side of the mountain, before we can call for help. Maybe even a different peak."

For starters, that meant a sheer climb of nearly a hundred feet.

There was a tangle of brush, but a good portion of that had been torn away by the chopper itself, leaving a lot of flat, bare rock.

"So who gets to make the climb?" Wilkes asked, looking up at the daunting ascent.

The group of them looked at each other.

Allison had shot Bud a look – *you're* not going *anywhere*.

Rosa was no rock-climber. Shanna had a broken leg.

"Well," Mr. Wilson said, "I'm sure not climbing that damn thing." He nodded at Maverick. "That's why I had *you*."

Maverick shrugged, putting his hands against the rock wall, testing for handholds.

"Hold on," Garner objected. "You people are still in custody."

"You keep not saying 'prisoners'," Maverick remarked, ignoring him as he tested his weight on some of the tangled roots.

Garner started to move towards him, but Cameron put a restraining hand on his shoulder. Garner rounded on him. Cameron pulled back his hand with a shrug.

"You know he's just going to hit you again," he said.

Garner's hand dropped to his sidearm.

"What if I shoot him first?" he said.

"Well, then *I'll* hit you," Mr. Wilson said, standing up and planting a stiff right fist square in Garner's jaw, knocking him flat on his back.

Without waiting, Allison grabbed a log off the fire, and with the smooth stroke of a softball batter, she turned and struck Wilkes dead in the groin.

Wilkes' eyes went wide, as he doubled over, blurting a glut of involuntary profanity. He stumbled back and dropped to his knees.

As he gasped breath, he glared at Allison, eyes streaming.

"What the *hell* you do *that* for? I was just *standing* here."

Garner let out a low moan and Cameron reached down a hand.

"Don't feel bad," he said, as he helped the soldier to his feet. "I've seen him do that to full-grown Holsteins back on the farm. It's actually impressive you didn't go out."

Maverick gathered a small pack from the chopper – rope, a few tools. He also dangled the service pistol he'd snatched off the co-pilot before he'd pitched him over the cliff, nodding at both soldiers, but most meaningfully at Garner.

"Either of you got a problem with me having this?"

Garner glanced at Wilkes, who was still on his knees, and then Mr. Wilson, who appeared to be polishing his knuckles. Resigned, Garner shook his head.

"Okay then," Maverick said, "then why don't we get everybody set up?"

Garner sighed. He grabbed up his rifle, and tossed the strap over his shoulder, but pulled his service pistol and handed it to Bud – who promptly turned and gave it to Allison.

Allison popped the clip into place with a cold snap.

Wilkes handed his pistol to Cameron, while shouldering his own rifle.

Maverick looked up, squinting in the sun, eyeballing the sheer rock wall.

"You know," he said, stepping back, "now that I look at it, this just seems foolish." He turned, tossing the rope over his shoulder to Garner. "Here. Which one of you wants to be a hero?"

Garner caught the rope with a frown. But he dutifully stepped forward, putting his hand on the rock, feeling for handholds.

The volcanic rock was layered, so while the climb was nearly vertical, there were grooves to latch onto. Unfortunately, there was also no way of telling what was solid rock versus what was ready to tumble loose. The ropes of root were likewise compromised.

With the sheer drop, simply pushing back from the wall would be to fall – maybe back to the rock ledge, or possibly into the chasm beyond.

Garner began to scale the cliff, feeling one hold at a time. After he'd gained ten feet, Maverick stepped up and began to follow behind him.

"I thought you weren't coming," Garner called down.

"No, I was just smart-assing," Maverick replied. "But I thought I'd let you go first."

Wilkes looked unhappily up at the cliff, but nevertheless followed along behind Maverick.

Cameron knelt beside Shanna, just touching her hand, as if all that need be said was in their physical touch.

"We'll be back," he promised.

Shanna smiled. "I know you will," she said, with no doubt.

Cameron looked up at Rosa.

"You're a doctor. You'll take care of her, right?"

Rosa nodded. "That's what I do," she said.

Cameron turned steadfastly, deliberately not looking up, and began to climb after the others.

Already nearly thirty-feet above, Maverick kicked loose a small cascade of rocks. Cameron covered up as the shards bounced off his head and shoulders.

"Owwww! Dammit!"

"Sorry," Maverick hollered.

Mr. Wilson shook his head apologetically. "That's his mother's son."

The climbers proceeded slowly; Rosa estimated that Garner was about fifty feet when a large pterosaur swooped in – one of the nastier-looking beasties, with claws and teeth.

It went for Garner, with his rifle strapped on his back, helpless to defend himself. Immediately below, Maverick tried to reach the pistol in his belt without letting go his hold on the rock.

Then a single shot rang out as Allison dropped the bird from the ledge beneath. The pterosaur crumpled, wings folded, as it bounced off the cliff into the ravine.

Maverick's voice bugled down.

"Thaaank you!"

And with the smoking pistol still in her hand, and Lucas bundled in her other arm, Allison started crying.

Almost immediately, little Lucas joined her, whether from the gunshot or by his mother's own tears. Allison turned to Bud, almost burning him with the pistol barrel as she wept in his arms.

Rosa put a tentative hand on Allison's shoulder. Allison could be a bit of a touch-freak when she got emotional, but this time she clasped Rosa's hand, squeezing out any comfort she could. After a moment, she sat up, making an attempt to dry her eyes.

She looked down at the infant in her arms, whose own sobs had subsided to concerned sniffles, as he looked up at the goddess who was his mother.

"What kind of a life is this?" Allison said. "I mean, what's the point? The world's over, isn't it?"

She looked around helplessly at the others, but none of them had a ready answer.

But Shanna shook her head.

"The world has only ended for *you*," she said. "*He* doesn't know it unless you tell him. For him, everything just started."

Shanna waved her hand out at the prehistoric new world.

"This was *my* childhood," she said.

Rosa shook her head. "What does that mean? Who *are* you?"

Shanna sighed. "Well, I guess you could say I'm the daughter of the apocalypse." She looked thoughtful. "It's ironic. All my life, I wanted to see the real world. But *this* was always my life. And now it's all there is."

For the first time since Rosa had met her, Shanna's face bent into a genuine frown, a dark expression that somehow looked hurtful on her features.

"I grew up alone except for my father. And the animals. That was all I had. I mean, I could *see* the outside world, I just wasn't allowed to touch it."

Now she smiled a bit. "Don't get me wrong, I was hacking into top-secret files since I was a kid. My father didn't seem to mind about that. I knew perfectly well who killed Kennedy by the time I was eight, but there was never anyone around to care."

Rosa perked and started to ask, but Shanna was already past it.

"Area 51 got their best stuff from us," Shanna said. "There was never a Bigfoot, or a Loch Ness Monster. And yes, the alien autopsy was a fake.

"But," she said, "Monster Island was real. It was my home."

CHAPTER 19

Kate's first reaction to the cryptologically mythological Professor Nolan Hinkle was dismay and shock.

She wasn't sure what she had expected. Kate had known he was an old man, but as Shanna bent to his side, the impression was of an RN assisting a resident of a nursing home.

Perhaps even a dementia patient.

Nolan Hinkle regarded Kate and her entourage with clear confusion – which was perhaps understandable, given Cameron's camera, and Maverick with his rifle slung over one burly shoulder – but there was blinking hesitance in his old eyes, and when he spoke, his voice was willowy and frail.

"Shanna? We have guests?"

Kate glanced sideways at Betty, who nodded back with a frown.

"Professor Hinkle?" Kate said, stepping forward. "My name is Kate Rhodes. I'm an investigative documentary filmmaker. I received footage via an e-mail in your name. Footage of this island."

But even as she said it, Kate was beginning to doubt it.

"Daddy," Shanna said, "did you contact this woman? Or make any outside contact at all?"

Hinkle shook his head, wide-eyed and bewildered. "I can't imagine," he said.

"We got here somehow," Kate said. "I didn't peg the latitude/longitude on a dartboard."

She reached in her bag.

"Here," she said, producing the thumb-drive. "I can show you the message."

Shanna popped the device into the nearest PC, bringing up the video – the images of the canyon they'd just driven past, and all the beasts in the valley.

She shook her head. "I don't understand."

"That's the main valley," Hinkle said, suddenly alert. There was an abrupt change in his posture, and he seemed to snap to attention. "We have three, where natural faults have split the island cap." He leaned forward, tapping on the screen, indicating the surrounding foliage. "It was actually quite difficult to duplicate a prehistoric ecosystem on such a small island."

The willowy tones were replaced by a professorial lecturer. Kate was reminded of her own grandfather, in the late-stages of senility, long past the point where he remembered who *she* was, but he had been an electrical-engineer for forty years, and could switch-on and discuss *that* stuff for hours, never once screwing up the math, right up to his final days.

"We are talking, after all," Hinkle continued, "not just about animals from different climates, but entirely different eras. In a fraction of their natural space."

Kate nodded to Cameron, who brought his camera to his shoulder.

"Hold on," Shanna said. "You shouldn't be filming."

"We're already here," Kate said. "They're going to arrest us anyway. And we're *way* past the point of *I-could-tell-you-but-then-I'd-have-to-kill-you*, right?"

Kate had meant the remark to be flippant, but Cameron glanced at her over his camera, a touch disquieted. Even Maverick frowned.

Betty, who hadn't even been told, displayed no external reaction beyond rapid blinking.

Oh well, Kate thought. No point dwelling on it now.

"Excuse me, Professor," Kate asked, simply moving forward as if the entire exchange was a scheduled interview, "you say this island is small. Why create such large animals? Every creature I've seen is the largest example of its type."

"Well, young lady," Hinkle said, responding automatically to the student's question, "size is very much a focal point. One of our first practical applications was the accelerated growth of crops and livestock."

Hinkle's grin turned briefly nostalgic.

"Do you know one of my original sponsors as a young man was Greenpeace? They wanted their condors back." Hinkle chuckled with the memory. "That was before the government stepped in."

Shanna put her hand to her head with a groan. *"Daddy..."*

But Hinkle was lecturing now.

"You will note," he said, indicating the screen, "the animals are not exclusively dinosaurs. We have representation of every single branch of animals that ever produced giants. Fish, mosasaurs, lizards, snakes, crocodiles." Hinkle pointed to several gigantic beasts that resembled rhinoceros with necks like giraffes. "We also have several large mammals."

"What about that big gorilla?" Maverick asked, raising his hand like a kid in a classroom.

"Congo." Hinkle nodded. "Yes, that was the next stage. Gigantism not simply reproduced in an existing, albeit extinct, species, but applied to an extant animal, from a line where gigantism never evolved."

Maverick nodded slowly, like that same kid who didn't quite understand the answer.

"Growth can be generated by many factors," Hinkle explained, "both in an individual and a species. The question is what activates it, and can macro-evolutionary catalysts be applied to the micro-scale of a single organism?"

Now Kate was nodding along with Maverick. Recognizing the blank looks on his students, Hinkle grinned.

"Would you like to see?" he asked.

"Daddy," Shanna said, "you're going to get *us* arrested."

Hinkle pish-poshed. "Nonsense. Shanna, we're being rude. We have guests."

Again, the here-and-now focus seemed to shift in the old man's eyes.

Shanna glanced at Kate. "Daddy, do you understand? These people are not supposed to *be* here."

Hinkle paused, turning to his daughter, holding up a corrective finger.

"Neither are we," he said. "Yet, here we all are."

Shanna frowned, starting to reply, but she was interrupted by a loud beeping, like a timed alarm.

"You need to set out the morning feed," Hinkle said. "You've got your chores."

Shanna sighed, throwing her hands up.

"I'll be right outside," she said, eyeing Kate meaningfully. "Everything's automated. I shouldn't be long.'"

With a last, reluctant look at the rest of them, Shanna turned to leave, tapping the sliding glass shut behind her. The motion-sensing cameras followed her movements and her image remained on the security screens, blinking to a new view as she walked past each building.

Hinkle sat down in front of the computer, and started pulling up files, his trembling fingers typing fast and sure.

"One thing I discovered," Hinkle said, "was that the slightest genetic flaw could create wild disruptions at the most basic chemical level of an altered organism. So one of the first things I developed was a purification process."

"Purification process?" Betty asked, learning over Hinkle's shoulder, observing the simulation on-screen.

"A method," Hinkle said, "of chemically eradicating imperfections in an organism's genetic structure. All animals on this island are the healthiest, strongest, most intelligent examples of their species that their genes could muster.

"And," he said, "that includes my darling daughter, Shanna."

Kate blinked. "You experimented on your own *daughter*?"

"Wait a minute," Cameron said, lowering his camera. "That girl, Shanna... she's a *clone*?"

Hinkle laughed.

"No, of course not," he said. "She was conceived and born in the normal way. All I did was administer a sort of super prenatal-vitamin. She was, in fact, the very first. And it was from her very DNA that I was able to move forward with all the rest of it."

Kate was shaking her head in disbelief. "You recklessly administered an experimental agent to an unborn?"

"Hardly recklessly," Hinkle replied, a bit miffed. "I knew it would work."

"Didn't you wonder," he asked, "how an old toad like me could have produced such a beautiful daughter? The prenatal agent weeded-out abnormalities at the chromosome-level. No defects, no deformities, every single cell healthy and full."

"Aesthetics," Hinkle explained, "are about balance. That's why athletes tend to be attractive people. The even-limbs that allow for physical talent also produce aesthetic balance. It is simply key to the binary-design, and translates to otherwise subjective aspects like facial features."

Cameron was shaking his head, watching the security cameras as they followed Shanna on her rounds. "She's an experiment?"

"Not an 'experiment'," Hinkle objected. "My wife and I used many advanced prenatal methods unavailable to the general public, all during her pregnancy. Always to the benefit."

Kate nodded. "I'm sure. And where exactly is your wife?"

Hinkle frowned. "Died," he said. "Many years ago. When Shanna was young."

"But she approved?"

"Much of it was her own work. She was my research partner," Hinkle said. "The original agent was originally intended as no more than prenatal health. It was only later, through happenstance, that my wife discovered the resulting potential in Shanna herself."

"What potential?"

"We found that the prenatal agent had a negative effect on *recreated* organisms. One of the difficulties in cloning is that *all* the genetic traits of the parent get passed on, including aspects like the organism's current stage-of-development. Genes that mix-up commands to age with those of adolescence are simply not viable. The organism ages quickly, and dies young, among a whole host of other problems. Unfortunately, when we attempted to solve this by administering the prenatal purification agent to our engineered subjects, the results were catastrophic, to say the least, massively accelerating the genetic defects."

"But," Hinkle said, "when the agent was extracted from Shanna's blood, out of a viable living organism, as opposed to a synthetic test-tube, suddenly it allowed us to adapt the purification process to clones as well. Once that viability was passed on, everything changed, and our research moved forward at light-speed."

Hinkle tapped up a new screen.

"And here," he said, "is where we are now."

The screen opened up into a virtual-reality simulation.

"This," Hinkle said, "is the Food of the Gods."

The group of them watched as the computer model spun like a Rubik's cube through the process of cell reproduction, from the initial chemical commands from the DNA-level to the outer effect on the organism itself. The virtual example on-screen was a simple houseplant. Once the reaction was activated, the plant began to grow.

In time-lapse, stop-motion, the stalks tentacled out, the roots broke the virtual pot, and the leaves fanned out like a parachute catching wind.

Betty was leaning forward, entranced, all thoughts of possible arrest and criminal charges momentarily forgotten.

"This is a simulation," Betty said. "You can do anything with CGI."

Hinkle smiled again. "Would you like to see?"

The old man stood up, puttering his way to the back of the lab, motioning them to follow. He tapped-open another series of sliding glass doors, leading out to an enclosure similar to those outside the main compound. This one, however, was fenced off, like a private terrarium.

Within were rows of cages, the size used to transport large dogs, except with heavy-duty construction more apropos for a pet tiger.

"I keep them back here," Hinkle said. "They tend to make a lot of noise."

Inside the first cage, lying on its side, its ribs rising and falling in apparent sleep, was a cute white bunny, with big ears and a wiggling pink nose.

It was better than four feet long and probably close to two-hundred pounds.

Other cages held mice, squirrels, chickens – all greatly enlarged. They all seemed to be sleeping.

Betty peered into the cage. The rabbit's lids fluttered open, and the irises reflected back fluorescent green, like phosphorus.

"Its eyes are *glowing*," Betty exclaimed.

"Yes," Hinkle said, musingly. "The chemical isn't perfected yet. That's one of the more minor side-effects."

"What are some of the less minor ones?" Kate asked, peering in over Betty's shoulder.

"Well," Hinkle said, "you'll notice all the animals seem lethargic. They're dying. At the late-stages, in fact. The animals all just die."

"There is also," he said, "the abiding fact that the chemical only seems to work on genetically-engineered organisms. All these animals are clones."

"What does it do to normal organisms?" Betty asked.

Hinkle shook his head. "It's fairly gruesome, I'm afraid."

"Any other problems?" Betty asked, peering in the cage.

"Well," Hinkle said, "the biggest flaw seems to be that the effect is passed on. If we grow a stock of corn, for example, ingestion passes the chemical on to whoever might try to consume it. Which, in effect, defeats the entire purpose.

"There is also," Hinkle acknowledged, "the matter of the affected animal's temperament."

At that moment, the apparently docile rabbit stirred in its cage.

There was a flash of movement, accompanied by a frighteningly deep-throated squeal, and suddenly there were chomping, eight-inch rodent-teeth, snarling through the bars to the cage.

Betty jerked back with a screech.

The rabbit latched onto one of the bars and began whipping its head back and forth like a bulldog, scarring the metal.

"Jesus," Maverick muttered, shouldering his rifle uncomfortably. Cameron zoomed-in his camera.

Then the entire enclosure abruptly came alive as the rabbit's mad-screeching roused the other animals. The caterwauling howls rose in pitch.

"My God," Kate exclaimed, holding her ears.

"They become highly aggressive," Hinkle said, raising his voice to be heard over the ruckus. "The effect is rather like rabies, except that it seems consistent in birds, reptiles, fish or insects."

Betty looked back at the cute two-hundred-pound bunny tearing savagely at its cage. There was little doubt what those chomping jaws would do if it could but free itself.

Around them, the other cages actually began to shake as their frenzied occupants attacked the bars locking them inside.

"Perhaps we'd best leave them be," Hinkle said. "This batch is due to be euthanized."

As Hinkle led them back into the main lab, there was a beep and Shanna's voice sounded over the intercom.

"Daddy? I'm going to be a bit longer out here than I thought."

"Malfunction in the equipment?" Hinkle spoke aloud.

"I'm not sure yet," Shanna replied.

"I'm going to take our guests over to the dining area," Hinkle said. "I'm sure everyone is hungry."

"I'm sure," Shanna replied tiredly. "By the way, Miss Rhodes, I just got word they're sending a ship to collect you. So you might as well relax."

Shanna clicked the intercom off.

"You know," Maverick said, "maybe we should try and fly the hell out of here."

Cameron shook his head. "I'd rather get arrested than shot down."

Betty raised a confirming hand. "I'm afraid I have to second that."

"Relax," Kate cajoled, as they followed Hinkle out of the lab, across the grounds to the living quarters. The accommodations were equally space-age, although rather spartan, with a simple rec-room, a small gym, and a TV.

"By the way," Hinkle said, as if with an afterthought, "I downloaded some more detailed files, to peruse at your convenience." He handed Kate back her thumb-drive.

Kate blinked, looking down at the device, and then handed it to Betty.

It seemed for a moment that Hinkle frowned as she did so.

Betty took the drive, and nodded, pulling her laptop out of her bag, and plugged-in the drive.

"Do you have a place I can sit down?" Betty asked.

After a slight hesitation, Hinkle opened his door to a modestly compact but well-stocked library.

"This is my study," Hinkle said. "You should have sufficient privacy in here." He pointed to the intercom on the desk. "Just push this button when you're done."

He turned to the others. "This way to the dining room."

The motion-detected cameras followed them as they went.

Once the screens were all focused on the small entourage at the other end of the hall, there was scuttling movement as Otto emerged from where he'd been hiding in a corner.

His head bobbing, he peered into Hinkle's study, where Betty bent over her laptop.

CHAPTER 20

The cafeteria was adjoined with a modest dining room, and with obvious ritual, Hinkle began prepping the kitchen. The very model of etiquette, he offered libation. Maverick accepted a pint of heavy draft, while Kate took a glass of chilled white wine.

Cameron asked for a restroom, but as he ducked out into the hall, he instead headed back outside.

Across the yard, Shanna was still struggling with the automation. She stood in front of an open control box mounted on a pole, outside the series of utility buildings built at the edge of the waterfall.

The feed-carts looked like the log-ride at Disneyland – rail-tracks leading down through the segregated canyons – a traveling food-trough.

Cameron turned up the light on his camera as he approached, waving his hand.

"Hey there," he ventured, zeroing the lens in for a close-up.

Shanna turned, her face unhappy and frustrated. She held up her hand against the light.

"Would you please not do that?" she asked.

Cameron lowered his camera.

"Sorry," he said.

He was struck again by her sheer beauty – the absolute symmetry of her form and movements.

"Well?" she said. "Can I help you?"

She had what Maverick called 'bright-eyes'. As he put it, "The sort you see on post-grad college-chicks studying psychology, or some shit."

And she stared right through you, too, just like a shrink. Cameron actually found himself blushing.

"I'm sorry," he said. "I mean, I wanted to..."

But then the assembly-line food-trough suddenly kicked alive. Shanna turned to the screen which was flashing 'reset-complete'.

Shanna tapped the screen, bringing up a menu.

"What's wrong with it?" Cameron asked.

"Well," Shanna said icily, as she tapped through screens, "it seems that right about the time *you* people arrived..." Shanna cast him an arch eye, "... apparently the feed-operations ran without receiving a command from me."

She peered onto the screen.

"Right here," she said. "The code and the voice command are mine, but I was with you people on the beach. I didn't do it."

Cameron shrugged. "Computers have glitches."

Shanna shook her head. "We don't *have* glitches."

She shook her head.

"I can't figure out why this load ran. And I can't find what was on it. It's like the record was deleted except for the fact that the rail-computer logged the trip, and the troughs have been dumped."

"So what does that mean?" Cameron asked. "The critters get overfed? If they're anything like my dog, they won't complain about that."

As if in answer, there was a hooting cry from somewhere down in the valley.

Cameron had done his time on Mr. Wilson's farm with Maverick, but he lived in town, where wildlife was generally restricted to deer and raccoon, which were mostly quiet critters.

Whatever made *this* low howl was no raccoon.

Cameron tapped down a few unruly hairs on the back of his neck.

Shanna caught the movement and smiled a bit.

"Don't worry," she said. "No dinosaur is going to eat you. Not up here. They don't like the hills."

"What about your gorilla friend?"

"He's around," Shanna allowed. With a sigh, she shut down her computer screen, turning to eye him directly. "By the way," she said, "you stopped your friend from shooting him. Thank you for that."

"Listen," Cameron said, "I actually wanted to say I'm sorry for us showing up like this."

"You should be," Shanna agreed. "They're going to arrest you." She checked her watch. "Probably within the next hour or two."

"That's not what I meant." Cameron looked down at the camera in his hand. "I've followed Kate on some wild jaunts. And when you're looking at it from behind a camera, sometimes you forget about the lives." He shrugged. "Truth to tell, I didn't expect to find one here."

Shanna stared back for a moment, her bright eyes blinking.

Then suddenly she burst into tears.

"Don't worry," she said, turning away. "You didn't."

Cameron paused, uncertainly. Shanna held up an apologetic hand.

"I'm sorry," she said, "it's just that... my father's fading."

She looked up at him through her tears, a perfect stranger, but at least another face to tell.

"I've been on this island my whole life," Shanna said. "When my father's gone, I'll be alone."

She shook her head helplessly, kicking at the empty trailer trough on its rails.

"I'm an experiment," she said bitterly. "Just like any of these animals. And they will never let me leave this island."

Cameron reached out a tentative hand, laying it comfortingly on her shoulder.

And that was the first time he felt... *it*... from her.

Their first physical contact. For an instant, Cameron started to jerk away, as if with a static shock, but Shanna reached up to take his hand.

Her fingers clasped softly around his own, and she turned, looking back at him, as if seeing him for the first time.

She smiled as if she knew him now, and rather liked what she saw.

Shanna held the contact a moment longer.

"You're a good man," she said.

The crackle in that touch was like a light turning on inside him.

Wow, he thought, *I think I'm in love.*

Just like that. Like it was a by-product of being around her.

Entranced, Cameron started to lean close.

But then suddenly there was a deep and guttural growl – deep and *loud* – above and behind him.

Cameron felt himself grabbed completely around his chest and snatched bodily off his feet.

He found himself staring into Congo's snarling face.

"Congo!" Shanna shouted, slapping at the big ape's feet. "You put him down this instant!"

Congo pulled Cameron nose-to-nose, his hand starting to squeeze.

His teeth looked pretty big from this angle too.

"*Now!*" Shanna shouted again, stepping back and signing 'down'.

The big gorilla's eyes narrowed, but he sat Cameron back on his feet, leaving him to wobble unsteadily.

"Congo!" Shanna admonished. "Why don't you take a time-out!" She pointed sternly in the direction of the valley.

With a sulking scowl, Congo turned, shuffling his way back to the main gate.

Cameron was patting down his freshly-compressed torso, making sure everything was still working.

"*What*," he stammered, "was *that* about?"

"I told you, he's jealous," Shanna said.

Then, seeing his wide-eyed expression, she burst into helpless laughter.

"I'm sorry," she said, "but the look on your face..."

Cameron guessed it had been a good look – it probably shaved ten years off his life, too.

Who *was* this woman? A jungle girl, raised on an island – a military-research outpost?

What does *that* sort of socializing process do to you?

At a glance, it gave you a farm-girl. One with a *Starship Enterprise* lab in the barn. And really BIG livestock.

But who were the *people* she had known?

Military-types, for sure. Probably *hard-core* military. Possibly, collaborating scientists. Her doddering father. Hinkle mentioned a mother as a young girl.

Cameron still felt a tingle on the spot where she'd touched his hand. And just standing in her presence, he felt... *whatever* it was... her *shine.*

It was rather like sitting in a comfortable chair, with a sunbeam and a breeze. It just felt *good* to be around her.

But it was like a splash of cold water when a loud, piercing scream suddenly echoed over the intercom through the compound.

CHAPTER 21

Betty was already a little on edge when she heard the door creak.

It had only been a few minutes, but she was already wishing she hadn't let herself be left here alone. The science-fiction surroundings were less fascinating and more creepy when you were by yourself.

She jumped, letting out a small shriek when the door pushed open and Maverick popped his head inside.

"Hey, girl? You seen Cameron? Kate wants some on-camera."

Betty let out a slow breath, shaking her head. Maverick cocked an eye.

"Didn't mean to scare ya, darlin'," he said, pausing at the door with his typical caveman suave. Betty eyed him back sourly.

She paused, waiting for the inevitable one-line come-on. Maverick had propositioned her in some form, subtle or overt, almost every single time they'd met – it was almost a running gag, like Bond and Moneypenny. Betty, with varying degrees of patience, always shot him down.

Self-respect would *never* let her succumb to the secret knowledge that she had *totally* been into him ever since she was a sorority girl and Cameron had brought him to that kegger – all the way, back in the day.

Of course, there were always *what-if* scenarios – like on a desert island. After all, it was the Lost World where an ape-man has his greatest appeal. And when in a cave, do as the cave-dwellers do.

But today, Maverick simply let her be, ducking back out in the hall.

Betty turned back to her screen, amused that she was actually a little disappointed.

Then there was another creak, as Maverick poked his head back in briefly.

"By the way," he said, "you look hot today."

Betty gave him her best Moneypenny. Maverick grinned, sliding back out, shutting the door behind him.

Thus mildly distracted, Betty started tapping through the files Hinkle had attached, pulling up one of the images he had highlighted – 'effects on normals' – a graphic JPEG of what looked to have once been a mouse, turned inside-out.

Any lingering schoolgirl, soda-pop thoughts quickly evaporated as the ghastly images stung her eyes. Betty had done gross anatomy, but this nearly caused a gag-reflex. Her own application of DNA research had been primarily medicine, so she understood the need for animal-testing but...

Betty shuddered, closing the image, and scrolling down to the next file.

This one was an image of Princess Leia, in her white gown – the glowing hologram projected by R2-D2.

As Betty tapped the screen, the image spoke.

"Help me, Obi Wan Kenobi," the recorded voice of Carrie Fisher said. "You're my only hope."

Betty smiled a little, puzzled.

The file opened, and a video started to play.

In place of Leia's hologram, up popped the image of Professor Hinkle himself.

Betty's smile faded, as the old man began to speak.

"Ms. Kathryn Rhodes. I've chosen you to receive this message because you are the daughter of General Nathan Rhodes, and it has become dangerous for me to attempt to contact him directly."

Betty's brows furrowed. Hinkle's speech and manner were clearly much more cognizant than the man she'd met only a short while ago.

She paused the message briefly, checking the date, noting the file was created only shortly before Kate had received her first e-mails.

Betty recalled how Hinkle seemed to frown when Kate had handed her the drive. And the first thing on the message was a summons to her father, the General?

She paused, indecisive, before hitting play again.

It took less than two minutes.

As she watched, Hinkle's measured tones made it all the worse – like Rod Serling's invocation into the *Twilight Zone*.

Betty let the video end, staring, blinking at the blank screen.

The implications of what she'd just seen demanded a thousand contradictory impulses, and she found herself simply sitting immobile.

Her first random thought was that Kate's *tell-you-but-I'd-have-to-kill-you* joke was no longer funny at all.

Behind her, there was another creak at the door. Betty turned, expecting to see Maverick.

But the open doorway was empty.

Then she heard a skittering, and a shadow darted into the room.

Betty jumped as the little lizard, Otto, hopped up onto the bookshelf beside her.

Except, *now*, Betty knew he was a bit more than just a parrot-talking lizard.

Otto cocked his head and opened his mouth.

"Help me, Obi Wan Kenobi," he said in Princess Leia's voice. "You're my only hope."

There was more skittering movement at the door and suddenly two more of the little lizards popped up on the bookshelf beside the first.

The sickle-claws on their toes tapped, and their arms spread like wings, armed with very sharp claws.

When they moved, Betty reached for the intercom, but all she managed was a scream before they were upon her.

CHAPTER 22

Betty's scream echoed over the intercom throughout the compound.

When they came upon her in the study, it was very obviously already too late.

Cameron and Shanna came running up to find Maverick bent over Betty's bloody, still form. Kate was standing behind him, hovering at the door.

Hinkle turned a sober eye to his daughter, shaking his head.

Wide-eyed, Shanna knelt beside Maverick, who looked gut-punched, and she lay a consoling hand on his shoulder. He blinked at her touch, moving aside to let her examine the wounds.

Shanna ran her finger along the cleanly torn throat.

A sickle-claw slash, from a claw no more than three inches long.

"Otto?" she whispered hesitantly.

But even as she said it, Shanna's eyes squeezed shut and she doubled over, letting out a yelp of sudden pain. Her hand stole to her temple. She tried to stand, but Cameron had to catch her as she wobbled and nearly fell.

Hinkle moved forward, concerned. "Shanna...?"

The rest, however, was drowned out as just outside the building, there came a bellowing *roar*.

"Um, people?" Kate said, looking up at the security screen. "We've got a problem here."

Staggering, eyes tearing as she leaned on Cameron's shoulder, Shanna tapped the screen bringing up a wide view of the grounds outside.

"Oh no," she breathed. "Congo?"

The big gorilla was standing in the walkway just in front of the building, reared to his full height, beating his chest, roaring angrily.

And from the other end of the compound, the challenge was answered, by a deafening bellow.

Shanna tapped the screen, turning the camera view towards the front gate – which was wide open.

Standing in the walkway were two big carcharodonts.

Shanna was shaking her head. "They can't get here from the valley. We have a dozen safeguards."

"Like an open gate?" Kate said, turning from the screens, looking outside to where Congo pounded the ground, not twenty-feet beyond those uncomfortably fragile-looking, transparent alloy doors.

The little group of humans peered like mice under a log as just outside their hovel, the big ape faced down the two advancing dragons.

Giganotosaurus carolinii was the largest theropod on record. Of somewhat lighter build than *T. rex*, its more gracile, kite-like frame allowed a significantly greater body-length, with a skull that *averaged* over five-feet.

And, of course, Hinkle bred 'em big. These two males probably both scaled near ten tons, with nearly seven-foot jaws.

Congo, mighty-muscled as he was, seemed outmatched.

Maverick unshouldered his rifle, looking unhappily at the diminutive firearm compared to the elephant-sized predators. He nodded to Shanna.

"Hey, jungle-girl," he said. "Can't you do your rex-whisperer thing?"

Shanna shook her head. "Not with carnosaurs. They have more primitive brains. Too reptilian. No pair-bonding yet. Not much room for empathy."

Then her eyes narrowed as the beasts drew near.

"Oh *no*," she whispered.

The carcharodonts' eyes were glowing green.

"They're infected," Shanna whispered. She turned back to the security monitor, switching screens over to the view of the three separate valleys. She tapped again, zooming closer to the roaming animals.

The beasts were agitated, and the cameras struggled to focus.

Then the image snapped sharp and they could see the animals' eyes.

All of them – from the roaming ceratopsians, to the lumbering sauropods – their eyes reflected back that tell-tale emerald glow.

"The food-trough," Shanna said, blinking with realization. "It was dosed."

With one arm still over Cameron's shoulder, she began dragging them back to the main entrance. Muttering curses, Maverick followed, sliding the safety off his rifle and locking shells in place

"Uh, what exactly are we doing?" Cameron objected as Shanna hit the switch, sliding open the front doors, and now they could hear the cavernous growls, as Congo faced-off the two dragon-beasts, not twenty-yards away.

Riding on the carcharodonts' shoulders, like birds on a buffalo, were half-a-dozen Ottos.

"Wait a minute," Maverick said, scoping them with his rifle. "How many of those things are there?"

"One," Shanna said, bewildered. "I mean, we've cloned a lot of them over the years. They're like hamsters. Like pets. But never more than one at a time."

Behind them, Hinkle spoke up quietly.

"I'm afraid this is my fault, Shanna," he began quietly.

On the back of the lead carcharodont, one of the Ottos squealed, leaping off the big carnosaur's back to the ground. A second later, the rest followed, hooting like loons.

The troop of them turned, dead-eyeing Shanna as a group.

For a moment, Shanna stared back, as if transfixed.

Then she let out a cry of pain, grabbing her head, and dropped limp as if she'd been hit with a stick. Cameron caught her weight as she slumped bonelessly against him.

Congo's voice also rose in a shrill roar. He grabbed his head, snarling, even as the two carcharodonts bellowed and charged forward.

The pair of seven-foot skulls seemed to split in two, yawning into a razor-toothed maw, gaped wide as a snake's, as both carnosaurs lunged.

A carcharodont's jaws were designed to take down the largest prey that ever existed – the gigantic hundred-ton titanosaur-sauropods. In order to take down these fantastic beasts, carnosaur skulls had evolved like the six-foot bladed blubber-knives used to carve up whales, capable of shearing away entire slabs of living flesh at a stroke.

Giganotosaurus had, however, jettisoned much of the clawed-forearm armament of more primitive carnosaurs – their hands were no bigger than a tyrannosaur's. That meant their primary weapon was their head.

Congo ducked aside, letting the first set of jaws snap shut on empty air. Bulling forward, Congo batted the razor-toothed skull aside, grabbing the beast's head like a wrestler, clamping the jaws shut.

The second carcharodont went for Congo's offered back while the big ape grappled its twin, but Congo pivoted, rolling his opponent over his hip into the path of the attack, and both carnosaurs tumbled over the top of each other.

Maverick fired several shots at the tangled carnosaurs as they scrambled back to their feet, but the bullets only seemed to aggravate the dragon-beasts further, and Kate pulled him back.

Cameron was trying to bring Shanna around. As she struggled in soupy semi-consciousness, Hinkle bent beside them, taking his daughter's hand. There was no hint of dementia in his eyes now.

"I'm sorry," he said. "I'm so, so sorry."

"Daddy?" Shanna blinked, tears streaming out of bloodshot eyes. "What's happening?"

There was another caterwauling from the troop of Ottos who were now standing at the sidelines as the carnosaurs tussled with the giant ape.

The carcharodonts were circling Congo more cautiously now. For a ten-ton animal, getting rolled was more punishment than either of them cared to experience twice.

It didn't matter, however, as the island itself took the moment to suddenly become involved.

There was a very abrupt and massive rumble, followed by a tremor that knocked everyone on the ground off their feet.

Congo's eight-tons landed heavily, nearly on top of Maverick, who rolled clear at the last second. Kate toppled bodily over Cameron, crouched protectively over Shanna.

Professor Hinkle's old bones were sent tumbling, and he lay unmoving.

Both carcharodonts were also down again, and this time, slower to rise.

Congo groaned as he regained his feet.

The island, however, was not done.

It was a volcanic cap, already split ages ago, three-ways across the middle – hence the triple canyons.

There was a second tremor, and with it, came the smell of sulfur and a plume of smoke coughing into the sky.

A third tremor was more like an engine getting started.

"Oh my God," Shanna mumbled, struggling to rise. "Otto."

Cameron attempted to hold her down, but she pushed him away.

"You don't understand," she said, "we have to get off this island."

Over the rumble of the quaking earth, there now came several staccato blasts that sounded like seismic charges.

"That was not natural," Shanna affirmed, leaning heavily on Cameron's shoulder as she looked around for the Jeep.

The rig was exactly opposite the yard. Congo and the carcharodonts, back on their feet and squaring off once more, blocked the way.

Maverick nodded. "I'm on it," he said.

"Keys are in the dash," Shanna said, as Maverick darted past the circling beasts.

But then they heard Kate's voice behind them, low and regretful. "Shanna."

They turned to find Kate kneeled over Hinkle's crumpled form. She looked up, shaking her head helplessly.

"I think he's hurt."

With a low cry, Shanna stumbled to his side, turning him over.

Only then did they see his throat was slashed – the same wounds as on Betty.

Dancing not thirty-feet away, their claws bloody, were the troop of Ottos.

The first of them hissed, hopping over the fence, followed immediately by the rest, and they disappeared into the surrounding brush.

Shanna bent over her father.

"Daddy..." she choked.

Cameron actually felt a tear squeeze out of his own eye as he touched her shoulder, absorbing the empathic pulse of her grief.

Across the yard, Maverick gunned the Jeep to life.

Both carnosaurs responded with gape-mouthed attacks, and were nearly upon him in three steps.

Congo charged to intercept, catching one set of seven-foot jaws, and shoving the saw-blade skull into the other, always turning one beast in front of the other, never allowing both of them to attack him at once.

The strategic tactics offset the advantage of the carnosaurs' killing weapons, turning the battle into a wrestling match that favored the muscular ape.

Maverick squealed tires past the trio's stomping legs, skidding up next to the rest of them.

"Come on, people," he said urgently. "We've got to go."

Cameron pulled Shanna gently away from her father's still form, feeling every bit of her grief as she broke contact.

Maverick revved the engine impatiently. Kate slid in the front, while Cameron helped Shanna into the back.

Unfortunately, now the path to the gate was blocked.

Congo had gained a momentary advantage, having tripped-up both his opponents at once, and pinning the second carnosaur on top of the other.

The big ape was currently raining massive fists in repeated blows down on both their heads – and starting to see some success, as his knuckles began to come up bloody – but the maneuver had trapped all three of them against the gate.

Maverick honked the horn.

Looking up with an exasperated snort, Congo gave up the mount, instead grabbing the top carnosaur's head, and leveraging it in a judo roll out of the gateway. The second carcharodont scrambled to its feet, leaping immediately to attack, as Congo gave ground.

The path now clear, Maverick stomped the gas, even as the monster threesome launched themselves at each other once again.

Shanna looked back, as the Jeep skidded down the slope. The sound of the battle carried well after they were out of sight.

As they left Congo behind, she buried her face in her hands.

Congo, however, was gaining an edge. Not being particularly bright animals, neither of the two carcharodonts made any particular effort at countering Congo's tactics, which kept them off-balance and in each other's way, and the big ape's powerful blows were starting to take their toll.

One of the beasts was blind in one eye, allowing Congo to approach that side unguarded, taking the opportunity to slip a more substantial grip around the carnosaur's neck.

Giganotosaurus was a large, but not overtly robust animal for its size – it was not built for sustained struggles with its giant sauropod prey – the slicing, blubber-saw jaw-blades were not intended for jarring impact, and its modest neck was only just thick enough to economically support the long, but gracile skull.

Congo encircled the carnosaur's neck and twisted, snapping the vertebra just behind the head. The beast dropped limp at his feet.

Learning nothing, the second carcharodont lunged over the twitching corpse of the first. Congo caught the gaping jaws in both hands.

No longer having to worry about an attack from behind, the big ape simply grappled the carnosaur off its feet, flipping the beast over one hairy hip, locking the jaws together as he bore the struggling dragon to the ground.

Another twist and a snap. The carcharodont kicked once and quivered still.

Then there was a soft 'phut' sound, and Congo felt a bee-sting in his backside.

He slapped reflexively, narrowly missing one of the Ottos as it darted away. As Congo turned, growling, the little lizard paused, bobbing up and down.

Congo reached and found the pneumatic needle still stuck in his buttocks. He pulled it out like a stinger. There were traces of glowing green.

Otto chirped once, and vanished between the fence.

Congo growled, poised for a moment, as if to chase after the little lizard.

But then he shook his head, his perception warping, as the effects of the chemical began to take hold.

The big ape turned and followed down the path where Shanna disappeared.

There was only one other animal on the island that was out of the normal food-trough train.

Big Rex lay, lightly sedated, through the caterwauling and continued tremors.

There was a skittering in its enclosure and another light *phut*-sound.

The rex blinked immediately awake, the nearly six-foot skull perked with the sudden awareness of a hawk.

A deep rumble sounded in the mighty beast's chest as energy surged through his system.

His eyes blinked emerald green.

The rex cocked his head, regarding the little lizard, hopping through its enclosure.

Otto looked up cheekily, no doubt as it had before mounting the carcharodonts.

The big tyrannosaur lurched to his feet and stomped the little lizard flat.

He paused to sniff at the squished splatter, wiping his foot disgustedly on the rock.

Then he reared up, blinking with new awareness.

With fourteen-foot legs, spring-muscled like a ten-ton ostrich, Big Rex kicked the door to the enclosure down, its head turning in the direction of the beach – and Shanna.

The squirreling Jeep engine was only just ahead.

It was less than two miles from the compound to the lagoon. But one of them was a mountain-mile.

Maverick kept the top-heavy vehicle on full-tilt. Kate gripped the roll-bar, teeth clenched, as their skidding tires kicked rocks into free-fall over the ledge.

Even Cameron's eyes were shut as he and Shanna were nearly thrown out the side.

There was another heavy tremor and a particularly noxious cloud of black smoke belched into the air.

Looking up at the terminal blackness encroaching upon the entire sky, Shanna groaned.

"You gotta go faster," she said.

Maverick glanced over his shoulder. "Lady, no one has *ever* said that to me before."

As if his ego was on the line, he took the next turn a little tighter.

The curve brought them to the overview of the main valley – the same vantage they'd passed only a short time before.

Less than two hours ago, this had been a recreated eco-sanctuary, a rather tranquil, if prehistoric, nature-scene by the river.

What they saw now could not even be fairly judged a stampede – this was a *rampage*.

Sauropods crushed smaller beasts beneath their feet, even as they were gored and raked by horns and spike-rimmed armor.

They seemed to attack the forest itself, as much as each other.

"Can they beat us to the lagoon?" Kate asked.

"There's no direct access through any of the canyons. Two of them are blocked by cliff walls. The main valley is split off by heavy jungle." She nodded meaningfully to the scene below. "Only partially blocked by canyon wall."

"You mean they can get there if they really *want* to," Maverick said as he reached the turn where the road veered off the cliffside back into the trees.

It was a lot worse surrounded by the heavy foliage, where they couldn't see anything but the road just ahead.

The trees around them shook with the tremors like capering rubber skeletons dancing in a brisk wind, and already they began collapsing into the main road as the earth beneath their roots began to break apart.

Maverick swerved, clinging to the road by sheer momentum.

There was the smell like burning brimstone as the deepest crevice splitting the island began to spark, like a long-dead engine trying to fire.

And again there came the deliberate staccato explosions of seismic charges.

It was beginning to seem like overkill.

Maverick burst through the trees, firing the Jeep out onto the beach like a shooting pinball, barely braking in time before sliding the full length of the clearing out onto the dock, right up to the edge of the lagoon.

Their renewed view of sky revealed a solid patch of smoke, spreading overhead, like a dark black wing. Bits of fire and rock sparked like fireflies amid the closing shadowy curtain.

The Cessna rocked against the dock as waves splashed over the pier. The pontoons threatened to tear away before the plane broke its mooring.

Maverick jumped from the Jeep, running for the floundering seaplane. Kate started to follow, with Cameron pulling Shanna on his shoulder, but then the trees behind them burst.

Kate let loose a reflexive scream as Congo bound into the clearing.

They could see his eyes were glowing green.

"Oh, Congo," Shanna mourned, as the big ape galloped after them to the end of the dock.

The Cessna's engine kicked once and died, followed by a volley of oaths and curses from Maverick. Kate paused at the dock as the waves crashed over the paneling.

Cameron pulled lightly at Shanna's shoulder as Congo reached out a paw to touch her.

"We've got to leave him," Cameron said, eyeing the big ape, and his newly emerald-eyes. "I'm sorry."

"He understands you," Shanna said through tears, holding her hand up to the giant ape's massive paw.

Congo blinked at her touch. Then he set back on his haunches, and signed.

Shanna nodded, tears streaming.

"I have to go," she agreed. "I'm so sorry."

Another sign with the giant hairy paw.

Shanna's voice broke.

"I love you too."

Behind them, the Cessna engine kicked alive as Maverick fired the propellers.

But now the jungle brush was broken yet again.

This time, as if in deliberate defiance, the trees that bordered the threshold were physically broken and knocked aside.

Big Rex stepped into the clearing – eyes glowing green.

Congo turned to face his long-time rival as the rex paused, eyeing the tableau of the big ape and Shanna together.

"Hey!" Maverick hollered from the cockpit. "Can we get the hell out of here?"

The rex took a step forward. Congo stepped away from Shanna to face him.

Cameron estimated the rex' stride. Five steps down the beach, onto the dock, and the rex could have a mouthful of sea-plane long before Maverick could have it in the air.

The rex advanced another step, blinking its glowing eyes.

Congo twisted a large branch from one of the fallen trees, brandishing it like a club.

Big Rex' lips pulled back into a snarl.

Cameron sensed Shanna's intention a second too late to prevent it.

With a sudden lurch, she pulled free from his hands, still stumbling off-balance, as she ran between the two posturing beasts.

There was another slew of cursing from Maverick in the plane.

"Please," Shanna gasped, out of breath and sobbing. "Please stop..."

The rex hovered over her, blinking down with its glowing eyes.

Congo paused, his tree-limb bludgeon held ready, growling warily.

Shanna stepped forward, raising her hand for the rex to sniff.

"That's right, Rex. It's me. Everything's okay."

The big tyrannosaur nosed her outstretched hand, nodding at Congo with a snort, but stepped back another step.

Then Shanna jerked again, as if being struck, staggering, with one hand to her temple. She dropped to the ground, apparently unconscious.

At the same moment, both Congo and Rex snarled, shaking their heads as if with a stinging shock.

Even Cameron thought he felt a taste of acid in his sinuses.

For Big Rex, Shanna's distress was catalyst enough – a genetically-embedded attack-command – and Congo was right in front of him, already long-hated and long-envied.

More than ten tons of *T. rex* lunged forward, jaws agape.

Congo caught the charge, shoving the tree limb into the rex' open mouth. The teeth clamped shut, expecting hairy flesh, but instead latched onto the branch like a dog onto a bone.

The two titans clashed, just over Shanna's crumpled form.

Cameron dashed forward, between the crushing feet, and grabbed her up.

Overhead, the black cloud was threatening to swallow the entire sky. The tremors crashed the Cessna against the dock.

Maverick was now broadcasting over his loudspeaker.

"Will you people please get on the goddamn plane!"

Kate turned, stumbling over the shaking wharf, even as roiling waves tried to wash her off either side. Cameron was close on her heels, carrying Shanna's limp form as they piled into the sea-plane.

Maverick jerked them away from the dock, snapping the mooring, before Kate even shut the cabin door. And then they were riding the chopping surf like speed-bumps, battering the already damaged pontoons.

Back on the beach, the rex chomped the tree-limb in half. The combatants pushed apart and circled menacingly.

But then they were knocked from their feet as a massive and final tremor shook the entire island.

There was a deep volcanic rumble, wafting out from the island's deepest crevice – no seismic charge this time.

Within the circular cap that had once been the mountain's broken peak, the trapped cove of ocean rocked against the surrounding walls like water in a bathtub, sending a microcosm of repeating rogue waves ricocheting back to shore.

Maverick jerked the sea-plane out of the water before the bucking breaker-waves could overtake them, pulling the aircraft up in a near-vertical climb, and sending his passengers tumbling.

And as he stretched out over the reef, struggling for altitude, the crashing ocean broke once again as seventy-feet of pliosaur surged like a breaching sub, snapping its crocodile-jaws shut less than ten feet from their wing.

"Knew you were coming that time, you son-of-a-bitch!" Maverick hollered as he angled away.

The pliosaur crashed back below the surface.

With the margin of a high-jumper, Maverick cleared the Cessna over the crest of the surrounding wall, just as the volcano erupted behind them.

For a moment, the entire sky seemed to light on fire.

Then came the blast of smoke.

Within seconds, the explosion caught up with them, fire and smoke, riding on the blast. The sound hit them half-an-instant early, deafening their ears, a moment before a tsunami of turbulence rattled their teeth.

They tumbled through the sky, with Maverick struggling to maintain a general forward trajectory.

Somewhere in the middle, the engine quit.

"Oh, you son-of-a-*bitch!*" Maverick roared as he wrestled the wing-flaps against naked wind.

The Cessna dipped, dropping into a dive, straight for the ocean.

'Oh, *shiiittt!*" Maverick groaned, straining.

The plane's nose arched up.

The sea below, however, had no intention of helping. The swells breached twenty and thirty feet high as the eruption displaced water for miles in every direction.

Without an engine, they were going down, sooner than later.

Maverick leaned his back into the arc, leveling them into a straight glide, coasting barely fifty-feet above the surface.

Uncertain if the pontoons were even still attached, Maverick touched them down to the water, just at the crest of the highest swell.

The pontoons caught, planting them face down and forward as the wave dipped. The landing struts bent in half, tearing partially loose.

Kate was thrown forward, nearly landing in Maverick's lap. Shanna was still unconscious, but Cameron had managed to belt the two of them in.

Which wouldn't matter if the pontoons broke away, and the plane sank.

The impact drenched the cabin, flooding them with icy ocean.

But the second pontoon held, and together they propped the main cabin between them, and the Cessna stayed afloat, riding the swells, its wings propped awkwardly like an injured bird.

Maverick, who had simply thrown the controls aside near the end, collapsed limply in the pilot's seat.

"Maverick," Kate muttered, crumpled at his feet, "you are *so* fired."

Behind them, the sky continued to darken with smoke. There were echoes of continued rumbles.

The chill of seawater had roused Shanna, and she looked up groggily at the burning pier that had been her home.

No one spoke as the ocean rose and fell around them, carrying their little wreck like a floating leaf.

They all jumped as the radio suddenly barked static.

A hailing signal. A summons.

"That's your Navy buddies," Maverick said. "Coming to arrest us."

He glanced around at the empty ocean.

Or at least a *hopefully* empty ocean. Who knew what dragon-beasts might be lurking about.

Maverick squinted as the first of the Navy vessels were now visible on the horizon.

"You know what?" he sighed. "I'm fine with it. I could use the rest."

He picked up the radio, clicking on the speaker.

"Okay," he said, "come and get us."

Cameron nudged Shanna, who lay, spent and listless in his arms.

"Well," he said, "it looks like you're going to see the real world after all."

Now there was the sound of choppers, as the first of their escorts appeared overhead.

Kate sighed, popping up next to Maverick, looking out the window.

"More likely a military base outside Washington DC."

Maverick waved out the window as the choppers circled. They spent twenty minutes extricating them from the crashed Cessna.

Then they were taken into custody.

CHAPTER 23

The ship that picked up Shanna and Kate's team was far from the only vessel that appeared to surround the smoldering remains of Monster Island. At least half-a-dozen destroyers patrolled.

Clinging to a bit of flotsam that had once been part of the dock, Congo heard the repeated sound of munitions.

Some of the other beasts had escaped the island, and were currently floundering in the ocean. There were steady canon blasts as the circling ships picked them off one by one.

Congo tried paddling away from the convoy, but before long he was spotted by a chopper, and one of the destroyers turned his way.

Helplessly, he watched as the ship approached.

Exhausted and resigned, he waited for the sound of the canon.

Instead, a soldier leaning out of the chopper above shot a tranq-dart into his back.

Almost instantly, Congo's eyes fluttered, and he started to slip from the floating pier.

On the destroyer, sailors with ropes dropped over the rail. As he drifted out of consciousness, Congo felt himself bound and secured.

And while the Navy occupied themselves with Congo, only a short distance away, Big Rex floated at the surface, riding the swells with only his eyes and back exposed. The furrowed brow rather resembled an enormous crocodile, although when the big rex began to swim, it was actually more of a dog-paddle, his powerful legs churning the water like a motor.

The blinking green glow of his eyes was the only tell of his presence.

He had taken a battering in the eruption, and been tossed and thrown with the surf. For a brief time, he had lost consciousness. When he had awakened, stirred by the sound of explosions, he had found himself floating like so much driftwood.

Knocked into a state of semi-apathy, as well as still feeling the effects of the sedative, the big tyrannosaur had watched impassively as the other surviving animals struggled in the surf, drawing attention from the patrolling navy ships.

The rex saw Congo loaded onto one of the vessels – spared for some reason.

Big Rex also sensed the presence of Shanna, growing quickly distant, like a rapidly-fading star.

His glowing green eyes blinked, locking in on that star, and with its simple-minded focus, began to follow.

CHAPTER 24

Kristie had been traveling through Montana for a week, and according to her map, the site up ahead was the Maelstrom nuclear base.

As she scoped the grounds with her binoculars, however, she could see it was now being patrolled by sickle-claws.

Kristie had picked up on cross-talk coming from the site within the last week. But as she perused the grounds, the base now seemed abandoned.

A sickle-claw raid? Kristie knew first-hand the packs of dromaeosaurs were particularly vicious – even mindlessly so.

That, however, was something Kristie had learned could be used against them.

Vacationing in the tropics, she had once seen native fishermen 'jigging' for four-foot Humboldt squid – mollusks that would swarm prey in aggressive packs – but the moment one of *them* was hooked, the others cannibalized it within seconds.

Sickle-claws were like that. Kristie knew if she could kill one quietly, the others would dog-pile.

At the distance, she would have preferred a rifle shot, but her pistol had a silencer.

She lined up her shot and fired.

Two-hundred yards away, one of the beasts dropped, twisting and kicking in spasms. Immediately, the others pounced, savaging their downed comrade.

Now that they were gathered together, they were easier targets. It was rather like herding mackerel.

Of course, the tactic didn't work if those *little* ones were around – the ones she sometimes saw riding the bigger beasts like birds.

Kristie wasn't sure what the little lizards were. They looked like a small sickle-claw, but she knew they weren't infants – adult dromaeosaurs ran with the hatchlings. These creatures were clearly different.

She'd encountered a lot of them on her path just lately. And Kristie, who would doctor a bird with a broken wing, had taken to pot-shotting the little vermin on sight – always with an unconscious shudder of revulsion.

There had been a troop of them not twenty-miles back.

Kristie had been keeping to the high-grounds – you tended to get the smaller animals there – and she stumbled onto what looked like a military unit, setting up munitions – a single vehicle and equipment scattered in a makeshift day-camp.

The soldiers were missing.

There were, however, nearly a dozen of the little scaled lizard-rats skittering all over the site. Kristie was reminded of cockroaches. With her scope, she was able to take out six of them in succession, like shooting gallery ducks before the others vanished into the rocks.

Kristie had salvaged what she could from the site. The Jeep's keys were missing, and there was no food, nor did she have much use for seismic munitions equipment.

As she searched the area, she found no human remains, not even bones.

She wondered what the military had been doing up there. Seismic testing seemed rather risky after what she'd heard over the airwaves about the San Andreas fault.

Over the last year, she'd felt more rumbles and quakes than in her entire life put together.

The dormant volcanic chain seemed to have been awakened.

Even the beasts succumbed to the rage of the Dragon under the Mountain.

She had left the abandoned munitions unit two days ago. And it seemed that whatever happened there had also happened at Maelstrom.

Kristie held her position on the hillside while she waited for more sickle-claws to reveal themselves, attracted by the scent of the beasts she'd already killed.

She pulled out her radio, dialing up military channels.

"Hello?" she said. "Anyone there?"

There was nothing but static.

Keeping a wary eye to the surrounding brush, Kristie began picking her way down the hill.

This had been a nuclear site. Now she found herself simply walking up to the main gate, which was standing wide-open.

It looked like it had not been abandoned all that long. There were still tire tracks leading out onto the main road.

Unlike the field unit, however, this time there were bodies.

Or more accurately, there were remains – piles of bones, some with scraps of clothing, but otherwise gnawed clean.

Kristie shivered as a gust of wind whistled through the empty ghost-town.

The base was organized in a typical military grid, which meant the communications building would be near the center. Kristie had seen little actual damage to the facility itself – it seemed a good chance the radio-equipment was intact.

As she made her way cautiously along, the rows of barracks opened up into the administration sector. A satellite-disc and radio tower identified the building she was after. And with the same, seemingly lax post-apocalypse security, she found the front entrance left standing open.

Kristie frowned. What did they do? Just go around and unlock every gate and doorway in the place? *Then* get slaughtered by sickle-claws?

She had no more finished the thought when a screeching cry suddenly pierced the silence, echoing down the empty sage-brush street.

Kristie turned and saw nearly a dozen dromaeosaurs trotting up in a pack.

They moved in formation, like flocking birds, scenting the air as they followed her path.

Then they spotted her.

Kristie slid her rifle from her shoulder.

She'd become quite an adept skeet-shooter in the last year – she didn't wait for the attack, but simply opened fire.

Three of them dropped in quick succession, but the rest launched themselves at her in a mob.

What did they call it? A *murder* of crows?

She took out three more, before stepping back behind the open door and pulling it shut behind her, locking the bolt.

There was impact half-a-second later, and the door vibrated on its frame.

That, Kristie thought, did not look to last.

She took the stairs – the upper floors were the likely location of any broadcast office. As she reached the top, she realized the lights were on.

At that moment, the radio on her hip blared static.

She heard her own voice say, "Hello? Anyone there?"

Kristie looked up at an answering echo coming from the broadcast-office – a windowed-off cubicle.

As she peered inside, mounted by the microphone was one of those little lizards.

The thing hissed as it saw her, flaring small but very formidable claws.

"Hello?" it said again in her voice, and leaped, its small sickle-claws outstretched, reaching for her eyes.

Kristie dropped it out of the air with a single shot – it hit the floor, twitching at her feet.

From the floor below, there was a loud creak as the main door started to give. Kristie stepped to the top of the stairs, holding her rifle ready.

Her radio blared once more. This time it called her by name.

"Kristie?" it said. "Kristie Morgan. If you're reading me, please pick up now."

Kristie blinked, hesitating, before grabbing up her radio.

"Who the hell is this?" she demanded. "This better not be a goddamn lizard!"

"My name's Tom," came the reply. "And I'm not a goddamn lizard."

There was another buzz of static.

"I'm in space," Tom said.

CHAPTER 25

Tom knew Otto.

Trapped in space for over a year, linked with every working satellite in space, and with little else to do, Tom had hacked a lot of files. Before the world had gone dark, or at least before the EITS had, he had broken down a lot of firewalls that were no longer being guarded, or even monitored anymore.

Tom knew Professor Nolan Hinkle. He knew the top-secret history of Monster Island. He knew Shanna.

And he knew Otto.

An unimpressive beast, considered a failure, albeit a minor-experiment.

Catastrophically underestimated on both counts.

The sheer scope would be hard to accept if it wasn't laid out so graphically, and with such brutal simplicity, right in front of him.

Screens and various open files were left open and organized like a child's playroom – the busiest toys laid out right in front for use.

It all told its story as obvious as a dog's footprints leading to the empty hamburger tray on the counter.

Otto was a parrot. He used the language and words in front of him. If you showed him math, he read math. If you showed him digital functions, he saw the basic binary codes. Tom imagined he would have been very good at counting cards in Vegas.

There were at least three of the little bastards on the ISS with him. Possibly more.

Quantum-level gremlins.

It was at least helpful that they made no effort to hide their intent, or their work in progress, although probably hadn't anticipated the need in space. They even used all the standard military language and codes.

Tom also found map-diagrams marked 'human-habitation', and 'Big Rex' – code-named directly from military files.

A gremlin, alright.

An ornery genocidal gremlin.

Tom had periodically been repeating his mayday to General Rhodes. He knew his message had been received, and was likely going through relays, but now he finally received his first reply, from someone identifying as Lieutenant Hicks.

Tom gave it to him in thirty words or less.

There was a pause, before Hicks responded soberly.

"I'll get you through to the General, sir," he said.

That had been ten minutes ago. Tom had spent it perusing Otto's little virtual dioramas, all of which stood every chance of being transformed into physical reality.

One file contained a list of documented blooms over the last year, along with containment efforts. Nuke a bloom, burn a bud, pretty much summed up the strategy.

Accompanying this response-list was an inventory of functional nuclear assets.

Again, lined out like a kid's toy-set – a submarine, a single silo, and a single squadron of planes armed with a dozen missiles – two operational.

Acting on a hunch, Tom checked the satellite cameras, and found most of them currently aimed right at the center of the Rockies – right at the Mount.

The maps all diagrammed segments of this region, and Tom pulled back the satellite resolution to encompass the surrounding three states.

That was the thing about the Food of the Gods – it generated tremendous energy within an organism, and it radiated out like excessive body heat.

Early on, he had learned to decipher the ultra-violet signature, and how it differed from energy generated from natural sources like geothermal.

When he scanned the targeted perimeter, the results stood out like florescence under a black-light – and sure enough, a pre-generated topography model popped up beside it, separating the geothermal from targeted areas highlighted in green.

The radio blared again, and this time it was the voice of General Nathan Rhodes.

"Major Corbett?"

"Right here, sir."

"Son, it's awful good to hear from you. We'd pretty much given you up for lost. We've had our hands full. Things seem to be heating up again."

"That's no accident, sir," Tom replied.

Tom glanced at the screens.

"I'm afraid you've got two problems, General," Tom said. "The first is that I've just detected a very large bloom on satellite. It's one of the biggest on record, and it's headed your way."

Tom shut his eyes.

"It's bait sir," he said. "As of now, all your nuclear options are compromised."

CHAPTER 26

Dr. Shriver placed the sound-proofed glass case over Otto's cage.

Sally leaned in, watching the apparently oblivious little lizard blinking back, absorbing their words like a sponge.

Lieutenant Hicks had rerouted Major Tom to the lab and Rhodes had him on speaker.

The General was already pacing. If the Major's report was accurate, the Mount itself could be in trouble.

"I've got satellite confirmation," Tom informed them, his voice echoing in the glass acoustics of the sealed lab. "About two-hundred miles west of your position."

Rhodes turned to Sally.

"I want a roll-call report," he said. "All our nuclear assets. *Yesterday*."

The sub was the first to report back – Captain Mason.

"Standing-by on alert, sir."

Which meant prepped to assume launch depth, pending targeting and launch commands.

"You got any tomfoolery out your way? Anything unusual at all?"

There was a pause on the line. "No, sir."

Major Travis from the Northwest site was next, reporting that he'd had a convoy attacked, and picked up a couple of refugees.

"However, sir," Travis said, "we do seem to have a problem with lizards."

Rhodes had glanced in Sally's direction. Shriver nodded.

"Hold that thought," Rhodes replied to Travis, "I may need you on-deck."

He switched the line to hold. "Anything from Maelstrom?" he asked.

Sally shook her head. "Nothing, sir."

Rhodes swore under his breath.

"Get Hicks over there with a combat-unit. I want boots and eyes on the ground. Tell them to let me know the second they've got *anything*."

Dr. Shriver checked the coordinates Major Tom had provided. He looked somberly at Rhodes.

"If we can't nuke it," Shriver said, "the Mount is in range."

Rhodes rubbed his eyes.

"We are still reacting," Shriver said, "as if this were all just a disaster, and not the actions of a deliberate, intelligent enemy. Now, remaining population centers are being targeted. We have to recognize our opponent and learn how it operates."

"And," Rhodes added, "it just so happens that our one high-intelligence asset that could maybe help us out with that, is *also* down in the area. We *can't* nuke the place even if we could."

The General took a deep breath, his feet set, back deliberately straight, like a man about to lift a difficult weight.

He turned to Sally.

"How many people currently living in the facility?" he asked. "Last census? And how fast could we realistically get them out?"

Sally blinked as she realized what she was being asked. Was Rhodes actually talking about abandoning the Mount?

Under what kind of time-frame?

That was not to beg the question of where would they evacuate to?

Rhodes took Sally's aghast expression for his answer, turning instead to Shriver.

"This site was built to withstand nuclear strikes," Rhodes said. "What would be its chances against a ground-zero bloom?"

"It's the nature of the beast," Shriver replied. "No pun intended. Beyond the blast wave, a nuke is less physical impact and more heat and radiation. Besides being one-and-done. This would be more like being attacked by a living earthquake that would dig this structure out like bears splitting logs after termites."

Rhodes stood silent.

"Sir?" Sally asked. "Should we... start to evacuate the Mount? As a precaution?"

Rhodes let out a slow breath.

"We are pretty limited on alternatives to the Mount, I'm afraid."

Rhodes looked down at the blinking lights, both Major Tom and Major Travis waiting on hold.

Then his eyes settled on Otto, staring back soundlessly behind the glass cover.

"If this is the enemy," Rhodes asked, "can we get intelligence from it?"

"They aren't like that," Shriver said, shaking his head. "It would be like trying to shake down a remote drone."

The little creature's head cocked as it blinked back at them through the glass.

What would it do, Sally wondered, when humans were all gone? Would it move on to something else?

Rhodes nodded to Sally.

"Route all my calls to my office," he said, turning abruptly for the elevator. Sally jumped into immediate heel beside him.

Shrinker's lab was giving her the creeps.

She glanced back at Shriver, already bent over his screens, as the elevator door closed behind them.

The good doctor was no doubt brainstorming on *advisable protocol*.

Nuke a bloom, burn a bud, had been his. So was most of the Arc Project.

Sally couldn't wait to hear what he came up with this time. It was certain he would be asked.

For once grateful for the claustrophobic well of the elevator, Sally still shuddered as the sudden pull of gravity mimicked the sensation of being dragged back below.

And speaking of the creeps, when they reached the command-level, they found a guest waiting for them.

Standing with Corporal Stevens as an escort, was Michelle – who Sally personally found the scariest member of the Coven.

Rather scarier, in fact, *after* her interrogation, and the deliberately obedient 'good-girl' act she'd affected since.

Michelle had been in Rhodes' office more than once in the past two weeks.

She eyed Sally challengingly, but had her obedient face on when she turned to Rhodes.

"Got something for me, Miss?" Rhodes asked.

Michelle nodded.

"Lizards," she said.

CHAPTER 27

Caesar was the philosopher among anthropoids.

Brutus embraced the ape.

As he led his troop through mountains, the rite of their passage shook the Earth.

In some way, looking strictly through the short-term parameter of the alpha male, the Food of the Gods was almost a blessing.

It was *power.* The very *ground* trembled at his steps; his roar was the gale wind of a god-beast.

Beating his chest never *felt* so good – a war-drum to silence every creature on the mountain.

Brutus was a smart ape, but still an ape first. He knew what value Caesar placed on being civilized. Brutus used his brains to be a better ape. He was already the biggest and the strongest, and he understood you didn't *have* to be the smartest, as long as you were smart enough to be in charge.

His own troop hadn't exactly drawn the intellectual elite, as apes go. His first lieutenant was a pigment-challenged moose of a beast with the shaggy hair of a burgundy-tinted orangutan, whose big trick was when the humans had taught him to say his own name, croaking out of his not-yet-evolved vocal-cords, "Grape Ape. Grape Ape."

It was enough to make him second-smartest in the troop. Konga and Big Joe were both jealous, capable of only gagging chokes of staggered consonants.

Brutus knew what Caesar thought. And Brutus could mostly care less what high-and-mighty Caesar thought.

In light of current circumstances, however, it irritated the *hell* out of him to know Caesar would think him a fool.

Brutus understood very well what had happened to him and his troop.

He could see the glowing green in their eyes – Konga, Joe, and Grape Ape – all of them.

It had happened under his watch.

Despite Caesar's not-quite voiced opinion, Brutus was not stupid – they hadn't eaten any funny bushes or infected rodents.

Whatever they had ingested had been saturated in the leaves.

Brutus had known something was wrong almost right away, although he was not immediately alarmed. It was, in fact, euphoric, like munching on coca leaves, a euphoria that had lasted up until the moment when Grape Ape had first shuffled up, belching with overfed decadence, to where Brutus himself had fallen into a light doze with a mouthful, still chewed into a cud.

And when he spotted Grape Ape's lazy, sated, glowing green eyes, he had spat the mouthful out into the dirt.

It had actually been *succulent* – he was full, and actually wanted *more*.

Over the course of the next day, the natural indigenous foliage they had been consuming seemed to have withered and died – although a new patch of growth seemed to be making progress on the ridge – something different, but modified to fit the climate, and thus, blending right in.

Brutus knew what was to follow.

His initial plan had actually been rather selfless – sort of a walk-into-the-woods-and-commune-with-the-Great-Spirit approach to what he knew would be a terminal end.

Brutus had seen the effects of the Food of the Gods unleashed. He knew his troop's simple presence would soon be dangerous – to Caesar's tribe, to the ecosystem of the mountain itself – and so he spent the next three weeks leading his troops on walk-about.

In the manner of an animal, it didn't occur to him to end his own life – the basic instinct of survival – but Brutus did intend to put a mountain range between them before the madness took hold.

It had been three weeks, and the infection was far-advanced when he felt *her* for the first time.

And while he did not know it, like Caesar himself, his first impression was that she was a presence that must have been there in his subconscious all along.

His troop felt it too. He had led them on a mostly meandering path north, simply following the mountain peaks as they drifted north and east.

And then one day they had *felt* her – flying overhead.

A plane – a lone blinking light in a night sky. The troop had stopped and stared like children mesmerized by fireworks.

In Brutus, there was a subtle change.

He hadn't started out as the brightest of apes, but as his intellect deteriorated, under the corroding burn of the chemical, the sheer energy enhanced certain other senses, flooding circuits not yet adapted to the load, but would continue to channel this new power until they melted and burned.

Now Grape Ape was trying to say her name, struggling with his primitive larynx.

"Shaahh-Naahh."

It wasn't just him. They *all* felt it – a light, they'd only been just aware of, like the warm background glow of the sun.

Already a creature of impulse, Brutus had followed, and he had led his troop with him.

And with his new awareness, he felt *others* who were drawn as well.

Brutus was not like Congo – he hadn't been raised on an island of tyrannosaurs – there was no *personal* animosity.

Yet, he could sense them, miles distant – burning, just as he was, with the Food of the Gods.

Not natural enemies, but rivals from the genetic code.

And clearly following the same star.

Tyrannosaurs were the first creatures whose DNA was engineered with the purification element. Along with Congo himself.

And, of course, Otto.

Brutus knew *that* little bastard too, and he could smell the scaly little rat *all* over this.

It seemed that nasty sinus sting had gotten worse just lately, even ambient.

Coincidentally, it seemed to coincide with this newer, brighter light, as if in aggressive resistance.

And didn't it seem like Shanna's light was like a balm for that vaporous acid burn?

Brutus could feel her, just over the mountain. He knew she was hurt and that put speed in his stride, as if with the sudden concern over a long-forgotten loved one.

His troop picked up the pace without urging, the thundering tons of their passage shaking the very mountains.

Brutus could not quantify the urgency that prompted him, or even what he might be hoping for. Did he expect Shanna to just touch his head and make his impending madness go away? Or the pain that would inevitably follow as the infection finally spread?

But Brutus had never been the type to overthink. And now, as the energy building within him began to distort his perceptions, to the point where it would gradually transform his world into an over-focused kaleidoscope of insanity, Brutus simply followed the star he'd been given.

His troop followed him unquestioningly towards the light.

A light that, just in recent weeks, had suddenly grown brighter.

CHAPTER 28

Jonah and Naomi had been sitting in the holding cell for nearly an hour as the base around them buzzed on high-alert. Jonah was beginning to think they'd been forgotten.

They could hear the rumble of jet engines being prepped. Jonah had counted six F-16s – all nuke-capable.

He wondered what their target might be. A single infected giant had caused them to burn down an entire forest.

Jonah shut his eyes. Speculation would only start his imagination running wild.

His cell-mate was very little inspiration. Naomi sat silent and morose.

She had once spent the night in a drunk-tank holding-cell – a bit of the personal knowledge Jonah had picked-up over the last year. It had been a DUI, after a fight with her husband, and she had been *deeply* humiliated – as much as anything, after being bailed-out the next morning by her oh-so-sober-and-responsible man.

Jonah knew about the incident because Lieutenant Lucas Walker had made the strategic mistake of jokingly referring to the incident as "the only argument I ever won."

Backfire was not the word – it was a remark that would live in infamy, and one Lieutenant Lucas' freshly-sprung young wife would *never* let be forgotten.

Jonah, himself, had been in trouble more than once, just being in the room when she thought of it.

The drunk-tank had been in downtown LA, and the company she'd spent that night with had been suitably colorful. A military-brat and pilot's wife, Naomi was no stranger to roughing it, but the concept of being *confined*, of being gathered up like refuse, because you couldn't be allowed in public – to be given a time-out against your will like a child? Naomi twisted just at the memory of it.

Jonah wondered if she was flashing back to that now, as she huddled herself in the tightest corner of the cell, pressed against the wall, legs folded-up into the little ball she always enveloped herself in.

It was her protective cocoon, and like so many things in living with her, it was something he'd learned not to touch.

The back of their little cell was walled-off to the outside, and did not allow for a view into the yard, but they could see well enough into the main walkway.

Something had really stirred things up.

Major Travis had told them several caravans had been attacked. He also said he believed them about Otto.

Now they were scrambling nukes.

And the two of them were locked-up, unable to even run.

Jonah was tempted to hang it on Naomi. It was her insistence to follow the military supply chain, right from the moment they'd out-distanced the forest-fire.

On the other hand, if *this* time, they were about to go nuke someplace, at least Jonah could be certain he wasn't going to be standing ground-zero on their target.

They were safe in a cage.

Although, Jonah did find himself wondering how long he and Naomi would continue to be caged together.

She had been right before. *He* was a redundant component – a dime-a-dozen male, getting a little long in the tooth. And he was never that good a pilot anyway.

Jonah suspected that this little interlude in holding might be their last time alone together before being tossed into the system. Major Travis had mentioned refugee facilities, indicating that, security breaches aside, this was where protocol typically dictated they should go.

Naomi would no longer need make do with his civilian company. She was going to be surrounded by nothing but American heroes, just like her ex.

Not EX, he reminded himself. Better not forget *that* again.

As he stole a glance at her, folded-up in her corner, head bowed and her face bent in the frown she wore far too often, Jonah wondered if she would miss him.

He was already starting to miss *her*. And it seemed that their final hours together would be spent in stony silence.

But then abruptly, she spoke.

"I owe you an apology," she said.

Jonah perked. *That* was a first.

"For what?"

Naomi sighed, resigned and tired.

"For *all* of it," she said. "You've been great. Through everything. Right from the beginning." She sighed. "And I've put you through your paces."

"You're a pace-setter," Jonah allowed cautiously.

Naomi unfolded from her ball, and turned to face him directly.

"I just wanted to tell you that you deserved better," she said. "After our night together, I mean. You deserved better."

Jonah sat back, listening. It was the first time she'd brought it up.

Naomi held up the ring she still wore.

"It was our anniversary." She looked at Jonah apologetically. "I should have told you that."

Jonah had actually surmised as much.

"You know what?" he said. "*I'm* sorry. I saw the wine..."

"It wasn't the wine," Naomi interrupted. "I'm a big girl. All grown up. You didn't take advantage of me. What I'm apologizing for is that *I* totally used *you*. And in the morning, I just utterly blew you off."

With extreme prejudice, Jonah thought. But he waved it away.

"Forget it," he said. "I've had more than one woman regret me in the morning. Like my ex-wife."

Naomi smiled a little.

"That was never a problem for Lucas. I was always so *proud* of him. I bragged on him with my friends. I *paraded* him about town. The way it *felt* when we were together. I thought we were *so* special."

She shook her head, puzzled.

"But with you," she said, "it was just the same."

Naomi paused a moment, looking strained.

"A deliberate drunk surrogate," she said. "And it was just the same."

Deliberate drunk surrogate, Jonah repeated quietly in his head.

"I'm not stupid," she said. "I understand psychology. Imagination. It just scared me that what I felt with Lucas... that I could have just projected that on *anybody*."

Naomi eyed him seriously, clearly wanting him to understand.

"It made me feel like I couldn't trust my own head," she said. "And I guess I needed to separate a little until I reminded myself what was real."

Jonah nodded stoically, saying nothing, but couldn't help note her unquestioned presumption.

If it's good with you, *it must be my imagination.*

Even his ex-wife wouldn't have hung *that* one on him.

And the hell of it was, the one night he got to step-up as *deliberate-drunk-surrogate,* was a night he wouldn't give up for his life.

He almost said it out-loud. Part of him wanted to.

If I died tonight, at least I got to be with you.

That was *his* reality.

Instead, he simply sat silent. Naomi said nothing more, satisfied the air between them was cleared.

Jonah supposed it was. And he supposed he had an answer to his question – you didn't miss a surrogate.

They sat quietly together, strangers who had been thrust together in a storm – perhaps finally about to separate once again. After all, the only thing that had ever held them together was the continuing crisis and lack of options.

The silence in the cell highlighted the sound of activity in the yard outside.

It also boosted the acoustics of the first gunshots, followed by the familiar warbling yodels of sickle-claws.

And just behind that, the echoing dragon-roar of a *Tyrannosaurus rex.*

Jonah and Naomi both sat bolt upright, exchanging alarmed glances.

An explosion of military fire erupted from the main yard – the gun-turrets from the towers now aimed down into the compound itself. Baying roars turned into screams as the high-caliber ammunition tore like a rototiller into saurian hide.

Jonah could imagine it all clearly enough – just like the convoy – the smallish dromaeosaurs darting through the grounds, drawing the rex pack to the chase, in turn, drawing gunfire.

It was the kind of behavior sickle-claws only displayed when Otto was around.

And this time, they were on a top-secret site, commanding nuclear assets.

Shouts echoed in the hall outside their cell, and a rush of soldiers filed in front of the main entrance, rifles drawn.

Jonah saw Major Travis himself, his hand pistol aimed and ready, as they faced the doorway. Beside him, Sergeant Meyers had his rifle shouldered.

Almost simultaneously, there was a crash as the main doors came down, followed by the eruption of gunfire, and a goon-squad of sickle-claws flooded the main hall like a wave.

Jonah and Naomi could see it from their cell.

In the close quarters, it was a massacre.

These sickle-claws were *big* – larger than Utahraptor – all arms and legs, with a small body, and slender neck and head – difficult to hit while moving – *definitely* hard to hit under pressure.

Major Travis shot two of the beasts before he was beheaded by a slashing foot-claw.

Sergeant Meyers was taken a moment later, disemboweled.

Most of the men barely had a chance to cry out. The two-dozen armed soldiers crowded into that hall might as well have fallen into a cage full of hungry lions. It was over within minutes. Absolutely and graphically over.

And as the sickle-claws hovered over the torn and scattered remains, with the main hall now secured like a trained infiltration unit, a troop of Ottos came scurrying in between their feet.

"Aw, shit," Naomi muttered. "You little *bastards*."

And the sound carried.

The sickle-claws perked at the bare whisper, uttered among screams and munitions fire, and the pack turned in the direction of their cell.

The troop of Ottos bobbed at their feet, and recited Naomi's voice back in stereo, "You little *bastards*."

In the blink of an eye, the sickle-claws moved, taloned hands wide and flailing, reaching for purchase, with their lethal foot claws poised and cocked.

Naomi and Jonah both fell back against the cell wall as the first of them hit the bars.

But the cage saved them. These dromaeosaurs were the size of tigers and the gap between the bars was not quite wide-enough.

Jonah looked around for anything to use as a weapon, but there weren't even pillows for the flat-stone bench.

The beast snarled, reaching with its claws, straining, as it pushed through the gap.

Two more hit the bars, with a heavy, crashing *clang*, jaws snapping, claws slashing.

Otto's chorus chittered again. "Little *bastards*!"

Then the entire front wall of the building crashed in.

Rudy, his hide splattered into bloody meatloaf from turret fire, burst into the main hall, bringing the roof and wall crashing down behind him.

There was a shriek from the Ottos, again broadcasting Naomi's voice, this time in a stereo-chimed, "Aw *shit*!"

The sound echoed as the little lizards scampered down past the jail-block.

But now the cell-wall crashed in.

Jonah and Naomi dived aside, dodging cinder and rubble, as Jughead stepped into the holding cell with them.

The hapless sickle-claws wedged between the bars shrieked horrible reptilian/avian curses as the big rex tore the entire wall of iron bars from their mooring, collapsing the cell-block.

Trapped beneath the bars, the snarling sickle-claws kicked and struggled, as Jughead dipped his massive jaws, and snapped both of the clawed beasts in half at a stroke.

There was a Hail-Mary screeching as Rudy was swarmed by the dromaeosaur pack. The big rex bellowed in outrage, as he began to thrash up against the remaining walls.

With sickle-claw feet still protruding from his lips, Jughead paused, looking down at Jonah and Naomi, lying stunned amid the scattered rubble.

The big eyes focused – binocular vision – and its nostrils sniffed.

From down the hallway, where the Ottos had disappeared, came another echoing chorus in Naomi's voice.

"You little bastards!"

Jughead turned, knocking out the neighboring wall in pursuit.

Rudy heard the echoes as well. He was already in a frenzy, as the swarming sickle-claws targeted his eyes and throat. Unfortunately for the dromaeosaurs, the cramped space worked to the tyrannosaur's benefit, allowing Rudy to simply crush most of them against heavy breakable objects, any lingering offenders to be snapped up as they tried to retreat.

With the wall to their cell now gone, Jonah and Naomi peered out into the yard, just in time to see one of the turret towers come tumbling down, landing in a resounding crash of mortar and brick.

Big Moose had simply just charged the tower, absorbing the hail of gunfire, and crashed face-first into the base. At six-tons, he was the largest of the JV squad and took the tower out at a stroke.

But Big Moose took his own damage, and was clearly staggering. He tried to roar, but his breath came out in bloody coughs.

The second turret opened fire, and angry spurts of blood exploded across the big rex' back and neck, running a race all the way up to the back of the giant skull.

At least one of the shots hit something vulnerable and Big Moose dropped in his tracks, his breath grunting out with the impact as he bonelessly struck the earth, his legs kicking briefly, as if attempting to run. But then he stiffened and lay still.

Archie took out the remaining tower, charging past running soldiers, stepping on the ones that he could, even as they pumped bullets into his thighs and ribs. Mimicking the tactics of his bigger brother, the five-ton rex hit the turret square at the base.

This time, the tower itself held, but the gunner was knocked loose, falling nearly forty-feet, right at Archie's feet.

There was a low moan, as the soldier, his back broken, cried out weakly, trying to move.

Archie's jaws dipped, snapping the man up, and tossing him down his gullet like a raw oyster.

Then the big tyrannosaur turned as a fresh hail of gunfire erupted from the dwindling troops.

Jonah wanted to shout at the soldiers to stop. All they really had to do was simply get the hell out of the way – the *T. rex* wanted the sickle-claws.

Most especially, they wanted the Ottos, and would do *anything* to get at those little bastards.

Jonah had said as much to Major Travis. If he were alive, the Major might have realized to call a stand-down order.

But he was dead. And so his soldiers instead did what they were trained to and kept fighting – and kept antagonizing the rex pack until they smashed the base flat – helpfully providing cover for the sickle-claws as they sprinted between the tyrannosaurs' towering legs, chasing down any remaining human resistance.

It was as costly for all sides as it could possibly be. It ended with a final burst of gunfire, and the sound of an aborted scream.

The warbling calls of the sickle-claws were quickly silenced as well. Steadfastly holding their ground, they were easy pickings for the teen tyrannosaurs.

The JV squad, however, had also taken their lumps. The turret-guns had done their work. *T. rex* were known by fossils to have recovered from seemingly ridiculous amounts of damage, but it was always about surviving the initial injury in the first place.

Operating on the adrenaline of their attack, and no doubt juiced-up by whatever antagonistic psycho/chemical reaction Otto's presence seemed to inspire, the rex pack had walked through weapons intended to take down fighter-jets.

To their credit, they seemed to have won their fight.

But once the skirmish was over, the JV squad's injuries caught up with them.

Jughead's hide was flayed open all along the ribcage, and his breath rasped through ragged holes blown clear into its lungs.

Big Moose was already down, and Archie, with the last sickle-claw's legs still dangling from his jaws, just stood panting, like a hard-run dog, with ragged munitions wounds scoured along his hide.

And Rudy, now that the dromaeosaur-pack seemed accounted for, simply sat down to wait.

There were still Ottos around somewhere.

T. rex were stubborn. They didn't mind dying, but they had to get *you* first.

For the moment, the little lizards remained hidden.

Naomi stole from the collapsed holding-cell out into the smashed hallway. Rudy had knocked away a substantial portion of the roof. What was left looked practically eager to drop on top of them.

Jonah followed as Naomi peeled a bloody rifle off the body of a fallen soldier. She turned and tossed the crimson-stained weapon to Jonah, who caught it reflexively, the impact knocking droplets of gore into his face.

Naomi purloined a second rifle for herself, and then hunted through the carnage until she found clips.

Without waiting for Jonah, she poked her way past the collapsed entrance, looking out over the demolished yard.

Rudy and Jughead both sat at a short distance, immobile, like lions under a tree, momentarily off-the-clock. In the yard behind them, Archie's eyes blinked their way, but the big rex continued to pant, as if trying to catch its breath.

Keeping a wary eye on all three dragons at once, Naomi started out across the grounds.

"Where are you going?" Jonah called softly.

Naomi pointed to the radio tower.

Cautiously, her rifle ready, Naomi made her way across the yard. Cursing under his breath, Jonah followed.

The sickle-claws had left a trail of corpses right up to the front steps. Jonah kept his eyes averted as Naomi pushed open the door.

From the broadcast booth upstairs, they heard the crackle of static, and a voice blaring over the speakers.

"This is General Rhodes. Come in. For God's sake, is anyone there?"

CHAPTER 29

Rosa could tell Shanna's leg was hurting her.

It was cold on the mountain, and despite being bundled by the fire, they had precious little cover from the wind beyond the vertical-hanging chopper, which itself rocked on the tenuously clinging vines as the gusts kept trying to snatch them all off the cliff.

Allison and Bud hung around Lucas, rocking together, unconsciously, a universal tempo of comfort.

Mr. Wilson occupied himself with keeping up the fire, frowning each time the vines holding the chopper above their heads creaked with the wind.

Rosa could picture him in the old world, out on the farm, one ear ever-perked for that malfunctioning sprinkler or pipe – a life of constant maintenance.

She tried to imagine young Maverick on the farm.

"That son of mine hasn't got a brain in his head," Mr. Wilson had told her. "But he's proven that he's damn hard to kill. Which makes it beneficial to be standing next to him."

He nodded, his tone one of giving fair praise.

"I'd say we've got better than even odds, if he pulls this off."

Rosa had tried to take the comfort as it was intended.

Shanna was a little more certain.

"All they need is to get a clear signal," she said. "I can promise you General Rhodes is looking for us."

Shifting under the mound of makeshift blankets, sacks, and tarps Cameron had wrapped around her, Shanna looked down into the valley.

"And he's not the only one, either."

Rosa frowned. As far as she could see, there was nothing but empty forestland below, bordered by sheer rock wall.

Shanna seemed to be staring at things unseen.

Rosa wondered if Shanna might be hallucinating as her own natural endorphins corralled around her injury. Her leg was discolored and swelling, and no doubt quite painful.

Even for someone with perfect genetics.

Rosa still wasn't sure how much of what Shanna was telling her she believed.

Scratch that – she believed *all* of it – she was just having trouble taking it in.

It was whatever Shanna *had* – whatever odd crackle that seemed to spark at her touch – but Rosa simply had no doubt.

She rooted around in the chopper's medical kit, pulling out a needle, and a bottle of clear-liquid. She turned to Shanna.

"This will help your pain," she said.

But Shanna shook her head. "I'm fine," she said.

Rosa frowned. "You're hurting."

She knew it. She could *feel* it.

But Shanna waved her off, shuffling closer to the fire.

Rosa knelt beside her.

"Shanna? Is something wrong?"

Shanna shut her eyes.

"Otto," she said quietly, her voice heavy with regret, even a pang of remorse.

Rosa could feel a pulse of it herself.

"We always had an Otto around," Shanna said. "When I was little, my father replaced them like gerbils. When one died, he just cloned another. I was eight years old before I realized they weren't all the same one."

Shanna smiled sadly.

"Otto was what the Area 51 guys used to sell it in the budget. The vocalizations sold it. He became an internal mascot, next to the dead alien."

"Wait a minute," Mr. Wilson interjected, "I thought you said the alien was fake."

"I said the alien *autopsy* was fake."

Shanna shook her head.

"It's funny. Otto was like a fake too. A genetically engineered novelty. Barely mentioned to the higher-ups. General Rhodes was probably peripherally aware of his existence, if at all. He was the little lizard wearing hats or wigs in the JPEGs the interoffice Area 51 guys sent each other. I never got one from them without an Otto in it."

Shanna shifted closer to the fire, pulling the ratty covers tighter.

"He was dismissed as an old experiment. A failure. Even by my father."

She shrugged, and Rosa actually felt the conflicting angst – uncertain whether she should feel hurt, or bereaved, or betrayed.

Or guilt? Because once there had been love.

"To me, he was my pet," Shanna said helplessly. "He was my childhood friend. Just like Rex and Congo."

Rosa glanced around the circle. Mr. Wilson had stopped poking the fire to listen. Bud and Allison settled to a slow rock. Even little Lucas regarded Shanna with a bit of puzzled concern.

Whatever she felt for the little lizard, it hurt.

"It's hard to forget a lifetime," Shanna said, looking apologetic for the simple fact of it. "Even after everything. It only makes it worse."

Rosa had worked the inner-cities as a doctor. She'd met more than one mother whose son lay dying from a bullet wound – along with another mother whose son had fired the shot. Sometimes they even killed each other.

So whose grief was more justified or sincere?

Or simply real?

"You know," Shanna said thoughtfully, "when I was young, my father and I always played *What's-Worse*?"

Rosa knew that one. "That was a running gag at my house," she said, smiling at the memory. "It always started with something my mother made for dinner. Or something bad on TV. What's worse? A re-run of *Days of Our Lives* or the stew your mother made?"

Shanna smiled back. "And it escalated. It always escalated."

Rosa nodded. It had. At her house, What's-Worse often ended pitting mom's stew against plagues or mythological horrors.

"My father," Shanna said, "was a scientist. We were splitting atoms. We'd be pitting thermonuclear destruction versus a nationwide pandemic of diarrhea." Shanna grinned. "I mean we had global tsunamis versus planet-sized asteroids."

Her grin faded a little.

"There's always something worse."

The remark hung unexpectedly heavy, and Rosa felt her brief warm memory evaporate in the icy air.

"I wonder," Shanna said, "if Otto listened."

Now Rosa felt a touch of goose-flesh.

The chill seemed to blow through the others as well. Both Allison and Bud shivered visibly, Allison unconsciously clutching Lucas tighter. Even Mr. Wilson settled up closer to the fire.

The gusts of wind were becoming shrill and impatient, grabbing at the fire, pulling the licks of flame dangerously close, even as it threatened to snuff them out.

"He always said his name," Shanna said. "'My name is Otto'. Always in my father's voice. The first words he ever learned."

She looked thoughtful.

"All of them did it. The very second they hatched. And after that, they all repeated it. Regardless of generation."

Shanna shrugged. "I was young. I never questioned. All the Area 51 guys tossed it off as a weird little glitch. No one ever imagined what that weird little glitch implied."

She shook her head. "I never did."

Then her eyes narrowed.

"But I think," she said, "my father might have. Right near the end. But by then, it was too late."

The fire cracked loudly, sending a spark, and Rosa jumped.

A moment later, the spark was answered by a flash of lightning on the far horizon. Two heartbeats followed before the corresponding rumble of thunder.

And somewhere, off in the near distance, something answered.

Mr. Wilson paused over the fire. Allison slowed her steady rock.

"What was *that*?" Rosa asked, not wanting *any* kind of answer.

Shanna's eyes were shut, as if listening.

Rosa tried to hear, but now the rising wind brought the first sheets of rain, a curtain of icy sleet that slapped into the cliffside.

Drums of thunder echoed through the canyons.

Overture to the approaching storm.

CHAPTER 30

Three weeks after the island disaster, Kate was back at her Manhattan apartment.

It was official. There *was* no Monster Island, and it never sank.

Her freedom was contingent on her clear understanding of that point – a message communicated bluntly from her father, through intermediate government lawyers, because he was still too goddamn mad to even directly speak to her.

As a General's daughter, Kate was afforded privilege. The others were still in custody. Cameron and Maverick hadn't even been given lawyers – not until security debriefing was completed. Which meant until they were damn good and ready.

Kate's own lawyer had actually broken down into helpless laughter over the sheer length of the list of charges.

Suffice to say, everybody was in a lot of trouble.

Except for Shanna, who, to be fair, hadn't actually done anything.

But Gosh-darned if it didn't turn out, her father just *loved* Shanna.

When they had boarded the Navy vessel, after being fished out of the wrecked Cessna, the ship's captain, an old veteran named Brody, had greeted Kate on deck. Kate's face was well known among officers.

"You've been at it again," Captain Brody said. "Your father's pissed-off on a national security-level this time."

"Wait a minute," Shanna said. "Kate *Rhodes*? You're General Rhodes' daughter?"

Kate's own brows raised. "You know my father?"

Although, after a second's thought, she realized that was a no-brainer – of course, she did. How could she not?

There was a brief reappraisal as the two women regarded each other.

Kate had grown up with top-level security as part of her daily life – a long-time point of resentment, dating back from when she was just a child and her father was her whole world, and ninety-nine percent of his life was an invisible black hole.

Shanna was one of the shadows that existed in that blank spot. It was like finding out about a half-sister lovechild.

And here she'd thought her father had shut her investigation down just on general principals.

Kate wondered what was it like to live on the other side of all that top-security? Shanna had no doubt grown up on a much tighter leash than even she had. There was, after all, a difference between even a high-security military base, and Area 65,000,000 BC.

And while Shanna was not being charged with anything, she was no more free than Cameron and Maverick. The difference was that instead of a risk, *she* was an asset.

The government had just lost its head mad scientist, and Shanna was heir-apparent.

Which meant everything Kate had seen on that island would continue to be real.

As far as she knew, all the animals had been killed. The Navy had toured the area with munitions for days. The island itself had been destroyed.

But they still had Shanna. And who knew what they had stashed away in Area 51?

There were stories, Kate was discovering, scattered across the Internet, about not-quite-remote areas that had encountered strange creatures.

Crackpot stuff. Most of it. Except Kate had found her perimeters widened dramatically on what she was prepared to believe.

And there *did* seem to have been a rash of them just lately – as near as Kate could tell, dating back to an incident on a tropical Pacific cruise-liner. When she searched the source, however, she found the websites scrubbed.

There was also the question of who had sent the e-mails to her in the first place.

Kate was beginning to wonder if it really *had* been Hinkle himself.

Like maybe there was something happening on that island he wanted the world to see, but for some reason, was afraid to step forward himself?

And what might he have to be afraid of? He was an old man. Kate couldn't confirm his exact age, but he had first started making waves in the sixties. Shanna was young enough to be a granddaughter.

Shanna who, Kate mused, might have been the one Hinkle was really trying to protect.

But from what specifically? The sort of legal/bureaucratical retribution that currently barked at her own heels?

Which begged the question, why send the e-mail at all?

Perhaps *that* was supposed to protect her.

Or was it that he believed he simply had to take the risk?

Because the elephant in the room was the two-foot lizard that was apparently a lot smarter than his keepers believed.

At least one of the stories she'd found had mentioned a talking lizard – nothing but a headline, and when she searched the story, she found it gone.

Kate was becoming nervous.

She couldn't put her finger on it, but she felt distinctly uneasy, the way animals are supposed to get edgy before an earthquake or some natural disaster.

Not just a military brat, but a General's daughter, Kate was hard-headed. She didn't believe in premonitions, or fortune-telling.

But after meeting Shanna, she certainly believed she could pick up on bad vibes.

Kate had a little secret – something she'd been holding as an ace-in-the-hole, her leverage with any prosecutors the government might send her way – and once she was legally in the clear, she could turn her attention to wrangling Maverick and Cameron out of limbo.

She pulled a small disc from her purse – the video disc she'd pulled from Cameron's camcorder after Hinkle's little walk-through of his lab – up to and including the giant savage rabbit with the glowing green eyes.

Their Navy ship had taken three days to arrive in New York. Kate had it in her possession the whole time. After already being in custody, and having just been pulled out of a crashed sea-plane, no one even thought to search her.

She'd had it stashed behind her compact-mirror, just in case.

It was supposed to be her get-out-of-jail-free card.

If she did what she was thinking of doing with it now, it would be *go-to*-jail.

It would also effectively destroy any lingering relationship she had with her father.

Kate plugged the disc into her computer.

On her e-mail contact-list alone, she had every major media outlet in the world.

That was the thing about the Internet – the w*orldwide w*eb – once it was out there, you couldn't get it back.

In a way, it was amazing there were still secrets. It just showed how dark parts of the world could be.

Kate was still not certain it had been Nolan Hinkle who sent that e-mail video. Or why.

She didn't believe in premonitions. But she had a world-class case of the creeps.

Kate wondered if Hinkle had felt those same creeps.

She tapped her keyboard, bringing her screen to life.

As she did so, she noticed she had a message.

A blinking picture of Princess Leia, floating in a hologram.

She tapped it, and the picture spoke.

"Help me, Obi Wan Kenobi. You're my only hope."

Then the image blurred to that of Nolan Hinkle standing in his study.

On screen, the image started speaking, but the voice-over continued to be Princess Leia's heart-felt plea, "Help me, Obi Wan Kenobi."

And then, almost right in her ear, the words finished.

"You're my only hope."

Kate jumped from her chair with a screech, nearly knocking over her desk as she turned to where a two-foot lizard was standing on her bookcase.

A lizard with *big* claws.

Otto hissed.

There was a rustling patter and suddenly it was joined by two others.

Kate backed up against her desk. She looked around for something to get in her hands, but she was cornered.

"Help me, Obi Wan," the little lizards said in chorus.

Kate screamed as they came for her.

CHAPTER 31

Shanna finally got to see New York.

When it went south on Monster Island, Rhodes had taken steps for both security and science.

One of those steps was a giant gorilla named Congo.

Another was a young man named Cameron, who Shanna had only just met – who had invaded her privacy on her island, and along with his friend, Maverick, now faced some very serious charges.

Kate was fine. Shanna had a feeling she would be.

But Cameron and Maverick currently didn't even exist, sequestered at a secret facility, the Area 51 guys called the 'east-coast shop' – a deceptively tame-looking warehouse lot off the south beach of Brooklyn.

Congo was there too – the only facility large enough to hold him while the chemical's effect ran its course.

Three weeks in and he appeared nearly at full-growth.

He was chained and heavily sedated.

Shanna herself was given a more gilded cage. A workshop in Manhattan – the East Coast shop's downtown office, not far from the Empire State.

Rhodes had done his best to duplicate her lab from the island, and to his credit, were it not for the armed guards at her door, the illusion might have held.

Rhodes had also re-established links to her Area 51-contacts.

Primary among them, Dr. Shriver, who had taken over the clandestine site, was extremely interested in Hinkle's work on the Food of the Gods.

Shriver had been Rhodes' primary adviser in regards to Nolan Hinkle's research, particularly now, in the absence of Hinkle himself.

At least, until he was comfortable with who Shanna was.

Shanna was just actually learning that herself.

For the first time in her entire life, she was around *people*. And not just people, but *millions* of people, all around her.

She still couldn't walk among them, but she could see them from her window.

In a way, it was intimidating, and a small, frightened part of her was actually glad for the lock on her door, giving her an excuse to stay in her own space and hide.

But she could *feel* them.

And even the handful of uniformed officers, the crew of sailors on the boat, or the odd assistant Shriver sent over – all of it still represented the most contact with her own species Shanna had experienced in her entire life.

Ironic that she actually felt more alone than she ever had before.

Her father was gone. Her whole island home was gone – not just left-behind, but *gone*. And in a city of millions, just on the other side of a window, the people around *her* were either virtual or armed keepers.

Shanna had not grown up with the human touch, and as such, had never been truly aware of her gift.

Now that she was in the world, she found she got a little bit of a glow from most people. Usually, it was just a vague sense of mood and temperament – some she felt more strongly than others.

When she had touched Cameron's hand, it was if she'd suddenly known all about him.

Not facts, not where he was born, his favorite color, but the essential *him*.

Even on her island, Shanna had not completely missed the attention of men. In fact, it had mostly been hard-core military studs, who had certainly made their appreciation for her face and form well-known.

So Shanna knew what she looked like. And even if she hadn't, her online nerd-contacts at Area 51 would have let her know. Among the pictures with Otto in Santa hats at Christmas, were a long line of propositions, should she ever make it state-side.

But with Cameron, all it had taken was a touch.

And now she found herself missing him.

Shanna wondered what Rhodes had in mind for him and Maverick.

She could only guess, because from Rhodes, she felt nothing.

Some people were closed off that way – like a dead circuit – a hardness that blocked them off. It wasn't necessarily a lack of empathy, so much as deliberately unemotional – doctors could be like that, people who couldn't let themselves *feel*.

It was different from *bad* people. Shanna had encountered a smattering enough of those to know the difference. Among the ships that had periodically come to her island, she'd met the odd soldier in it for the wrong reasons – but a man who liked to kill was no less emotional or empathic than the next, sometimes more so. Sadism was simply a matter of taste.

Which turned Shanna's mind to Otto.

Otto was not like Rhodes – she always felt the little lizard's presence. But in terms of higher emotion, he emitted only the most basic reptilian stimulus. If not for the fact of his direct creation from her DNA, Otto likely would have been like the big plant-eaters or the more primitive carnosaurs, where she only felt the barest glow.

With Otto, it was general awareness and not much else.

But clearly, there was more there.

What happened on the island – what it implied?

Shanna had not seen it coming.

General Rhodes had several long discussions with her on that point.

Rhodes also informed her that they had in their possession a lot more footage than just Kate's thumb-drive. They were, in fact, keeping a number of incidents under wraps.

As he put it, "We seem to be having a bit of a crypto-zoological crisis."

Incidents had been reported all over the world. Not in remote areas, either, but just outside some of the biggest cities.

It didn't seem likely until you looked on a map.

In North America alone, seventy-five percent of forest-lands were protected and off-limits, and the largest concentration of these protected forests surrounded the big cities, where local lawmakers were more inclined to pass laws locking them off.

Which meant there was a blind spot there, and close to major population centers.

And 'crypto-incidents', as Rhodes called them, were on the rise, with a spike starting six months ago, after a cruise ship went down along its Central Pacific tour – an incident that had no casualties until the shipwrecked passengers made it to shore.

"A hundred castaways," Rhodes said, "according to two survivors, were eaten by monsters."

Then there was the matter of Kate's e-mail video from Monster Island. They never did quite figure out where that leak came from. Kate herself swore she didn't know.

"She's my daughter," Rhodes had sighed. "And she's been a handful all her life."

Shanna felt a blip from him then, when he talked about Kate – a single note of regret.

Then it had dried-up like a tear-drop and he had turned his direct eyes, focusing cybernetically on Shanna.

"What about you?" he said. "Do you have any idea where that leak might have come from?"

Shanna, who had suspicions, told him no. She had not told many lies in her life, so she wasn't sure if he believed her.

Not that it mattered. Rhodes had other plans for her.

It had been her first day in the states, still sitting on board the ship, docked at the Brooklyn shore opposite the river from Manhattan, looking up at the skyline of New York City – a dream all her life, and now near enough to touch – staring through port-windows not much different than a prison wall.

But she wasn't a prisoner. She was an asset. Rhodes had told her so.

And then he had showed her what they wanted.

He had taken her to the nondescript warehouse on a quiet corner of the Brooklyn docks – a three-mile stretch of storage lots bordering the East River.

These buildings, however, were a lot bigger on the inside, dug many levels deep.

Rhodes had taken her to see Congo.

The makeshift cage was a re-purposed weapons-bunker, well-fortified and *big*.

Congo lay slumped against the far wall, drugged near-comatose. His eyes were half-closed and glazed. Shanna could see the green glow between his slitted lids.

It had been a week since the island. The big gorilla had been infected via direct injection – clearly not a large dose, as the infection seemed to be progressing slowly – perhaps Otto had been using his stores sparingly in order to contaminate the whole island on short notice – but the chemical's effect was still obvious.

Measured at full maturity, Congo had stretched nearly twenty-three feet tall, and just over eight tons. Now he was at least twice that.

"He's growing," Rhodes said.

"He's dying," Shanna said.

"Maybe," Rhodes said, "you can do something about it."

Shanna sighed. Without having to hear it, she knew what they wanted.

"Dr. Shriver," Rhodes continued, "says that your father was working on an antidote."

"Not an antidote," Shanna corrected. "There's no way to reverse the growth effect. The intent was to alleviate the rabies-like madness that *killed* the subjects."

Shanna shook her head. "But it doesn't matter. We lost everything on the island."

"Dr. Shriver," Rhodes said, "believes you can extract the chemical from your ape friend's blood. And he has back-up files."

Shanna knew what Shriver had. She had been the one who sent in reports. Her father's efforts had been theoretical – nothing put into physical practice.

Although, she supposed, the idea was simple enough, an approach intended to work not much different chemically than an analgesic.

But the idea that she could develop something workable, when her father hadn't even attempted it, within time enough to save Congo?

Shanna knew psychology well enough, and understood the big gorilla's life was being dangled in front of her as incentive.

She also knew she was going to try.

And so, she had settled down in Rhodes' mid-town lab/bunker – likely an intended act of kindness on the General's part – after all, she had always wanted to see the city.

She could still feel Congo, just across the river, his aura ever stronger as the chemical reaction within him continued to build.

And now, three weeks since his exposure on the island, his growth-phase was peaking. Soon madness would start setting in.

Shanna knew she would feel his pain along with him.

And as she sat before her computer, trapped in simulations, no further along than her father in anything that might manifest, even experimentally, in the real world, Shanna knew that Congo was going to die, and that she wouldn't be able to stop it. It was just a fundamental fact.

The hell of it was, she actually believed she had a viable idea. Given time, she really thought a cure was possible – or at least she could stop the cycle of madness and death, and with it, the key to the chemical's transmissibility.

She *believed* it was possible.

But she *knew* it was in the early territory of *someday*. The chances of saving Congo's life were non-existent.

Part of her had already started to grieve, on top of still mourning her father.

It was such a general sense of malaise, that it made sense she would be progressively on edge.

Except...

This was the sort of feeling of unease she'd felt on the island, right up to those last days.

But this was different. It was bigger.

It was... *everywhere*. From every direction.

There was nothing she could focus on – the pressure in her head was like an allergic reaction.

Except Shanna didn't have allergies. She was genetically perfect.

She was picking up on something.

It actually felt more like a dampening sensation – like an antiseptic numbs a sting.

And Congo's presence, growing brighter by the moment, as the Food of the Gods continued to build within his blood, was also a blinding influence on what else might be more subtly lurking around her.

In fact, the big ape's aura had grown so strong, it almost caused Shanna to overlook the growing presence of another.

Congo had been the third creation that had been taken directly from her genetic footnote. Otto had been the second.

The rex had been the first.

Shanna turned from her computer to the window.

Her vantage was high. Rhodes had given her a view of the city, along with the southwest coast of Manhattan. She could see the Statue of Liberty and the Atlantic Ocean beyond.

"Oh no," she breathed.

Shanna tapped her intercom, her heart beating as realization dawned.

There was no answer.

"Hello?" she said, pushing the button again. "Is anyone there? I need to get hold of General Rhodes right away! It's urgent!"

Then there was the ding of the elevator. She turned, expecting to see her morning-shift guard.

But the elevator was empty.

Except as she looked, she saw that it wasn't.

The guard was crumpled on the floor, slathered in blood, his throat slashed.

Even as Shanna stood, she felt the sulfur-sting in her sinus.

Otto hopped off the soldier's body out of the elevator.

He was followed by two others.

They hissed, baring their claws, and without formality, they came at her.

CHAPTER 32

It all started in New York when a two-hundred-foot *T. rex* walked out of the East River, just north of the Brooklyn Bridge, into the lower East Side.

Night had fallen on the city, and New York's nightlife was coming alive. Crowds in the streets were filling up all the usual hot-spots.

Manhattan Island was about to receive a most unexpected visitor from out of town.

A low fog covered the water, and for all practical purposes, the creature was invisible.

Big Rex swam with surprising efficiency, its massive legs churning the water. His craggy brow broke the surface like a giant crocodile.

And like a croc's eyes under a night-light, his eyes shined in the dark, glowing like an emerald jack o'lantern.

The rex' nostrils flared. The water in the river was fetid – slimy and horrible – nothing like the sea's cool embrace.

But despite this particularly foul gateway, Big Rex knew he had reached his destination. The beacon he had pursued unerringly, like a psychic north star, was bare miles ahead. A light he followed like a flower follows the sun.

Her. Shanna.

Just as clearly, he sensed the presence of the *other* – his rival.

Congo was here as well. Someplace close.

And somewhere behind it all, that familiar sting in the sinus – that foul psychic stench...

Otto.

Big Rex would swim across an ocean for Shanna, but he would walk through fire to smash *that* little bastard.

But now he could sense them converging around her.

Just as he could sense it when she screamed.

And Big Rex' glowing green eyes saw red.

The energy within him was already building to a head as the growth-cycle peaked and the chemical started to eat at his primitive brain.

Now his pace quickened, bearing down on the very city itself, his body tensed in the water like a shark poised to attack.

The rex rose from the East River like a tidal wave.

CHAPTER 33

Across the river, Congo's reaction wasn't much better.

His keepers had been forced to administer progressively higher doses of sedatives in an attempt to compensate for both his steadily increasing mass, combined with the sheer energy pumping through his system.

At Shanna's scream, Congo's glowing green eyes snapped open.

His roar echoed through the facility and he immediately began banging away at the bunker walls. The impact of his blows shook the entire complex.

Alarms sounded, and there were shouts in the hall, just outside Cameron and Maverick's cell.

Maverick leaned against the door, peering out.

"What the hell is wrong with that big ape?"

He turned to find Cameron holding one hand to his head as if responding to a shout in his ear. When he turned, his eyes were wide.

"It's Shanna," he said. "She's in trouble."

Maverick eyed him dubiously.

"Getting a psychic flash or something?"

Cameron nodded.

"I think so. And I think that big ape feels it too."

"*Okay,*" Maverick said, agreeably enough, turning to hit the cell's alarm, banging on the bars, and shouting down the hall for the guards.

It was an effort that went completely ignored as, several levels down, a freshly-roused Congo smashed down the wall of the bunker that contained him.

The vast majority of the complex was underground. Congo's makeshift cell had been basement-level, and now the raging ape crashed through the ceiling into the floors above, as he dug his way back up to the surface.

Cameron and Maverick heard gunfire.

Even more alarming, the ground-level of the warehouse-shell seemed to rattle on its foundation, an underground skyscraper about to collapse in upon itself.

The floor beneath their feet shook like an earthquake.

Maverick stepped back warily from the center of the cell, glancing nervously at Cameron.

Then the rumble escalated and the walls around them broke apart, as Congo burst out onto the main floor, smashing his way up through the false warehouse into the open air.

His roar echoed across the starlit sky, out over the water.

And from somewhere within the towers of Manhattan, just the other side of the river, came the answering roar of Big Rex.

His eyes glowing, Congo beat at his chest, bellowing his response.

With his roar building to a crescendo, his pounding fists tearing up the remaining facade of a warehouse like a silverback tearing up the brush, and ignoring the mosquito-taps of hand-held weapons, Congo charged off the dock and leaped into the river.

Displaced water crashed over the Brooklyn docks like a Tsunami, washing over the razed warehouse, taking a number of hapless troops over the edge into the tunneled-out crevice Congo had left behind.

The surging river poured down into the tunnels in a flood. Cameron and Maverick's entire level was demolished, with three of their four walls simply collapsed. Only the bedrock of the wall behind them kept them from being crushed along with the majority of the personnel on their floor.

They could still hear gunshots up above, and something that might have been a bazooka, but Congo's roars were already echoing with increasing distance.

Their floor had been completely knocked away. What remained of Cameron and Maverick's cell amounted to a circular ledge against the back wall, and the two of them were forced to climb along broken rafters up to the surface.

Once up top, the grounds were abuzz. No longer a simple warehouse, troops materialized out of nowhere.

Cameron and Maverick found themselves momentarily ignored as the mad scramble was torn between rescuing survivors and mobilizing against the threat.

But then an MP in a Jeep squirreled up beside them.

"Hey! What the hell are you two doing here? This is a restricted area."

"That's okay," Maverick said. "We were just leaving."

He leaned through the window and knocked the MP cold, pulling the door open with the other hand to let him tumble limply out. Maverick slid into the driver's seat, hollering over his shoulder.

"Let's go!"

Cameron jumped in beside him, looking back at the stone-unconscious figure crumpled behind them as Maverick sped away.

That was a thing with both him and his dad. Besides the odd, unsuspecting MP, Cameron had seen them knock-out cows, horses – any livestock that might get uppity. Maverick had once climbed into the pen with his father's bull – when Maverick said bull-fight, he meant *fist*-fight.

And God forbid the neighbor's cat get in front of one of his farm rigs.

There was a brief moment at the security gate, where the guard attempted to block the road with his body – actually drawing his gun before diving aside, as Maverick piled through, knocking the gate loose as he skidded out onto the road.

They could see the skyline of the city.

Already there were news-helicopters circling over midtown, holding a cautious perimeter, as police choppers hovered over the long stretch along Broadway, where the city now burned.

Framed in the spotlights, looming among the towers like a monolith, was the rex.

Maverick turned a sideways eye to Cameron.

"Do I even have to ask where we're going?"

Cameron just pointed to the city.

"I'll know when we get closer."

"What is it with you and this broad?"

Cameron shook his head.

"Honest to God, I don't know."

Maverick sighed, squealing tires as he turned north, up the seaport to where the Brooklyn Bridge led into the city.

CHAPTER 34

One thing Shanna *had* noticed about Otto was a total lack of impulse control.

Her father had gotten her a puppy once and the little lizard had slaughtered it. Then he had hopped on Shanna's horrified shoulder, with blood slathered on his claws, and said, "Mine?" the way Shanna had when she was a little girl.

Perhaps that should have been a bit of a tell. But Shanna had felt no malice. In truth, she *still* didn't – even now, as they came for her out of the elevator.

What she *did* feel was implacable – a total lack of empathy – in fact, seeming to zero-in on empathy – perhaps because of their very inability to perceive it. An instinctive counter-force.

For Shanna, these were the creatures who killed her father.

But Shanna was not an old man, nor was she a mousy tech-nerd. She was, for all practical purposes, a farm-girl used to dealing with livestock that weighed fifty-tons or more.

She also happened to be a physically perfect human female, with athletic reflexes to match.

As the little bastards came for her, foot-claws outstretched, reaching for her throat, Shanna snatched the folding lamp off of her desk and caught it in a wide-open swat, catching the two-foot lizard flush, batting it clear across the room, where it twitched like a broken toy.

The other two were on her in a flash, one going high, slashing for her eyes, the other bringing its foot-claw in low for a disembowelment.

Shanna side-stepped the belly-strike while bringing up her monitor screen to block her face, knocking the offending Otto aside. With a follow-up strike, she brought the flat-screen down on top of the other one, pinning it to the floor. She stomped her weight on the monitor and heard the lizard's bones crack.

Shanna turned to the last of them.

The little lizard hissed and Shanna felt pressure in her head.

Whatever it had done to her before on the island, it was trying to do again.

This time Shanna pushed back.

The sensation was like holding your breath underwater too deep. She felt Otto resist.

Then the little lizard staggered back with a squawk.

"Not this time, you little bastard," Shanna whispered.

The little lizard eyed her, claws spread.

But then it turned and made a dash for the elevator. Shanna chased after, armed with her keyboard, but it turned, hissing, claws spread, holding her at bay until the elevator doors closed.

Shanna, however, had now gotten a better look at the guard's body lying in the elevator car behind him. The man's throat was gone – large wounds, more in line with a tiger-sized beast.

Otto had not killed that man.

The little lizard hissed as the doors blinked shut.

Shanna glanced back at her desk. Her intercom was still beeping, with no answer – not from the desk downstairs.

This was a big facility – a lot of people worked here – even some civilians, mostly scientists and researchers, all oblivious, working from the museum just up the street.

Shanna pulled up the security monitor on one of the surviving PCs, bringing up the overhead view of the lobby levels.

It was a slaughter.

And as she tapped to the screen in the main hallway, over to the security desk in front of the elevator that took you to this very floor, she saw a pack of sickle-claws waiting patiently for the light.

Behind her, the elevator light beeped.

She was trapped.

The windows didn't open, and even if they did, it was a thirty-story-tower – minor among the Manhattan skyline, but a two-hundred-foot drop to the street from her own perch on the twentieth floor.

She pulled the control box on the wall, yanking the circuit that controlled the door so it would not automatically open.

Which meant all they had to do was push the doors apart.

She looked around desperately for a weapon. A keyboard wasn't going to help her versus a full-size dromaeosaur.

The elevator dinged. There came a snarling from inside and banging on the metal door.

As distracting as all that was, Shanna could perhaps be forgiven for failing to sense the approach of another, even though his very footsteps shook the ground.

But then the entire building shook, and he now commanded her full attention.

Shanna turned to the window as Big Rex nudged the building, like a dog pawing at a cabinet.

Twenty-stories high, the rex stared her nose-to-nose through her window. His eyes blinked, glowing green.

"Hey, big guy," Shanna whispered – pointlessly, the glass was as soundproof as it was bulletproof. Nor could the Big Rex smell her. But he knew she was there.

He bumped the building again, and now there was a crack in the unbreakable glass.

The elevator door slid partly open. Pushing between the six-inch crack, Shanna could see snapping jaws and reaching claws.

Apparently, Big Rex did too.

He hated sickle-claws.

The window rattled with his very roar, before the massive spike-toothed jaws smashed in, this time stepping with his weight, rocking the very building.

It was hard to know the mind of a rex, or if he perceived the danger to Shanna herself – most likely, he thought he was moving to her aid.

But the building shifted on its very foundation.

The elevator door was pushed all the way open – a moment before the cable snapped.

One sickle-claw made it halfway through before the descending car chopped it in half against the floor, leaving its top half to quiver and squirm at Shanna's feet.

She could hear the elevator sing along its rails as it sailed twenty-stories down, before landing with an impact that reverberated all the way back up to the roof.

The rex bumped the building again – not an attack, not yet, or else it would have already tumbled down – but it wouldn't matter soon.

"Rex!" Shanna called through the now broken window. "Stop!"

And for a moment, Big Rex did, his glowing green eyes blinking, his roars settling to a low rumble.

The chemical, Shanna knew, was just beginning to addle his brain. The madness hadn't settled in yet – and a rex would always follow his nose.

With the window broken, he no doubt smelled her. Big Rex cocked his head, looking crazily like a giant Labrador as he peered in the window.

Then he bumped the building again.

Shanna felt an alarming tremor ripple up through the foundation.

"Rex," Shanna whispered. "Please."

But then there came another, challenging roar.

With the impact of his steps shaking the streets, his head rising above the surrounding towers, Congo stepped into the square.

Rearing to his full height, staring the twenty-story rex in the eye, the giant gorilla beat his chest, and then dropped to all fours, smashing his fists like pistons into the city streets.

Shanna could see the green glow in Congo's own eyes.

Big Rex almost seemed to smile.

After all this time, this was the fight they *both* wanted.

Shanna knew she had to get out of this building before they brought it down.

With the doorway pried open and the elevator car itself now gone, Shanna had access to the empty shaft. She stared down twenty-stories.

Climbing into the narrow corridor, she latched onto the service ladder and began to climb.

She had barely gone two stories when she looked down and saw sickle-claws working their way up from below.

The clawed devils scaled the walls the way Shanna had seen bats climb trees. There were too many to count.

There was no way through.

With no other choice, she turned back and started climbing for the roof.

CHAPTER 35

Congo and Big Rex circled in the street.

This battle was personal. And a long time in coming.

When they came together, there was nothing like it in the history of the Earth – and the world indeed shook to attention.

Circling choppers broadcast the images worldwide, even as police choppers gave up on useless gunfire, and simply turned their attention to diverting the citizenry out of their path.

So far, that wasn't hard – their path had been straight as an arrow.

And now they faced each other, the chemical in their veins amplifying a long and mutual animosity into a panting rage.

It was the rex who attacked first, and also drew first blood.

Congo had been watching for it. *T. rex*' armaments had evolved into one massive super-weapon – its jaws. Where an allosaur might have kicked with clawed feet or slashed with clawed hands, a rex attack was like the big carcharodonts, and came from the head.

Oh, it could kick alright, but the claws were blunted like an ostrich, or a horse's hoof.

This was a killing battle, and the rex came after Congo with bio-armament that had raised its kind to the top of the food chain. Back on the island, Congo had seen tyrannosaurs drop ceratopsians with a single bite, and cripple a full-grown titanosaur.

But your greatest weapon can become a weakness if you rely on it overmuch, and Congo had mastered a tyrannosaur or two in his day – usually skirmishes with the smaller, albeit aggressive adolescent males, but occasionally he had battled the big female pride leaders.

The trick was simple wrestling – evade the massive jaws and go for the powerful but unarmed legs.

Of course, this was no juvenile male or even a female pride leader. Big Rex was a fully-mature, dominant rogue.

He was experienced, as well, lunging forward with the suddenness of a striking snake. Congo had been on his guard, but the teeth still snagged his shoulder, chopping out a divot.

Congo returned with a mighty blow of his own, a truck-sized fist that crashed against the rex' jaw, shaking the beast's entire frame.

The blow echoed in the streets. The impact might have crippled a carcharodont – broken its jaw, or possibly its neck. But the rex, with a skull designed to absorb the headlong impact of its own attacks, merely rounded back, landing a heavy return stroke with its bony brow.

Congo caught the head, grabbing with both arms and clamping the lethal jaws shut.

The titans grappled, widening the city block as they crashed into the buildings around them.

Congo was attempting to take his opponent's back, pulling himself beyond the reach of the jaws, to where his long arms could encircle the thick bulldog neck. The rex responded with simple brute force, bucking like a bronco-bull, slamming his rider against the base of the tower.

The impact knocked out Congo's wind. Sensing advantage, the rex dug forward with both legs. Congo maintained his hold on the jaws, but now he found himself pinned.

The rex snarled in anger and Congo felt himself answering in kind – and in doing so, began to realize his own disadvantage.

Instead of the tactical battle that might have allowed him to hold his own, Congo found himself fueled by a mindless rage, an urge to meet the rex' brutality with his own.

That was a battle he simply couldn't win. The rex was larger and better-armed – a true primordial engine of power. Congo had to get control of himself or the matter would soon be finished.

As he struggled against the base of the tower, Congo was also well aware that somewhere, not far above, Shanna was feeling every tremor.

Fortunately, the building was sturdier than it looked. A normal to-code structure would have already collapsed, but this was an Area 51 branch office.

The rex pushed forward, and Congo slipped suddenly aside, sending the lunging jaws face-first into the building.

Stepping in quickly, the big ape delivered another bludgeoning blow to the rex' head.

Taking the impact cleanly, Big Rex whirled, bent low, connecting heavily with the bony ridge of its massive skull. Congo was knocked backwards, and sent rolling into one of the neighboring towers – a more modest ten-story structure that crumbled under him like a sandcastle.

Congo was on his feet in a moment, shaking off dust, pounding the street in anger.

Both combatants circled, both unbowed.

But the rex had a shade better of the battle. Congo's shoulder was bleeding and he found himself backing up, forced on the defensive.

The rex allowed no quarter, moving in relentlessly.

It was a second too late when Congo realized the cagey tyrannosaur had again maneuvered him against the tower.

The moment his back touched the concrete, the rex launched forward, its massive jaws yawning wide.

Congo realized he couldn't get out of the way.

The jaws closed over his already-wounded shoulder. But this time, the teeth sank down deep, piercing into bone, clamping down like a vice.

In another moment, it would begin to shake and rip, and the cookie-cutter-action of the teeth, combined with the torque from the powerful muscles in its neck, would sever Congo's arm from his body, along with most of the meat and bone across the big ape's shoulder and back, leaving a wide-open, hollowed-out wound. Congo would not survive it.

Evolution had curved rex-teeth inward and back – pulling away would sink the hold deeper.

So instead, Congo pushed forward.

The unexpected shift in direction gave Congo one last chance to regain the offensive.

His massive paw swept along the street, scooping up a semi-trailer, and brought it in a wide, sweeping arc against the rex' skull. Big Rex let out an angry grunt, but did not release his grip.

Congo hit him again. And then a third time, his strength fading fast.

The third blow, however, happened to strike the rex in the eye, the hard metal digging past the protective bony brow, into the soft tissue of the iris.

Big Rex screamed, releasing his grip, and Congo rolled clear.

The rex danced madly in the street, pawing at the bleeding socket, which was blackening like a prizefighter's, and starting to swell shut.

But Congo was badly wounded. His right arm was clutched tightly to his side, nearly useless, tendons and muscles completely severed, perhaps bone as well.

Blood splashed the streets at his feet. As Congo moved, the wound yawned.

It was enough, he realized, to kill him.

But he knew he was already dying. That's what the Food of the Gods did.

The rex was already advancing again, glaring at his longtime rival with his one good eye.

If this were merely a hunt, now would be the time to sit back and wait for the wound to do its work, letting the prey expire on its own.

But this was personal. So the rex stepped forward menacingly – albeit with a touch of caution, blinking his damaged eye – an experienced killer who knew a wounded prey was the most dangerous.

Still, Big Rex sensed he had scored a telling blow and that his opponent was fading.

As he retreated, Congo again found his back pressed against the tower wall. He looked up over his shoulder, where he could still sense Shanna somewhere up above.

He could feel her fear.

Worse, he could sense that nasal stench as well.

Otto – somewhere near.

No doubt it was egging Big Rex on as well.

Congo, however, still had his mind.

He pitched the trailer at the advancing tyrannosaur's face. And by happenstance or good aim, it struck the already-injured eye.

The rex turned away, stamping its feet, roaring in pain – for a brief window, fully distracted and vulnerable.

But Congo was beyond counterattacks. In the seconds before the rex rounded back in angry pursuit, the big ape turned to the tower behind him and began to climb.

The rex realized Congo's escape a moment too late. The big tyrannosaur charged, striking the building, its jaws snapping shut mere yards from Congo's retreating foot.

Big Rex smashed his head against the tower, roaring in frustration. The foundation shook.

Reinforced or not, the structure wasn't going to last much longer.

Shanna was somewhere above, and Otto was up there with her.

Keeping his injured arm tucked at his side, Congo climbed.

CHAPTER 36

Shanna could hear the sickle-claws coming up fast.

The service ladder took her to a small platform leading out onto the roof. The doorway, however, was locked. Shanna cursed under her breath – only in a government building did you get locks going in *and* out.

Shanna glanced over the railing. The nearest of her pursuers were less than two floors below.

She had never seen this kind of coordinated behavior before. Dromaeosaurs weren't particularly smart animals – just bone-deep evil.

But she knew the answer, even as she again felt that throb of pressure in her skull.

There was a jolt of pain, but now Shanna was ready for it. She flexed back – and that's really what it felt like – straining a muscle.

As if in response, a warbling hooting echoed in the corridor, as the sickle-claws all catcalled out together.

The first of them made the leap, catching the access ladder deftly, like a squirrel.

In another moment, it would be standing on the platform next to her.

But then the building itself was rocked, accompanied by a crescendo of savage roars and bellows from out on the street.

The sickle-claw perched precariously on the ladder was knocked loose, tumbling nearly fifty feet before snagging its claws along the wall, and arresting its fall.

Without missing a beat, it began climbing again.

Apparently oblivious as the tower itself shook around them, two more sickle-claws leaped for the platform, one catching the wall just below, and clinging like a spider.

The second caught the railing, and like a giant crow, hopped up on the platform beside her.

Shanna knew her life could be counted in seconds.

Then the roof above her was suddenly torn away.

Concrete and rubble tumbled past, bouncing down the narrow shaft as the rooftop was peeled like a sardine can.

Congo peered in from above.

The sickle-claw screeched, but instead of fleeing, it moved on Shanna, claws up.

Congo's massive paw reached down, squashing the clawed beast like a bug.

Shanna looked up at the giant ape's glowing green eyes, even as she saw the terrible wound the rex had left across his shoulder.

She could feel his pain.

"Oh, Congo," she said, touching his hand. "I'm so sorry."

The building shook again, and now Shanna felt herself snatched-up bodily.

Congo cradled her in his giant paw as he leaped from the tower to the top of the next building over.

There was a loud and angry objection below from Big Rex.

Congo hooted down from the neighboring rooftop.

With a roar, the rex charged, even as Congo turned to retreat.

Tucking Shanna in the crook of his injured arm, the giant ape leaped from rooftop to rooftop, straddling the New York skyline like a cat running along adjoining fences.

In the streets below, Big Rex followed.

Shanna clung to Congo's fur as she felt herself flying through the cold night air.

She could clearly see their destination – the Wall Street district of lower Manhattan, and the single tallest structure in the city.

Once it had been the World Trade Center, but it had been destroyed, ushering in a new era of violence and hate.

The twin towers had given way to a single monument – a steeple that once again dominated the city.

Perhaps in keeping with the dangerous new era, the original name 'Freedom Tower' was replaced with the rather more ominous 'One World' Tower.

But whatever the name, it was the highest spot in the city, and Congo was still, at his heart, a mountain gorilla. As his wound bled him dry and the chemical continued to eat at his brain, he went where he felt safe – as high up as he could get.

With the rex in hot-pursuit, Congo leaped from the neighboring spires, catching the tower at its lower floors and began to climb.

In the square below, Big Rex crashed into the building's base.

Shanna felt the impact, even as Congo scaled the tower, cresting quickly to the top, clinging with his one good paw. Shanna clung to his fur, her head spinning with vertigo from the sheer dizzying height.

It had been less than thirty minutes since the rex had first walked out of the East River, and already it was the worst disaster in the city's history. From her vantage, Shanna could see the path of the destruction leading straight through midtown.

There had not even been a military response yet. The choppers that circled the air-space were all either police or local news.

Another tremendous impact shook the tower.

Shanna remembered 9/11 – the way the buildings had suddenly seemed to simply dissolve and crumble apart.

The circling helicopters seemed to remember as well. They held a respectful distance.

Except for one – a news-chopper that abruptly separated, rapidly zeroing in on the tower's steeple.

The buzzing bird drew close, and even as she felt the building below her begin to totter, Shanna realized who was on-board.

CHAPTER 37

Cameron was quite surprised to learn Maverick had never once flown a chopper before. Turned out it was completely different to flying a plane – a balancing act with wind-gusts, always in a constant state of near-crashing.

Maverick had offered up this little tidbit as he was starting the bird up.

When they had first skidded their purloined Jeep up to the Brooklyn Bridge, they found it jammed with emergency barricades blocking the route back into the city. Police were escorting people from their cars, ushering them out on foot.

Reporters milled at the east end of the bridge, peppering the directing officers with questions, including a local reporter, whose traffic-chopper had been flagged away from the bridge, and landed on the nearby docks.

Surveying the blocked-off bridge-access, Maverick parked the Jeep, hopped out and started jogging over to where the pilot waited in the chopper for his team.

"Hey!" he shouted, waving.

The pilot looked over just as Maverick pulled open the cabin door, stepped up and pumped a fist precisely on the helmet-strap of his unsuspecting chin. The pilot emitted a brief grunt before Maverick tossed him semi-conscious out onto the dock.

Cameron stepped discreetly past the dazed, blinking pilot, and climbed into the co-pilot's seat. Maverick fired the rotors and jerked them into the air before Cameron even got his door shut.

"Sorry," Maverick said, mulling over the controls. "Let's see. Lift versus rotation. Can't be that hard."

Neither was it hard to determine their destination.

Congo stood atop the highest tower in the land.

Two-thousand feet below, bellowing like a hound who had treed a cougar, the rex smashed into its base again and again.

Cameron had seen this before. He had been in Midtown when the original towers had gone down.

Already the steeple Congo clung to seemed to tilt.

"That's where we're going," Cameron said. "Right there."

Maverick nodded. "Of course it is."

With an abrupt, skating-rink, mid-air spin, Maverick turned them towards the tower.

Congo hung from the steeple by a single hand. Even from the distance, they could see the grievous wound that had nearly severed his arm at the collar.

And as the rex pounded away, it was also obvious the building would not last much longer.

It wasn't until they circled in close, however, that they saw Shanna, looking no bigger than a pocket-pen, tucked in the crook of Congo's injured arm.

As they drew near, the big gorilla snarled, but they could see Shanna patting him down.

His glowing green eyes blinked, with shifting awareness.

"Take us down," Cameron said.

Maverick eyed the giant ape dubiously, but dropped their altitude, riding the wind-drafts in steps. Cameron pushed open the hatch. With one hand latched grimly on his seat, he stepped down onto the landing gear.

The whirling rotor blades buzzed dangerously close as Maverick hovered just above the giant ape's head.

"I get any closer," he said, "I'm gonna clip his ears."

Congo, struggling with one good arm, latched onto his perch with his feet, and plucked Shanna from the crook of his shoulder, holding her cupped gently in his palm as he held her up to the chopper hovering above.

Maverick dropped them lower as Shanna reached up for Cameron's hand.

Two-hundred stories below, the rex crashed into the base of the tower one final time.

Almost from the moment the original twin towers had collapsed, there had been talk of a monument – but with such constant, and ever-more politicized legal wrangling, it had taken so long, it seemed as if it would never be built,

Now the monument was coming down too – just as its predecessors had, the fates simply denying the towers' right-to-be.

Cameron would daresay it would stay down this time.

As the building started to crumble, Congo began to fall.

For a breath of a moment, Shanna fell with him – and Congo reached his hand up, even as Maverick dropped the chopper abruptly.

The rotors chopped one of Congo's extended fingers, prompting a snarling yelp, and an involuntary jerk.

Even as the chopper spun from the impact, Shanna leaped for Cameron's outstretched hand. He caught her grip in mid-air, hauling her up next to him onto the landing gear.

Below them, the building collapsed on itself, crumbling into rubble.

Congo disappeared into a billowing cloud, as hundreds of thousands of tons of steel and concrete went crashing to the streets.

By happenstance, right on top of the hapless rex itself.

The mighty beast's own roar was drowned out as the collapsing tower tumbled down, burying him in an avalanche of rubble.

Circling above, the chopper spun crazily, its rear-rotor knocked askew.

Cameron pulled Shanna into the seat beside him, yanking the door shut, as Maverick struggled to level them out.

He took them up over the rooftops, arrowing out of the city.

They were out over the river when the main-rotor started to chop.

"Awww, *shit*," Maverick muttered. He glanced sideways to Cameron and Shanna.

"Hang on," he said.

Maverick cranked the throttle, prompting backfires from the motor, but a surge of speed as he launched them towards the west docks, opposite the East River.

They just made the beach, when the chopper engine quit and they crashed, right where the ocean met the sand.

CHAPTER 38

As the tower collapsed, Congo felt himself falling. Then he was blind and couldn't breathe as he was enveloped in a cloud of debris, crashing two-thousand feet down to the street.

Countless tons that landed hard.

Big Rex realized his own peril too late. The collapse seemed to come in slow motion, but the rex barely had time for a startled roar before the cascading avalanche of the man-made mountain caught him square and he was buried beneath all of it.

Eventually, the last piece of rubble settled to a stop, and the cloud of powdered concrete filled the square like a fog.

For several minutes, the two-hundred-foot pile of rubble remained absolutely still.

Then something stirred.

From near the top, heavy chunks of concrete and steel were tossed aside, starting a fresh avalanche as displaced debris tumbled to the street.

Congo emerged, slowly and painfully, from the wreckage.

The big ape's breath was ragged as his life's blood leaked away.

As he reared on his haunches, Congo felt his head go light. His vision blurred.

He was about to die.

But it was not done yet.

Congo began digging through the mountain of rubble until he found the rex.

The big tyrannosaur lay stunned and bleeding. Its breathing was rapid and shallow, likely with internal injuries.

He was pinned beneath countless tons.

Congo stood above his long-time rival, and the rex' eyes rolled in their sockets, defiant to the end – and the green glow shined bright as ever.

The emerald gleam in Congo's own eyes were full of grim resolve, as the big ape bent to do what had to be done.

He picked up a piece of rubble, as massive as his fading strength could manage, raised it above his head, and brought the bludgeon down.

Again. And again. As many times as it took.

When it was done, he lay down in the dust and debris next to his lifetime enemy.

His eyes turned to the sky as a single chopper circled above, turning to make its way out of the city.

For the moment, at least, Shanna was safe.

As he died, Congo's simian lips turned up in a very human smile.

CHAPTER 39

In the lull after the battle, the city of New York stopped to catch its breath, believing it was over.

It was not.

The two fallen titans and the destruction they left in their path was but a preamble.

From the surrounding buildings and sewers, scores of Ottos suddenly swarmed like rats.

Their hand, as it were, had been conclusively shown.

As a troop, they threw their heads back in a hooting caterwauling that echoed in the abandoned streets.

Ten miles away, a young allosaur, that had been living within a strict territorial range for years at the edge of federal land, suddenly turned and walked into town.

It was the first, but it was not alone.

Worldwide-coverage of the 'New York incident', as it was being called, was barely forty-five minutes old, but now new broadcasts began breaking in.

From everywhere.

Chicago. LA. London. Paris. Moscow. Friggin' Beijing.

All simultaneous.

First the beasts had come out of the forests.

And then behind them, with glowing green eyes, the marching giants.

New York was ground-zero as blooms began to sprout worldwide.

KT-day had begun.

When it was over, the world of humankind would be gone.

CHAPTER 40

As the storm darkened the sky, the Rocky Mountains were lit by strobe-flashes of lightning. The wind picked up as the storm clouds rolled in.

Along with whatever else loomed on the horizon.

Not all the thunder echoing through the canyons came from lightning.

Rosa looked around their wide-eyed circle, clinging to their little ledge on the edge of this freezing cliff.

They had all heard these deep, echoing bellows before, as had every surviving human on Earth.

There were the beasts that populated the forests – and then there were the blooms of giants.

Shanna's ordeal in New York ended just as it began for the rest of the world.

"We actually crashed within half-a-mile of the east-coast shop," Shanna said. "Which was lucky, because that was the only stretch of beach that wasn't jammed. That way we were able to get out of the city."

Rosa nodded. She herself had been in San Francisco on KT-day, and had not been so lucky. Her refuge had been a half-collapsed underground parking garage with a vending machine for almost two-weeks.

Although, the edge of a freezing cliff was definitely worse.

"We were lucky," Shanna said, "Mr. Wilson had Maverick's plane in his shop."

"Lucky, my ass," Mr. Wilson said. "Lucky he crashed it, or it wouldn't have been there. That damn kid of mine has actually turned *dumb-ass* into a survival skill."

Mr. Wilson had filched a pair of binoculars from the salvaged cargo and scanned the surrounding peaks and the canyons.

The trading bellows were echoing ever-closer.

But Mr. Wilson lowered the binoculars, shaking his head.

"I can't see anything," he said. "But this is a pretty clustered range."

"They sound close," Rosa said.

"Maybe they'll pass," Allison volunteered, hopefully.

But Shanna sighed.

"No. They won't."

She looked back at them apologetically.

"I'm sorry. But it's me. They're coming for me."

"Who is?" Rosa asked, hoping she didn't already know.

Shanna smiled, sadly.

"With Congo and Rex, it was personal," she said. "But they were both the first of their genetic lines. I guess the animosity just seemed to bleed through."

Her brow furrowed.

"Somehow, it's still over me."

Shanna shut her eyes.

"I can feel them," she said. "And just lately, it's like..."

But she was interrupted by another Gatling-gun blast of thunder.

The storm was upon them, and the rain came down in a sudden torrent, threatening to extinguish their fire. Mr. Wilson and Bud jumped up, throwing a tarp over the opening, even as the chopper rocked in the wind, tugging at the restraining vines that held it in place. Allison hugged her little bundle close, as Lucas began to sniffle and cry with the cold.

And amid the clouds breaching the mountains, and the trailing curtains of sheeted rain, the first towering shadows separated from the storm.

CHAPTER 41

"What the hell do you mean you're in space?" Kristie shouted into her radio. "And how the hell do you know my name?"

She could hear the sickle-claws one story below banging furiously at the door.

"My name is Major Tom Corbett," the radio said. "I'm on the International Space Station, I've been picking up on your broadcasts for a year. And I've got a satellite camera on your location right now."

"*Ohhhh-kay*, 'Major Tom'," Kristie said, looking uncomfortably out the window up at the sky, "I've actually got kind of a situation here."

"I know, I'm zeroing in on your building. Wait just a second."

There was a beep, as if he'd switched lines, and dead-air for thirty seconds until he came back on.

"You've got help coming," he said.

Downstairs, the pounding on the door grew louder, and was now accompanied by a widening *creak*.

Kristie picked up her rifle, standing ready at the top of the stairs.

Then she heard the air-blast of a chopper passing low overhead, the sound of its engine seeming to trail a half-second later,

The chopper landed just outside the building. Within moments, there was the sound of gunfire and the squalling of sickle-claws.

Kristie looked out the window as troops fanned from the chopper, laying out a barrage of bullets, dropping the surrounding packs of clawed dromaeosaurs like ducks in a shooting gallery.

These were all big ones. The little talking lizards seemed to have vanished.

After thirty seconds and a lot of shooting, the path to her building was clear and Kristie heard the downstairs door being battered down.

Troops flooded the hall, guns up and drawn.

The leader turned his rifle sights up the stairs and found Kristie, who held up her hands, wide-eyed.

"You must be Kristie Morgan," the soldier said. "I'm Lieutenant Dwayne Hicks, and you're going to need to come with us."

But as he spoke, a large sickle-claw appeared at the door behind him, unerringly catching its prey in its one unguarded moment. Hicks brought his rifle up, even as his team turned towards the door.

The sickle-claw, however, never reached its target before Kristie shot a hole in its chest, blowing it back, just as the foot-claw slashed within six-inches of Hick's throat.

Hicks glanced up at Kristie as the creature twitched in death-spasms at his feet.

"You are definitely coming with us," he said.

Hicks' radio scratched static, followed by Major Tom's voice.

"Did you get her?"

"Got her, sir," Hicks replied. "We're moving onto the silos now."

"Due north," Tom said. "Satellite image shows empty grounds."

Almost the moment he said it, another entire pack of sickle-claws materialized from the surrounding buildings.

"Oh for..." Hicks blurted as he dropped his radio, grabbing up his rifle.

There was another eruption of machine-gun fire, and Kristie could tell these troops understood the mobbing tactics employed by dromaeosaurs – they gave no quarter, spraying the clawed devils in a solid blanket of gunshots.

Hicks grabbed up his radio. "Does it still look clear?"

"Uh, no," Major Tom responded. "Actually, now it looks like they're crawling out of cracks all over the base."

Kristie was reminded of one of those old karate movies, after Bruce Lee single-handedly kills a hundred ninjas, but they just kept coming anyway, right down to the last man.

Sickle-claws were evil bastards on a good day, but Kristie had never seen them this aggressive.

And where were they all coming from? It was as if every last dromaeosaur in the territory was converging on the site.

Hicks and his team maintained a steady fire until the second attacking wave was chopped into carrion.

But even as the troops began to move across the grounds towards the silos, more of them began to appear at the perimeter.

A few came running in, only to be shot down, but most of the others held back, waiting for greater numbers to launch another mob attack.

As they reached the first of the silos, the squadron formed a perimeter, continuing to pick off individual sickle-claws as Hicks bent to access the entrance-key. After a moment, he cracked the lock and kicked open the door, filing in with his troops behind him.

And as she followed close behind, Kristie saw where all those little lizards had gone.

The warhead was crawling with them.

"What the hell?" Hicks breathed, before the first of them attacked, claws outstretched.

Hicks caught the little lizard in a single shot, and a moment later the silo echoed like a rat-shoot as he and his men started picking them off.

"Please, take care," Hicks instructed over the ricocheting bullets, "to not shoot the nuclear missile."

It shouldn't matter, but why take chances?

One of the soldiers kicked at one of the twitching lizards.

"What is this thing?" He looked uncomfortably up at Hicks. "Lieutenant, I let one of these loose just last week."

Hicks turned, frowning. "What are you talking about?"

"This girl back at the base. She said she wanted to set it free. I thought it was a lab animal." The soldier's expression was pained. "She said she couldn't bear to see it put down." He held up his hands helplessly. "What harm could it do?"

"Um, actually sir," another soldier spoke up, "I did too. Same thing. There was this girl."

Hicks turned towards the rest of the troops.

Several raised their hands, nodding.

"What harm could it do?" Hicks muttered.

"I've seen these things," Kristie said. "They talk like parrots. I found them in the broadcast booth."

Hicks nodded. He pulled out his radio.

"You seeing this, Major?"

"On high-definition," Tom responded. "I'm guessing they've been at every missile on this site."

Hicks turned towards the soldier who had spoken before.

"A girl you say?" Hicks shook his head. "Why do I think I know exactly who?

He tapped his radio.

"This is Lieutenant Hicks, urgent for General Rhodes. I think we've found our leak."

CHAPTER 42

When Lily left Dr. Shrinker's lab, she had gone right to Ginger.

That way, when Rhodes had appeared at their door with a dozen armed soldiers, there was nothing out of order.

Having been introduced to the Mount as a group, the Coven had more or less commandeered the majority of the lodgings on their hall, and most other civilian refugees tended to avoid their entire area.

Each hall had its own rec-room/laundry facility, and this was where Rhodes found them.

Lily found the General intimidating any old time. Today, he wore his war face.

And beside him, Corporal Stevens, who Lily had left only a short time ago with soda-pop flirts and smiles, now glared back at her with real anger.

That was not a good look in a man. That was another thing the Coven had taught her early – be careful how far you push your mark – no one likes being suckered.

Doubtless, that was particularly true of a General.

Ginger stood as Rhodes entered with his armed escort, but he had frozen her with a raised finger, motioning her to sit back down. Ginger complied readily enough.

"Can we help you, General?" she asked innocently.

Rhodes nodded to his men. "Look around," he said.

Ginger exchanged a brief glance with Luna, and then to Lily, herself. Lily was uncertain if the look was of confidence, or if she were again taking the rap for circumstances.

Stevens and the other soldiers started turning the place up, pulling out drawers, turning over furniture.

The room, however, just wasn't that big.

"I'm not finding anything, sir," Stephens said.

Ginger and Luna blinked at the General, completely deadpan. Lily began to believe the fates were working in her favor this time.

Then Michelle walked in.

Rhodes raised an eyebrow in her direction. "Well?"

Michelle pointed to the grating in the wall.

This time, it was Christine who rose to her feet – the Coven's *other* enforcer – stepping up to intercept Stevens as he reached for the grating.

Minus her pistol, however, she was somewhat declawed, and Corporal Stevens sat her down roughly. Making no bones, he brandished his weapon in her face, before turning to pull the grate cover off the wall.

There was a sudden squealing, and movement like scurrying rats.

Scaly clawed rats. The little lizard's toe-claws scraped metal as they vanished down the ventilation shaft.

Rhodes himself shoved the grating aside, peering inside.

It looked like a hamster-habitat – pack-rat and animal like – which seemed totally incongruent with what you *knew* about them.

Lying among the scattered pellets and torn bones of what looked like *actual* rats, there was an empty torn pack and several scattered pneumatic needles – all empty.

Christine was staring an evil-eye right through Michelle, who stared right back. Two enforcers now at odds, although both knew, unarmed, Christine was nowhere near the handful Michelle was.

"*Bitch*," Christine hissed venomously.

Michelle's lips crooked in a rough smile.

"*Duh.*"

Ginger and Luna both seemed utterly taken aback – Ginger, in particular, who was the keeper of the scrolls and utterly scandalized. Michelle had always been their stalwart. This was an almost ultimate betrayal.

"*Why?*" Ginger asked.

Michelle was utterly unabashed.

"Because I'm not going down with you."

And at that, Lily understood. Michelle had been their warrior for the same reason she had been a dancer – and a gangster – she was in it for the perks, and the lust to indulge her every fleeting desire – an utterly amoral creature of pure passion.

Personal sacrifice was not in her character. The only authority she recognized was power, and only followed where there was personal benefit.

Lily didn't know what Rhodes had done to her in that interview, but he'd obviously convinced Michelle where *that* lay.

Michelle saw Lily looking at her, brokenhearted, the way a girl looks at an idolized big sister fallen from grace.

"I can't believe you did this to us," Lily said.

Michelle's hardened face suddenly looked haunted.

Her eyes stole to the hole in the wall where Otto had disappeared.

"That little lizard," she said, "it really IS the dragon."

She eyed Lilly meaningfully.

"And don't think for one second that he's going to spare you."

Rhodes nodded to Stevens.

"Take the group of them up to the detention level."

The General eyed the gathered Coven.

"Ladies," he said, "that will be your new home for the immediate future."

Lily felt herself snatched-up roughly as Stevens angrily yanked her to her feet.

"Easy, soldier," Rhodes cautioned.

There was a brief scuffle as Christine had to be restrained, but the rest of the Coven acquiesced obediently enough.

Luna, always the philosopher, had scowled.

"It wasn't like we weren't prisoners already," she said.

"Well," Rhodes countered mildly, "if you weren't, you are now."

CHAPTER 43

The news from the Maelstrom site was every bit as bad as Major Tom had expected.

There was no telling how long Otto had been there – likely checking into the Mount via radio reports in chirps and quips taken from the slaughtered troops. That left more than five-hundred individual warheads unguarded for weeks. The little gremlins had no doubt been into everything from the launch-systems, to targeting, to the warheads themselves.

Tom shuddered to think what might have happened if Rhodes had provided the launch code. And likely *would* have, because with the impending bloom, there was nothing left to them *but* nuclear options.

Options which had now been narrowed down to one submarine and a handful of planes capable of delivering warheads.

The sub, theoretically, was the most viable. By its very nature, it was least affected by the EMPs that had nullified most modern tech – they were their own Faraway cages, and retained advanced targeting programs that could launch anywhere in the world.

The Anchorage currently waited to assume launch depth, holding upon orders.

Rhodes, however, had kept them on stand-by. And Tom knew why, well enough.

So far, the only nuclear option they'd been able to employ successfully at all since KT-day was the most hands-on, and the most dangerous – piloted jets. And while that was also their sparest resource, circumstances allowed for little margin of error with untested options.

Hail Marys were for last-ditch of desperation. And while that might yet be hanging in the wings, for the moment, Captain Mason waited on-call.

Their saving grace was that this time they had the advantage of satellite-imagery, otherwise they wouldn't know where to shoot until the bloom was upon them.

Otto's screens were helpful too, having zeroed in on all his preferred targets. Among the spinning digital global models detailing nuclear sites, volcanic/thermal hot-spots, along with oceans and active weather patterns, almost every screen at least had a pop-up with satellite views keyed to the energy signature of the Food of the Gods.

Tom glanced over his shoulder at the security-screen, which was still empty.

The little bastards seemed to have disappeared for the moment. But Tom knew that only meant they were up to something.

Tom had already resolved to destroy the station. It simply couldn't be left in their hands.

That required a few logistics to work out – the most viable option would be flammable gas and fire. Setting it up, however, could prove problematic. He had no idea how many of the little lizards were actually on-board, waiting in some hidden compartment to spring out and slash his throat.

There was also the fact that the escape pods were docked off the Russian cargo-module, right in the direction the escaping Ottos had disappeared.

If push came to shove, he would tank ISS, and go down with the ship, but he would at least *try* to get to the pods.

But he couldn't go anywhere yet. For the moment, he still had to coordinate with Rhodes.

The situation on the ground, however, just kept getting worse.

It was actually the sheer boldness of it that kept Tom from seeing it straight out.

Otto had several screens running simulations – all global models.

The big bloom Tom had spotted sprouting earlier had been on the central screen – a localized view covering maybe a hundred square miles – the risk to the Mount was based on a helpful projected model Otto had running right next to it.

It wasn't until he pulled back the view that he realized that the model next to it, running simultaneously, wasn't actually a model at all.

Tom zoomed back the view of the first screen and realized they were both live.

Things *weren't* worse, he realized.

They were a LOT worse.

Rhodes wasn't going to like this.

Tom tapped the comm, but before he could bring up the General's line, there was a squawk over the speakers.

When he looked up, the toothy lizard faces were back in front of the security screen, gibbering like monkeys for the cameras.

A moment later, the lights in the ISS went out.

CHAPTER 44

Rhodes had his men crawling down the ventilation pipes as far as they could, finding a long trail of rat-like scraps and feces.

They also found the gnawed bones of Nurse Rose.

Sally wondered if *that* had come up during Michelle's little interview concerning the nurse's disappearance.

As the Coven was escorted out, Christine made a move at Rhodes with a palmed steak knife. Michelle stepped forward, catching the thrust, and swung her hips into one of her snappy spin-kicks – made famous at Susie's Bar – catching Christine full in the face, knocking her cold. Ginger and Luna caught her as she fell, both of them glaring at Michelle, who responded with a complete snub.

Sally wasn't sure who she should hate more. Nurse Rose had been her friend.

Michelle was led away with the rest – although, presumably *not* to detention – while Rhodes oversaw the ransack of the entire hall.

Then the radio on his hip beeped.

"General?" Dr. Shriver's voice said. "Something's come up. I need to talk to you right away."

Rhodes glanced at Sally. There was urgency in the doctor's normally deadpan tone.

"Meet me up top in my office," Rhodes said. He nodded to his men. "I want the entire complex swept. Warehouse, barracks, everything. You find anything, you let me know."

Sally hurried to follow as Rhodes turned for the door.

The General was in his fifties, and solidly over two-hundred pounds, but Sally found herself struggling to keep up as he took the stairs to the upper floors – perhaps impatient for the elevator, or possibly just energy to burn.

When they stepped into his office, they found three of the little lizards standing on his desk.

Along the wall, the safe was open and the documents inside – targeting codes for nuclear launch – were spread out on Rhodes' desk and shredded into confetti.

The Ottos hissed.

"Son of a bitch!" Rhodes blurted, and in a flash, his sidearm was up and firing.

Two of the scaly little vermin were blown off the desktop, as the third made for the open grating in the wall.

Letting out a deceptively calm breath, Rhodes cracked off one more shot, sending the little rat spinning into the corner.

Sally blinked – it was over before she even reached to turn on the lights.

Rhodes bent over his desk, looking at the torn documents, rubbing one hand on his temple.

"Well," he said, "let's see how bad they've screwed us."

"Oh. Pretty bad, I'm afraid," a voice said from behind them.

They turned to find Dr. Shriver standing at the elevator.

"The situation might be worse than we thought."

"I already thought it was pretty bad," Rhodes said. He turned to Shriver in his combat pose, like a fighter waiting to see what his opponent might throw.

Sally had always been a little scared of Shriver, but now the doctor actually seemed nervous.

"Well, sir," he said reluctantly, "it looks like we're missing a few bottles of the Food of the Gods."

Rhodes blinked once. "Come again?"

Shriver shifted uncomfortably.

"Um. It seems several containers have been replaced with... well, it looks like shampoo. Prell, I think. It matches the emerald green and the inherent glow is not obviously absent when placed among other bottles."

Rhodes looked at him mildly.

"Let me get this straight. You're actually telling me *several* containers – in your care – that should be loaded with the most destructive chemical ever known, are instead filled with Prell?"

"Or possibly a designer brand," Shriver said, nodding.

Sally saw one of Rhodes' hands drift to the still-smoking pistol at his belt.

The General took a deep breath.

"Wow," he said. "I almost just shot you over that one."

His hand, however, did not move from his waist. And when he spoke, his calm voice was deadly matter-of-fact.

"We can still get there." Rhodes eyed the doctor seriously. "You better start being real valuable real soon. What exactly is the potential damage?"

Shriver cleared his voice.

"The amount that's missing," he said, "released over a widespread area, even in small doses, could infect an entire region."

Dr. Shriver noted the dead twitching lizards on the floor, and then the torn documents on the desk.

"What happened here?"

"Those," Rhodes said, "are the rats in the walls you were telling us about. And that shredded pile on my desk is all the launch codes for every self-delivered missile we have available to us."

Sally, however, noticed one scrap on the floor, right next to the grating where the last Otto had tried to escape.

"This one isn't torn," she said. "What is it?"

Rhodes frowned. "It's the combination to Captain Mason's safe on the Anchorage."

Submarine firing-codes were always kept on-board because of the potential for lost contact. The combination would be wired to the Captain of the vessel in case of a launch order, including instructions of which firing package to activate.

"Get Mason on the horn," he said. "Right away."

"Already got him on stand-by, sir," Sally said.

"Put him on speaker."

"Mason here, sir."

"Captain," Rhodes said, starting his relentless march around his desk, "have you received further contact with me since your stand-by order?"

"Negative, sir."

"Captain," Rhodes said, "this is not a reprimand, but we must consider your option compromised. Under no circumstances initiate any launch mission within the next forty-eight hours. Even on orders from me. Understood?"

There was a pause.

"Yes, sir."

"Withdraw to safe ground until further notice," Rhodes said. He turned to Sally. "Get Major Travis online. Tell him he's up."

"Sir?" Sally said, "I've got incoming from Major Tom, sir,"

Rhodes tapped his speaker.

"General," Tom blurted, out-of-breath, "you've got a big bloom coming, sir!"

"You said that already, Major. We're dealing with it."

"No sir," he said. "I've got it on satellite. It's bigger. I mean a *lot* bigger."

Rhodes turned a dark eye in Shriver's direction.

"It's already sprouted, sir," Tom continued. "And on simple biomass alone it will easily engulf the Mount."

"We're not ground-zero?"

Tom paused.

"No, sir. It tracks about two-hundred miles west."

Rhodes shut his eyes. "Of course it does. And I think I know why."

"General," Tom said, "if you can't nuke it, you're going to have to evacuate."

"We've got personnel in the area," Rhodes said. He turned to Sally. "Get Hicks on. Tell Johnson's search crews I know where our chopper went down."

"Sir?" Tom interrupted. "I'm sorry, but I have to tell you, I don't have much time. They've turned off my life-support."

Rhodes paused his pacing.

"Son," he said, "we've got a human race to save. I need you to hold out as long as you can."

"That won't be long, sir. And I have to make sure the ISS goes down before that, or it gets left in their hands."

Rhodes resumed his march.

"Understood," he said. "Do what you have to do, son. But remember, there's not a lot of the world left to spare."

Rhodes turned to Sally. "Where's Travis?"

"He hasn't reported in yet, sir."

"Oh, for Christ's..."

Rhodes stopped himself. It wasn't the first bit of temper Sally had seen from him, but it was one of very few. He reigned it in immediately.

"Where is he?"

"I don't know, sir. His line's active, and he checked in earlier, but now there's no response."

Rhodes was silent.

Too much of a coincidence.

"There isn't time," Dr. Shriver volunteered, "to evacuate the Mount. Should we perhaps start securing essential personnel?"

Rhodes smiled thinly. "I think essential personnel will remain essential for the mission at hand," he said.

"Still no response from Major Travis, sir," Sally said.

"Alright then," he said. "We'll have to send in what we've got. Napalm and conventional missiles."

"None of that ever worked before," Shriver said.

Rhodes frowned, but didn't answer.

Sally knew why. Rhodes would go down fighting.

In its way, it was the ultimate optimism – he would keep trying to win.

Sally had seen a cartoon once – a frog reaching its hands out of a pelican's mouth, choking the bird's throat, with the caption, 'It ain't over, 'till it's over'.

But Sally also understood futility.

If this bloom spread, if it really threatened to overtake the Mount, would he run?

Would he let his *people* run? Sally found herself wondering if *she* was 'essential personnel' who would be sticking it out to the last.

Now Rhodes stopped his endless pacing, and finally sat down at his desk.

He smacked the speaker phone, as if that would make it answer, hitting Major Travis' line.

"This is General Rhodes," he said, in a tone that sounded to Sally frighteningly close to despair. "Come in. For God's sake, is anyone there?"

And then, almost like the voice of an angel, someone answered.

"Hey there, General," a woman's voice said, "my name's Naomi. How can I help you today?"

CHAPTER 45

Tyrannosaurus rex – Tyrant Lizard King – named sixty-five million years after its extinction.

Resurrected and monstrously distorted, the rogue stood perched at the edge of the canyon, framed in the strobing flashes of electric light, the thunder announcing his arrival in a drumroll.

Josie and the pussycats galloped up beside him, shaking the ground beneath their feet.

Their eyes glowed green, reflecting back the lightning with an energy all its own.

The rogue peered through the storm, its eagle-like acuity picking out the surrounding peaks.

Shanna was up there somewhere, just ahead, perhaps looking down, even now.

The rogue could *feel* her, a light he couldn't even see.

His flock sensed it too, along with all the other heightened sensory input that seemed to accompany this strange energy pulsing through their veins.

But now the rogue growled.

Because he could sense the *others* as well – and even if he hadn't, their scent would have come to him on the wind.

The apes. In his own primitive way, the rogue understood they were following the same star.

T. rex didn't think. If the rex had a goal, he would advance on it – if he had a rival, he would attack it. More than anything, a rex followed its nose, and acted instinctively to the sensory input. It was all very cause/effect.

The rex had never heard of Congo – or *any* of the ape-clan, yet something beyond his eyes and ears sensed their presence, and seemed to share in Shanna's light.

And with the dog-like jealousy of a *T. rex*, those same instinctual reactions perceived a competitor and a rival.

Simple cause/effect – a chain-reaction – the path they followed was like a fuse leading up to the moment when they would finally come face-to-face – two marching clans of twenty-thousand-ton bombs.

And somewhere in the background, the rex still felt that little sting in the sinus – that psychic stench.

A *T. rex* would walk through fire to step on an Otto.

Perhaps it was a testament of sorts that the rogue instead decided to follow the light.

Josie and the pussycats filed into step beside him.

The earth trembled in homage.

Their star was just ahead somewhere, hidden by the clouds and the storm.

CHAPTER 46

Caesar could not be in a bigger hurry to leave these mountains.

Besides the blow stirring up, the freezing, torrential rain, *and* the lightning strikes, he could hear the bellows of giant rage-infected *T. rex* echoing through the canyons.

And if he couldn't hear them, he knew they were there anyway.

Whatever empathic link that tied them to Shanna also made them aware of each other.

He also knew the infected giants were not the only *T. rex* in the area.

But Caesar could evade the giants. More problematic was the presence of at least a small pack of normals prowling about somewhere right up here on the mountain.

Even a normal-sized average adult Tyrannosaurus outweighed him. Then to have three or four of them?

Naturally, he had to come alone, the stoic leader, delivering strict orders that his tribe stay as far away as possible.

In retrospect, Caesar might have felt a little better to have Cornelius or Zaius at his side just about now.

The little rex chasing that human had snapped at his finger like an angry turtle. A pack of adults would attack him on sight.

Caesar would have been happy to keep his distance. Unfortunately, he knew he couldn't expect the same from a rex – they just hadn't evolved that far. Tolerance wasn't a necessary quality in a super-predator.

But more than that, it wasn't even really about conscious decision. *T. rex* simply followed an impulse – a very basic shine. Tyrannosaurs were very advanced for their *era*, having evolved pair-bonding, and the rudimentary emotional ties that go with it.

But they didn't *think*. Most often, they simply followed their nose.

Or in this case, they followed their shine, no different than a moth to light.

Caesar supposed he was no different, other than perhaps the self-awareness of it.

He knew perfectly well why he was on the mountain, enduring the storm, braving the thunder and lightning.

Shanna was up there somewhere – she was hurt, and he could feel her pain.

Knowing that, Caesar presumed the rex did too.

At the very least, that would make them protective and edgy.

And for better or worse, bringing up the rear, not much further distant, Caesar knew Brutus was bumbling his big, stupid way, right behind.

A testosterone-bloated moron to begin with, Caesar shuddered at the thought of Brutus in the later stage-infection of the Food of the Gods.

He could already hear the echoing bellows trading back and forth, like marching war-horns, leading an incursion.

Brutus was clearly intending to meet the rogue rex and his pack head-on.

Caesar would very much like to be off this mountain before that happened.

Shanna was not far ahead. Caesar had nearly reached the peak, and he could see a trundle of smoke billowing not half-a-mile away. If he moved quickly, there should be no need for confrontation of any kind.

The big ape stepped out of the trees into the open and was greeted by a lashing of lightning and thunder.

And standing in the path, directly in front of him, was the human who had shot him.

Mark turned, greeted by the sight of the giant ape framed in the electric backdrop of the storm.

In a flash, he brought his rifle to his shoulder.

Caesar had to hand it to the hapless hominid – he had fast reflexes.

At this close range, Caesar found himself looking at a likely head-shot. Unless he could squash him first.

Mark, for his part, didn't seem all that confident in the stopping power of his weapon, holding off on the trigger until there was no choice.

Caesar raised his arms. Mark tensed on the trigger.

The big ape's vocal-cords struggled, as he held open his hands.

"Shaahh-Naahh," Caesar growled.

Mark lowered his gun, staring up disbelievingly.

"Shaahh-Naahh? Who the hell is Shaahh-Naahh?"

"Actually," a voice said from behind them, "she's over here."

Caesar turned to see four more humans – two of them soldiers, *all* with guns – separating from the brush.

The two soldiers raised their own weapons, but the human who had spoken waved his hand.

"Hold it," he said, stepping in front of their line of fire. He also nodded to Mark, who had already lowered his rifle, before walking up to Caesar as if to shake the big ape's hand.

"You understand what I'm saying, right?"

Caesar made the international sign-language gesture for 'yes', but the group of humans looked at him blankly. With a grunting sigh, he simply held two fingers together in the okay-sign, while nodding his head.

"I don't believe I'm seeing this," one of the soldiers muttered.

Caesar rose to his full height.

"Shaahh-Naahh!" he insisted.

"That's right," Cameron said. "Shanna."

He pointed back the direction they had come.

"Can you help us?" he said.

Caesar again held up the *okay*.

Without waiting, Caesar began loping up the path towards the peak, leaving the humans to hurry along behind.

There was more than a storm on the horizon, and they didn't have much time.

CHAPTER 47

"A bunch of *T. rex* destroyed your base, General," Naomi said.

There was a long pause from the radio.

"And who might you be, Naomi?" Rhodes asked.

"Civilians onsite, sir," Naomi said. She glanced at Jonah. "Two of us."

"Where's Major Travis?"

"He's dead, sir," Naomi replied. "Everybody's dead."

There was a longer pause.

When Rhodes responded, his voice reflected a cut-your-losses calm.

"Okay," he said. "Naomi. Here's the situation. The largest bloom ever recorded has just sprouted, and if we can't stop it with a nuke, it is positioned to wipe-out the single largest surviving population of human beings left on the planet, along with the bulk of our remaining military assets."

Rhodes gave this a moment to settle.

"You," he continued, "are sitting at the site of the only non-corrupted nuclear asset left at our disposal. And you're telling me there's not one living pilot left on that base?"

Naomi turned and looked at Jonah.

"Oh God," she said. "Maybe."

Jonah's eyes widened.

"Wait a minute," he said. "I can't fly a fighter jet."

"Maybe?" Rhodes prodded. "Ma'am, I'm gonna need a little better than *maybe*."

Naomi handed Jonah the radio.

"*You* tell him," she said.

Frowning, Jonah grabbed up the speaker.

"My name's Jonah Kirkland, General. I'm a goddamn river-guide pilot. I've never flown anything like this in my life."

"Fair enough," Rhodes said. "Just letting you know what the stakes are, son. In case you missed it, the world already ended. Maybe you can keep our whole species from going out forever. Or maybe you can't. Maybe you'd just be giving your life up trying.

"It might even be," he said, "that you'll be safe out there. At least for a while. But I can assure you from the highest level, the apocalypse *will* finally come for you. This is an enemy that does not take prisoners."

Jonah shut his eyes. At this point, they all knew that enemy.

A parrot-talking little ghoul – a scaly little rat that called itself Otto.

God, he hated those little bastards.

"What are you made of, son?" Rhodes asked. "What do you want your life to mean?"

Jonah could feel Naomi's eyes on him.

The General was right on both counts. They *would* be safe here.

But sooner or later, the final purge would come.

Without opening his eyes, he clicked the radio.

"I'll do it."

Without missing a beat, Rhodes read off the mission perimeters – payload, coordinates, airspeed, firing mechanisms – all of which Naomi jotted down while Jonah sat rubbing his temple.

"God bless, son," Rhodes said.

Naomi took the mic.

"Yes, sir," she said, clicking off. She popped a new clip in her pistol.

"We've still got to get to the runway," she said.

"Assuming the planes are still there," Jonah muttered unhappily, following her back out onto the street.

The runway was perched over the cliff at the very back of the compound, and actually hadn't been touched.

On the other hand, that meant crossing the main grounds, right past what were still at least two live *T. rex*.

It seemed Jughead might have died – as if in sudden exhaustion, the teen rex had abruptly lain down his head, and there was a thick bubbling as labored breathing through bullet-holes rasped to a stop.

Archie still sat in a near trance, panting like a winded dog, lost in the pain of his injuries, the last sickle-claw's' legs still dangling from his jaws.

Rudy just sat silent, perhaps dozing... or perhaps eyeing them through that catlike slit in his eye.

If he decided to move, the big rex could be on them in a few steps.

That was assuming there were no more sickle-claws waiting in ambush.

And they knew there was still a troop of Ottos skulking about. That was undoubtedly why the tyrannosaurs still remained, waiting them out like cats outside their hole.

After a moment, Naomi stepped out into the open, her eye on Rudy, and began skirting her way past.

Mouthing silent curses, Jonah followed.

Rudy's slitted eyes were like a portrait's that just seemed to follow you.

Naomi glanced back impatiently, motioning Jonah to hurry.

Jonah found himself shaking his head, not for the first, but perhaps for the last time.

He just wasn't built for her speed. There was a fearlessness there he just couldn't relate to.

Jonah doubted Lieutenant Lucas Walker would have been trailing along behind her.

No – he actually knew *exactly* what Lucas Walker would have done – he would have gotten in that plane and saved the day, even at the cost of his life. He would have been a hero.

Would? Had. *Did*.

But he'd already given his life *last* time. Someone else had to step up.

The base had been on alert – the jets had been prepped for this very mission.

Two F-16s were parked on the runway, missiles already loaded.

The hatch was open and waiting, as if inviting him into his own coffin.

As he climbed into the cockpit, Naomi crawled into the seat behind him.

"What do you think you're doing?"

Naomi strapped herself in.

"You think I'm getting left behind here? I'm going with you."

"Of course you are," Jonah said. "We're going to crash, you know."

Naomi sat back.

"Who knows?" she said. "You might pull it off. You haven't killed us yet."

Jonah supposed that was faith of sorts.

"Not yet," he agreed.

"Besides," she finished, "you're going to need all the help you can get."

Jonah strapped himself in. It took him another minute to figure out how to close the hatch.

His hand literally trembled as he ran his hand over the controls.

As he did so, he caught skittering movement just outside.

"Jonah," Naomi said. "Look."

Scampering like three scaly gremlins along the wing of the second jet, also waiting prepped beside them, was that last little troop of Ottos.

They bounced into the cockpit. A second later, the hatch started to come down.

"That plane," Naomi said, "is loaded with a nuke."

Jonah shook his head.

"You can't possibly believe those little lizards can start that thing..."

The jets fired.

Jonah jumped at the sudden roar.

A roar that was answered a second later as Rudy was suddenly on his feet and moving towards them, jaws agape.

Archie started awake as well, clambering upright, his wounds suddenly forgotten.

"Oh shit, Jonah...!" Naomi blurted.

Jonah lit up his own jets. The roar and sudden burst of power was right up there with the most terrifying moments of his life.

Beside them, Otto's jet launched off the runway, arching into the sky.

With Rudy bearing down upon them, Jonah launched.

Naomi screamed aloud as the big teen *T. rex'* jaws smashed shut not a yard from their tail, while Jonah skidded them off the edge of the runway like a stunt-car leaping off a bridge, before arcing upwards in a struggling, wobbling climb, leaving the frustrated tyrannosaur roaring and stamping his feet on the tarmac behind them.

Jonah was nearly screaming himself, cussing a blue streak, as he wrestled the joystick, fighting to pull them out of the sheer climb.

Battling centrifugal force, Jonah strained until they bent into a gradual arc, and finally leveled out.

"Can I open my eyes?" Naomi hollered from behind him.

"I don't know," Jonah hollered back. "Can *I*?"

But as they angled south and then east, they saw the retreating jet wash of the other plane.

The sky ahead loomed dark – the entire eastern horizon looked like a brewing storm.

"Jonah," Naomi said again, "behind us."

Jonah turned his head to see the sky to the west had darkened as well.

These storm clouds, however, were alive.

It looked to Jonah like every damned pterosaur in the world – normals - circled like bats around the massive flying dreadnoughts of infected giants.

The winged-dragons' eyes glowed green like targeting missile sights.

They filled the entire sky.

Ahead of the flying horde, Jonah followed after Otto into the eye of the storm.

CHAPTER 48

The rex posed like a monolith on the precipice of the nearest peak. The storming clouds whipped like angry poltergeists as the raging colossus announced its claim on the mountain.

"Yes," Shanna whispered, "I see you."

Rosa guessed Shanna's age at no more than twenty-five – at least six years her junior. Yet, *Doctor* Rosa Holland found herself just like the others, gathered around this slight young woman, as if sitting at the wizened knee of her own grandmother.

She could clearly see it in the others as well.

Allison was always cool under pressure – a dangerous lifestyle left you less likely to get rattled in a crisis. But this was different – this wasn't her being stoic. Allison simply rocked under Bud's protective arm, taking the echoing bellows below in the same stride as the thundering storm clouds above – and her calm translated to Lucas, who had spent the hours as if by the living room fireplace.

Rosa supposed it was exactly as Shanna had said – at one time cave-children would have huddled just like this, soothed and rocked before the fire, with the bellows of beasts in the background – they had to be *taught* to fear the circumstances, and Lucas didn't feel it from his mother.

Nor from any of them, Rosa realized.

They all might be looking at the end of their lives, but in Shanna's presence, they weren't afraid.

The giant rex standing atop the mountain was the harbinger, as a rex had been in New York.

As Shanna told it, *T. rex* was the wild-card – on one hand, the foil – on the other, the catalyst that had forced Otto's own hand.

KT-day had always seemed a bit... rushed.

Once the Big Rex had touched down in New York, only then were belated blooms initiated all over the world.

At what point did Otto recognize the rex' defiance?

And to what degree was that defiance exacerbated by the presence of Shanna herself?

That was another thing Shanna suspected her father knew.

"Someone," she said, "leaked footage off that island."

Shanna had nodded affirmatively.

"My father was... fading. His dementia was advanced. But he had his good days too."

Shanna shut her eyes.

"My mother died when I was young. I wonder now if that's why he was afraid."

Rosa actually felt a sense of closure in her own mind as Shanna connected long-separated dots for the first time.

"That," Shanna said, "would explain why he contacted Kate Rhodes. The daughter of a General. *And* a crusading evangelic journalist known for blowing big, loud whistles." She shrugged. "Maybe he even intended to use her to get me off the island."

Shanna smiled a little.

"He was looking out for me," she said. "And he was in his right mind."

Shanna fell silent, ceding to the wind.

But the wind itself ceded to the roars of the beasts.

And as the lightning lashed down on the neighboring summit, they could see that the rex had not arrived on the mountain alone.

Josie and the pussycats lined up beside him, facing down into the canyon, spotlighted by the electric light-show.

The first of the five armies, Rosa thought.

And what yet waited, still hidden in the storm?

"My father knew," Shanna whispered, seemingly to herself. "He was just too late to stop it."

After a moment, Mr. Wilson asked, "How come *you* didn't know? I mean, couldn't you *feel* them out there?"

An ironic smile touched her lips.

"I *did* feel them," she said. "Every day of my life. Concentrated on that island. I never knew anything else. On the mainland... I just didn't notice.

"And," Shanna said, thoughtfully, "Otto. I think he's been learning to hide from me for a long time.

"Although," she said, "just lately, it's been different."

Shanna shut her eyes as if scenting the air.

"I can feel him out there again. And I can feel him trying to get to me. Those smelling salts in the brain."

Her eyes narrowed. "Those mind-zaps of his – they get stronger when there's a lot of them." She shook her head. "But before, they were able to drop me in my tracks. They can't do that anymore. I can feel them trying. I can feel *pressure...*"

Shanna put her hand to her head. "But I can push back now."

It was Allison who said it.

"Are you pregnant?"

And Shanna nodded.

"I think so."

"Does Cameron know?" Rosa asked.

Shanna smiled. "I haven't said anything, but I think so." She shrugged. "We really don't have secrets."

Rosa supposed they wouldn't. She actually found herself a little jealous – having known a conniving bastard or two, that was the sort of thing that couldn't be measured.

"And," Shanna said, indicating the towering shapes on the mountain, "I think *they* know too."

The second army had arrived.

Brutus and the apes lined the opposite peak, staring across the chasm at the rogue and his pussycats.

Grape Ape, Big Joe, and Konga all beat their chests as Brutus pounded the earth, as if to bludgeon the mountain into submission with his bare fists.

It was a gesture the rogue clearly took personally.

The giant rex began to move forward, down into the valley. Josie and the pussycats flocked beside him, jagged maws gaping wide and eager.

Brutus rose to his full height, answering with a mighty bellow as he led his own charge down the mountain, reveling in the rumble in the ground, as his troop came galloping along behind.

Sitting there helpless, front row to a death fight in her honor, Shanna covered her eyes – a single tear rolled down her cheek.

A second later, Allison did the same, followed by sniffles from Lucas.

It wasn't fear. Rosa could feel it herself. It was deep and painful regret.

The world itself seemed to quake as the beasts came crashing together, the echo ricocheting through the canyon, their enraged bellows drowning out the storm.

CHAPTER 49

This was not like the battle of Congo and Big Rex in New York. Brutus had never seen a tyrannosaur in his life, and the rogue had never once encountered a giant ape.

Yet, neither questioned what set them at each other's throats.

For the rogue, it was the instinctual response to a rival.

For Brutus, who was never the smartest of apes, it wasn't much more than that.

But neither of them had experienced each other's weapons.

The rogue's first strike was very near Brutus' last. The massive jaws lunged at him like a running tackle zeroing in on a runner.

On pure reflex, Brutus dodged, catching the rex' head in his brawny arms.

Now, the rex discovered the ape's own advantage as he found his jaws clamped shut.

With few other options than pure explosive power, the rogue pushed forward with its powerful hind-legs, slamming Brutus into the cliff wall.

At the very same moment, the rest of the ape-troop descended into the canyon, colliding with the pussycats, crashing together with impact enough to shake the entire mountain.

Grape Ape was not as nimble as Brutus, and Josie latched onto his wrist as he attempted to ensnare her jaws, sinking her armor-piercing teeth deep.

The giant gorilla screamed, reflexively pulling away, sinking the teeth deeper.

Big Joe came to his aid, smashing Josie across the skull with an uprooted tree.

Josie responded to the blow by clamping harder and shaking her head like a bulldog, biting Grape Ape's hand clean away. The giant ape screamed, rolling away, holding the spouting stump.

Big Joe struck the female rex again, even as the other two pussycats pounced on the wounded Grape Ape, bearing him to the ground.

Konga had joined Brutus against the rogue, leaping upon the giant rex' broad back. All three beasts crashed together against the canyon walls, breaking repeated avalanches off into the river.

The rogue thrashed wildly, like a bull trying to gore two rodeo-clowns at once. Brutus clung desperately, holding the deadly jaws shut, with Konga simply hanging on for dear life.

Josie swallowed Grape Ape's severed paw, turning her attention to Big Joe. The giant ape brandished his uprooted tree, this time thrusting it forward like a dagger, catching the female rex in her forward-facing eye. Josie howled, backing-up and nearly tripping over the pussycats as they tore Grape Ape apart.

Big Joe pounced on the advantage, charging Josie's unguarded legs, sending her tumbling to the canyon floor.

Joe brought the tree down again, this time aiming the sharpened edge for the downed tyrannosaur's throat. For Josie, it would have been over, except for the two pussycats who turned from Grape Ape's twitching corpse and attacked.

This was not predator-prey action – this was clan-warfare.

The jagged tree-trunk missed its mark on Josie's jugular, but still slashed her throat deeply. Bleeding badly, she staggered to her feet, while Big Joe turned to engage both pussycats as they circled, aggressively, jaws agape.

Brutus felt his grip on the rogue's jaws slipping. Bucking like a wild bronco, the rex threw Konga off his back, leaving Brutus wrestling the king tyrannosaur alone.

Konga landed hard, nearly at the feet of the pussycats. The two females immediately pounced, and would have sunk their teeth into the big ape's unguarded hide, if not for Big Joe charging suddenly forward, tackling both dragon beasts at once, sending them all three tumbling, while Konga scrambled to his feet.

Brutus felt himself lifted and slammed into the canyon wall.

This time the impact broke his grip.

With a grunt, Brutus threw the suddenly loose jaws aside, slipping clear, and circling back out into the center of the canyon.

The rex turned, its eyes blinking with a green glow that Brutus knew was reflected in his own.

He looked around. Grape Ape was clearly dead, although Josie also looked worse for wear, stumbling, and apparently blinded in one eye.

Konga and Big Joe squared-off with the two slowly advancing pussycats.

And for Brutus, the rogue.

As it should be.

Brutus beat his chest. *This* was what he was good for.

Caesar could be a philosopher all he wanted.

Brutus was in it to be king. That's what alphas did.

A sentiment clearly shared by the rex itself.

With a roar to cower the thunder, the rogue charged again.

CHAPTER 50

Mark was a dozen steps behind Caesar as the big ape burst from the trees, out onto the drop-off overlooking the cliff.

Once they were out in the open, the first thing that assaulted them was the rain, followed by blinding flashes of lightning and the roar of thunder.

But then, as Mark hiked up behind Caesar, they beheld the spectacle of the battle in the canyon below.

For several seconds, Mark found himself staring in awe. Even Caesar let out a subdued moan.

Then a voice called up from below.

"Hey!" Mr. Wilson shouted. "Is there an idiot named Maverick up there with you?"

"Right here, old man," Maverick shouted, jogging up with Garner and Wilkes on his heels. Puffing, as he brought the rear, was Cameron.

"Jesus," Garner said as they looked down into the canyon.

They could feel thunder of the battle in their feet, reverberating up through the ground as the impact tremors of their footfalls shook the entire mountain.

The view was... surreal – flashes of lightning cast a strobing effect like old-time stop-motion puppetry.

"Well?" Maverick said, looking down to the ledge below. "Any ideas?"

Caesar grunted, simply hopping down over the edge.

"Holy shit!" came Mr. Wilson's voice, wafting up, followed immediately by "Wait! It's *alright!*" from Shanna.

Caesar's approach, however, proved a little too direct as the big ape's weight pulled at the vines supporting the dangling chopper, yanking the roots free.

Perched over the hapless survivors on the ledge, the chopper started to drop.

With a herculean grunt, Caesar caught the metal bird's tail.

Straining, one hand clinging to the rock, he held on until everybody below pulled themselves clear, before dropping the chopper with a crash. It hit the ledge, tilting briefly, before tumbling over the edge, rolling and bouncing off the cliff wall, as it tumbled into the canyon.

The bonfire was dragged over with it, and without shelter, the sleet and the wind bore down mercilessly. Immediately, there was the sound of a crying infant.

Shanna looked up at the big ape, who she had never met.

Congo was really *all* their fathers. Caesar had his eyes.

"Take them first," Shanna said.

As Rosa bent to secure Shanna's leg, Caesar grabbed up a startled Allison, tucking her and Lucas into the crook of his arm. He grunted at Bud and Mr. Wilson, who exchanged glances briefly, before climbing up on the big ape's shoulder and grabbing a handful of fur as Caesar loped back up the cliff.

Allison had her eyes squeezed shut as Caesar handed her over the edge to Maverick and Garner. Cameron and Wilkes caught Bud and Mr. Wilson by the hand, pulling them up.

Caesar turned, ready to drop back down, when a sudden roar rattled the clearing.

Standing at the edge of the forest was Trix, with her own pack of pussycats.

The rex queen stepped forward, sensing Shanna just beyond the ledge.

She did not appreciate Caesar standing in the way.

Female tyrannosaurs didn't waste time with bluster – when she moved, it was right for the throat.

The group of humans leaped aside as Caesar stood up to meet her, grabbing the big female's jaws, and wrestling her away from the others.

At the forest's edge, little sister Velma and the two unnamed daughters moved in.

Garner and Wilkes raised their rifles, looking for a shot, but Caesar growled adamantly over his shoulder.

"Shaahh-Naahh!"

And from the cliff below, Rosa's voice echoed up over the wind.

"Hey! We're freezing to death down here!"

Garner frowned, before shouldering his rifle, and turning to the cliff.

Tumbling his length of rope over the edge, he handed one end to Maverick.

"You're anchor," he said, turning to Mark and the others. "All of you. Grab hold and get ready to pull for all you're worth."

With that, he slipped the rope around his hips and dropped over the side, sliding down, touching his feet off the cliff wall as he went.

Caesar, meanwhile, struggled to keep four *T. rex* occupied. His powerful arms latched around Trix' lethal jaws, keeping her turning, using her own massive frame to shield him from the other three, as they snapped at his haunches.

Allison huddled with Lucas, her pistol drawn, looking utterly useless as the eight-ton combatants dueled right over their heads.

On the ledge below, Garner jury-rigged Shanna's make-shift stretcher, tying her off, and motioning to Rosa to climb aboard.

"Hang on," he said, before hollering up the cliff. "Okay, bring us up!"

The four men holding the rope grunted as one, yanking them into the air.

A hundred feet, dangling by a rope in a storm.

Trix was working her way free of Caesar's grip.

As the big ape struggled to maintain his hold, he lost his balance and stumbled.

Caesar desperately clung to Trix' jaws, pulling her with him to the ground. There was a heavy crash as they hit the tarmac together.

But now Caesar was on bottom, and the rest of the pussycats circled in.

Behind them, Mr. Wilson reached down, catching Garner's hand, pulling them in as Maverick, Wilkes and Cameron hauled Shanna's stretcher over the edge.

Caesar caught Shanna's eye as Trix broke free on top of him, turning her massive jaws towards his throat.

In another moment, Velma and the others would pounce and the four of them would tear him apart.

Pushing Cameron and Rosa aside, Shanna sat up on her stretcher, her voice rising up into a scream.

"STOP IT!"

And they stopped.

In the breath of a moment, with Shanna's words echoing in the clearing and off the surrounding peaks, Trix paused, her jaws poised at Caesar's throat.

Sister Velma and the daughters cocked their heads like giant birds.

And down in the canyons below, with Shanna's cry bouncing off the canyon walls, the thunder of the battle rumbled to a stop, as even the infected giants paused, turning their glowing green eyes to the mountain peak above.

Even the storm seemed to hang on the moment, the very absence of thunder deafening by itself.

Cameron looked down at Shanna, wide-eyed.

"I didn't know you could *do* that."

"I didn't either," she replied, wide-eyed right back.

Shanna took Cameron's shoulder, pulling herself to her feet. Cameron's eyes cut nervously to the blinking pack of tyrannosaurs as she led him to where Trix still had Caesar pinned.

There was a brief murmur from the others as Trix' head dipped towards Shanna's outstretched hand – and sniffed it like a dog.

"Easy, girl," Shanna whispered.

Trix stepped away from Caesar, who rolled back warily. The other pussycats murmured.

"*Oookay*," Mark whistled through his teeth.

And at the edge of the trees, not five yards from his feet, the bushes suddenly burst like a flushed pheasant.

Mark caught the flash of miniature tyrannosaur teeth as Junior darted right past his leg over to Shanna's side, hopping up and down like an excited puppy.

Shanna reached to touch his snout and the little rex preened.

Mark glanced back at the bushes behind him. The little sonofabitch had been five feet from his ass this time – he'd never seen a rex turn away from a target before.

Eyeing the gathered rex pack warily, Mark edged away, only to be met with a growl from Caesar, who stared down at him threateningly.

Mark jumped back, looking at Shanna.

"What's *his* problem?"

Caesar signed briefly, and then held up two fingers.

"He says, 'the little bastard shot me'," Shanna interpreted. "'Twice'."

There was a crack of thunder, breaking the brief interlude.

Down in the canyon, the rogue rumbled a brief response.

As if sparked by the crack of lightning, Garner's radio suddenly barked static.

"... this is Captain Johnson. Come in. If anyone can read me, come in."

"Oh *hell* yeah," Garner said, grabbing up his radio. He clicked transmit. "Johnson," he said, "boy am I glad to hear from you."

"Garner! Hang tight. We're coming to get you."

But now Shanna turned to the canyons, as if listening.

The pause in the storm ended with a renewed blast of staccato lightning and thunder.

This time it was answered from beyond the canyon.

Brutus and the rogue turned their green glowing eyes to the surrounding mountains, where echoing bellows now sounded over the thunder.

"What," Rosa whispered, "is that?"

Shanna shut her eyes.

"Escalation," she said. "Exponential escalation."

The earth beneath their feet trembled.

Over the peaks, the first of the titans appeared.

Sauropods – infected giants – some of them carrying their heads over a thousand feet high. Armored and horned ceratopsians and ankylosaurs, dreadnoughts designed to fight tyrannosaurs. And flesh-eaters – carnosaurs, megalosaurs, giant carcharodonts.

The first of them were still indistinct, misted by the billowing clouds.

But their glowing green eyes shined through.

Up on the edge of the cliff, Junior suddenly hissed, turning to the forest, back arched like a dog pointing out a hidden bird.

As they all turned, the trees at the edge of the clearing were suddenly filled with sickle-claws.

And skittering among their feet, warbling like loons, was a troop of Ottos.

In a squawking mob, the sickle-claws attacked.

CHAPTER 51

"What's happening out there, Hicks? Where are you?"

Rhodes was standing, facing east, honing in on the battle like a divining rod. Hicks' voice scratched back over speakers.

"We're about fifty-miles out of Maelstrom, sir. We've picked up a survivor. We're bringing her in with us."

"Bring in whoever you want, Lieutenant," Rhodes responded. "But all other considerations are secondary to recovering our asset. Understood?"

"Johnson's already in the area, sir."

"Time counts, Lieutenant. You've got incoming, both on the ground and in the air, both enemy and friendly fire. You've got the biggest bloom ever recorded. Best-case scenario, the whole area is a nuclear dust-cloud in thirty-minutes or less. You've got until yesterday to get in and out, with less margin for error than that. Understood?"

"Understood, sir," Hicks responded.

Sally took quiet note of that word *asset* again.

"Who's Shanna?" she asked.

Rhodes turned to her slowly.

"How do you know that name?" he asked.

Sally blinked.

"I don't know."

Rhodes glanced to Shriver.

"Shanna Hinkle," Shriver said, "is perhaps our single most important asset, and our biggest hope for the future lies within her mind."

"And," Shriver added, "perhaps within her DNA, as well."

Shriver's brows furrowed as he spoke, like a far-sighted man trying to spot something on a detailed chart.

Perhaps with a touch of obsession.

"The human race," Shriver said, "is now an endangered species. Within her lies the potential to eliminate genetic defects. She would be an invaluable asset to the Arc Project."

"At the moment," Rhodes interjected, "that is still secondary to eliminating the threat that damn near wiped us out in the first place." He eyed Shriver seriously. "And if we get her here, you're working for *her*. That clearly understood?'

Shriver nodded. "Absolutely, sir."

Rhodes turned to Sally.

"What's the word on our jet-pilot?"

"Nothing, sir."

Rhodes shut his eyes.

Major Tom's follow-up estimate was also not encouraging.

"I've got a convergence, sir," Tom radioed in. "I've got satellite-imagery onsite. It's... it's an army, sir. Biggest I've ever seen."

"Where did they all come from?" Sally asked.

"From everywhere," Tom replied. "At a steady walking pace an infected giant can cross most states in less than a day."

"The rate of infection," Shriver said, "indicates direct injection." He shook his head. "The missing pneumatic needles."

"That jibes with data, sir," Major Tom confirmed. "I've got no normals visible at all."

"How soon before they overtake our rescue site?" Rhodes asked.

"They're already there, sir," Tom replied.

CHAPTER 52

Mega-beasts – that's what the press called them in the first days after KT-day.

Of course, the first few days were all the press had, so the phrase never really went viral.

But Rosa was reminded of it now, as monolithic monsters seemed to materialize out of the storm, like Lovecraftian Elder Gods manifesting across some dimensional plane, marching to an entourage of lightning and an accompaniment of thunder.

There was no way to guess their numbers, but they were legion.

The already-unstable earth rumbled as the first of them hit the valley floor.

Titanosaurs – largest of sauropods – infected beast-gods.

At their heels, were the shields and horns of ceratopsians.

It certainly looked like coordinated behavior.

Otto's beasts had the madness, but they didn't attack each other.

The united front of apes and *T. rex*, however, proved a tougher nut to crack than the sheer overwhelming numbers and pure physical mass might have indicated.

Ceratopsians were designed to kill *T. rex*, but they had no particular adaption to the giant apes who ran among them, grabbing their horns like over-muscled cowboys wrestling steers, twisting their necks until they cracked.

And sauropods, while indomitably powerful, had receded from the fossil record as tyrannosaurs came on the scene – big meant slow, and an easier target for those jaws. The rogue and his pussycat entourage savaged their giant legs and calves like wolverines hamstringing elk.

Most importantly, the canyon was narrow.

There were only so-many thousand-foot sauropods that could shoulder through at a time, and once the first of them went down, they started tripping over each other.

Brutus and the apes twisted the heads off the fallen ceratopsians, creating impromptu spiked shields.

The rogue and the pussycats simply bit anything that moved.

It was on the cliff above, however, where the more crucial battle was fought.

Otto had clearly learned not to send carnosaurs on commando missions. Besides being a good degree or two dumber, even the big carcharodonts simply couldn't match a tyrannosaur tooth-to-claw.

Sickle-claws, on the other hand, operated like a band of ninjas – especially effective if your target was *just* past a rex' giant ankles.

This was where the human contingent finally earned its keep, as Garner and Wilkes picked them off like shooting ducks.

Allison also acquitted herself quite well, handing Lucas off to Bud as she dropped one attacking dromaeosaur after another in single shots.

Cameron and Maverick contributed a lot of fired bullets – some of which probably landed.

Maverick paused to reload, for a moment inattentive. When he turned, he found a sickle-claw already in mid-leap.

Huddling just behind him, hovering over Shanna, Rosa abruptly bolted forward in a running shoulder-charge and physically knocked the beast off its pins.

The sickle-claw righted itself quickly, only to be blown permanently off its feet by Maverick, in three successive shots.

Maverick cast Rosa an approving eye.

"Owe ya dinner for that one, honey."

In the midst of it all, he actually had the sheer gall to wink. Rosa took her own moment to shudder.

Caesar had purloined the trunk of a large tree, and was swatting the mobbing dromaeosaurs aside in wide, sweeping back-and-forth strikes.

From the *T. rex*, it was actually Junior who did the most significant damage.

In true rex-fashion, he darted past the sickle-claws, going unerringly for the Ottos scurrying among them.

That in itself served to break the ranks of the dromaeosaurs.

Rosa had seen it before. She was not sure if it was precisely mind-control, but you put a couple of them on a big carnosaur's back, it went the way they wanted. There were always gaggles of the little lizards scattered across the backs of infected giants, scurrying like lice.

And normal sickle-claws just seemed to become like trained attack dogs.

Rosa had noticed a spike in her sinuses whenever the scaly little rats were about, like a mote of virulent pollen, sometimes even painful, watering her eyes. Allison had remarked the same thing. Bud had shrugged, oblivious.

Every indication was that the rex felt it too – except it just made them mad.

Junior had taken out two of the little bastards before being chased aside by the larger dromaeosaurs, who sent the little rex tumbling.

The sickle-claws' target, however, clearly was Shanna.

In utter careless disregard, they braved the stamping feet and jaws of the rex pack, as they tried to slip even one of them past.

Bullets were no deterrent, nor were the kicking corpses of their fellows – Mr. Wilson clobbered one skulking individual with a stick – but the clawed-devils had arrived in numbers, and they just kept coming.

Over the din of gunshots, warbling shrieks and reverberating bellows, Rosa almost didn't notice the additional blast of wind from overhead.

Even the roar of the rotors was almost muted by the crash of battle and the rumble of the storm, as the military chopper suddenly appeared, circling above.

CHAPTER 53

The temperature in the ISS was dropping.

Tom knew he had to abandon ship – he just had to make sure the ship went *down*.

Load the neighboring compartments with hydrogen gas, set a fire. That ought to do it.

There were two lifeboats set to a default re-entry trajectory. All he had to do was push a button.

If he could make it to one of the boats alive.

Otto had gotten into the life-support – or at least one of them had – he still didn't know how many there were.

It was getting cold. He didn't have much time.

Rhodes had asked him to hold out as long as he could, but he was about there. Bottom line, he had to be alive enough to destroy the station.

He took one last look at his screens. There was nothing more he could do. The silos had been shut down. The sub-launch had been put on hold.

Tom glanced at the sub-screen again – the one piece of equipment in the modern US navy arsenal that could interact with the ISS on its own tech-level – while Tom talked to a General on radio, he had a video screen for Captain Mason.

The sub's launch was active and appeared to be counting down.

Rhodes likely had no way of knowing.

Tom punched up Mason's line.

"Captain? Why are you counting down? You were confirmed on stand-down."

The image of Mason blurred.

When the screen returned, it was still an image of Captain Mason – except now he was a half-eaten corpse lying across his desk, probably weeks old.

Gibbering and dancing onscreen beside him was Otto.

Tom took a slow breath of cold air.

Nuclear sub-launches were actually both harder and easier than people thought.

The codes both for firing and targeting were already on-board – you just had to get into the safe.

It also required the participation of almost every member of the crew to achieve launch depth, activate all the appropriate keys – and any change in targeting would require PhD-level understanding.

Check on all counts.

Otto had just become a nuclear power.

And one about to announce its presence with authority.

Otto left the feed open as he counted down.

Lack of concern? Or perhaps perverse sadism – wanting him to see?

Tom looked at the screens – all the highlighted targets.

Remaining human enclaves. Rex populations, in particular.

What would be the first target?

Or would they just fire all of them, hail-Mary, all at once?

And why the hell not? This was pure nihilism.

Tom punched up Rhodes' line, even though he knew it was already too late.

CHAPTER 54

It turned out there was a reason the USS Anchorage survived the Megalodons. And it wasn't by hovering at the bottom.

Sharks are extremely primitive animals with no trainable behavior to speak of, but they could be counted on to respond reliably to certain basic stimulus.

Megs, like pretty much any fish, would hit anything they perceived as prey, and ignore anything that wasn't and didn't pose a threat.

Neither of those were particularly difficult buttons to push.

Otherwise, a submarine simply assuming launch depth would practically be waving a red flag.

Within the sub itself, the little lizards skittered about, flitting like birds from perch to perch, station to station, as the Anchorage counted down its launch.

There were a dozen warheads aboard, and every one of them was ticking down.

Clawed hands began to turn the launch keys.

Large shapes circled the sub as it approached the surface, but the Anchorage moved with impunity.

Blooms sprouted underwater as well as on land, and once the Megalodons were infected, they effectively became an impenetrable barrier – there were extremely few other sea-monsters that would brave Meg territory. One of the largest shapes turned in the direction of the Anchorage.

A normal Meg could reach seventy-feet – the Food of the Gods magnified that tenfold.

This creature, however, was no Meg.

It was, in fact, perhaps the one sea-beast that could swim among them unconcerned.

Pliosaurs were technically short-necked plesiosaurs. In practical fact, they were like seals with the jaws of a crocodile.

And for whatever reason, they shared with tyrannosaurs a particular resistance to dominance – a resentment – and they did not at ALL like that psychic stench on the brain.

Jaws bigger than the Anchorage itself split, as the pliosaur bore down, clamping onto the sub like a gator snapping up a trout.

The sub exploded in the pliosaur's jaws, seconds from the first launch.

Two-hundred and twenty miles above, Major Tom, who had just raised General Rhodes, shrugged.

"Well," he said. "Never mind. I guess we don't have to worry about that one."

CHAPTER 55

The canyon was bloody slaughter – rabid titans killing each other.

In the narrow valley, giant corpses piled between the cliff walls like a dead-fall, damming the flow of the invading army.

Brutus and the rogue stood atop the mountain of carrion, facing off the relentless march of beasts.

The storm yet masked their numbers beyond the canyon, but they went on for miles.

Brutus and the rogue were the last of the defenders.

Big Joe had gotten between two carnosaurs and a bull Triceratops. He managed to break one of the big meateater's necks – a large Allosaurus – before the trike gored him. He might even still have gotten away except for the second carnosaur, this one a much larger carcharodont, got a free strike with its saw-blade jaws from the back.

The teeth cut deep across his shoulder into Big Joe's neck, and might have caught his jugular, but it quickly became irrelevant as the trike bored in again, spearing the big ape deep in the chest, and finally bearing him to the ground.

Konga had tried to trip up a titanosaur with his horned-ceratopsian shield and gotten himself trampled.

Josie and the pussycats had the most difficulty with the trikes – *T. rex* simply hadn't evolved to fight a ceratopsian face-to-face – it would have been stupid. A hunting tyrannosaur bit Triceratops from *behind*.

Circumstances, however, put them nose-to-nose. Worse, there was the sheer fact of numbers.

To their credit, the pussycats got their bites in.

Josie accounted for two-dead trikes, with the horns and shield bitten away from two others, before they surrounded her, gouging her legs in the manner of modern boars, before taking her down.

Not one of the pussycats fell without at least a *piece* of someone's ass in their teeth.

But now it was almost over.

Having gained the high-ground, through the sheer accumulation of piled corpses, Brutus and the rouge had so far held off the horde. But the relentless march hadn't slowed, and the invading beasts continued to funnel into the valley.

Brutus knew they were fighting to the end. Perhaps it was even a blessing, as the cycle of madness need not run its course.

And he knew he had given Shanna her window – a chance to get away.

That's what he was good for.

The rogue knew none of this. It had followed a light. Now it was being attacked. All its actions were cause/effect.

It would fight to the end, because that was all it knew to do.

And so it stood beside Brutus, the two of them framed in the storming electric light-show, staring down from the mountain of their slaughtered foes, daring ever more.

Brutus glanced at his impromptu ally – only a short while before, the rogue had been at his own throat.

Now he prepared to die fighting beside him.

They turned together to face the horde...

... even as somewhere in the sky above, there came the roaring sound of twin jet engines approaching fast.

CHAPTER 56

"There's our ride," Garner shouted, as he waved at the chopper.

His radio barked alive. Captain Johnson's voice.

"Anyone left alive down there, Garner?"

"Not if you don't get us the hell out of here," Garner shouted back.

From the chopper above, gunfire erupted.

Trix roared in outrage as bullets dotted her hide. Caesar growled, covering up.

"Hold your fire, goddamn it," Garner yelled into his radio.

Johnson's voice coming back was incredulous.

"Are you kidding?"

"Shoot the sickle-claws," Garner shouted back. "Leave the big ape and the tyrannosaurs alone."

With more directed fire, the chopper was able to clear a path to land.

Garner and Wilkes both waved. "Let's go!"

Ducking under the still-spinning rotors, Allison climbed on board, clutching Lucas, followed by Bud and Mr. Wilson.

Still exchanging gunshots, Mark glanced at Maverick.

"Maybe this is a bad time to mention this, but I'd really rather not end up in military custody."

Maverick glanced up at the chopper, eyeing the pilot and the soldiers helping the others on-board.

"Don't worry about it," he said, pulling another shot.

Rosa climbed aboard, reaching for Shanna as Cameron carried her on one shoulder. But Shanna stopped, turning to Caesar, even as the big ape cleared the way, waving his broken tree trunk at any encroaching sickle-claws that remained.

Caesar glanced over his shoulder.

In that same growly voice, he said, "Go-ohhh. Ru-uhh-nnn."

Shanna turned to the canyons, where Brutus and the rogue faced-off Otto's advancing army.

It didn't matter for them. They were already under a death-sentence.

Shanna turned, climbing on-board. Cameron hopped up behind her. Then Maverick and Mark, as the craft lifted into the air, buffeting in the heavy crosswind.

Caesar stared up after the departing chopper as it was carried away in the storm.

Beside him, Trix and Velma and the other two pussycats stared up as well.

And somewhere over the buzz of rotor blades, the crash and bash of the storm, and the battle yet raging in the canyons below, Caesar's sensitive ear picked up the sound of a jet engine.

Turning to the west, he saw approaching twin flares.

Shanna was safe and away. It was time to get the hell off this mountain.

And as if it was an option, he somehow felt he couldn't leave Trix behind.

As the rex pack's attention focused on their fading star, Caesar turned and bounced his broken tree trunk off Trix' broad nose.

Then he turned and ran for the hills, with the furious rex pack hot on his heels.

CHAPTER 57

The two F-16s spun together as they charged into the billowing black clouds.

Jonah didn't know where that goddamned lizard learned to fly, but he was a sight better at it than *he* was.

He could see them in the cockpit as the twin jet made sweeping passes like a hawk. Jonah wasn't even sure which one of them was flying – maybe they *all* were – they danced in the pilot's seat like monkeys.

"He's coming in again!" Naomi shouted as the F-16 dogged their tail like a thing alive, alternating between trying to shoot them down, and driving them into the flocks of pursuing pterosaurs – some of the infected giants with wingspans reaching four-hundred feet or better.

An F-16 could handily beat even an infected giant's top air-speed, but they were swarming out of the trees, all along their path, threatening to cut in front of them. To avoid the seemingly suicidal mobbing pterosaurs, Jonah was discovering the fighter's full-range of capabilities.

He had met a few fighter pilots while gaining his own license, and had watched them run their exercises. Never once had he the *slightest* urge to try it – it was terrifying to watch from the ground.

Jonah wondered if Naomi was as scared as he was. She had shrieked at their initial take-off, but had manned the rear cockpit mostly with open eyes.

"Watch it!" Naomi shouted into his headset.

Otto's plane twisted acrobatically, this time bee-lining physically right at them, apparently happy to crash them both.

Which caused Jonah to wonder about the nuke on Otto's own wing. He knew they weren't supposed to go off in a crash, or even an explosion, but it didn't seem prudent to test it.

Otto sure didn't seem concerned.

And as they flew into the heart of the storm, and visibility quickly dropped, it was harder to see them coming – not to mention the giant pterosaurs.

That was another thing – you never saw pterosaurs, or birds for that matter, out in harsh weather – yet the flocks of flying dragons hung doggedly on their tail, no matter how many of them were battered down by the winds, or electrocuted by lightning strikes, or simply drowned in mid-air – and they *had* to be flying blind.

Jonah sure was. The artificial horizon blinked on the screen like an arcade-game.

Their target was twenty-miles ahead – he was firing by virtual line-of-sight at a target he wouldn't even be able to see.

Although, he supposed close *counted* in nukes and horseshoes.

They had the coordinates entered into the artificial horizon.

For all Jonah knew, he might as well shut it off and use the Force.

Above and to the rear, Otto's jet broke through the clouds, like a hawk.

"He's getting behind us," Naomi shouted into his ear.

The warning came just as bullets riddled their right wing. Jonah spun them off before the engine was hit.

But the pursuing jet was on their tail in seconds. Jonah was waiting for the shots when the radio suddenly blared in his ear.

"Rhodes wants an update," Naomi said, grabbing up the radio. "We're a little busy, General," she said into the mic.

Rhodes wasn't feeling patient.

"Where the hell are you? What the hell is going on?"

"Coming up on our target, sir," Naomi replied, with even less patience. "And right now we're being attacked by lizards in an F-16, and giant flying dragons, so can we call you back?"

As terrified as he was, Jonah almost snickered over that one.

Rhodes was silent a moment, and Jonah could almost hear him steaming.

Nevertheless, his voice was steady.

"We're counting on you."

Naomi clicked off, turning to look as Otto moved in again.

Jonah glanced over his shoulder – they were in gun-range.

"Well," Jonah said, "saw this in a movie once. Hit the brakes and they'll fly right by."

Jonah turned the flaps, jerking them upright as if they'd hit a wall, at the very moment Otto opened fire.

Bullets riddled the wing again, but the pursuing jet overshot, and went sailing past.

"Son of a bitch," Jonah said, with Otto now in his sights. "It worked."

As he opened up his guns, he wondered again about the nuclear payload.

Oh well – it *shouldn't* go off.

Jonah's bullets caught Otto's engines and the plane exploded.

The wreckage went spinning earthward, disappearing quickly in the storming clouds.

Now, that just left every bat-winged monster out of hell.

At this point, only the infected giants were successfully battling the storm.

"We've got a big one on our tail," Naomi said.

Jonah glanced over his shoulder as the massive shadow descended down like a winged-dreadnought. He could see the glowing green eyes through the storm.

They were nearing firing range – their target, the expanse of valley beyond the highest peak.

On their starboard, the bullet-riddled engine flamed out.

"Jonah..." Naomi began.

"I know," he said, already feeling the F-16 slipping out of his control

Jonah fired.

This missile streaked away, leaving a tracer-trail through the clouds.

Jonah veered off.

That's when the giant pterosaur caught them, on the curve – just barely catching their wing with its snapping beak.

The engine was ripped loose.

They were soaring in free-fall as the nuclear cloud mushroomed on the horizon, for a single moment more powerful than the storm.

And then the blast wave came, blowing the clouds along with it.

Jonah felt the wave hit them and the jet was sent spinning.

Then Naomi screamed in his ear.

"Jonah!"

The pterosaur was coming in again, riding the wave, its jaws outstretched, and Jonah saw that it was going to reach them.

He hit eject.

The hatch blew and both their seats fired into the air just as the giant beak smashed into the fuselage. The F-16 exploded.

Naomi's automatic chute opened, immediately catching in the buffeting wind.

Above her, she saw the pterosaur arcing away, spitting out smoking pieces of jet.

Below, she saw Jonah's chute open, spinning in the gale like a seed-leaf.

He hung limp in his harness, his face covered in blood.

Naomi called his name as they were carried into the storm.

CHAPTER 58

Brutus saw the missile sailing past overhead. He was probably the only one left alive on this side of the mountain who knew what it meant.

Oblivious, Otto's inexorable marching army had begun to pile upon itself as they crowded into the wall of corpses, until they were starting to flood their way over the top like gigantic swarming insects.

The rogue stubbornly held its ground. It perceived the missile as clearly as Brutus, even registered it as a potential threat like one of the sky beasts, but dismissed it quickly once it passed on, arcing past the edge of the canyons where the invading army's true numbers lay.

The rex also sensed Shanna's fading aura, and perhaps some part of it perceived that this battle was on her behalf.

When the blast came, the rogue was still at the top of the hill, still swinging, still king under the mountain – for a rex, that was enough.

Brutus paused right at the last, watching the dark, storming horizon in the moments after the missile passed out of sight.

Then there was the flash of light – a sense of warmth and wind.

He felt no pain.

CHAPTER 59

Major Tom saw the nuke from space.

Then the lights in the ISS went out.

It was not a complete power-cut – computer screens still blinked, but the heat was dropping fast. He had minutes.

He had already gathered several hydrogen tanks and had gone module by module, setting them on slow release, propping the sealing doors open with pieces of machinery. The last one he planned to set near the orbit-stabilizer engine at the far end of the station, one module over from the nearest lifeboat.

Then start a fire – that should do it. He had a butane torch ready.

He'd already covered the Japanese and American sections of the station.

The hard part was going to be getting to the rear engine at the far end of the Russian modules.

The two Ottos who'd escaped were skulking somewhere on the other side of that sealed door, somewhere along the tunneled path to both those modules.

He didn't even know how many of them there really were. They were small enough to hide in the walls or inside pipes, and they had gotten into the electrical, for sure.

Tom had been doing a last minute search of each module on the security monitor when the lights shut off.

His monitor blinked and the screen was suddenly filled with the faces of toothy gremlins – definitely more than two – small, but with *big* claws.

And now he was going to have to get past them in the dark.

The compartments behind him should be full-up with gas. Catching a quick breath, he opened the rear of the module, while slipping out and sealing the front hatch behind him.

Tapping the wall console, he programmed a five-minute reset on the air-lock.

Then he turned, shining his light down the dark corridor as he tapped his way cautiously along the walls, the last gas tank held out weightlessly in front of him, like a cameraman underwater.

He passed over the first of the lifeboats on the way to the engine, and was sorely tempted to just drop below and abandon ship. But if the remaining components simply broke away as the gas lit, the independent modules could quite possibly survive.

As Tom shined his light down the dark corridor, he saw the connecting airlocks between each section were all open.

The little bastards were waiting for him somewhere.

On the walls, all the little blinking lights looked like eyes reflecting in his flashlight.

He pushed through the first module, over the second lifeboat hatch, and into the rear component connected to the engine.

That was when they came at him in the dark.

His light-beam caught the flash of claws as they went for his eyes, slashing at his face. Tom spun, swatting with the flashlight, and then he turned on the torch.

A burst of flame shot out, illuminating the compartment, and barbecuing one of the little bastards like a crow on a power-line. He fired a torch-blast after the others, who scattered. He kept the flame on until they retreated the module.

He waited another moment before moving on. He couldn't let the torch run empty, and he couldn't use it once he set the gas – unless Otto forced this into a suicide mission, and that hadn't been decided, yet.

Tom turned on the gas, letting the canister spin slowly, as he reset the door behind him.

Now right above the first of the lifeboats, he turned the torch on the walls, lighting the insulation, before spreading it to the counters and equipment – anything that would burn.

They were waiting for him as he started down the hatch to the first lifeboat.

In the dark, it was hard to tell how many – he felt their claws digging his chest and arms as he covered his face.

The tight-quarters, however, gave Tom the advantage, provided he was willing to bleed. He braced against the walls and started kicking and thrashing, crushing the seagull-sized lizards with sheer physical strength. Then he fired another blast from the torch, this time down the hatch as the Ottos fled into the escape pod.

Leaving the flame on, Tom wedged the torch in the lifeboat's air-lock as it automatically tried to close, preventing it from sealing, and flooding the compartment in fire. The trapped Ottos screamed.

Pushing back up into the main module, Tom pulled himself over the second lifeboat.

The door to the Destiny module would be resetting soon, opening and flooding the rest of the station in gas – a touch of flame would be all that was needed.

There were more of the lizards waiting for him in the cargo-block as he made his way to the second lifeboat. They pushed off the walls, coming at him, claws outstretched. Tom batted them away with the flashlight, grabbing hold of one that latched onto his leg and simply breaking its neck like a chicken's.

As he slid down the hatch into the second remaining lifeboat, he again felt their claws in the dark.

Taking the cuts, he crushed them against the walls, seeing droplets of his own blood floating in the air like soap bubbles, reflected in the flashlight's beam, even as he bludgeoned the scaly little rats back and forth.

Tom heard the seal to the Destiny module reset and slide open. In another moment, the rest of the air-locks throughout the station would follow.

There was a poof of wind as the gas caught, igniting an explosion of fire from above. There was the squealing warble from the lizards.

Tom pushed back into the lifeboat, still choking one of the little bastards in one hand, as he sealed the hatch behind him and pressed the emergency launch.

The lifeboat fell away from the station as each compartment first exploded into flame, rupturing, and then imploding.

As the module above him lit up, Tom thought he might have been a bit too late.

The hatchway behind the sealed pod-door burst at the very moment the pod broke away, and the lifeboat went spinning, its control board going haywire with the abruptly broken contact.

Tom looked out the window as the ISS finished destroying itself.

In his hand, that last little Otto twitched.

Slow and deliberate, Tom twisted its neck until it snapped.

"Bastard," he muttered.

He shut his eyes, waiting for the life-pod to right itself.

After an excruciatingly long several minutes, the computer reset and the craft straightened out.

The life-pod was now poised over the planet below.

Tom wondered what might yet be waiting.

How many apocalypse-events did one world need?

The lifeboat began its slow tumble to Earth.

CHAPTER 60

Rosa didn't think they were going to make it – the winds were too strong.

The pilot strained at the joystick, keeping them on a steady climb, but Rosa could feel the crosswinds trying to flip them completely over.

The soldiers clung to their seats alongside the passengers, their part of the mission accomplished, now just praying with the rest of them that the pilot could pull off his.

Maverick glanced over at Mark and the two of them suddenly both rose, moving for the cockpit.

Rosa saw the look of purpose in Maverick's eyes and the small smirk that she was already learning to worry about.

"Hey..." she started, before Maverick stepped into the cockpit, turning the pilot in his seat and slugging him dead in the chin.

"Ow," Maverick said, shaking his hand, and tossing the pilot aside. "Hard jaw."

The pilot groaned, starting to sit up. As Maverick took the controls, Mark shrugged, turning and knocking the dazed pilot the rest of the way out.

Rosa hadn't even finished her inhale as one of the soldiers started to his feet.

"What the hell..."

But he stopped as Allison's pistol was suddenly pressed against his ear, Lucas, wrapped in a bundle, still hanging nonchalantly off of one arm.

The second soldier turned to find Cameron holding a rifle, comfortably straddled across his lap, aimed dead at his chest across the cabin.

Bud and Mr. Wilson nonchalantly relieved the two soldiers of their weapons.

The first soldier, whose badge identified as Johnson, turned to Garner.

"Are you just going to let them do this?"

Garner glanced back at Shanna.

Then he shrugged, nodding to Maverick.

"Well," he said, "we're already in the air, and right now, he's our only pilot."

At that, the chopper suddenly skewed sharply with the crosswind. Maverick cursed under his breath as he wrestled the joystick.

Mark looked at him sideways, and then back at the pilot he'd just knocked-out.

"Say," he said, belatedly, "you *can* fly this thing, can't you?"

"Crashed the last one," Maverick admitted. "But I think I've got the hang of it now."

Mark promptly buckled himself in.

The console radio barked General Rhodes' voice.

"Johnson? Are you there? For Christ's sake, we've got confirmed incoming, are you away?"

"Well, well," Mark said. "General Rhodes."

He picked up the radio.

"Johnson here, sir."

"What's your status, son? Incoming is imminent. Are you in the clear? Have you got our asset?"

Mark glanced back at their asset. Shanna smiled back, holding her fingers in an *okay*-sign.

"We've got her, sir," Mark said. "We are in the clear and we are on our way. Keep a candle burning for us."

Maverick took them up in altitude, and finally seemed to be outracing the storm.

The weather, however, suddenly wasn't the problem anymore, as the darkened sky abruptly lit up like a torch.

Now the heavy winds were all of a sudden at their back, as the blast wave hit, forcing the storm right along with it, evaporating the very water in the air, igniting bursts of lightning like charging electrodes.

Maverick rode the chopper like a surfer on a suicide wave, his voice a long, howling yodel.

"Ohhhhh *shhheeeiiiiittt!*"

Rosa squeezed her eyes shut, not certain if this maniac was her new hero, or if he was going to kill them all yet.

The chopper spun crazily, the passengers clinging to their seats.

Around them, the world had gone white, the water-vapor burned into a soup of fog.

The chopper leveled out and they hovered somewhere in the middle of the smoky mist, hanging in a ghostly twilight, utterly blind in the solid white.

Maverick let the chopper ride along the buffeting wind-currents generated by the blast wave.

Finally, the fog began to dissipate.

The high-energy still sparked balls of lightning and cracks of thunder, but the storm itself had been literally blown-out.

"I think we're clear," Maverick said, eliciting a collective sigh from the cabin.

Shanna, however, still had her eyes shut.

Rosa caught the sudden frown.

"Shanna?" Cameron said, alarmed. "Something wrong?"

But before she could speak, there came another rumble, this one louder than the thunder.

An explosion, coming from below, followed immediately by another.

Then there came a whole series of blasts, ever louder, like a run of firecrackers, all lighting up each other.

"Those aren't munitions," Garner said. "Those are demo-blasts."

Now there was a whole cacophony of explosions.

Rosa looked out the window as the chopper held steady, looking down at the mountain below.

"Oh my God," she whispered.

As far as the eye could see, the surrounding peaks began to explode – staccato blasts that kept on growing, echoing for miles.

There was a geothermic belch as the mountains responded.

"What's happening?" Rosa breathed.

"Escalation," Shanna said, without opening her eyes. "Exponential escalation. Beyond all possible reason."

She shook her head.

"What's worse?" she whispered.

Below them, the earth visibly rocked, as the very geography itself seemed to blur – the vibrations of a massive quake triggered by seismic blasts along the entire range.

They watched from above as the world seemed to break itself in half.

CHAPTER 61

Naomi pulled on her harness, trying to follow Jonah as he was buffeted in the aftermath of the blast wave.

The wreckage of the jet impacted the jagged precipice below and exploded in a flaming ball that immediately lit the surrounding forest.

Jonah, hanging limp in his harness, was following the same trajectory, and barely missed the flames as his parachute piled into the trees.

Straining on her own chute, Naomi angled in after him.

She hit the rocky slope, bracing the impact with her feet, cutting her harness away lest she get sucked by the wind right back up into the sky.

Jonah had been caught in the trees, and she could see him dangling ten feet from the ground.

Below him, ready to leap, were three sickle-claws.

Naomi was reaching for her pistol before she even blurted her first curse.

She dropped the first of them with a single shot, but missed the second as it leaped, catching Jonah's harness with its claws, and pulling him down.

"Bastards!" Naomi screamed, starting to tear-up.

She aimed her pistol again, fighting the tremble in her cold hands, controlling herself as her Lieutenant Lucas had taught her.

You had to be cool to be an effective killer, and Naomi found herself emotionally involved.

She let out a slow breath, shutting her eyes for one second.

When she opened them, both dromaeosaurs were perched on Jonah's chest, claws extended, cutting at his harness.

Naomi dropped them in two shots.

Sucking her breath, staying cool, she holstered her pistol and ran to where Jonah had fallen.

She kicked away the dead sickle-claws and bent over him. She tried checking for a pulse, but her own hands were too cold and numb to tell if it was there or not.

But as the straps fell away, his head dropped, utterly limp, making a loud *bonk* on the rock.

It was a chilling sound – colder than the ice in the storm.

Then she heard a groan.

Jonah's eyes blinked. *"Owwww."*

Naomi chirped a brief laughter, almost limp with relief, until she looked in his eyes.

He wasn't focusing. And his breathing was shallow.

Eleven months ago, Naomi had watched her husband die in a fiery explosion.

Today was more intimate.

She felt unwilling tears start to fall.

"You did it," she whispered. "You pulled it off. And you still haven't killed us."

Jonah tried to smile.

"Not... yet."

His voice was a failing whisper.

"If I died tonight," he said, "at least I got to have you."

He reached up and squeezed her fingers gently.

Then his hand fell away.

Naomi huddled over Jonah's still form.

She found herself remembering what she'd said to him back at the base – about their night together. At the time, she had thought she was being honest.

What she had actually been doing was rationalizing, trying to preserve a memory.

Lieutenant Lucas Walker had been her husband – he had been the best man she had ever met – ever *dreamed* of – her *hero*.

Every girl believes her man is special, but *her* man was one-of-a-kind.

The very idea of being happy with someone else, let alone some bush-pilot, threatened to cheapen the shrine she kept to him in her heart. And her memory was all she had of him. She didn't even have a picture.

Therefore, Jonah *had* to be an illusion.

Only now, here at the end, when it didn't matter anymore, did it finally occur to her that she might have simply been lucky enough to have found another good man.

After the end of the world.

Naomi lay her head down on his harness and wept.

And somewhere in the distance, she heard an explosion.

A military brat all her life, Naomi recognized a seismic charge.

There came another. And then a whole string.

Beneath her feet, she felt the first rumbling response in the earth.

Naomi looked up at the sky, where there was nothing but blank, misty white, and decided she was just too tired to run anymore.

As the earth began to shake, she held Jonah close and waited for the end.

But before that happened, she felt the rush of wind and the misty fog directly above was swept away by the blast of a rotor-engine blade.

Naomi looked up as the chopper circled down.

Half-a-dozen armed troops filed out, circling quickly, securing the area.

She'd seen Lucas do this in drills. She could tell this was a tight unit. All-American heroes, just like her man had been.

Naomi felt hands on her arms.

"Ma'am?" one of the soldiers said. "My name is Lieutenant Hicks. Are you injured?"

Naomi looked up at him, shaking her head, then back down at Jonah.

Hicks bent beside him, touching under his chin.

"I got a pulse," he said. "He's alive."

Naomi's heart skipped a beat.

"This the guy who was flying the plane?" Hicks asked, running a quick field check, looking for broken bones or obvious bleeding. "The General's gonna wanna meet this fella," Hicks said. "Let's see if we can keep among the living."

Beneath them, the ground was shaking harder, and from the nearest peak, came another series of seismic explosions, detonating all across the mountain.

This region was already unstable. It was always a volcanic range, but when the West Coast had broken loose, it triggered tectonic movement across the entire continent.

The Rockies were a natural break point.

"Sir?" one of the other soldiers said. "I think we better be getting the hell out of here."

Hicks nodded to Naomi.

"On board, ma'am," he said. "I'll take care of your fella."

"He's not my..." Naomi began, reflexively, but stopped and simply nodded.

"Please," she said.

Two other soldiers helped Hicks stretcher-up Jonah's unconscious form, and load him onto the chopper.

As Hicks pulled Naomi on-board, the earth was suddenly rocked again, and this time the quake didn't stop.

"Let's go!" Hicks shouted.

The chopper rose up into the air, even as the mountain began to break itself apart.

CHAPTER 62

The seismic blasts continued from the Midwestern United States all the way up through Canada.

Tom could see it from space.

And as he watched the mountains literally split the continent down the center, he now recalled all those topography maps, with thermal highlighting.

Kristie said she'd seen the lizards along her trek – and what she'd *thought* had been a military munitions unit, setting up seismic charges.

Tom was willing to bet those detonations were being set up for months, and no military, no *human* hand, had anything to do with it.

All those models, he thought, with thermal hotspots highlighted.

Detonation points. Spread out for five-thousand miles.

The semi-dormant volcano range was rumbling back to life. The skies filled with belching clouds of black smoke, from simultaneous eruptions along the entire length of the chain.

Circling in orbit, following the lifeboat's pre-programed path, Tom could see it all.

Tom tried to imagine what was happening on the ground. So far, his hail-frequency on the lifeboat had drawn no response.

He wondered what was waiting for him down there. He wondered if Rhodes would be able to find him once he touched down.

He *hoped* he landed in water. He also hoped there weren't any giant sharks or crocodile-toothed reptiles.

Perhaps more than anything, Tom hoped he'd get to meet Kristie, who'd been like a snapshot on the wall of his solitary prison cell for almost a year.

The first flames touched the metal of his lifeboat as the pod began re-entry.

After more than eighteen months in space, Major Tom was coming home to Earth.

CHAPTER 63

The upheaval lasted for the better part of a day.

It was doubtful anyone would ever be able to catalog the total number of eruptions along the entire chain, but the sky had grown nearly black with soot – black as sack-cloth made of hair.

Wildfires ran rampant, and when it was done, a new fault split the continental United States down the middle.

In spots, the broken chasm was separated by miles. All along the break was devastation.

Perched on the east side of the breach, Caesar looked out where the abrupt new canyon had fallen out of the earth.

Across the divide, staring back at him, was Trix.

Velma and the last two pussycats were gone, lost somewhere in the destruction.

Junior hovered at Trix' ankles, mugging at Caesar like a belligerent wolf-pup.

Shanna's aura had faded, but it was not gone. Caesar looked to the west.

He wondered if the rex would follow.

For his part, Caesar had left his tribe behind, and he had no idea how far the seismic upheaval might have spread, or how his people might have fared through it all. That was where his first duty lay.

But he believed he would see Shanna again.

For now, however, the west belonged to the rex.

Trix eyed him back – a dominant pack-leader, full of pregnant hormones – perched on her own side of the divide – simultaneously accepting those terms and claiming the entire region.

The big female rex let out a long trumpeting bellow that sent the message clearly enough.

That's your place. This is mine.

Caesar hooted back – just one parting taunt, before turning and disappearing into the tattered brush.

Trix stood at the opposite peak a moment longer.

And because tyrannosaurs don't think, she just followed her first impulse.

She still felt the light, somewhat more distant now, but having no further concern, Trix began to follow.

Junior tagged along at her heels.

CHAPTER 64

Maverick took them west as the wall of volcanic ash rose like a cloaked reaper, bigger than the sky.

Still latched in the co-pilot's seat, Mark cautiously unclasped one hand to point forward.

"I was on my way to the coast," he said. "That was my home."

Maverick glanced back to the others with a shrug.

Shanna had nodded. "I like that," she said. "Sold."

"First star to the left and straight on 'till morning," Maverick agreed.

Rosa tended to the deposed pilot – Bradbury, according to his badge. A young guy, he eyed Rosa doubtfully while she dabbed the blood off his lip, even as Cameron held him good-naturedly at gunpoint.

Johnson and Cooper, the two accosted gunners, found a decidedly less-friendly face as Allison leveled her pistol at the both of them.

At one point, Johnson shifted his feet, as if coiling to make a move, and Bud had uttered one sardonic chuckle, shaking his head mildly.

Cold-bloodedly deliberate, Allison pulled the hammer back on her pistol, even as she bounced Lucas on one knee. Johnson remained compliantly still.

Before long, they were passing over a new range of mountains.

Many of the peaks along the Northwest Cascades had already experienced minor eruptions over the last year, and most remained active, burping periodic smoke.

But the initial break-point had been almost eleven months ago, after San Andreas had broken away, and most of the local peaks were currently winter white.

Further west, the Cascade mountains gave way to what had once been a fertile valley.

Like everywhere, seismic upheaval had left its mark, not to mention giant trampling feet.

The terrain was scarred. New canyons existed where none had before, and entire swaths of forest had been stamped out and burned.

But this one little valley seemed largely untouched.

"There's a commercial airport near here," Mark directed. "We can refuel."

That almost got Johnson on his feet, but for the immediate hammer-cock of Allison's pistol.

"We've got to stick to the high-ground," Johnson objected. "The valley floor's not safe."

Behind him, Shanna shook her head.

"Not here," she said. "Not now."

The air-park was easy to spot among the surrounding farms. Maverick circled them down, cussing at the unfamiliar back rotor, as the chopper's feet landed heavily on the runway.

But they at least settled to a stop without flipping over.

Wilkes and Garner slid open the cabin door.

Garner turned to Johnson and Cooper, holding up their confiscated weapons. "So," he said, "you with us, or do we shoot you?"

Johnson and Cooper exchanged glances, then back at Allison's levered pistol, and shrugged, reaching for the rifles.

The four troops fanned out of the chopper, weapons drawn, forming a perimeter as the others deboarded.

Sitting up abruptly, just on the other side of the tarmac where it had been dozing in the sun, was a young adult male *T. rex*.

Its head cocked in their direction, atilt in that oddly birdlike way.

With an abbreviated curse, Johnson jerked his rifle to his shoulder, but Shanna shouted out behind him, "Wait!"

Johnson was wide-eyed incredulous as Garner pushed his gun-barrel down.

Rudy stood up, and began to pad in their direction.

The big tyrannosaur looked the worse for wear, riddled with munitions fire, and it looked burned.

Johnson jerked at his rifle. Garner held him down. "*Wait.*"

Still clinging to Cameron's reluctant shoulder, Shanna raised her hand.

The five-ton *T. rex* sniffed it like a dog.

Then it lay down on the runway beside her, its head at her feet.

Johnson shook his head, unbelieving.

"What the hell *is* this?"

"*This*," Shanna said, "is why we came here."

She ran her hand along Rudy's bony brow.

"The northwest," she said, "is tyrannosaur territory."

"Come again?" Mark blanched, gawking at this gangly teenage version of the beast that had chased him for six-hundred miles – not to mention its biting baby offspring.

Shanna turned to the others, beckoning.

"Come on," she said. "Come meet him."

Amazingly, it was Allison who stepped up first, Lucas still crooked in her arm.

Bud actually reached out to stop her. Allison paused uncertainly, but cautiously held out her hand. Bud stood helplessly at bay as she ran her fingers lightly across the massive fanged jaws.

Then Lucas himself reached out to touch Rudy's snout, his eyes goggling.

It seemed the rex twitched a little.

But Shanna's voice was soothing, and her hands never broke contact.

She waved to the others, and one-by-one, the soldiers shuffled forward, all touching the big rex, as if on a dare.

Mark hung back. Mr. Wilson did likewise.

Maverick smiled as he patted the thick, muscular neck.

"I wanna ride him."

Shanna smiled. "Let's make friends first," she said.

Rosa held back with Mark.

Not that she sensed any threat from the prehistoric super-predator, but because she found herself wondering what might come next.

Rosa guessed Shanna was in the first trimester of her pregnancy – and correlation suggested an ever-increasing influence on the new wildlife.

They'd seen what followed her to the mountain. Clearly, for at least some of the resurrected beasts, she was a beacon.

But *T. rex* meant no other predators – like having a king snake under the house to eat the rattlers.

Shanna reached out to touch Lucas' cheek even as he ran his delighted little hands over Rudy's speckled hide like the fur of a giant Labrador.

Rudy let out a slow sigh, like a dragon's purr.

Shanna's hand fell to her own barely-showing belly.

Cameron's arm curled over her shoulder, squeezing softly, as they looked around at the surrounding peaks that sequestered the little valley all by itself.

"We can live here," Shanna said. "We don't have to hide in the hills."

She patted the bony crest on Rudy's massive skull, not yet even fully grown. "We don't have to be afraid."

Maverick shrugged. "Fine by me."

He reached into his pocket, and tossed the chopper key to pilot Bradbury.

"Here's your helicopter back."

Bradbury frowned, glancing at Johnson and Cooper, before simply putting the key in his pocket.

Maverick turned to Rosa.

"That reminds me," he said. "I owe you dinner. I don't suppose you can cook?"

Rosa blinked back earnestly. "Not if you really *were* the last man on Earth."

Mr. Wilson snickered. "I *like* her."

On the ridge, a development of houses circled the hillside around a modest lake.

Like the rest of the valley, it was abandoned but intact.

Rosa had always wanted a house on the water. Now she had her pick.

These days you had to take your blessings where you found them.

A year ago, the world had ended, and she'd been left almost without hope.

But this might not be the worst of lives.

CHAPTER 65

The Mount was designed to protect from a nuke – *not* an assault from the mountain itself.

Sally was getting reports from below. So far, they had not yet gotten a full tally on the damage.

Nor had they counted the dead.

The mountain had shrugged off a single splintered segment from the cliff upon which the Mount had been built, dropping the chunk into the canyons, and taking the attached portion of the facility along with it.

It had been living quarters, mostly – they hadn't lost as many soldiers, who were scrambled and on-duty.

Their civilian numbers, however, had taken a hit. No survivors found – or expected – from the section that had broken off the mountain.

Ironically, the Coven, in detention at the time, were just fine.

Rhodes had been unequivocal in judgment of their actions – he called it treason.

Sally, personally, would have called it what it really was – attempted genocide.

Sacrifice your own for the Dragon.

She had spent one night in the woods with this cat-crew of psychopaths, and that was all it took.

Rhodes still didn't seem to fully appreciate the vengeance nihilist, the pursuit of total blaspheme.

Sally had told Rhodes she believed their 'men-folk' had been led right to the dragon's fangs.

What she hadn't told him was how Lily had also mentioned children with these men.

Sally suspected that was the *real* sacrifice – the symbolic transition to their new Lord – the progeny of their past lives had to go.

It was just a suspicion. A creeping suspicion that Sally believed with all of her heart.

She wondered what Rhodes would say if she told him.

Sally knew she wasn't the only one bending the General's ear anymore. It now seemed Michelle was always around – lately, the deceptively obedient, good-girl.

If Sally was Rhodes' adopted daughter, then Michelle was what? Hot-tail on the side?

She'd not seen anything overt. On the other hand, Rhodes had been similarly succinct on his position towards the Coven.

They were still fertile women, and therefore, still their most valuable resource.

Lily, in particular, had come out as pregnant. Corporal Stevens seemed to believe he was the father, and Lily had done nothing to dissuade him. Sally, however, found herself somehow doubtful.

Dr. Shriver had taken over the infirmary, and particularly the nursery, where Lily and Sally were currently the only pregnancies on the Mount.

Shriver wanted direct supervision on any potential births. Lily had been granted a stay from the holding cells to a bed in the infirmary, on the doctor's recommendation – for the good of the baby's health.

The young girl/woman said little, just stroking her still-flat belly self-consciously. And she never seemed to meet Sally's eye, her face always turned down and away, like a little girl with a secret.

Dr. Shriver was also attempting to rebuild his lab. The lower levels had collapsed.

Rhodes currently had a crew attempting to dig it all out. Important assets had been buried there too – among other things, a sealed cabinet filled with vials of the Food of the Gods – enough to infect the entire continent.

So far, tons of rubble blocked their way. Unstable rock continued to collapse.

They were also still trying to locate Major Tom, who had not reported in since re-entry. Kristie, the young woman Hicks brought in from the Maelstrom-site, had been pestering Rhodes anxiously over any news there.

Rhodes, himself, had not said much in conversation, speaking only in monotone orders.

Johnson's chopper had disappeared. Shanna had disappeared with him.

Their *most* valuable asset.

The last contact with Johnson's rescue chopper had been right when the seismic seizures hit – reported safe and away... and they had not been heard from since. Presumed dead.

Sally, for her part, didn't think so.

'Johnson's' last report said to 'Keep a candle burning'.

Sally had recognized the voice. And it wasn't Johnson. It was actually someone else Rhodes thought long-dead.

The turn of phrase was the last thing Mark had said to her.

And Sally also knew right where he would be going.

The northwest coast was his home and where he'd been trying to get back to for two years.

If this 'Shanna' was with him, that's where they would find her too.

A woman Sally had never met, who seemed to be of her own mind about being anyone's asset.

Sally could get behind that. And so she said nothing.

And Mark would never even know. One more time, he had unknowingly left her behind.

One more time, Sally was forced to stay silent, and simply let him walk away.

Her hands stole to the lump in her own belly, just starting to show.

This was *her* value as an asset.

The Arc-Project remained. And would begin again.

If for no other reason than defiance in the face of extinction.

CHAPTER 66

Jonah woke up in the infirmary.

The first thing he was aware of was bright light. The second was throbbing pain.

He had fallen out of a tree once as a kid, hitting every branch all the way down, and landed on flat hard earth. He'd lain for several minutes, battered and stunned, and when he finally climbed to his feet, it was as if every inch of his body had been beaten with a hammer.

This was like that. It hurt to move the tips of his fingers.

The effort forced a low groan, and he blinked the room into focus.

He saw Naomi leaning over him. Behind her was a man in a lab coat, who seemed to be preparing a needle made for a horse.

"Hey," Naomi said softly. "Welcome back."

Jonah started to speak, now realizing an even more throbbing pain in his head.

The third man in the room stepped forward, square-shouldered in hard-worn military fatigues and four-stars across the shoulder.

"General Nathan Rhodes," the man said, extending his hand.

Jonah started to reach out reflexively and grimaced. Rhodes turned the reached hand into a salute.

"Rest easy, son," he said. "That was a hell of a gutsy move you pulled." The General nodded to the gaunt-looking man in the lab coat. "Dr. Shriver says you're going to live."

Dr. Shriver approached with the giant needle, hovering briefly – and then injected it into the IV tube beside the bed.

"You've taken quite a beating," Shriver informed Jonah, unnecessarily. "You have a broken femur and shin. Assorted cracked ribs, and a humerus. Most problematically, you took a hard blow to the head, a fairly significant concussion, and some nasty lacerations along the scalp."

"These days," Rhodes said, "we call those 'flesh-wounds.'"

He turned to Naomi, indicating her wedding ring.

"Mrs. Walker," he said. "I knew your husband. Lieutenant Walker was a hero."

Naomi nodded.

"I know," she said.

"Speaking of that," Rhodes said, turning back to Jonah, "we're damn short of pilots these days."

Naomi shook her head.

"I keep telling him – they still are."

Rhodes smiled, nodding down at Jonah.

"Heal up, son. You've just been drafted."

Jonah absorbed this silently as the General turned to leave.

Hicks met them at the door, popping his head in after Naomi.

"Ma'am?" Hicks said. "We've got some temporary quarters set up for you. Clothes and a shower."

Naomi's eyes brightened. She wasn't sold on General Rhodes, yet, but Jonah could tell she liked Hicks – certainly cut in the Lucas Walker mold – highly-trained and disciplined, testosterone-military.

Probably, she was going to be around a lot of them now.

Naomi rose to follow Hicks, but stopped at the door, looking back at Jonah with an odd look on her face, as if there was something she wasn't sure she should say.

"Get some sleep," she said instead. "I'll come see you later."

But Jonah had lain awake in the time since.

Whatever Shriver had given him brought his pain down to a duller ache – not *quite* enough to relax. And if there was any sedative, it was kept at bay by his red blinking eyes as he contemplated his future.

Drafted, Rhodes had said.

Heal-up quick, so you can make *sure* and get yourself killed.

He'd used up at least eight of nine lives just this time.

But he'd pulled it off.

Why couldn't that mean he could just rest?

He supposed it simply wasn't that kind of world anymore.

Jonah shut his eyes, feeling the swelling capillaries in his bones pulse like a background organ-beat.

It at least kept him from wondering what Naomi was waiting to tell him.

While on this particular occasion he *thought* he'd finally won her respect, he had little doubt that the headline was something to the effect of *thanks-for-everything*, and *good-bye*.

Somewhere over the next several hours, Jonah finally drifted off to sleep.

He was awakened sometime around midnight by a nurse in whites fidgeting by his bed.

The lights in the infirmary were out. Groggily, Jonah watched apathetically, as the nurse detached his IV from the wall.

Then she popped the wheels on his bed, rolling him out into the hall.

Jonah blinked.

Dr. Shriver was lying on the floor, his leg twitching. Corporal Stevens lay next to him.

The nurse held up the taser she had in her hand, zapping up a couple sparks, and Jonah realized it was Naomi.

Jonah started to speak, but Naomi pinched his lips.

"You just keep your mouth shut," she said. "I got this one."

In the hall, she transferred him to a wheelchair and rolled him down the hall at a quick jog.

A couple more taser-zaps got them into the upper decks and the vehicle warehouse where she had an RV waiting.

The power was still out over large parts of the compound, and the upper grounds were dark. Naomi kept the lights off until they reached the front gates.

Then she revved the engine and the unsuspecting guards jumped to attention.

"Hang on," Naomi said, flaring the brights, flooring the gas, and blasted through the gate.

Jonah heard shouts from the guards as they dived aside, but Naomi was already squirreling past, down the road.

It occurred to Jonah he'd never actually driven passenger-side with Naomi before.

He never knew how lucky he'd been.

She skidded back and forth, down the narrow mountain road, until the bare-moment the terrain flattened enough for her to turn the rig directly into the trees, where she angled downhill and just kept going.

The bumping Jeep kept Jonah's full attention on his every damaged bone.

They were miles down the mountain before Jonah thought to disobey Naomi's edict to keep quiet.

"*What*," he managed, "are we *doing*?"

"The General was right," Naomi replied, bumping them along. "Lucas was a hero. Turns out I've been lucky that way."

She glanced at him.

"That's the thing about the military," she said. "You sign-up, your ass belongs to them."

Naomi shook her head.

"You're *mine*," she said.

Jonah considered.

He decided he was fine with it.

"Any idea where we're going?" he asked.

Naomi pointed ahead into the blind dark.

"That way," she said.

Jonah nodded, settling into his seat.

If I died tonight, he thought.

But he hadn't.

Not yet.

He glanced at her sideways as Naomi carried them away into the night.

The forest was dark and deep.

Jonah had no idea what beasts and monsters might yet wait, hidden in that darkness. Or what other dangers might lie ahead.

But the future could bother him tomorrow.

For now, he was content.

CHAPTER 67

Mark stayed a week in the valley before continuing on to the coast.

When Trix came traipsing over the hill, that was the last straw. He didn't care how well-behaved tyrannosaurs were around Shanna, Mark was like a postman around dogs – they just didn't seem to like *him* much.

Besides, it was the coast that had been his home, the last place he'd seen his family, before that cruise-trip job, forever and not so very-damn long ago.

Who knew what he might find?

No doubt devastation and not much closure, except perhaps for seeing the final stake driven into his last associations of the old world.

But it seemed like it was something he had to do.

Besides, these damn *T. rex* scared him.

The little lake community was remarkably well-preserved and Mark had been able to find a stored four-by-four, and a stock of canned goods to load it with. He even found an old-style Walkman radio and headphones, and CDs to go with it.

Shanna had asked him to stay.

When she had touched his hand, he felt that odd internal glow.

It reminded him a little of Sally – still so recently lost.

And of course, Lily, who'd turned that glow into the lure of a Venus fly-trap.

A glow was something you fixated on – for *you*, it seemed a personal experience, but it was actually a light shining down on everything and everybody.

In his heart, Mark couldn't help believe Lilly was a punishment for letting Sally down. And whether it was or it wasn't, he would continue to punish himself accordingly.

Mark had thanked Shanna, and even though he knew he already loved her, just like everybody else did, he turned and left the valley behind.

He followed the road for an hour until he came to a gas station, a last-stop-on-the-mountain shop. Mark already had several full containers in the back, but there was no telling how long before the next one.

Pumping gas was more of a production than it used to be, and Mark fussed about with sealed tanks and siphoning hoses, his new Walkman headphones on, whistling along as he worked.

A birdlike warbling in the brush thus escaped him.

The tall grass parted, as the little lizards hopped out onto the road.

It was a small troop – they always seemed to move in threes – perhaps base nuclear organization.

Twenty miles outside the valley, they were beyond Shanna's immediate perception.

Besides, they were learning how to hide from her – all she should feel would be a mild sense of unease.

That's what Otto *was*.

He did not have higher cerebral functions.

Memory storage, on the other hand...?

With reptilian motivations and mind.

What's-Worse? That was the game Nolan Hinkle played, with his exponential genius of a daughter.

Invariably, it led him to lecturing about all the possible ways the world could come to an end – and of course, what humanity might attempt to stop it – along with comparable world-destroying events from the past, from the KT extinction, to the Black Plague.

Nolan Hinkle destroyed the world in his imagination a dozen times every night of his life.

And perhaps this is what Otto absorbed. If Shanna was the soul of the empath, what Otto had taken was the id.

In each of the little lizard's hands were pneumatic needles, all glowing bright emerald green.

The lizards eyed Mark with his headphones on, and his back to them, their avid eyes turning speculatively to his truck – easier travel through tyrannosaur territory, and a car-jacking was the last thing Mark would expect.

The bushes rustled as they skittered closer, their wicked foot-claws tapping, their hand-talons spread.

Mark opened the door, fiddling with the keys.

There was a flash of movement from the brush.

Behind Otto, the bushes exploded and Junior darted out, jaws agape.

With Mark still completely oblivious, the little rex totally ignored his vulnerable leg and latched onto the first of the Ottos by the throat, ripping like a bulldog.

The other two squawked, brandishing both their claws and needles – an effort that lasted all of three seconds as Junior launched at them, fangs first.

In moments, the little lizards were torn to shreds.

The loose needles and their glowing liquid contents went spinning into the overgrown leaves.

Mark climbed into his driver's seat and started the engine, still whistling.

Junior stared longingly as Mark trundled off down the road. The little rex had been following the four-by-four all the way from town.

With single-minded tyrannosaur stubbornness, Junior had once again gotten *so* close – his target unmindful and unguarded – he had been but seconds away – he had been *tasting* it.

Junior bent to tear loose a piece of lizard drumstick.

But he *hated* these little bastards.

So he guessed he had a few minutes.

In perfect gluttony, Junior gobbled up the rest, leaving not a scrap behind.

And then, with his stomach bloated, his eyes blinked in the direction Mark had gone.

A rex didn't think – it just followed its nose.

Besides, Mark was just simply taking the highway. That made it easy.

His lips still bloody, and scraps of Otto still in his teeth, Junior scampered out onto the road and followed.

THE END

CHECK OUT OTHER GREAT DINOSAUR BOOKS

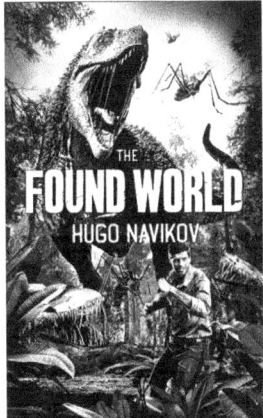

THE FOUND WORLD
by Hugo Navikov

A powerful global cabal wants adventurer Brett Russell to retrieve a superweapon stolen by the scientist who built it. To entice him to travel underneath one of the most dangerous volcanoes on Earth to find the scientist, this shadowy organization will pay him the only thing he cares about: information that will allow him to avenge his family's murder.

But before he can get paid, he and his team must enter an underground hellscape of killer plants, giant insects, terrifying dinosaurs, and an army of other predators never previously seen by man.

At the end of this journey awaits a revelation that could alter the fate of mankind ... if they can make it back from this horrifying found world.

HOUSE OF THE GODS
by Davide Mana

High above the steamy jungle of the Amazon basin, rise the flat plateaus known as the Tepui, the House of the Gods. Lost worlds of unknown beauty, a naturalistic wonder, each an ecology onto itself, shunned by the local tribes for centuries. The House of the Gods was not made for men.

But now, the crew and passengers of a small charter plane are about to find what was hidden for sixty million years.

Lost on an island in the clouds 10.000 feet above the jungle, surrounded by dinosaurs, hunted by mysterious mercenaries, the survivors of Sligo Air flight 001 will quickly learn the only rule of life on Earth: Extinction.

SEVEREDPRESS

 facebook.com/severedpress
 twitter.com/severedpress

CHECK OUT OTHER GREAT DINOSAUR BOOKS

PRIMORDIA
by **Greig Beck**

Ben Cartwright, former soldier, home to mourn the loss of his father stumbles upon cryptic letters from the past between the author, Arthur Conan Doyle and his great, great grandfather who vanished while exploring the Amazon jungle in 1908.

Amazingly, these letters lead Ben to believe that his ancestor's expedition was the basis for Doyle's fantastical tale of a lost world inhabited by long extinct creatures. As Ben digs some more he finds clues to the whereabouts of a lost notebook that might contain a map to a place that is home to creatures that would rewrite everything known about history, biology and evolution.

But other parties now know about the notebook, and will do anything to obtain it. For Ben and his friends, it becomes a race against time and against ruthless rivals.

In the remotest corners of Venezuela, along winding river trails known only to lost tribes, and through near impenetrable jungle, Ben and his novice team find a forbidden place more terrifying and dangerous than anything they could ever have imagined.

PANGAEA EXILES
by **Jeff Brackett**

Tried and convicted for his crimes, Sean Barrow is sent into temporal exile—banished to a time so far before recorded history that there is no chance that he, or any other criminal sent back, has any chance of altering history.

Now Sean must find a way to survive more than 200 million years in the past, in a world populated by monstrous creatures that would rend him limb from limb if they got the chance. And that's just his fellow prisoners.

The dinosaurs are almost as bad.

CHECK OUT OTHER GREAT DINOSAUR BOOKS

FLIPSIDE
by JAKE BIBLE

The year is 2046 and dinosaurs are real.

Time bubbles across the world, many as large as one hundred square miles, turn like clockwork, revealing prehistoric landscapes from the Cretaceous Period.

They reveal the Flipside.

Now, thirty years after the first Turn, the clockwork is breaking down as one of the world's powers has decided to exploit the phenomenon for their own gain, possibly destroying everything then and now in the process.

A MAN OUT OF TIME
by Christopher Laflan

Five years after the Chinese Axis detonated an unknown weapon of mass destruction off the southern coast of the United States, Special Ops Sergeant John Crider and the members of Shadow Company have finally captured what they all hope will lead to the end of the war. Unfortunately, the population within the United States is no longer sustainable. In an effort to stabilize the economy, the government enacts the Cryonics Act. One hundred years in suspended animation, all debt forgiven, and a chance at a less crowded future are too good to pass up for John and his young daughter.

Except not everything always goes as planned as Sergeant John Crider finds himself pitted against a land of prehistoric monsters genetically resurrected from the fossil record, murderous inhabitants, and a future he never wanted.

www.ingramcontent.com/pod-product-compliance
Lightning Source LLC
Chambersburg PA
CBHW070745180626
46818CB00007B/2996